The Master

The Master

A novel of golf and death

Nathan Edmondson

PALMETTO
PUBLISHING
Charleston, SC
www.PalmettoPublishing.com

First Edition

Cover illustration by Margarita Fedorenko

Hardcover ISBN: 979-8-8229-4601-9
Paperback ISBN: 979-8-8229-4602-6

While many historical events and facts are referenced, this is a work of fiction. Names, characters, places and incidents either are products of the author's imagination or are used fictitiously. Any resemblance to actual events or locales or persons, living or dead, is entirely coincidental. For example, the conversation with Bubba Watson never happened, and may not have gone the way I wrote it.

AUTHOR'S NOTE:

This is a work of fiction. It is born of my love for and admiration of this grand institution and competition that preserves among many things one of the last bastions of etiquette in sports. I have fond memories that will last forever from my time at tournaments over the years, including standing on the 18th rope in the rain watching the electrifying showdown between Angel Cabrera and Adam Scott.

Any references to staff or departments at the Augusta National are entirely made-up, as are policies, procedures and practices. Some inaccuracies are intentional; all fiction is intentional.

This work has, if anything, made me more of a fan of the Augusta National and the Masters Tournament.

For Bill

"On the golf course, a man may be the dogged victim of inexorable fate, be struck down by an appalling stroke of tragedy, become the hero of unbelievable melodrama, or the clown in a side-splitting comedy."

Bobby Jones

PROLOGUE

Sunday

The 'Golden Bell' is a small shrub with a yellow flower that hangs with four petals that fan out as if they are arms welcoming pollen-laden bumblebees. The first buds blossom when winter gives way to spring; canary-yellow flashes pop from within the thick and dark green leaves of the mother plant. The bush is a Chinese import to the United States, and in the south it fares well with the ample sunlight and frequent thunderstorm-born rains; it is particularly well suited in the humid, seasonal weather of Georgia.

On the world-famous Augusta National Golf course, in Augusta, Georgia, a thick Golden Bell shrub grows in the partial shade of towering Loblolly pine trees just off the green on the 12th hole, just up a rise from iconic Rae's Creek which is crossed by two stone bridges there. Once called "Three Pines," the 12th is a Par 3 hole at the heart of the famous (or infamous, to some golfers) Amen Corner, the tight turn on the course where players' fortunes are often made or broken on spring weekends while the world watches. It is the shortest hole on the entire course at 155 yards, and yet many pros have dubbed it the most difficult or misleading, due primarily to the whirlwind effect made by the geography as winds crest over National Hills from Washington Road, Augusta and the piedmont hills beyond.

THE MASTER

It was here on the 12th hole that tournament competitor Tom Weis-kopf slipped ball after ball into the water, dropping thirteen points for the highest score-to-par in the history of the Masters. Rory McIlroy's infamous collapse in 2011 began on the 12th hole as the pine shadows were just beginning to creep onto the rough. In 2016, Jordan Spieth, favored to win a second time fell into a quadruple-bogey on the 12th hole; it was a modest slip over the creek in that cozy Augusta clearing that earned him the tears and ridicule of fans worldwide and altered his career trajectory.

The 12th has humbled some of the greatest pros in the game. Jack Nicklaus said the 12th hole was "the most dangerous par-3 in the game." It can be a simple hole to shoot, but if the winds — if the Gods of golf — are against you, then Golden Bell can be the death of even the best players.

On the morning of March 29, the Golden Bell was in full spring bloom, though there was still a chill in the air on the morning before the first day of Masters Tournament practice rounds at the Augusta National. Dawn was breaking quickly as it does in the piedmont of the south in spring; the sun blazes over the horizon and ignites the humid air. On any morning the air was thick also with the smell of fresh cut grass, azalea and pine pollen, and the paper mills to the south.

But before the sun crested over the tops of the pines, and while all of the Augusta National grass was still in shadow, teams of groundskeepers exited the maintenance compound and began to swarm the grounds for a final day of tune-ups before the course is opened to the public. Even today, golfers from around the world, competitors at golf's most exclusive, invitation-only tournament, will walk the grounds, feeling the wind and grass and looking at the play of sun on rough and fairway.

Still in the dim haze of dawn, groundskeeper Adrian Castillo drove along the pine-covered walkway in his tool-heavy Club Car, heading to the 12th hole, to Golden Bell, to begin trimming the grass and foliage with surgical precision and tender care. Castillo was in fact a course superintendent at another course - Macon, Georgia's Bowden — but he, like so many others was working as a volunteer for the week, partly for the bragging rights, partly for the experience working firsthand on the world's best-kept course. At least a dozen men and women would work on Golden Bell this morning. Some above ground, like himself; more specialized staff would focus on the underground network of pipes that could water or drain the grass by invisible subterranean means. There was always more happening at the National, Castillo knew, than one could see or imagine. His work was more traditional, though. Despite the science and machination behind the most spectacular golf course in the world, the grounds had to be maintained by rake, clippers and by hand. Castillo felt fortunate to blow the leaves, rake the sand, or prune the Azaleas, and he was moving early and eagerly to be the first one to the "Amen Corner." He was eager. This was his fourth year and he could hardly sleep the night before walking the hallowed grounds. Hence he had been first in the gate, and was first to pull up to the Amen corner that morning, where already brown thrashers and finches were calling out to one another with hurried songs from the dark of the woods leading away from the fairways and greens. They announced the sun as it began to break through the trees where the early light found passage; where it did it shot hot and bright like fiery blades.

Some of that golden light caught the TV camera tower that was painted green and hidden back behind a sand bunker in the shadow of a dogwood tree. Castillo was just getting near that spot with a soft rake in hand. He began to work as the sunlight warmed the air around him. He stood to admire the trees, which was when he noticed it, hanging there beneath the TV tower, barely moving in the breeze. It didn't look real at first, but then again, nothing in the tableau of the Augusta National feels real. It all feels like some kind of fantasy, a dream, more reminiscent of J.R.R. Tolkien's Shire than an everyday golf course.

But the body hanging from the camera loft wasn't a dream; it was something out of a nightmare. At his feet was a bottle of whiskey. The eyes were grotesquely swollen and yellow, staring up at the morning sky. The man's tongue was thick and dry as it hung out of his mouth. As Castillo watched, a mourning dove flittered over and landed on the man's shoulder and cooed.

ONE

Jonni Lombard felt the sun on his neck and watched the last bit of dew steam off the grass. He studied the distance between the ball, dazzling white in the dry grass, and the hole, a small cup recessed with a shadow. The distance was irrelevant in meters; he measured it in effort and energy. Tension in his arms and the smooth slide back before everything became automatic and the motion carried the putter forward as it connected squarely with the ball and then the whole world seemed to turn and he felt a kind of dizziness at the events he set in motion until the ball tipped into the cup.

He heard the low guttural growl-like sound from down the hill at the pond where the hippos were enjoying the break of day and birds stood by the pool looking to pick up water bugs stirred up by the animals' breakfast. A little closer down toward the water and the gentle animals would turn ungentle and the dangerously cantankerous hippos might charge him and that would be the end of Jonni, most likely. On a dime the curved shapes in the water turned to runaway freight cars, snarling with pink and brown mouths bared and shining huge teeth.

On this course there were other dangers. Snakes, like the mamba — one bite from which meant death within a couple of hours — and occasionally a leopard, a greater danger as daylight faded. South Africa was a beautify country with more than its share of crime and predators. This was only a semi-wild course. He was invited by a resident of the reserve to practice here before his trip overseas. Across the green he could see the next hole, a small herd of impala grazed twitching and occasionally studying the golfer and his father who stood a few meters back with the golf bag. Dad was his caddie today.

All of this, though, the young man of twenty-four tuned out as he tightened, then relaxed his hands on the club's grip and let his body drift in place. He could feel the weight of the putter in his hand and arms and neck as if they were all connected. He let the putter swing. It connected with ball which was sent toward the cup where it dropped and disappeared. He lowered his head, walked to it and stooped to retrieve it. His father commented on his shot, but he tuned him out, as well. Dad was more eager sometimes than Jonni. His enthusiasm could be a bit obnoxious. He couldn't let that distract him.

Dad tossed out another ball for him to putt.

"The grass will be different, remember. Smoother, less frayed on the ends. You'll get less resistance and if you strike it high it may spin back on you. Certainly it may veer." Jonni knew this; Willy had prepared him extensively about what to expect in Augusta. Willy had never been there, but researched it thoroughly. His father did his best to throw out tips, but he was a poor substitute for Jonni's caddie, and Dad wasn't adept at keeping Jonni cool and focused as Willy could.

Jonni worked the past few years washing dishes at a local restaurant; now he did so at the golf club restaurant, which also afforded him free practice time on the course. He heard his father's tips, but ignored them. He wasn't really a technical player.

Jonni swung with feeling and instinct and the ball went where it should. He felt good with a club in his hands and better when he took a shot and best when he first arrived on a course and felt the quiet settle over him and the world fade away.

The club where he worked and practiced was fifty kilometers south. His caddie Willy wasn't here. He had gone a few days early to study the course in Augusta. Jonni would leave on a flight this evening, traveling with his Dad. They would drive to Johannesburg and from there they flew to Atlanta. Jonni had played in a number of amateur and professional tournaments before but never one in the U.S, which was unusual, they told him, for someone invited to the Masters as a pro competitor.

He walked to the next putt, anchored his feet and relaxed his knees and leaned over, letting the brim of his hat shadow his eyes. His father was currently negotiating with Oakley to get him as many pairs of glasses as possible, some for all their family and friends, as part of the new endorsement. Jonni preferred not to wear sunglasses. They distracted him as he took in everything and felt the wind and grass and determined his shots. Jonni wasn't sure how much time had passed. He sensed his father looking at his watch. It was almost time to go. He tensed at the thought, and forced himself to be calm. This time tomorrow, he'd be halfway around the world.

TWO

Just ten miles from Augusta National Golf Club in South Augusta off of Peach Orchard Road, inside a brick house with an unkept front yard and a faded American Flag hanging from the porch, Detective Ryals Hall tried a sport coat on over his t-shirt. His daughter recommended that he wear a sport coat more often, so he thought he would lay it out for work tomorrow. What was that on the collar? Toothpaste? Mayo? He rubbed it but it wouldn't come off. He avoided dry cleaning anything and he was going to lose his jacket pretty quickly anyway this time of year as he avoided long sleeves when the weather climbed into the upper seventies as it would this week. He put the jacket away. Maybe he'd wear it tomorrow. Today was Sunday. He would only work a half-day, admin at the station.

His daughter was in the kitchen eating Raisin Bran for breakfast at the counter. He sat and reached for the cereal.

"I thought you were going to quit," she said without looking up from the box. Angela was fifteen going on twenty-six, and recently on a health kick which meant assigning guilt to any of Ryals's few remaining joys. She had been the woman of the house since she was nine years old. Last night at the restaurant she had lectured him on saturated fats and processed meat and bovine ethics and, of course, sugar. It would be cute, he thought, her learning all about where food comes from, if it wasn't ruining his hard-earned hamburger and his Sunday morning

Raisin Bran. Since her mom left them, he had faced the herculean effort of dealing with her big disappointments in life; now he was also fighting her small ones.

I am quitting. It's a process," he answered as he poured himself a bowl.

"It's loaded with sugar," she said. He eyed her bowl.

"You're eating it, too."

"I'm a kid. I burn sugar, like fast. You don't. You could use the fiber but not the sugar."

He sighed. He put the cereal away and opened the fridge to find another option, simply to avoid the lecture.

"What time will you be back today?"

"After lunch sometime. Unless you want to skip and ride along with me today. Catch some bad guys."

"I thought all you did on Sundays was paperwork."

"I'm an investigator. I investigate things."

"Is that what you're doing today?"

"No, today I'm doing paperwork."

"I'll stay here. Maybe I'll walk to Kroger and get some food that works with your diet."

"I'm not on a diet."

"Exactly." She sat and looked at the newspaper. Most kids her age probably read the funnies. She read the front page, then politics and sports.

"I hope Rory kills it this year," she said. "It's his year."

"Who?"

"Rory McIlroy. The Masters. C'mon dad."

He shook his head. "You don't even like golf."

"I like the Masters. Everyone does. It's our thing."

"Whose thing?"

"Augusta's thing. Our highways are named after Masters golfers, dad. You have to care."

"I don't."

He settled on a piece of toast. He pulled out the peanut butter. He waited for the toaster.

"Peanut butter is loaded with fat," his daughter said, flipping through the pages. "Egg whites are better for protein."

He was glad to be getting out of her crosshairs. She'd be alone at home, but she was a resourceful kid, and used to it. They were a team.

He sat at a light midway across town, the empty wrapper from a McDonald's breakfast sandwich bunched up and shoved into the cupholder.

It was that time of the year: the traffic all over town increased dramatically during Masters Week. For a week every year it was a nightmare to cross certain neighborhoods and streets. Many schools used this week as spring break (which meant Angela had plenty of energy to pour into being his mother). He passed through the light and saw Club Car golf carts parked at the corners in anticipation of the tournament. Every local business advertised special prices. This week the town was occupied, as if in war time, but rather by an invading army of green and pink and plaid pastels and khaki shorts, a few high-priced escorts, cigars and money and love for a game that Ryals found fundamentally unlovable.

The downtown Sheriff's station usually smelled like water damage and Lysol, despite a renovation four years ago. Today it smelled like donuts, and Ryals snagged one on his way to his cubicle. He sat and flipped open his computer and thought about spring cleaning his desk. Another investigator usually sat beside him, but she was apparently out on assignment. All investigators were at one time guaranteed an office but then came the consolidation between city and county a few years before and now the Sheriff's department was restricted to one floor on the Telfair Street eight-story building, and space was at a premium. At least parking was easy here.

Richmond County covered most of metropolitan Augusta, including the downtown and oldest areas of town — "The Hill," much of the Washington road corridor, South Augusta, downtown, National Hills — a checkerboard of residential and metro, of old government housing and new subdivisions, of shopping centers and restaurants, of parks and golf courses and schools; it was the heart of the second largest city in Georgia. Ryals worked all over the county, and he lived now just ten miles from where he had been brought up an Army brat living on post at Fort Eisenhower (then "Gordon"), his parents moving from across the Savannah River in South Carolina two decades before he was born.

"Detective Hall," Mary, the department secretary, called to him from across the bullpen. He looked up and over at her. "Call for you. Got a body."

"I'm not up."

"Sharon's not back so I guess you are."

Ryals did not feel like hitting the road today. He had a mountain of paperwork to climb out from under and he didn't want his lower back stuck to the vinyl seat with the lousy a/c in the car fighting the Georgia sun. He answered the call which Mary patched through to his desk phon.

Behind him, a young lieutenant listened in. Sundays were typically slow and dull.

"Hall here." He listened and jotted a note on a pad. Bored, trying not to sign into the receiver. The person on the other end was talking fast. Too fast. He stopped and lifted his pen. "Wait. Go back. You found a body where?"

THREE

This was a golfing town. When Ryals made detective, he was often invited to play golf, at least at first. He went once. He wasn't invited back after that, and wouldn't have accepted another invitation. He had no patience for the game. He had no finesse, nor did he take any time to learn anything. After a year or two of making promises to himself that he'd try again to learn the game, knowing that "promotions happen on the course," even after being invited by the mayor, he gave up. It was expensive besides, and he could never spare six hours, not while raising a teenager on his own. Now he paid little attention to the game, but it was hard to avoid in this town this time of year.   The industry was in part built on Club Car; the locals all played and around Easter golf fans from around the world flooded into town and so did their money — but to Ryals, it all only meant that traffic sucked for a week every year.

He might have enjoyed playing it if he had ever really invested the time, but he certainly didn't care to watch it. It was as dull a spectator sport as anyone could ever sit through. He could enjoy baseball with a beer. Baseball was a sport he could get behind, as it offered just the right combination of speed and rest. He went to local Green Jacket games (the local minor league team) and occasionally up to Atlanta to watch the Braves. Angela loved going. He liked college football, too, and he supported the Falcons. Sports to Ryals was meant to be exciting and emotional; it was meant to involve cheering and lively crowds. Golf was dull and unrewarding. And as for cheering and lively crowds, The Masters was too proper for all of that.

Most locals ignored or simply accepted that along Berckmans or Washington roads, behind the walls of deep green bamboo, lay the rarified greens, the "secret garden" of sorts that was the most exclusive golf club in the world and hosted the world's most exclusive sporting event. Many Augustans were proud of the town's golf heritage and boasted about the tournament, but most were resigned to it. Hall just sighed at the traffic.

Nor was there much crime during Masters week. Not violent crime, anyway. The Sheriff's department did, though, spend plenty of time looking into reports of badge fraud. Reselling Masters Badges was illegal within a half-mile of the course, but there was still an intense black market outside the gates that Richmond County patrolled diligently. Badges were sometimes stolen. Even where they were sold legally, selling them was against Augusta National policy, and a fate worse than a fine and a week in the county jail was the loss of the privilege of entry. Ryals was at least familiar with this criminal fringe, though beyond helping traffic near the gates during Masters Week, he personally didn't care about National's badge policy. Effectively, though, the Sheriff's Department worked for the National during Master's Week.

Locals avoided the area around ANGC during this week, but he was all too familiar with the desperate look of the would-be-buyers on the sidewalks and grass edges of Washington Road, holding out their hands, whispering to passers-by needing badges like tickets to get into Heaven. Pop-up counterfeit gear shops disappeared when Sheriff's patrol cars rolled by.

So, it was a truly strange thing to be driving down to the gate at the entrance to Magnolia Drive. It seemed absurd, but he couldn't ignore that he was essentially a common cop invited into a royal court. He arrived at the gate and an agreeable man in a uniform jacket and slacks approached Ryals while holding a tablet. Ryals provided his credentials and after some consultation via a radio, the man opened the gates to reveal the straight, shaded driveway between towering Magnolias that led to the world-famous clubhouse. As he drove in, Ryals passed teams of groundskeepers blowing, raking, cutting and fertilizing the drive and the grounds beyond. Beyond the white, colonial guardhouse he had a glimpse of the course that stretched away down gentle sloping hills. With each pair of Magnolias he passed, casting a dark shade, the busy, five-lane Washington road behind and the shopping centers and restaurants felt increasingly distant, almost a world away.

He showed his credentials to a second guard who stood in front of the clubhouse. He was directed to guest parking. Undoubtedly word of the death had spread amongst the staff here like a creeping dawn fog and surely it wouldn't long be contained. On the phone, the woman had stressed that this be kept as quiet and secret as possible for the sake of the club. She said it was an unfortunate matter, and they wished to be thorough, but discretion was paramount. Seeing the place from the inside, the white facades and brass knobs and security all in jackets, he wished he'd worn his blazer.

He parked in the shade of the trees. He drove an unmarked sedan as a detective but they apparently were wary of even that alerting the press, who were likely gathering in anticipation of the practice rounds beginning tomorrow, so he was directed to the furthest space.

They didn't tell him much but Ryals was sure he knew what he was likely dealing with. Kids occasionally tried to jump the fences and break into the course, despite aggressive security and severe penalties. Ryals was certain he would discover a dead, drugged kid from the area who had climbed over on a dare. From the woman's description, the body was discovered near the trees and close to the fence.

Ryals emerged from his car and wiped the sweat from his nose beneath his Ray Bans and saw a woman with long black hair, pants and blouse, with a yellow Augusta National flag pin walking toward him. She wore sporty sunglasses and bright new sneakers. She extended her hand when she was still several cars away and walked up to him at a quick pace.

"Allison Roy," she said. "Director of Operations, Augusta National. Is it just you?"

"Ryals Hall. Richmond County Sheriff's Investigator. The coroner is on the way."

"You won't need the CSI... type people? I apologize, I'm not familiar with all the offices and terms." Implied was that there was no need for such things out here. Until now, of course.

"That shouldn't be necessary, I wouldn't think."

"I figure you need to go to the scene of the suicide? No one has touched the body."

"Suicide? You didn't mention that on the phone. It was you I spoke to, wasn't it?"

"Yes, I'm sorry, I suppose alleged, or presumed, suicide. He was found hanging."

Hanging? Ryals thought. This was unexpected.

Ryals removed his notepad and jotted a few brief notes. She directed him to a golf cart and, as they climbed in, he saw staff standing outside the clubhouse watching. She drove them in the silent cart around the clubhouse, down a path toward the gift shop and then turned downhill; Allison pointed — to the left was the first hole, to the right was the second; then that was the extent of her guided tour and they drove in silence down a path under pine trees and by cherry blossoms and toward the bottom of the hill.

"This has never happened here before. Break-ins, you know, theft and trespassing and vandalism. Never something this."

"I can imagine," was all he said.

"Locals as I'm sure you know, they try to sneak in, to take selfies or a cut of the grass. That's all we deal with typically."

She was worried. He could feel her tension like atmospheric pressure. They continued downhill. Birds were chirping. A squirrel ran across the path. A gardener with a bag of seed and gloves looked up from the edge of the fairway through the trees.

"Of course, this wasn't a local."

"It wasn't?" Ryals looked at her. "Then who?"

"It was a caddie."

"A caddie?"

"It was Jonni Lombard's caddie."

FOUR

Jonni Lombard, following in the tradition of Rory McIlroy and Jordan Spieth, was a bright-eyed young prodigy. He came from South Africa and he had won his first pro tournament at age 17. Only son of a salesman, his mother had passed years ago. Jonni grew up outside of Hoedspruit in the northeast of the country. His father, who traveled with Jonni everywhere, often told the story in interviews about how one night Jonni couldn't get a ball to drop into a hole and stayed out until three hours past bedtime trying to make the shot. "He came in so covered in mosquito bites that we had to get him an injection," his father would proudly explain.

Jonni had a world ranking of seventy-six, and his virtuosity was rivaled only by his aversion to press and cameras. His success on the course did not help him overcome his shyness. He was a quiet kid and a golf pro. With sandy hair that tufted out from beneath his Adidas-sponsored hat, coral blue eyes, and a short nose accented with a few freckles he looked the part of shy youngster.

This would be Lombard's first Masters invitation; his first time competing on the legendary 84-year-old course known for tricky, hidden slopes, lightning fast greens, and contours reshaped every year so that no returning pro would ever hold an advantage. Top amateurs could be invited to the Masters; but the top fifty spots were reserved for the

Pros. Jonni's invitation followed his win at the Latin America Amateur Championship the year before.

Jonni had worked with the same caddie — Willy Shepherd — for six years. Willy was a pro caddie in South Africa who had helped develop Jonni's game. A divorced man himself, he had seen the raw talent in Jonni and even more than the pro instructors, he believed in Jonni's potential. In one of his few interviews, given in Sydney, Jonni had said of Willy "there would never be a Professional Jonni without Willy."

"I haven't met Mr. Lombard yet," Allison said as she finished briefing Ryals. She bit her lip.

Currently Jonni and his father Martin were on their way. Allison referred to her iPad frequently and Ryals could see the precisely organized schedule. Shepherd arrived days before, she explained and had been accommodated. He had walked with a representative across the grounds yesterday and studied the course as many caddies before him had done.

Allison waited for her phone to ring. The Chairman had met with the board and they were inclined to downplay the incident, and she tended to agree that the world didn't need to know of a caddie's personal tragedy, particularly not when they would be reporting to the family. They also had a tournament to put on. The cost and logistics of delaying it even an hour were too extraordinary to even imagine.

Allison had dealt with so-called "extraordinary" things at the course during her four year tenure—which in Augusta National terms, was not a long time. But "extraordinary" at the National would be mundane anywhere else. The most typical and pedestrian issue was the occasional fence jumper hoping for a peek, a picture, a divot of grass or just a drunk gallivanting across a green. Or there were the disgruntled employees — it was rare, as they paid even the lowest-tier groundskeeper better than any comparable job, and most considered working at the National a privilege — but occasionally they had bad apples, attempting theft or even minor sabotage.

There was one more dramatic incident, well before her time — in 1983, a drunk interloper crashed the gate in a blue Dodge pickup with a bottle of tequila bouncing on the seat and threatened Ronald Regan's Secret Service detail with a .38 revolver. He was able to disarm and detain seven hostages as he demanded to speak to the president, who was playing the course. There was a black and white framed picture of the truck being towed in the director's office. The National still used the same tow company—Kendrick—all these years later, whose name was painted on the door of the tow truck in the grainy photo.

Allison was hired the year following the famous expansion across Berckmans Road (the road named for the family that sold their indigo orchard to the founders of the Augusta National): the clearing for the new parking lot, the construction of the new media center, gift shop, entrance and other facilities. All of these done without compromising any of the of the legendary course elements nor any aesthetic, but it was an overhaul and it brought with it a new boundary to be secured, new staff, new responsibilities and new dynamics. She was part of that "new." Four years new, now.

Her phone rang. Not the director. Not yet.

It was her travel logistics coordinator, informing her that Jonni Lombard had landed in Atlanta, and was on his way to Augusta by charter to Augusta's Bush Field.

Of course, he hadn't been told anything yet.

Ryals and Allison stepped out of the cart. They were on the small maintenance path to the back of the 12th. Green tape blocked off an area near the edge of the green and around the woods where trees hung over the grass and orange-brown pine needles spread over the ground but stopped in a neat edge as if held by magic there. A man who introduced himself as Lawrence, head of Augusta National Security, was already there, waiting. At the cross path to the hole, seventy or more yards up the hill on the stone bridges, maintenance and ground staff were gathered watching. Allison looked at them.

Four security guards helped two Sheriff's deputies patrol the area. Allison told the nearest guard,

"Please tell the staff to get back to work. We have a tournament this week," with a sharp edge of aggravation in her voice. She was a woman who liked control and needed to maintain it now more than ever.

Ryals knew the deputies. One typically worked swing. Likely he was returning to the station at the end of his shift and got the call. His eyes were red and wide. Ryals nodded to them as he retrieved his small digital camera from his left front pants pocket. Lawrence was quiet, professional, and took his own notes.

"I took my own pictures this morning. Video as well. Anything you need please ask." Ryals nodded and kept walking.

"Heck of a thing," the second deputy said, hooking his fingers in his belt and looking around. Then added, in a near-whisper "Can't even believe it."

Ryals followed the deputy's gaze. The sun beat down now and Ryals was beginning to sweat. He could imagine the Sheriff's call complaining about him crawling around here without a jacket. He looked to see if there were any cameras. He saw none. Even cell phones were not allowed. He could see much of the course from here, and it was a strange sight with all of it so empty and pristine. Almost like Eden before Adam and his wife showed up.

He took in the scene, a sweeping look over the bordering azaleas, the pine groves, and the green hills and the semi-hidden TV towers, and the leaderboard yet devoid of names and he finally saw the bit of yellow dangling rope from the corner of the TV tower and an empty bottle of liquor on the ground beneath it and then the white cloth that covered the body. He turned his camera on, and he began taking pictures.

Allison stood beside him. "The Chairman recommended we cut it down. Demanded, rather. He was concerned about the birds, and the, well, it was really morbid. I hope that's okay." She spoke nervously. Her eyes to-and-fro quickly. Ryals was calm, slow, and quiet by nature. She was the sort who made others nervous by proximity.

Ryals took a stroll, looking up and down the trees, shrubs, paths, but focused mostly on the ground. Rules and protocol clicked through his head like a Geiger counter while he looked around. He studied the footprints. He didn't have any reason to gather evidence, but he was the responder and everyone would want a thorough report. There were many footprints, whether from staff or groundskeepers or his own deputies, but the ground was unnaturally immaculate. Even footprints were purged to preserve the picturesque tableau. One print was a bit off the path, where pine straw had been shoved aside, and he took a picture of it. It was an aggressive print with an "S" in the heel. He laid a small ruler from his pocket by the print and took another shot to establish size. For some reason it stood out to him. Again, the ticking of protocol sounded in his head, but now a little faster.

Indeed, the politics were radioactive. This may be one drunk foreigner's suicide, but given that it happened here, every detail of his report no matter how routine would fall under immense scrutiny. He crouched and snapped more photos, took a step, took pictures of the rope and then a close-up of the bottle. Allison paced, on her phone, texting, and taking calls constantly while Lawrence stood like a sentry. Ryals remembered the news a few years back in the Chronicle—when the National wanted to move Berckmans road, and annex part a neighborhood, the city said it was impossible. The National loaned the city of Augusta thirty million for the road and bought the neighborhood. Reportedly, the National had spent $200 million in the last couple of decades on additional real estate. 270 acres worth.

"You have cameras in this area?" Ryals asked him.

"Not exactly. We have one up the hill there," Lawrence pointed, "and back in there among the trees watching the fence. But here, other than the tournament cameras, you can't see much."

Ryals walked to the base of the TV tower from which the rope hung and looked up the ascending steps. The rope swayed slightly in the soft breeze. He snapped pictures from this angle and then looked around, but for what, he couldn't imagine. The tower catwalk was several yards out from the center of the tower. The caddie would had to have climbed out onto it to tie the rope and then stepped off the edge. Ryals shook his head. The caddie obviously loved golf to go through the effort to die on the course. Or hated it.

Finally, Ryals went to the body and removed the sheet enough to get a good look. A white male, early forties, reddish hair and a graying beard; he was thin and vomit was dried in his beard over his chin. He was pale, his neck was reddened from rope burn, and his eyes were now closed.

Ryals began to take pictures; the forensic team would do so as well, but he wanted his own. This was more precaution than he would have given the body of a meth head downtown on a Sunday morning, but the Operations Director stood and watched him nervously. He wasn't thinking foul play, but he was thinking of some bereaved family filing a lawsuit that would be passed through the channels and he would end up in the spotlight. He used a pencil to lift the man's hands; he found some dirt under the fingernails of the right hand, but not the left. The caddie wore a sweatshirt and sweatpants and slip-on shoes; Ryals felt through them and found a wallet with his South African ID card and credit cards, identifying him as "Willy Shepherd."

Ryals could smell booze on the late Mr. Shepherd, and flies explored his skin and shirt.

"I'm going to call in a forensic team, just to be thorough." Ryals kept close to the corpse, sweat growing on his hairline.

Allison seemed flummoxed but didn't argue. She adjusted the earpiece that connected to her secret-service-like dangle that came from beneath her collar and connected to her radio. Ryals removed his latex gloves and stood.

Ryals looked again at the yellow rope. It was at least ten feet off the ground, and out on the corner; Shepard would have had to have jumped. He was lucky — or unlucky, Ryals wasn't sure which — the rope hadn't snapped when he had jumped. Ryals looked at the ground again, then said to Lawrence,

"Let's just keep the perimeter until they get here, and they'll turn the body over to the coroner. Just be thorough as possible. God knows I'll get a call from the Mayor." Lawrence only nodded.

Ryals was sure Lawrence had an extensive resume and had Ryals had seen far worse in his kind of position. Lawrence had the steeled look and posture of former military.

Ryals wiped his sweat and walked back into the club car with Allison.

"I have to admit. Hell of a place to go if you have to." He regretted saying it as soon as he did. So, he added, "Just a beautiful course."

It didn't matter; everyone was preoccupied. But Lawrence looked at him after a moment.

"You've never been in here, huh?" Lawrence seemed surprised. Allison wasn't; she acted as if he should probably leave as soon as possible.

"Lived in Augusta my whole life. Never set foot in. Not really a golf person."

She just nodded and kept on her phone. "Yeah, I wasn't either," speaking of some distant time, some person now gone. She walked away on her phone and one of the other deputies stepped close, hooking his thumbs in his belt and puffing his chest as if posing for the cameras that weren't there. Of course, they would be soon. Somehow or another.

"I guess it's what they get," he said, lifting onto the balls of his feet. He was full of energy. "Spirits come back to haunt."

"What does that mean?" Ryals asked, not looking directly at the young deputy.

"Well, they say they built the Augusta National on an Indian burial ground. You never heard that?"

Ryals hadn't. There was plenty he didn't know about Augusta's most famous piece of history.

He hoped to get out of here before he needed to know much more.

FIVE

Jonni watched the trees pass beneath them; a river, some swampland, industrial plants, the interstate, but mostly dark green, pine as well as oak, elm, sweetgum and sycamore along the river. He did not know them all by sight, but Willy had studied up and made sure Jonni knew what grew in Georgia. Even when he landed he could feel the humidity settle on him like a sticky layer and thick air in his lungs.

The leased five-seater Cyberjet landed at the regional airport in Augusta. His dad was taking pictures and video with his phone as they exited the plane. They were on board with one other golfer, Cameron Smith from Australia, who had been quite friendly when they boarded before but both had gone quiet to focus on what lay ahead.

The Masters was the Shangri-LA of Golf Tournaments; the green Jacket was the Holy Grail. It was monumental to receive an invitation and nearly impossible to win. Jonni imagined the drive up the famous Magnolia Lane — he had read about it in books and on the internet for years. He was not far from that passage.

There were a number of ways to become eligible for an invitation, none of them easy. The most obvious were to have been a previous champion or competitor ranking in the Masters top twelve; other options included winning PGA championships, being in the top 50 in global golf rankings, or to be a British, Latin American or other regional amateur champion. Jonni's Latin win followed three Asia-Pacific tournaments. Still the letter and call came as a complete surprise. He wished his mother had been alive for him to share the news that day.

They landed, taxied, exited the plane into bright sun.. His dad ushered him through the airport where fans were waiting, taking pictures, getting autographs — several shouted his name but he kept his hat down, signed an obligatory autograph and kept moving while he held his breath.

"They're excited for you," his dad said in their native language, Afrikaans, a bastardized form of Dutch evolved among settlers in the 17th century; now an official language of South Africa. He knew Jonni needed encouragement when interacting with fans. It did not come naturally. He told Jonni as well that it was part of the game now; sponsorships were earned on and off the course.

They made it outside and climbed into the black SUV that awaited them.

Whenever Jonni began to think of things like this — endorsements, products, commercials, press tours — he got dizzy and felt like he wanted to quit the whole thing and go back to washing dishes. His dad seemed to soak it up, and sometimes spoke at press conferences in Jonni's stead. Not that they had many. Five minor wins, two major second-places, one major win. Jonni shied quickly from the camera.

Jonni watched the trees on the other side and felt the jet lag. His eyes fluttered shut against the morning sun as it flickered on his face through the window from behind the pine trees as they pulled onto the freeway.

The driver's phone rang and he passed it back to Jonni's dad, who listened. Jonni opened his eyes and looked. His dad thanked the caller and hung up and returned the phone.

"What is it?" Jonni asked.

"I don't know," his dad said, shrugging. "They want us to come to the clubhouse before we go to the hotel." Dad patted his son on the shoulder. "Must be an informal welcome."

SIX

Ryals watched as the CSI scoured the pine straw and shrubbery, then moved to the rope and body, which was soon taken down. There was a small crowd of onlookers, including the poor man who had found the body, and whom Ryals had just finished interviewing. The sun was overhead and hot and his neck was sweating, but he didn't remove his jacket. There was a strict no electronics policy set by the club, including cell phones, even on the employees, and particularly now, they had stressed, and had security out to enforce it. He felt nearly obliged to follow those orders, and thought they would prefer that he did. His phone buzzed with calls from the Sheriff and DA. He couldn't answer his phone until he had answers himself. Allison had been hanging around, nervous like a bird when you get between her and her nest, but he wanted to thoroughly canvas the scene and then get the hell out and report in.

The CSI guys soon wrapped up, apparently finding nothing remarkable, and the body was taken away by the coroner. The assistant director had requested there be a truck with no markings but the coroner only had the one. So that was by now beginning to generate some speculative headlines, he supposed. He cared — only because the inevitable storm would be that much worse if the National didn't have it their way.

He tucked his notepad into his jacket and walked up the hill wiping his brow with his thumb and thumbnail, flicking the sweat off on the grass. He didn't know how the golfers walked around in long pants all day.

He answered his phone this time. "Yes sir," he said. "Just wrapping up here. Yes, sir. All done, all easy. Oh yes sir. Hell of a thing." The Sheriff was a fan.

Ahead he could see the Allison awaiting him, her hands clutched together moving a stylish ring from one finger to the other between glances at her watch. He didn't envy her job today. But it wasn't his problem.

"They're here," she said.

"Who?"

"The golfer," she said. "Jonni Lombard. He and his father."

"His father?"

"He's young. Twenty-four."

"Really."

"Yes, they're waiting in the clubhouse, a private room. The director has been with them."

"Okay, what's that to me?" Ryals asked.

"For you to speak with them," she said, falling into pace with him as they climbed the long hill up. Ryals looked around. The course was massive; the rolling hills like jade and an unending blanket brown pine straw contrasted with the green, the bright white sand traps and neon azaleas; it was like being in some fantasy world.

"I don't need to speak with them, Miss Roy."

"You don't?"

"No. There's no crime here, and they aren't immediate family. They are welcome to call the department or coroner if they have a need to see the body or ask any questions about arranging transport, but no one will release anything except to family."

"Oh," she said. He wasn't sure why she was disappointed. Maybe she just wanted him to do the hard part for her.

As he turned, he asked her, "Most golfers bring their caddies?"

"Yes, competitors do for the tournament. Since 1983 anyway. The course provides caddies for members."

Hell of a long way to come to die, Ryals thought.

Jonni had his first drive up Magnolia lane. It was something like a baptism, or a walk up the line of pews for confirmation. For a moment all of his jet lag dissolved like fizz in a cup and he nearly asked the driver to stop so he could get out and take a picture. Nothing could ever compare to this moment, he thought. The clubhouse ahead, the shadows of the trees on its white pillared facade; it was like a dream.

Of course, he didn't share his thoughts. His father took pictures and posted them to Jonni's social media accounts, which much to his father's chagrin Jonni had little interest in. Jonni just stared without blinking, wanting to remember all of it, forever. He felt that he truly didn't belong.

They were greeted by a woman named Allison, who took them inside, down green-carpeted hallways lined with photos of the Masters history. She was friendly and seemed to bounce, as if her athleticism was always being contained; she sat them in a room of mahogany wood and dark green with white trim and simple gold and white patterns. There were beautiful paintings of the course, which Jonni had yet to see but knew was just outside on the other side of the building. Allison offered them both water served in a pitcher with crystal cups. Then, the Chairman of the Augusta National, a tall man with silver hair and a high forehead and glasses that sparkled in the room's clean light sat, opposite them and shook their hands.

"There's something I need to tell you. Both of you," the Chairman began.

Jonni heard the words and found himself staring at the Chairman, then at Allison, then his dad. He thought he must be dreaming; still asleep on the plane.

"It wasn't Willy," Jonni said. "I just talked to him from South Africa. Let me talk to him again." Jonni took his phone out, everything seeming slow and quiet as he typed a text to Willy. He knew his dad, mouth hanging open, was watching him and saying nothing. Jonni typed a text and halfway through he stopped and looked up. His phone didn't work here. Everyone stared at him.

"Does everyone know?" Jonni asked. He wasn't sure why.

"Right now it's contained, Mr. Lombard," Allison said. "Word has not gotten out."

She knew that would not continue to be the case. The National maintained notoriously strict control over the dissemination of information related to all operations, from groundskeeping secrets to the membership list. For decades they controlled what was televised and renewed the exclusive contract with CBS for TV rights only one year at a time. Outside of the Masters, this was a very private club. Its finances were not disclosed.

In 2017 the National opened its state-of-the-art media center. The stately building welcomed reporters with antebellum-inspired staircases and flattered each news entity with a brass plaque, and provided journalists four-star meals, gratis, in a fine dining room with curved wood ceilings. It was a way to welcome the press — but also to control the news. Reporters wore RFID tags from the moment they walked on the grounds (as do patrons). The media building cost north of sixty million dollars to build and operated only ten days out of the year. They were now three days into that window. Allison wanted to keep secret this sensational and horrible event at a time when they invited all eyes onto the course, but news would break very soon. This morning she instructed the National's media team to prepare a release. Except the national didn't issue press releases like another organization. Going back to its founding, only one person was authorized to speak on behalf of ANGC — and about matters relating to the Masters. That was the Chairman. And since uncharacteristically hot-blooded comments about the Saudi LIV tour and its predatory sponsorship recruitment methods, he had said very little at all. That was three years ago.

"It doesn't make any sense," Martin Lombard said.

"I'm sure it will at some point," the Chairman said. "We wanted you to hear this from us. Not in any other way."

Martin turned to his son and sat beside him. He embraced him. "I'm sorry, Jonni. I'm so sorry." His dad said. He looked with teary eyes at Allison. He fought words and none came out. Jonni saw a mix of emotions on his face. He was at a loss.

Jonni could barely think. He replayed the Chairman's news over and over. Dad held him but there was nothing his embrace could do. It couldn't be true. Willy was here. Surely, he was here somewhere.

Jonni looked from face to face, and saw how grave it all was.

"The Sheriff's department will need you to ID the body," Allison said. "Just one of you," she added, hoping to soften the blow.

Jonni said nothing. He sat back against the chair and stared at the ceiling. Father said nothing for a moment and they both listened to the noise of the staff and golf carts outside. Any minute, his dad was sure, other golfers and managers and staff would be looking for them as word spread. It was just a matter of time before they were surrounded by shouting press. Before they were the center of the world's attention. It was coming.

"Why would Willy do this?" Jonni asked, echoing his dad, the one thing he wanted an answer for, his voice cracking.

The Chairman adjusted the glasses on his nose then removed them and rested them on his knee. "I didn't know Mr. Sharpe, I trust and understand he was a wonderful man. People can be sick, and we don't even know about it. I've experienced it in my life. There's no rhyme or reason to it."

It made sense. Jonni heard it. But it didn't, either. Willy wasn't sick. He was simple. About as simple as they came, but just about as good, too. His Afrikaans accent thick like a farmer. His teeth crooked and his laugh deep.

"He liked his rum and coke," his dad said, which wasn't helpful. But Willy did. Willy drank all the time, but only after work. Never on the course. Never on the grass. To him the grass was sacred. He taught Jonni that. Then his dad shook his head, as if in argument with his own thoughts. "How could he simply walk out on the course like that? Just stroll out drunk? You haven't got better security than that?"

"We're evaluating the situation," the Chairman said.

Jonni felt distant from everyone. If it was real, it was real. It did not feel real. They were alone. He and his dad. That was it. Just them in this foreign place. He wished he was back home. It felt very, very far away and the tournament suddenly not very important.

There was a tap at the door and then a woman entered. His father stood.

"I've just spoken with the investigator from the police. There's not much more to say than what we've told you. After we ID, his family can reach out, and we will need some of their details to pass along to the authorities to make necessary arrangements."

Jonni looked at her. Then he looked to Martin again. "Willy wouldn't have done that." He thought he would choke on the words. "He wouldn't have killed himself. There's no way." Jonni looked at his dad, but his dad shook his head again.

"There was a lot of pressure, son. On this tournament. You know Willy. He takes things on himself. He had a side to him that you and I couldn't easily see. But he loved you. He loved the game, he loved you."

She gave him the look again, but this time he felt no comfort. "I'm so sorry," was all she said. He could read her expression. Or he thought he could.

"He wouldn't abandon me," Jonni said. "Not now." He thought of Willy, showing up at dawn with a coffee for himself and a chocolate milk for Jonni, ready to go hit the "dew grass." He thought of Willy pumping his fist and doing a spin when Jonni eagled on the Hippo Course, then again in Sydney. He thought of Willy at their dinner table, his father with takeout, it was Jonni's birthday party, and Willy winked at Jonni when the singing started — Jonni hated singing. Finally Jonni began to sob. Quiet tears, he did his best to hold his face steel, but the emotion broke through.

Willy was his only confidant, the closest one in the world. Jonni rarely spoke, but he spoke to Willy when they walked between holes; they talked shots and irons and wind and humidity and breathing techniques and Jonni you're tensing up when your club is at noon and then they would talk about everything else, a girl Jonni liked or how nervous he was to fly or whenever he missed his mom.

Willy cared about him, was a close friend and an excellent caddie.

"I'm so sorry," Allison said. "We are here for you, though. Anything you need."

"I just need my caddie," Jonni said, and felt the room spin.

SEVEN

Monday
First day of Practice Rounds

Angela was supposed to have put herself to bed at nine-thirty — her exhausted Dad told her before crashing at eight-thirty. He knew she hadn't because when he walked out to make coffee he could smell popcorn and she only made that when she was staying up well past her bedtime. He was glad he went to bed early anyway, though, because his phone began to ring before five. He answered it and felt his bones and muscles groaning as he heard the familiar voice. But he still had to ask.

"Who is this?"

"It's Lauren. Your coroner."

"What can I do for you?" Ryals yawned.

"Listen, this case is still on your desk, right? Ball still in your court, so to speak?"

"The caddie?" Ryals asked.

"Yeah. Maybe I need a different sport metaphor."

"Yeah."

"Okay, I wanted you to know this before it goes anywhere else and anyone else sees it. Because it's you. I get — I know what a big deal this is."

"What are you calling me about?" Ryals asked, sitting up but already feeling the cold wash of horrible realization...

"It's not suicide," She said.

"Say that again," Ryals asked, sitting up completely. One, so he could process it. Two, so he could be absolutely sure.

"The hands, they were bound. Ankles too. There's rub marks —they tried to hide them but, there they are — he didn't hang himself. Someone wants us to think that he did. Or at least wanted it to look that way."

"So—"

"Yeah, buddy. That golf course is a crime scene."

Ryals dialed the Sheriff repeatedly while driving with his lights flashing. No siren, and thank God he was ahead of the traffic, but he hadn't a moment to spare. He didn't, however, have any kind of plan. He was simply on an errand to create mass hysteria. Thank God, he thought, thank God he had called the CSI guys. That would prove very, very important, at least as far as potential liability was concerned. Of course, they hadn't found anything. Then again, they hadn't really been looking, had they? They would tell him that they looked for anything, regardless. But right now, Ryals was asking himself, what would he have done yesterday if he knew it was a murder scene? So far, nothing.

That didn't change the fact that the clock had been ticking on a murder investigation, and he had literally slept on the clock. It was barely light out but in only moments the sun would come in blazing with ferocity. Today was a hot one, too hot for April.

He came to Washington Road where crowds were already moving on the roadsides, walking with water and chairs, crossing at crosswalks—no jaywalking allowed this week— gathering around stands selling coffee and breakfast. Many locals, but this was an international tournament. Augusta was flooded with people from every corner of the globe, and many celebrities. Ryals once bought groceries behind Mel Gibson who was getting milk. Heads of state were often spotted. Here in the heart of Augusta. It was a funny thing.

His phone finally rang. It was the Sheriff. He explained the situation. The Sheriff was quiet for a long moment.

"Well, Christ on Crutches," he said.

He moved around, getting into better position, maybe sitting up out of bed. "Okay. Listen. Where are you?"

"Getting to the National."

"Okay. This is still in your hands and we may need someone to blame when the Mayor or the Governor calls. But also because you know your stuff, Hall. So do not, do not mess this one up. Everything by the book. Every letter of the book. We don't bend one rule for them. Not that they'd ask us to but — well hot damn. This is a thing."

"Yes, sir," Ryals said with emphasis. "And yes, sir it absolutely is."

"Tell me what we know."

"Nothing. Looks like a suicide, but wasn't. I didn't interview the golfer, this Lombard, but I will this morning. I'll get their head of security in on it, too." Ryals said, reaching for a coffee cup that wasn't there.

"Do you have a theory? Anything to go on?" The Sheriff asked.

"Honestly, sir, no, but there wasn't much cause to look further. The golfer he worked for is just a kid."

"They say this is the last gentleman's tournament in the last gentleman's sport, but who knows what these celebrity golfers get up to. Did he travel with anyone? Girlfriend maybe?"

"No, he didn't. Came alone. Isn't married."

"You may need to get on an international phone call or two. Okay. I'll get the mayor and DA on the phone. Do this thing right, Hall."

"Sheriff," he said. "To do this thing right I'd have to close it down for a day."

Already a thousand people walking up the road to the entrance. Ryals pulled onto the Magnolia Lane drive. He could see pedestrians crossing in his rearview as they walked the long way to the entrance. The Sheriff just sighed.

"That's not going to happen, Detective."

"I know."

He hung up just as he flashed his badge at the guard shack. The guard made a call. Ryals began to move but the guard kept a hand up. "Please wait, sir."

"I'm Richmond County..."

"No one in without permission." Then he winked. "You'd be surprised, sir. People will use any excuse to get in."

"Tell Allison Roy or — Lawrence, uh, head of security—"

The guard stepped away, looking at Ryals's badge and ID. He made a call and returned.

"You're cleared," he said. And Ryals drove in, seeing the activity around the clubhouse now: if yesterday the whole place was alive, today it had taken a few shots of espresso.

Allison came around to meet him. Her face curious, overwhelmed, stressed. What he had to tell her was not about to make her day at any better. He felt like he was about to toss a hand grenade onto the Augusta National.

Jonni showered. He laid on the bed and his feet were on the ground and he had a putter in his hands laid across his body. It was like a security blanket to him. He'd been dressed and ready since two a.m. Wide awake and staring at the ceiling. He simply felt numb. Now he was going through motions like some kind of automaton.

He rolled the leather grip from one hand to another across his chest and tried to remember Willy's instructions; not just his tips, but his style. The way he taught Jonny to think. "Just feel it, Jon boy," he said once, playing late into the evening while they swatted mosquitos. "In the dark, middle of the day, you got to just feel that hole's gravity. And all you gotta do is help the ball fall into it. It wants to go there. Just help it." Then Willy spat. He chewed on toothpicks, and he spat.

Willy hadn't amounted to much in life—he would be the first to say it. He wasn't a renowned caddie. He worked the grounds at a golf course up north in the country, just a poor local Afrikaans gardener who had grown up around golf and grass. He began helping Jonni offering advice after Jonni's first local tournament. He took a shining to the kid, and his advice helped and Father had hired him after the first sponsorship. That was six years ago; Willy had been their faithful friend and caddie since.

All of a sudden, on the eve of this momentous week, Jonni had a new caddie. He agreed to it in a daze. The club had offered to find him one. Several other golfers offered, indirectly, to loan or seek one. In the end he went with one the director knew and recommended. The caddie went by "Buster." His last name was Crawford. He was from South Carolina. His hair was thinning on top and thick at the back. He squinted perpetually with one eye and he had a kind face. He was clean shaven and his nose was sunburnt. He and Jonni had met briefly the night before. Buster offered to walk the course and get to know one another but the jet lag had returned with a force like a wave knocking him over and Jonni said thank you, but he just wanted to go sleep.

Yesterday he felt like he had a direction in his life, a plan and some confidence but all of that was gone today like a forest fire that had swept over it all.

He didn't know what he was supposed to feel. He didn't cry much, not since his mom died. Once someone asked him if he had Aspergers but he didn't think so. It wasn't that he didn't feel sad. He felt so sad he didn't know how to express it. It was more that he simply didn't know how to process any of this. Didn't know how, and didn't want to.

Yesterday there was press waiting around the course, gathering and setting up inside and some taking note of him. A bigger spotlight than he could remember. He was the youngest competitor this year by five years. That was news enough, but it didn't mean anything to him.

Now the press was outside. He could see them on the roadside from his window, gathered like hyenas. Their faces were superficially sympathetic but they shouted their questions and snapped their pictures all the same.

Jonni fell asleep finally, some minutes before his dad was knocking at his door.

The practice rounds started today. It was time to get ready, he said. Jonni sat up quickly. Play? He thought. He hadn't decided yet that he would. He didn't know if he should.

EIGHT

Ryals walked back up from the 12th hole. He had learned nothing new other than admitting to himself how difficult it would have been for someone to tie the rope by himself and then jump with it. Difficult but not impossible. Of course, it was perhaps equally difficult for someone else to do it but maybe there was more than one suspect. Willy was no shrimp and maybe it had taken two to restrain him. Ryals had called back for the toxicology report but it wasn't ready yet. He didn't need to stress the priority.

Ryals returned uphill to the waiting cart and then rode to the club-house where Allison told him that Jonni Lombard and his father waited inside. The massive square house was immaculately white, almost blinding. There were people everywhere. Outside, inside. Staring. Ryals ignored them all.

He beelined for the open door.

Ryals entered the clubhouse.

He walked through, on perfect carpet, past a line of photos.

Ryals's first impression of Jonni Lombard was that the kid should have played more team sports in school. In fact, he thought the boy should probably be in school. He was despondent in his sponsored Adidas long-sleeve shirt and athletic pants. His Oakley sunglasses were in his blue hat with three white stripes beside him on the couch and he had a bottle of water at his feet. His father, who introduced himself as

Martin, paced the room. The father wore khakis and an Adidas t-shirt and sneakers. He was a tall man, but thin; Jonni had his lankiness but not his father's height.

Jonni's leg had been shaking. Now it was still. Martin stopped his pace and turned to face the detective.

"It's a big day for us, detective," was all Martin said. "For my boy." His accent was thick, and odd; Ryals wasn't sure he could name another South African he had ever met. Ryals held open his notebook and adjusted his pen, which bore the name and logo of his favorite lunch spot The Village Deli. Just looking at it Ryals craved lunch already. He felt like he could not wait to get out of here. He felt the pressure of the gathering press and knew he was in the middle of it. The word was out — but was it out about the murder? It would leak quickly if it hadn't. If they were smart, they would announce something. This would make for an interesting "so that happened" sort of story when he told relatives about his job, and perhaps even give his daughter reason enough not to lie to her friends about what her dad did that had him stuck on the south side of Augusta. (For a time being a cop was a matter of prestige for Angela, but after meeting a couple of the bad apples Ryals worked with, she made up other stories. Ryals liked many of his coworkers, but he didn't defend them to her.)

Ryals stood by the door and thought about what his daughter was up to while Martin paced and talked to Jonni or to himself. Then Ryals stepped in and sat in a chair opposite them.

"I just need to get some details from you both," Ryals said carefully.

"Details for a suicide? We weren't there. Who was there? No one. Someone should have been there, but..." Martin was impatient. Ryals studied him. Then Jonni — and he realized...

"Has anyone spoken to you this morning?"

He gestured to Allison, who was gone, on calls and talking to others. Lawrence was outside in the hallway now, speaking to someone unseen through a doorway. Allison occasionally appeared, moving in her OCD fashion.

"This is an investigation now. A murder investigation." For several moments nothing happened at all. The air conditioning kicked on. Ryals spoke slowly as a habit, his voice was deep. He could hear it echo in the room. Martin sat down slowly on the chair adjacent to Jonni's sofa and looked at Ryals.

Jonni was perplexed. He looked at Ryals directly. "Why would anyone want to kill Willy?"

"That's what I'm meant to find out. I need just a few details from you to help me do that."

There was total silence again.

Ryals cleared his throat and looked toward the door as if he were being graded. Surely, he was. "Yes, in light of new evidence we've reclassified the case and are proceeding now assuming criminal motive..."

He caught himself from saying more. He folded his hands and searched for words. "I'm very sorry,"

"Who? Who would do this?" Jonni asked again, his thoughts obviously coming in a rush, jumbled up. He stood, and clinched his fists and stared at Ryals. Then he looked at his hands as if realizing he had forgotten something.

"I don't..." He looked at his father. Then at Ryals. "Willy?"

No one said a word for a moment.

"Who did it?"

"I'm working on that. Maybe you can help me."

Jonni stared dumbly. His father sat beside him. "Of course, officer," Martin said. "Of course, whatever we can do."

"Just a few questions," Ryals continued, looking at his pad. "You knew Mr. Shepherd for—"

"Willy," Martin interjected. "He preferred Willy, would prefer that." There was an edge in his voice. He was angry, Ryan could see it. Angry at the system here. That somehow, they had failed to look after Willy.

" 'Willy.' So, how long had you known one another?"

Jonni finally responded. "Willy's been with me for six years."

"He travels with you?"

"Yeah. Everywhere."

"And do you..." Ryals paused on that one for a moment. "Is he close with anyone? I think I heard about a girlfriend."

"Yeah, Monique. I mean, sometimes. Sometimes she's around. She doesn't travel."

"They're on again, off again," Martin said. "She has never traveled with us. She's in South Africa."

Ryals nodded, jotted notes. It was hardly relevant. He lived in another country. Ryals didn't know what to ask. He cut to it.

"Do you have any idea what could have happened? Or why..."

Martin shook his head. "No. Not at all." Jonni sat, then stood again. He looked at Ryals. "We were told he drank and - but now..."

Ryals suggested they all sit. He tapped his pen twice and looked finally back at Martin. "Anything may be important. Even something that didn't seem important before," Ryals explained.

"I can't fathom," Martin replied quickly, putting his hand on Jonni's arm. He nodded at his son who Ryals could now see fought tears.

Martin put an arm on his son's shoulder. Ryals closed his notepad. There was nothing more to ask. He didn't bother with any more feeble pleasantries. He excused himself. Martin called after him,

"Tell them Jonni needs to practice. We need to get his gear and get out on the course."

"I believe they said he had the day off," Ryals said, glancing back at Allison in the hallway.

"No," Jonni said. "I'll play."

"They have him a new caddie," Martin said flatly. Ryals marked that in his notepad too. He stood and quietly spoke to Ryals, leveling up, father to father. "He needs to play. He needs to." Ryals looked past at the boy. He held a club, shifting it front hand to hand.

Allison was outside by the front. Ryals pocketed his notepad.

"All done here."

"They're free to do whatever they need to?"

"Yes, they are."

"We just asked them to wait for you there." She explained for no reason. He could tell she felt helpless. She shook her head and looked out at the course. "Do you need anything more from us?"

"Not really. I'll drop down and check on the coroner. Waiting on toxicology."

She said nothing, bit her lip. They both looked out over the Hole One tee, a view that carried over the long hill so that they could see hundreds of yards down the slope of the course. Golf carts whirred by criss-crossing on walk-paths while hundreds of groundskeepers trimmed and sprayed and raked. The place was alive now, buzzing, pulsing, humming as if it were some giant living organism. Men climbed towers and worked on video cameras; the leaderboards, still operating manually after a century, were being prepped with cards naming the first players to tee off. Ryals knew the practice rounds began today. They were open the public.

"When do you let players onto the course? Like Jonni."

"An hour before they tee off, give or take. They're invited in."

"They can't come in before?"

"Except for ceremonies."

"And the caddies?"

"They come in once before the practice rounds, for a meeting and briefing. That's new, more for the age of social media."

"There are cameras allowed in here today, correct? For the general public?"

"Yes," Allison answered. She set her phone down like it was a statement. "What's next?"

"I can speak with your head of security," Ryals gestured to him, standing by on the phone. "And see what he has from security feeds." Lawrence finished speaking into a radio and walked over to them. Allison relayed the camera request.

"As I said, that patch is in a blind spot, but we can review what we have. I've been over them and I can't find much."

"Yeah," Ryals said. "I think we need to know."

The National was monitored from a sophisticated security room, with AI-analyzed video feeds, motion sensors, and perimeter drone security. It was easily the most high tech, expensive room Ryals had seen in Georgia. Or anywhere, he thought. Lawrence pointed at one screen with a series of green lines and numbers.

"If someone climbs a fence, we know where and can approximate his or her weight. The CIA had that before us," Lawrence winked.

"Impressive."

"But really, Lawrence explained, we're on the Good Ol' Boy system. Someone jumps over the barbed wire and twelve-foot fences, we scoop em up and dump 'em out. There's nothing to hide here, just grass to protect, and the legacy."

"But that's different during the tournament."

"Absolutely. We have guards posted all over. Some hidden, many not. We have motion sensors and patrols outside, aerial surveillance..."

"That mostly stops people from getting in, right?"

"Correct," Lawrence said, fidgeting. "We watch the perimeter carefully. But the interior — not as well. It's covered, I'd say, thirty percent."

"Who runs your security? You use a private outfit as well?"

"I'm director of in-house security operations, but for patrol and everything else we contract Securitas. They run the Pinkerton guards, but you'll also see some of our security with a Securitas badge."

"I'd like to talk to whoever your point person is there."

"Absolutely."

"You keep it dark at night? Or is it lit up?"

"Usually dark. Saturday the lights were on for the workers until at least 11. Otherwise, we illuminate the perimeter and the facilities."

Ryals gathered Lawrence was a bit of a perfectionist and didn't like weaknesses exposed. The National's weaknesses were necessarily his. If there were any they could identify.

"So it's most likely that whoever it was, was already inside."

"I would say so."

Lawrence helped scroll through feeds from Saturday night. Ryals took a seat beside him. Lawrence's radio buzzed incessantly. His phone was vibrating. He checked it once.

"How long do we have?" Ryals asked.

"It's all starting up now, but gates open in two hours for practice rounds."

Ryals thought about that. Of course, there was no stopping that. No force could delay it. No investigation. Nor a loose murderer.

"How do you get tickets to practice rounds?"

"You need a pair?"

"Just curious."

"They're sold through a lottery. One hundred dollars per, if you're lucky enough to buy."

"That's it?"

"Four-fifty all four days of the tournament. One buck forty for each day."

"I would have thought more."

"The cost of concessions is still quite reasonable as well. It was meant that way from the beginning. Bobby Jones insisted."

Lawrence attended to several screens, seeing multi-colored crowds gathering on exterior pathways. Congregating with anticipation.

"Here," Lawrence announced. "This is what we have. One camera, with an angle here," he pointed above the leaderboard that was visible, and further down the green, "was down for the evening."

"Is that unusual?"

"Yes." Ryals noted it in his notebook.

"I didn't think anything of it before. We've upgraded our system, yet again. Third year in a row. There's bugs." Lawrence said as he worked forward in time on the feed, "but now..."

Yeah, Ryals thought. Now it was all in a different light.

"So here is what we do have," Lawrence said, calibrating the time.

"See, there's lots of activity, even at night. Carts moving, maintenance, prep, watering, you know. It's a busy night before hell week. Here's where the, ah..."

What they see on the screen is macabre. Willy, from the waist down, moved out of shadow and climbed up the camera tower post. A moment later his body drops into view, jerks, and then moves only by swaying from the noose.

"Not good bedtime entertainment," Lawrence observed.

"Play it again," Ryals said. Something about the video confused him. He wasn't sure what. He was starting to wish he had watched this the night before. Lawrence played it again. Ryals studied every detail. The body climbing up. Then swinging into view. "One more time." Lawrence had barely begun it again before Ryals caught it.

"There, look." Lawrence paused it and Ryals took a snapshot with his phone. "His shoes. Now, in both moments he's wearing black pants, black, boots or sneakers, not sure — but here. When he climbs up, they're jet black. When he's hanging, here, there's this silver swatch."

"I think — I think maybe I see that."

"It's a different person," Ryals said.

Lawrence pursed his lips and squinted his eyes. He played the video back and forward. "I think you're right. But if that's the case, where did the other guy go? And what — it doesn't make sense. One guy goes up, another comes down?"

"No. We can't see the other corner. Once he's up there he moves around. So supposing he climbs up, and on the other side pulls up Willy's body, then drops it down and jumps down the far side..."

"It must be the only place on the course where we have a blank spot like that," Lawrence said slowly as he studied it. "I'll be damned."

Ryals didn't know what it meant at all himself.

"I'll check other feeds. Got through them. You can as well if you like. They had to go in and out of the woods somehow." Lawrence flipped through video files quickly. There were two other video technicians nearby, busy with many tasks, so it was slow going, and Ryals had a sinking feeling that the crime scene was wider than it had first appeared — and the killer clever.

They looked for another forty minutes on separate screens. Ryals hunched unnaturally like a caveman. Lawrence with a straight back, thin arms and long fingers expertly manipulating the controls. He knew all aspects of his security domain intimately. The kind of guy who could do it all, just in case he had to. Ryals felt overwhelmed by the sheer volume of footage. Slowly going through two hundred cameras, every hour. This might take days.

Eventually he stepped out and updated the Sheriff and the DA, also Allison. Whether he or Lawrence were meant to speak to her, he wasn't sure.

He had texts from Angela, asking if she could meet friends for a movie. He would answer that in a moment.

He went back in the room, checked his watch. One hour until the gates opened. The Sheriff gave Ryals no direction. His was a political position, and he was clearly keeping at arm's length right now. He would take credit for whatever success and would avoid any blame. Ryals knew the DA was getting calls. Surely the mayor too. He had minutes to decide, he told Ryals. This thing is hotter than a tin roof.

"Here," Lawrence said. "I might have something."

Ryals sat again. Lawrence slowed the feed and they saw a truck full of pine straw bales roll to a stop under some trees close to the edge of the lit area by the deep shadows of the woods. A door opened. A man exited, wearing a hat and dark coveralls. He was large and imposing even on the grainy screen with the hues of digital night vision. The man unloaded bales of straw and it became clear — to Ryals, now that he knew what he was looking for — that the straw was meant to conceal something. The man moved something out of the bed — a plastic bag, large enough to contain a body — and carried it with the straw into the darkness.

"I wouldn't have picked this up. They're constantly moving bags of greens and mulch and potted plants." Lawrence was matter-of-fact, not apologetic.

"He's strong. He tossed it like it was nothing."

"This is about four hundred yards up from the 12th hole. Not far from one of the grounds facilities, number two."

"So he disappears into the woods, and then reappears at the 12th?" Ryals asked.

"Seems that way."

"How long is he gone?"

"Well..." Lawrence scrolled forward. "Looks like he comes back..." On the video the man reappears carrying nothing. "Eighteen minutes later."

"Okay. So. We need to find out where this guy came from. And hopefully that tells me why he went through the crazy trouble of hanging an already dead guy."

"In what was about to be one of the world's most public places."

"Yeah," Ryals said. "That too."

Lawrence scrolled back in the feed, looking at other cameras.

"The cart came from here," he said, pointing at a maintenance shed. "But the problem is..." Ryals saw it. It was a den of activity. Men coming and going, carts rolling in and out. They eventually saw the man with the cart drive it in —

"No cameras inside?"

"Afraid not."

—and then as they watched, at least two dozen men arrived at once, before that, another half dozen, moving in waves. All in coveralls, most wearing identical hats. Ryals studied their shoes, when they were visible. Most wore dark boots of some kind, and the feed here — and that of the trees and the camera tower — would make matching the boots nearly impossible.

"Do we have video of these guys coming through the gates?"

"Yes, but they all come through at once and get briefed. We're talking three hundred guys."

"Do they stick around through the whole thing, or they're just here for prep?"

"Most are not here for the tournament, but some either stay or return for work afterward. Allison can provide you with those numbers. I will say we have three hundred on the grounds during the tournament, another three hundred overnight and add another two hundred in the months and weeks approaching the tournament. Two hundred are permanent staff during the year."

"Is there any way to tell if this guy is permanent staff or if he's a recent hire?"

"Absolutely. But I can tell you I don't think he's either."

"Why is that?"

"His shoes," Lawrence said. "No groundskeeper is wearing sneakers like that. And to be honest..."

"Yes,"

"Our groundskeepers have a — how do I put this — a respect for the grounds. The way they walk, the way they even move the straw. This guy, he just doesn't act like he is on hallowed ground."

It was safe to assume the killer didn't show up to trim the azaleas after the murder. They also had less than an hour to get on the grounds before the crowds arrived. After that, any hope for material evidence would be gone.

NINE

Jonni stood at the edge of the practice range. He could see, and hear his idols, famous pro golfers, just a few feet away— Vijay Singh, Rory McIlroy, Kazuki Higa, Alex Noren from Sweden and Tyrell Hatton, already warming up and who had recently made a comment that some thought would have gotten him excused from the tournament. He complained openly about how much of an insult it was for the National not to recognize his LIV title win. The National didn't recognize the LIV as having the credibility to be included in players rankings and statistics, and flatly ignored it. More arrived soon. The air was dense here; it carried all the smells of the river and grass plants and a city that were unfamiliar to him. He felt an alien, brought in to an unfamiliar land with an unfamiliar atmosphere. He had played out of the country before, away from home, but this time he felt further away than ever.

"We will not let this godawful thing take this opportunity away from you," his father had said, hours ago when Jonni stormed away from his father to find a quiet place in the clubhouse, nearly violating critical etiquette. "We don't quit. That's not who we are, that's not what Willy would want. You play the course at home, you play the same as here. Grass is grass and Willy didn't bring you here to quit." Jonni disagreed. He wanted to argue. To shout and prove his point but his thoughts came together like tangled threads and he didn't say anything. He dressed and walked out automatically. He knew his dad gave him tough love when he needed it. His dad thought this was one of those times and Jonni needed a firm push to give him courage. But it wasn't at all what Jonni needed right then.

Buster was beside him now. He was tall, bald with a semi-transparent gray and chestnut goatee, he had a quick laugh that he stifled with a horse-like grunt. A Southern accent. He was more talkative than Willy.

He had taken Jonni to the practice range where he had Jonni chip, ranging from close in to about twenty meters away. All just for a nice warm up.

Jonni wasn't loosening up, though. His grip was tight because the sweat in his palms was soaking the leather, making it even harder to feel the club in his hands.

He practiced swinging straight with a crisp descending blow through the ball, a brush of the grass and an open club face. His toes dug in, his knees were bent but tight. A good chip meant keeping a level and low club, swinging straight through the grass, and using the open face of the iron against the ball. The follow through direct but not too high, easing into a rest parallel to the beginning of the stroke. Jonni tried to chip, but nothing seemed on the right path of the club, no solid connection. Dirt and grass covered the ball with each poorly timed chip. With each duffed chip, he simply went at the ball harder, causing even worse problems.

After a moment, he stopped and caught his breath. Buster didn't drop another ball. Jonni looked at Buster, who seemed to just be looking at the divots.

After a moment, Buster said, "People all over the world talk about Augusta National grass, and for good reason. The greens here are measured by a stimpmeter for a green speed of thirteen and above.

That's fast, real fast, for a putt. It's pro grass. You'll glide over it like ice skating. It's oversewed perennial rye grass, brought in from across the country. Recreational golfers are dreaming to think they can play surfaces that fast; they would quickly find themselves in an emerald green nightmare. It's grass for the elite professionals, like Olympic figure skaters carving a fresh sheet of ice. Have you ever felt grass like that?"

"No," replied Jonni, in a huff.

"Okay. It's extremely consistent. Which means you have no one to blame but yourself." He smirked, then studied Jonni. "You know what — am I giving you too much?"

Jonni hesitated. "I don't really know about grass. I like to feel it."

"Fair enough. It's your show. This place just ain't like others. You ever been somewhere where they bring in the pine straw, and ship out the pinecones? I'll give you some tips as I see them, you take or leave them. How's that?"

Jonni said nothing. He could feel sweat on his brow. Buster produced another ball. He set it down on the grass where it rested without sinking.

Jonni felt how his feet sank in the grass, felt his cleats catch the dirt softly, with plenty of give; the soil was rich and saturated but not like clay. There was no stickiness. There was no mental calculation, but there was a sense. It was like he just wanted to think about nothing.

He drew his putter back, far earlier than he was ready. He was so nervous that he had zero timing and while he could connect with the ball, the face of the putter was wide open, sending the putt far wide of the hole. He almost had a YIP, that involuntary, tragic wrist spasm that terrifies golfers. It was a lousy shot.

"That's okay," Buster said, setting down another ball. "Walk your mind into the game, don't run it. Jonni looked up to see a golfer he didn't know taking his own putt the next green over. Then he saw his father watching from the side—he had just arrived. Jonni looked at him and then studied the other golfer. "Just you and the ball here, there's no one else, no one else matters," Buster said. Jonni tapped the next putt, far too hard, overshot. He heard his dad breathing through his nose like he did when he was nervous. His dad was anxious and his anxiety was spilling over on Jonni.

Ryals and Lawrence exited the club car in the same place at the same location the man in the video, as best they were able to determine. Ryals look up to find the camera. For a moment he couldn't, even though he thought knew where to look.

"They really are hidden, aren't they."

"Yeah, we don't want to advertise the security here, save for the Pinkertons," Lawrence answered.

"And what about the Pinkertons?" Ryals asked as he snapped pictures. He'd heard of them, but didn't know much.

"Private security, kind of a legacy here, they stand at each hole and escort the golfers. Many are volunteers, come back every year. They're hall monitors, to be honest, but they keep things in check. Company started with Abraham Lincoln in response to assassination threats, actually. But more recently the entity was bought out by Securitas in Sweden."

"I see." Ryals looked around the straw on the ground. He studied everything and felt frantic doing it. Time was ticking. Fast. He wasn't a forensics guy, but he needed to find anything to justify bringing them in again. Lawrence seemed to know his stuff. He was looking, snapping, studying the cameras as well. Squared away, Ryals thought.

Ryals looked up to stretch his neck. The dogwood blossoms were so bright they were blinding.

"Hardly looks real," Ryals observed.

"There's many who believe it isn't. You should hear the conspiracy theories."

"Oh really?"

"Yeah. People say our azaleas can't be real, because they all bloom at the same time."

"But they are real."

"Of course. The grounds staff go through remarkable lengths to be sure they prune, fertilize, whatever they must do, including, as I understand it, swapping out plants for the ones that cooperate best, like some sort of unnatural selection."

"I see," Ryals said, looking it all over. Then he looked again at Lawrence. "You were military?" he asked.

"Navy."

"As?"

"SEAL; Navy Special Warfare. Eight years. Then FBI. Then worked for an international outfit out of Vegas before taking the gig here."

"Gotcha." Ryals moved into the woods now. He was shorter than Lawrence, shorter still because of the difference between Ryals' habit of hunching over, and Lawrence's pine-straight posture. They followed the path. Ryals felt his phone ringing. He needed to focus. It was all straw back here, as far as he could see. All manicured and brushed and trimmed and maintained even beyond what the eye could see. "Has anyone been back here since?"

"Most likely. But I'd have to check the cameras to be sure."

There was no evidence of footprints, no evidence at all. But they kept walking. Down the hill, close to the fence. There was a path there, for security and maintenance, behind the scenes. It was dirt and it was brushed clean. Ryals wasn't sure the killer would have used it, though. He was likely too smart for that. He would have walked on the straw to conceal his footprints.

They came to the bottom of the hill, a long walk and Ryals was sweating and his knees hurt. Lawrence, he noticed, wasn't even breathing hard. Nor did he sweat. He was a model of fitness, and Ryals involuntarily glanced at his gut, which he quickly sucked in. At least he wasn't wearing his jacket now, having left it at the club car. And there was a refreshing breeze down here.

They looked up at the leaderboard, and Ryals studied the base. Imagined the killer's path. There were a pair of young men on the board itself, readying cards with players names. Ryals grabbed the ladder and climbed up and they were surprised to see him.

"It's fine, just go about your work," Lawrence said. Ryals got up and looked up and down the short catwalk. He then looked at the camera station not facing the shimmering course. In it a green mesh covered camera was now set up, the operator testing it and readying the cables.

There was nothing to see. In the video the man was wearing gloves, so there was not much point in fingerprinting the structure. Still, he considered it. To be thorough, he thought, it made sense.

He was torn, though. Doing that would require shutting the place down. Or at least handicapping their operations. How quickly could he get a team in here?

Not worth it, he concluded. He climbed back down, and looked at the ground. All straw. He began to walk back. Slowly now, looking at everything from a different angle. He had one shot. This might be the most important walk of his career.

Ryals walked in the straw, imagining this to be the killer's path. He looked at the azaleas, some hidden holly bushes. Hoped for a shred of clothing, a dropped receipt — but that would have been cleaned by now, for sure.

Then he saw — something. A patch, beneath a bush, where there was no pine straw. Bare earth, soft, and in it a boot print, or a partial boot print.

"Here," Ryals said, crouching. It faced downhill, and the heel print was at the end of a slide. Someone had slipped here, at least a bit. "Maybe from carrying weight downhill?" Ryals thought out loud. He snapped pictures of it from every angle. He backed up, looked for more. The boot wasn't much, but enough to match. He could see the letters 'SA' on the heel. Of course, it could belong to any gardener. Or it could belong to the killer.

Lawrence's radio went into his ear through a transparent wire and he was constantly adjusting his volume, occasionally responding. Now he said, "we're on the North side of Two at the moment. Yes, ma'am, copy that."

Ryals could find no other prints, or anything at all. Just the heel, just right there. "You think it's something?" Lawrence asked.

"No, yes, who knows. It's all I can find though." He looked back up the hill. "We need to know where Willy was before this. He was tied up somewhere, killed somewhere."

"I'll get someone looking through all the video feeds trying to find him, see where he was. There's lots of places not to be seen on camera, but I'd venture not a lot to kill someone."

"Let's hope."

Lawrence checked his phone.

"Miss Roy is waiting for us up top," Lawrence said.

"No problem. I'm done here. We can ride up."

They walked back to the cart and turned back. Ryals saw even more people now, including the Pinkerton guards and volunteers and photographers and journalists and other staff all beginning to spread out onto the course. Birds: robins, sparrows, finches, and Georgia's State Bird, the Brown Trasher, all chirped and sang excitedly, as if even they were aware of the onset of the tournament. There was palpable energy as the grass warmed and the dew evaporated. Ryals couldn't help but feel it.

They arrived back at the security center beside the clubhouse and Allison was there. She was athletic, and in her sneakers and business suit she made for an odd marathon runner figure, but that's exactly what she was about to undertake, a week-long marathon. There was still some alarm on her face, though. Understandably.

"So," she said. "Where are we?"

Ryals lifted his jacket off the cart and held it in his arms. "There's lots I need to do."

"Right now, I just need to know if we can open the doors."

"You're willing to keep them shut?"

She was uncomfortable. "Well, no. It's not an option."

"I figured." Ryals nodded, turned and looked at the course, and sucked his teeth as he thought about it. He understood there was little he could do. In one sense, the entire Augusta National was a crime scene. He truly didn't think, however, that he would solve this thing by digging in azaleas. Cameras, cell records, those were more likely avenues. More than anything Ryals, expected the truth to emerge in an interview. Whatever happened here wasn't random. It seemed to Ryals deeply personal.

"Not that I could stop it, but you can go ahead," he said. "I'm not about to get fired for telling your Chairman — and the mayor, and everyone else otherwise."

"Okay, thank you," Allison said, and she was off again. He had given her the excuse.

Ryals took a breath.

"What do you need now?" Lawrence asked.

"I need to find out who the guy is, and how he got in here."

"Yes. I have one of my guys scanning the video feeds for anything. We don't recognize him at all." Ryals had a sense the answers were in the video. He hoped.

"How do we see personnel files, or whatever you have on all the groundskeepers?"

"I can get you over to the office where they would have that."

"You do some kinds of background checks?"

"Yes. References. Many are notable gardeners or groundskeepers at other facilities. Many are repeats, coming every year, some for decades."

"I think that's my next step," Ryals said. "Maybe he's on the list, maybe someone on your list helped him." Lawrence nodded and produced the cart keys.

"Okay, let's go," he said. Ryals looked at his phone. Twenty minutes until gates open.

TEN

Jonni sat on top of the toilet lid and closed his eyes. After a moment he leaned against the wall of the stall. He was in the clubhouse bathroom. The other players were gathered in a prep room outside. More legends there: Mark O'Meara, Zach Johnson, Fred Couples, Charl Schwartzel from South Africa, who lived just a little north of Jonni and who had his own green jacket. Outside he'd smiled at Jonni sadly — he knew Jonni from occasional South Africa events and had come over to give him a hug and offer his support. Everyone else treated Jonni like some sad puppy, all with their own sad eyes. Former champion Bubba Watson even came over and shook Jonni's hand and told him he was praying for the kid and Willy's family. It was the gathering of the greatest golfers alive in the world today and it was too much, just too much. So Jonni escaped the room.

Jonni heard them come and go in the bathroom, and he just faded away.

Eventually there came a knock at the door. It was his dad. "Jonni, come on, pal. Showtime, let's get moving." Jonni didn't. He looked at his golf shoes, the glove in his hand that he had pulled from his back pocket. By now the world knew about him, about Willy. It was on TV, his dad had told him, and then had watched it in the corner of their private dressing room while Jonni tried to ignore it. He didn't want to know what the world had to say. His dad was moving constantly, stepping from one foot to the other outside the stall. Jonni knew he was letting his dad down right now, but Jonni hadn't the energy for his dad.

Buster was outside, talking with the other caddies. He was nice and Jonni liked him and he felt bad for not opening up to the guy. He knew he meant well and Jonni had been downright rude to him, not even replying. He didn't know how.

He made up his mind, and opened the stall door. "I'm not playing today," he said, avoiding his dad's gaze. No one would blame him, but then again he didn't care. He left the bathroom and passed his dad who waited for him outside and neither said a word.

Jonni avoided the gazes of the caddies, the golfers, the staff in the room, all of whom watched him even if they didn't mean to. He walked down the short hallway to the private rooms and then found his way to the private dressing room and locked the door when inside.

He laid on the couch and felt tears forcing their way out but he also felt fatigue and jet lag and he closed his eyes and turned into the couch and wished he was back home even as his dad rattled the knob and knocked at the door.

The Sheriff was getting asked for updates every half hour.

"Of course," he told Ryals, "I told them that would just slow things down. So leave that to me. I'm sending several more investigators up to help you, however. The Augusta National Chairman has called my office, twice, instead of speaking to you on the ground. I need to tell him this isn't a one-man show." That was fine with Ryals, even if just to spread the blame around when it dragged on. This was a different category of crime than he had ever investigated. "GBI wants in as well, but the Chairman actually prefers to keep them out of it. He doesn't want the investigative footprint to get any bigger, if we can help it."

"I'm not sure what I'd have them do." He did have work for the rest of the team, however, as he looked at a few hundred personnel files in front of him, and more coming. He sat at a table in the personnel management office, not far from the clubhouse, and he was dizzy already from considering it. He didn't know what to look for, exactly, but if he had several other investigators, that would be a big help.

"Send them over," Ryals told the Sheriff. "We'll keep a low profile."

He had a window and outside he could see spectators streaming in like they were some kind of varicolored migration of shirts, chairs, umbrellas and hats.

Ryals needed to know where Willy had been when he wasn't on the course. Allison was supposed to have that information for him. Ryals needed to paint a picture of where the victim had been from the moment he touched down in Augusta until the moment he died. In that timeline he would find answers.

The Augusta National — and the Masters tournament — were one of the most private sporting organizations and events in the world. Membership is by invitation only, play is limited to certain times in the year; the merchandise is sold only during the tournament week, and many of the details of the course — including the provenance of the grass seed—are not disclosed. The tickets to the event aren't expensive relatively speaking, they're just very hard, if not impossible, to come by. Illegal resell prices could range into the tens of thousands. Nowhere is the preference of privacy over revenue more obvious, however, than in the TV air time: the Masters comes on TV only 3-7:30 pm the first two days, then 2-7 pm tournament days. A news publication once compared Masters airtime to "a renowned fancy restaurant," while other broadcast events were "Thanksgiving dinner."

Ryals learned this on his phone, googling facts about the tournament, trying his best to understand what message the killer might be trying to send with the murder. And to whom? If he wanted it to look like a suicide, then why make it a public one?

Ryals could only guess that it was because the message wasn't meant for everyone; the killer had a specific audience in mind.

The best guess was the South African golfer. But who would want to send him a message? Was it possible — Ryals suddenly thought that it was very possible — that someone had gotten Jonni to take a dive, to secure bets on him? Did golf even work like that? Ryals wasn't sure.

He googled 'golf and betting,' then 'gambling on golf,' and other variations. Indeed, there was a market. Most bets were head-to-head bets, pitting two golfers against one another. That was a possibility. Convince the kid to take a dive for a price, the kid gets cold feet, the mob — or whoever — sends a message.

It fit, though Ryals knew not to trust the apparent logic of an early theory. He didn't know much. Easy explanations were an easy way out.

He needed to talk to the Lombards again. At least now he had two avenues to pursue, he thought, as he began to flip through the personnel files of the paid and volunteer groundskeepers. Maintaining this grass, he realized, required an army.

It seemed that Jonni Lombard wasn't playing today at all.

Ryals met Jonni's father Martin again in a reception area in the clubhouse. Martin was agitated, stressed, and worried about his son.

Ryals decided to sit and talk with just Martin for now. Martin wasn't all that interested in talking to him, but then seemed to soften a little and welcome the distraction.

"I'm just—this is just the biggest week in my son's life. I'm trying to remain focused on that. Trying to help him find his way out to the course. What else can I do?"

"I understand that," Ryals said. "My daughter isn't a professional athlete, but I don't know what else I would do in your shoes."

"He'll rally. He won't miss his opportunity to show the world what he can do," Martin added with forced confidence. "He will make Willy proud." Martin wiped a tear.

Ryals tapped his notepad. He was trying to figure out how to phrase the question. "Is it possible," he said, almost as if thinking out loud, "that someone would make a large bet on your son? Or against your son?"

"A bet…"

"I understand he's something of a phenomenon, Jonni. I don't follow golf very closely. I'm wondering if someone might want your son to lose, for reasons of a bet. Could that be possible?"

Martin stared at the wall and then the TV across the room, his face blank. He didn't answer for a while. Finally he shook his head. "No," he said. "That doesn't seem possible. Then again, we've won juniors, but haven't played on this stage before. That level of malevolence — I can't fathom it." Martin watched the TV feed a minute longer. It was set to the Golf Channel with Masters coverage, which was unfortunately completely preoccupied by discussion of the murder. The word was out, but they only had the story; no photos except of the Twelfth Hole.

Ryals watched it for a minute as well. Details about Willy were on screen, pictures of him with Jonni, playing various courses and tournaments.

"Of course Jonni wouldn't know about anything like that. He just wants to play. Do you have any evidence?"

Ryals nodded. "The murder can be interpreted to be a signal of some kind, a public message. So that's one possibility." It wasn't smart to voice theories to an outside party. Ryals was punching well over his weight class.

Martin pulled his gaze from the TV and stared at the ground. "I don't know, I just, I don't know. It's all so sad."

Ryals was getting nowhere here and he was already wondering who else he could ask about this. If the boy and his father knew nothing about the threat, though, if they didn't know what it was about — well, who else to ask? Was it possible, Ryals wondered, that someone wanted to send a message to a different golfer? 'See what we can do to you?' And they chose, therefore, the youngest member's caddie, the most disposable in some eyes? There were lots of players here. He couldn't interview them all. He didn't even know if he could interview any of them.

Ryals would have to get direction and permission; he would start with Allison.

"Jonni is still in his room?"

"He's asked to go back to the hotel," Martin said, anxiety or something like it creeping into his voice. "Today is a wash. They've said he can start tomorrow."

Ryals thanked him. "I'll have more to chat about soon, but I'll leave you be for now."

Ryals didn't know golf, but he followed basketball, and played it in high school and college. Back in his slimmer, more active days.

He remembered the evening news speculation and gossip about Michael Jordan's retirement. Was he really just leaving the game, or was he under pressure from the NBA and maybe even his gambling debtors to get out for a while, let things cool down? Some even suspected that Jordan's father's murder was a warning, that MJ owed money to the wrong people.

There was lots of money involved at this level, probably more than Ryals was aware of. These people lived by different rules.

Golf just seemed a realm untouched by the same corruption evident in other sports. Maybe only up to now, Ryals thought. In his line of work, no criminal act was a surprise. Even some of the cops he worked with were lousy — beat their wives, lied on reports; there were good ones of course but the sleaze was a part of humanity.

So who knows. Jonni and his dad were in a very bad corner. He speculated they could file a lawsuit against the National, and almost certainly the National knew that.

Ryals walked back toward the front of the clubhouse — flashing his badge to a guard by a rope, who was perplexed at first and then his eyes grew wide as he realized. He was red-faced with a gut, sunglasses and a bald head protected by a straw hat. Ryals turned to pause a moment to see the crowd gathered around the top of each hole — the tee — that filtered down all around the course. There was an air of expectation and awe. Also many face were wrapped up in deep conversation, with eyes moving around quickly. There was something in the air. The news and gossip. Ryals asked the guard on the rope,

"Why do you have practice rounds?"

"They're meant to get the players ready for the tournament. Get to know the course, make it a real competition where they ain't stumbling all over themselves. I'm sure a big part of it is psychology. This place can get to you. Right into your head."

"Got it," Ryals said.

"The players can come other times of the year, you know. They are invited at specific times for private play to prepare."

"Do you work here all year?" Ryals asked.

"No, I'm a critical care nurse at the VA Hospital three-hundred-and-fifty-seven days of the year."

"You think people take the tournament too serious?" Ryals asked. They stood in the shade of a massive oak tree behind a rope that isolated club members from other patrons.

"Nossir; these days I don't think they take it serious enough."

Ryals had one other question. There was a building he hadn't been briefed on, and he passed by it . "What's the place behind the Fifth Green? Sits back a bit, large house." He'd seen much security there and only a handful of patron were allowed to excuse themselves to it.

"That's Berckman's Place," said the guard. "Since 2013, it's the VIP area of the club."

"Isn't the whole thing VIP?"

"This is the creme of the crop. 1% of 1%. There's a Scottish restaurant inside, TV, catering. Has a room named after Bobby Jones' putter — they called her Calamity Jane."

"So what goes on in there?"

"Golf," he said. "Watching it, talking it, keeping cool."

Ryals thanked the guard and was reminded how much more there was to educate himself about the course and how it operated. He didn't know exactly what Allison's job was, for example. Some of her duties were undoubtedly secret. She was a liaison and problem-solver for club members.

Ryals kept on. He wanted to get the team working on the personnel files, and he wanted to get to his desk for a while to make some calls to South Africa, and find out anything he could from people there. What people, he wasn't sure yet. He would ask Allison for suggestions on where to begin. Maybe someone knew something. Had heard something. Something he could confront Jonni with. Jonni might be too scared to speak.

He had two avenues of inquiry now. He would continue to peruse the personnel files files for anything out of place. Second, he could explore the gambling theory, though in that case he didn't even have a starting point, other than something that might be revealed by Willy Sharpe's finances. Looking into those, however, would require access to his bank in South Africa. Ryals knew nothing about how to navigate that. Outside of those two questions, he had nothing to go on.

ELEVEN

Allison obtained Willy's itinerary. She met Ryals in her office in the main clubhouse.

"I'm sorry it took so long. Everyone here is occupied with the usual mountain of work." She handed a folder over. "He landed Thursday evening, arrived at the Hampton on Washington road, by I-20. He was on the course all day Friday and Saturday."

"And you have this because?"

"We keep track. Especially when our guests arrive and depart, and when they visit the course."

"And outside?"

"We don't keep track of them outside."

"Except Jon Daly," Ryals joked, but Allison didn't react to it. Daly was well known to set up at Hooters on Washington Road after his play where he drank and signed autographs.

Ryals perused the folder. There wasn't much in it.

"You book his room?"

"He did that. Players book their own lodging." Ryals needed to go check his room, but he had to get a judge to sign off. He didn't have anything further on the National property at this time, so he would go see the Sheriff about it directly, and see about getting the deceased man's cell records and credit card statements. Ryals thanked Allison, and left. He drove downtown.

He met with the Sheriff who agreed to get the warrant expedited. Ryals could see the Sheriff was frazzled; the man was a wide-jawed, slow-tempered man with a thick southern accent and gray hair with a strong cowlick in the front. He was easily overwhelmed. He did not multitask well. He was mediocrity in motion. Slow motion.

"I'm getting state-level calls, maybe higher. Congressmen are checking in."

"What does that mean for us?"

"Keep doing what you're doing until they take it out of our hands."

"Will they?"

"God knows," the Sheriff said, reaching for his coffee cup and finding it empty. Ryals said he would be working from his desk for a while.

He worked from his chair until late afternoon and Ryals knew nothing more than he had at the beginning of the day. Often in investigations it was the accumulation of negatives that solved a case. A detective relied on the process of elimination.

Ryals often found that working at the station wasn't productive for him. That was even more the case this week. His coworkers leaned over as they passed by, frequently asked questions — he had a desk, not an office to shut them out — and there were constant press calls and reporters outside, including, as of this morning, national correspondents. The station had rarely seen anything like it. Notable excepts were the Reynaldo Rivera case, which was pursued by Major Crimes. Rivera was a serial killer who assaulted and murdered women between Georgia and North Carolina in 1999 and 2000.

In 2021, the press converged to cover the Augusta Spa Shooting, in which eight Asian Americans were shot and killed.

The press covered the search for LaTania Carwell in 2017 that tragically ended in December of 2018 when her remains were discovered off of Golden Camp Road.

The media presence was growing bigger this time than any time before.

So he left and drove through downtown and took Green Street to Washington Road and made calls from a restaurant near the course. It was busy place but he kept his back to the hubbub.

He had few places to try, but he called local police in South Africa near Willy's home to start. He found Willy's girlfriend's number; she spoke between sobs and had "no idea, no idea, just no idea." He had a brother, who mentioned only that he knew Willy cared a great deal for that kid, wanted to see him succeed, and that the relationship with Jonni had given Willy great opportunities and he wouldn't have ever looked that gift horse in the mouth, so to speak. He was grateful.

So far, Ryals had not even been able to rule anything out.

Ryals returned to the course to speak with Allison. He found her in a control center, working furiously, not a hair out of place and not a drop of sweat. She was a runner, no question. She was competent, but how could anyone have been ready for what they now had to deal with?

He pulled her aside and she offered him a bottle of water as she took one herself from a clear-front refrigerator.

He explained that he thought the murder was a message, and he was trying to understand what that message could be, or more importantly, to whom.

"You know this game well?"

"In the last four years, I've come to know it, and the business here. I..." She hesitated, drinking and thinking. "I can't say at all. I have no idea. This isn't that kind of game, not that kind of tournament. It would boggle the mind."

"Doesn't it already?" He asked. She drank and nodded.

"I can't think of anything," she said. "I've met I believe every player here, conversed with them at considerable length. It's a good group; we pride ourselves on the character not just of the institution but of the players we invite. I mean, we've got the occasional golfer," she said, lowering her voice, "with a checkered personal life, but they are all gentlemen here, and this tournament, it's so hard to get into, you just don't risk anything. Or I can't imagine how anyone would."

Ryals nodded. It made sense, though it sounded a bit like a sales pitch.

"Who's in charge here? Who's the top dog?" He was embarrassed not to know. The only person he could think of was the man whom he had met as a deputy when Ryals was asked to respond to a group at the gate protesting the historic male-only membership a decade or two back.

"The Chairman, who is also CEO. There are two corporations here, one that owns the Augusta National — Augusta National, Inc., the other that runs the tournament. For reasons going back to the founding."

"No president? Isn't that how corporations work?"

Allison smiled a bit. "The club voted a few years back that Bobby Jones was to be President in Perpetuity."

"And it's a club with — how many members?"

"Around 300, never more. They don't have voting power."

Ryals nodded, taking it all in. It was like finally learning details about a neighbor whom he'd live beside all his life.

"How's it coming with the personnel files?"

"Slow, but if there's anything there it's in the details. Thank you for accommodating the team."

"I told the staff in the office to keep them fed and watered."

"Always welcome with cops," Ryals said, realizing that he himself hadn't eaten today — he only had coffee at the restaurant.

His phone was buzzing. He checked it — it was Angela. He declined the call. He would try her again in a moment.

"So what's next?" Allison asked. He tried his best not to look clueless.

"Continue with personnel files. I'd like to speak with Lawrence, perhaps interview a few more members of his security team that worked Saturday night. Continue with the family."

"We're obviously — you know — getting pretty busy here, but I'm still at your service, anything you need."

"Thank you," he told her, meaning it. He almost asked where he could get something to eat. Then his phone rang; Lawrence responding to him. Lawrence had two of the security team Ryals wanted to question, he could speak to them at the security building.

Ryals made his way over there.

Neither of the men knew anything. One Ryals in fact knew; he was a former Sheriff's Deputy himself, from some years back. One worked the gate, the other had been on a patrol that night, walking the perimeter and driving it in a cart. Neither had anything at all to offer; they hadn't noticed anything out of the ordinary.

They left and Ryals was alone with Lawrence for a moment.

"Nothing yet?" Lawrence asked.

"No, but it's not unusual. The only unusual thing—"

"Is the setting."

"Yeah. Normally, you know, you wait for the brother, whom you suspect robbed his in-law, to sweat a bit and then something spills over. You do your due diligence and find something in a credit card transaction or on a camera," Ryals turned and glanced toward the camera room. "None of that works out here," he admitted. "Which makes me think..."

"Whoever it is, is very smart."

"Yeah."

Lawrence lowered his voice, stepped to the side. "What do you think about the mob? Could the mob be behind this?"

"I don't even know who the mob is. Mob in Augusta? We've got a few gangs. Not the mob. Boggles the mind. My mind anyway."

"This isn't really Augusta, though, is it? It's the Augusta National."

Lawrence was right. Ryals was out of his element here. This was a major crime, an FBI matter, really. Except that the National wasn't another state, or country, or anything else. Its membership was global, but it belonged to Augusta. Before Ryals left him, Lawrence explained that in fact, for all the secrecy of the member rolls, during the tournament, members were required to wear their Green Jackets while at the club or on the grounds and were obligated to help any patrons in need. They wore not only their jackets, but name tags as well. So it was with a bit of irony that senators, governors and CEOs might walk around occasionally acting as ushers.

The National was a local entity — but not this week. This week the course and the city were open to the world.

Ryals needed to speak to someone who understood that world.

Ryals had another notion, then. He remembered as with the Michael Jordan story, much of the truth was revealed following a book written by a sports journalist — someone who knew the players and wrote about them as people, not just statistics. Ryals returned to the course and found his way to the massive press building. He walked in and was overwhelmed by its opulence. He found it a buzz of activity, but all controlled and polite and professional. He made his way further past the double-stairway and toward the operations center, which reminded him more of the NASA control room than any press room he'd ever seen. No one seemed to recognize him, which was good. The second he became a celebrity in this madness, his job would get much harder. He realized of course that if Allison or anyone else knew he had walked into the press building, his job might be forfeited.

He found a man in an ESPN shirt working a phone, three cups of coffee in front of him. Ryals interrupted his call when he got a moment and asked who the most seasoned golf writer was in the room. The guy thought a moment, then pointed to the back, to a mostly bald man with a white mustache. Ryals walked over to him, and flashed his badge, making sure no one else could see him. This was a risky move but Ryals had to trust his gut on this one.

"Yes?" The man asked. His badge identified him as Sam Ingot.

"Could we speak outside?" Ryals asked with a low voice.

"Am I in some kind of trouble?" Ingot asked with irony.

"Nothing like that." Ryals glanced around, then nodded to a side door. Intrigued, Ingot set his computer down and the pair walked out of the building casually.

Outside Ryals walked with him, making sure they were well enough away from the press building. They came to the rope behind some trees, beyond which was a hole where players were practicing. Past that was the main gate, through which people were pouring and walking a path. Ryals was sure no one would pay them any mind.

As they walked, Ryals commented on the media center.

"It was quite unexpected in one sense; inevitable in another. Did you know the clubhouse sits atop the best wine cellars in the world?"

Ryals did not.

"The clubhouse has been around since the 1850s. Sure it has been renovated and expanded. There's a lot of people who don't know." Ingot stood in the sunlight outside with Ryals. They stopped in the grass. "What can I do for you, Deputy?" Ingot asked.

"Detective. And I want to be clear that this discussion is completely off the record."

"I'm not sure I can agree to that," Ingot said.

"You can. I'm not revealing any information, but I need some background."

Ingot considered this.

"Do I get an exclusive out of this?"

"No. Not from me."

"What is this about?" Ingot asked.

"I need context. About players and politics. Off the record. I need to understand this game."

"I'd like to think I know about as much as anyone about the Masters, and golf. I've been doing this for thirty years." Ingot said, pushing his clear rimmed glasses up on his nose. "What do you need to know?" Ingot asked. "General information? We can start with the four majors."

"The four majors?"

"There are four major tournaments in golf. The U.S. Open, the P.G.A., the British Open and the Masters. The Masters is the only major with a home base. Played in the same place every year."

Ryals didn't need a golf lecture. He interrupted Ingot.

"I need to know about gambling in golf."

"As in, do people gamble on golf games?"

"Right."

"Of course. Go out to Vegas, rooms of people betting on the tournament. People bet on anything. Matsuyama, 80-1 odds this week.

Rose, Fowler, in the 70s. Here at Augusta, it's more or less been outlawed, of course. But there used to be the Calcuttas."

"The what?"

"Calcuttas. In the old days of the Augusta National, gambling events. Club members and other friends gathered and made their bets and threw parties and watched as black boys from downtown punched one another in a boxing ring. If you can call it boxing. They stopped, I don't know, in the fifties? Maybe earlier. But at one time it was part of the whole shebang."

"Not anymore, though."

"Not here, no, it wouldn't be tolerated for a minute. Not among members I mean. Like I said, though, there's plenty of gambling on sports."

"Who's highest? This year, I mean. Who's the favorite?"

"Oh, I don't know really. In my mind Spieth again; he's been on a streak with three wins in a row and his life is really good off-the-course — but in the mind of Vegas, I'm not sure. People are talking about Rahm and Jason Young."

"What about Lombard?" Ryals asked.

"His ranking? He's young, this is his first tournament, his fourth major. He has a lot to prove. Top 20, maybe. 30 sure. Odds, I don't know. And look," Ingot said, turning to watch the players warming up. "This course is different. People like to say the National makes champions out of amateurs and amateurs out of champions."

Ryals took it in. Tried to find any thread and chase it.

"How dirty does it get?"

"Dirty? like gambling? Doping?" Ingot asked, looking around as he responded. A smirk on his face.

"Like making bets with the wrong people, fixing games, that sort of thing."

Ingot thought about it. "Well, look. This is golf. It's a white collar game, there's class to it. Requires more effort and patience and quiet skill to get here than just being tall and athletic, or able to push on an opponent. What I mean is, no one gets here cheaply, and no one would lose it cheaply. Bad behavior off the course usually results, quickly and dramatically, in poor performance on the course. It's a different animal than other sports. Doping? No. Some of these guys are fat. There's no point in doping. It's a mental game, all the way through. Can't dope the mind. As for betting — sure, some guys have been known to be gamblers. I don't know of anyone getting in so deep that they were in trouble, but a gambler is a gambler and so who knows. Is that what you think this is?"

"I need context. That's all."

"I couldn't begin to tell you where to look. This just isn't the game for that kind of thing." Ryals didn't know what more to ask. He gave the man his card.

"So, if you know something."

"Of course. And look," Ingot said, removing his glasses and wiping sweat from the bridge of his nose. "Lombard is special, really the raw kind of talent you only once in a decade or more. Bubba Watson never had a lesson and hits like a blind man but he hits true and he wins. Lombard is instinctive like that. He plays like a raw Rahm. He plays without thought. One can imagine what he'll be when he has experience. If the sport doesn't consume him first." Ryals looked at him, thinking more about Jonni and his talent than he expected. He wasn't sure why the man had mentioned that to him. He realized he wanted Jonni to make it. Whatever that meant. The kid was innocent. At least he seemed innocent.

Ryals checked his phone as he walked away. It had been buzzing in his pocket. He looked at it. Calls, then a text from the chief. Ryals was granted access to Willy's hotel room — but the GBI wanted to check it out too.

Ryals trudged over flattened and manicured pine straw to his car, which he realized, walking under the shade of the Magnolias, was parked under those trees that golf fans would kill for the opportunity to stand beneath. He then realized that was an unfortunate expression.

He paused a moment before getting into the car and he looked at the trees and considered the row of them down the drive. It looked like Augusta to him. He climbed into his car and drove to the hotel directly — as soon as he hit the Washington Road traffic, he flipped on his lights.

TWELVE

It was late afternoon, nearly evening as Ryals stood in Willy Shepherd's hotel room. The hotel manager stood just outside, waiting like a sentry. Compared to the expanse of the course where Ryals had been one hour before, the room was deathly still.

Yet it wasn't a bad place for Augusta. It boasted a view of Riverwatch Parkway, a new movie theater that Ryals didn't even know existed, and several restaurants. Just this past year the National bought the property where Ryals' favorite restaurant, the Olive Garden, stood, and tore it down. He had his own grudge for that reason alone. Of course, Angela told him he shouldn't eat there anyway. Carb overload, she called it.

Ryals stood and looked a moment and reminded himself to touch nothing. The GBI team would dust the room and do whatever else it was they did and he didn't want to contaminate it in any way.

He leaned over the trashcan: nothing. The maids had emptied it out. He used a pen to push the refuse aside and check beneath. He saw nothing.

He saw the Caddie's suitcase, open, clothes laid out in a drawer that was cracked open. Nothing of note in the suitcase. The safe was locked. The hotel manager would open it but Ryals wanted to wait for the GBI team to do that. No one ever put evidence in safes, though. Valuables, passports, but evidence they hid.

He checked the bathroom, turning the switch on with his pen. A leather shaving kit, nice, with "W.S." on it in gold. A gift from Jonni? Ryals made a note to ask.

Nothing more in the bathroom. He looked in the mini fridge. Inside were a few cokes and a bottle of rum tilted to fit. He flipped up the sheets and comforter. Looked beneath the bed and in the cushions of the small sofa. Finally, he stood in the dim entryway. He sighed. There was nothing to go on here.

Ryals thanked the manager and decided not to wait on the GBI team. They would do their thing. He would hear about it later. Ryals guessed that the powers-that-be wanted them involved just to express to the board of the Augusta National that they were "using every available resource."

Ryals knew the power the National wielded in this town. He was under no illusions who was calling the shots. It was also no surprise to him that the Chairman of the National avoided Ryals. His conversations were with the Mayor, Governor, maybe even Senators and the White House. Who knew, Ryals thought. He was meant to do his part. The Chairman outranked him by twenty rungs.

In his car he remembered to call Angela back. It was after five now.

"Dad," she said. "Where on earth have you been? I went ahead to Olivia's. We're seeing a movie tonight." It was no longer a question.

"I'm sorry," he said. "I've been knee deep in a case. It's..."

"Oh my God," she said. He winced. He wanted her to say 'gosh.' He didn't correct her this time. "Is it the Masters one?"

"Mhm."

"Are you — are you lead on it?"

"Mhm, I am." He said with fatigue, not pride. He could hear her squeal.

"Oh my God! I'm going to tell Olivia. That's huge dad! Huge!"

"It is if I can figure it out," he said.

"Oh, you will. You will, dad. You always get them, remember." Yes, usually he did. And usually it was a kid robbing his employer right in the line of sight of a camera, or someone murdering their ex-girlfriend. Those were more about filing paperwork than playing Sherlock Holmes.

"Thanks, Ang," he said.

"I'm going to stay over at Olivia's, is that okay?"

"Of course," he said, relieved. He didn't know if he would even make it home tonight.

He picked up Burger King driving back, feeling every minute of his day was being accounted for by some auditor somewhere, that he couldn't risk wasting a moment. He had the sneaking suspicion he was being set up to hang out if anything went wrong. That's why there was so little communication and oversight. This case was radioactive, and they sent him in with the Geiger counter.

Fortunately the drive-thru line moved quickly.

He was starving but felt worse after the food.

So what now, he wondered. He ticked off what he was waiting for.

The personnel files.

The toxicology report.

The phone records.

Finding Willy on the video screens.

The videos. Where had Willy been?

What else? He didn't know.

He reminded himself that big crimes were solved in small ways. He couldn't think of this as anything different than any other murder. Sure, there was an element here, something spectacular, showy; and, of course, the setting — as Lawrence had mentioned — was more than unique. It was still a murder, though. It had still happened in this town — in a closed environment, no less. It was personal, too. This wasn't a mugging or motel robbery or random knifing on the street. This was a highly personal killing with significant and specific motive.

And yet, the entire thing remained an enigma.

The killer or killers were sophisticated, to be sure.

Jonni laid on his bed and watched American TV. It was just noise; a distraction. His hotel phone was off the hook. The press had found his room and the phone had started to ring nonstop as reporters called so Jonni just took it off and set it down. He hadn't eaten, but he wasn't hungry.

He heard his dad get in; they had adjoining rooms. His dad didn't knock, but he heard the TV go on in the other room. He watched the Golf Channel; Cara Banks and Grant Boone talked side by side. Jonni knew them; he watched them from around the world and now they were in the same town as he was. Jonni didn't want to listen to them. He hoped his dad didn't answer the phone.

Dad was all about press. "It's the key," he said. "You have to become a star to get all of this paid for, to make this a career. You can't ignore the press." Dad could handle that for him. It was too much for Jonni.

He hated interviews, hated explaining what was in his head or how he felt when he made this shot or that. The game was personal to him. The course existed in his mind and he existed in the course and it felt like he was betraying something by divulging their secrets.

He reached off the bed and reached for his putter that he kept in the room. He pulled it onto the bed and over him like it was a security blanket. He rolled it between his hands and imagined the tap of it as he helped the ball "fall into the gravity" of the hole where it clucked against the cup. He imitated the sound with his tongue on the roof of his mouth.

He knew his dad tried his best. He would be disappointed if Jonni didn't play. Jonni wanted to play. He could see it, though. The thousand stares, ten thousand; not just watching him play, but scrutinizing him, wondering how he was feeling, how he was dealing with it, how could he even think of playing? He would hear the million voices in his mind as he tried for a single putt. The cameras didn't care about him, they cared about the murder. It would be an insult to Willy if Jonni just picked up a club and went to play the game that he was supposed to play with Willy by his side? A betrayal. Willy had earned it too.

Jonni just wanted to sleep and to be home. He closed his eyes.

That night, Ryals worked until late at the station. He explained to Angela by phone that he was working on the case, to call him on his cell if he needed anything, and that he would be home in the morning.

Ryals did some research before he finally crashed. He discovered that the Augusta National property was worth around $85,000,000. There was no published list of members but there were a number who were public: Warren Buffett, Senator Sam Nunn, the founder of Coors, then head of the NFL, the former secretary of state, Lou Holtz, Condoleeza Rice and Bill Gates, who reportedly had to wait three years to join because he committed the faux pas of saying aloud that he wanted to join — one could only be invited.

40,000 people would attend each day this year. That meant close to $160 million in ticket sales. One could double that that in the payment for TV rights.

Ryals drifted off soon, but not before realizing that this behemoth of an institution, perhaps the most famous one in all the south, was far more significant, complex and powerful behind the bamboo screen than he had ever considered, despite having driven past the entrance countless times.

THIRTEEN

Tuesday

Jonni was up an hour before sunrise. He sat a while. Paced. Swung his putter in the room, then produced a ball from his bag and began tapping it toward a plastic cup, barefoot in his pajamas with no lights on. Just feeling it.

Before he knew it, he was showered and he opened his bag for the third of six outfits provided him by Adidas and Oakley. His preferred colors were green and white, represented here in variations of patterns and combinations. He preferred a ball cap to a visor. His cleats were slightly loose; comfortable was how he liked them. He tried on the sunglasses; he would wear them on the back of his collar if not on his face. He wore socks with the South African flag.

He dressed and then sat at the end of the bed and recalled everything Willy had ever told him about the course. Willy hadn't been, but he had researched it — ordered every book, read every article, watched replays constantly.

"This is a second stroke course," he said. "Oosthuizen, that second stroke double eagle on number two in 2012 — I mean look at the hill, Jonni!" Willy showed Jonni videos excitedly in the shade at the bar on his old dusty laptop. "And then he was beat by Bubba on his second shot, after Bubba sent his first stroke into the trees." From there Watson made a miraculous shot. Jonni watched that one as well. The playback reported that Bubba's wife, at home with a newborn adoptee, watched as he turned his luck around in spectacular fashion.

"You lose after a double eagle, boy ,what other tourney could do that to you?" Bubba had said. "You get it moving, Jonni, and then you play your feeling. Left, right, they move the hole, you might not even be able to read it. So you play your sense." Jonni was two days behind. But Willy had caddied hungover, maybe once drunk. He would want Jonni to play, no matter what. Willy was an encyclopedia of golf history. He'd read every book, even if Willy sitting to read anything was a comedic notion. "Of course, there's no shot that mattered more than the double eagle by Gene Sarazen in 1935 — the 'shot heard round the world' on the 15th. It led to a 36-hole playoff. Willy made Jonni study these moments. It was another thirty years before someone else managed a double eagle — then it was 1967 by Australian Bruce Devlin. The next "albatross" would come in 1994 on the 13th by Jeff Maggert with a three iron. Then it was Oosthuizen, fellow South African, and Willy was more proud of that one than the others. "See what we can do?" He told Jonni. His enthusiasm was infectious. Jonni remembered watching it over and over with Willy. It was a two-hundred-and-fifty yard shot.

Hole-in-one's happened here too. They were achieved more often than an albatross, in fact. There was more excitement in a double eagle in a way. There was a build-up. It never happened by chance.

The Augusta National was no longer a world away — it was just down the road. Even if he missed every putt, shanked every drive, even if he played the worst game of golf in his life, he was still playing the Masters, on the world's premier course.

He had to do it. It would make his dad happy. It would make him happy.

He stood and saw that the sun was rising outside and that the clouds were clearing. Partly cloudy day, high humidity. Sticky on the fairway, as Willy would say. But watch that downhill.

He sat and then stood and filled a cup with water and drank it. He wasn't hungry — in fact he was queasy — but he knew he had to eat something.

He went to the adjoining door and knocked for his father.

Ryals kept a change of clothes at the station, but now he wished he had gotten something a bit more suitable for the notoriety of the investigation.

This morning the Sheriff would give a press conference updating the press on what they were doing. Hopefully split the attention from the tournament keeping the criminal investigation under the Sheriff's umbrella; let the golf coverage focus on golf.

It wouldn't work, but sure, and either way it was nothing for Ryals. He ate a breakfast burrito and shaved in the station bathroom with an electric razor on gray and brown stubble.

Last night he had worked until — he wasn't even sure, but late — researching online to find anything he could about any business deals or anything that might help him. He found out plenty about Jonni and golf stats and qualifications but he gave up eventually and called about the personnel files — they were halfway through, doing their own background check along with the GBI for each one.

With nothing else to do until more information came in, he took some time to pass his other cases off to other investigators, at the Sheriff's request.

He checked his phone and found a message from the coroner — come by, earliest convenience, it said. The coroner's office was a block away. He would walk, he needed to stretch out and wake up.

He called Lawrence to ask about the video.

"Nothing yet," the man answered, already up. Ryals checked his watch: it was only six. He didn't apologize. "We've got him on a few cameras, but he's walking the grounds. We're still looking. I could only afford one guy so it's been slow going but I'm helping him this morning before we open."

Ryals thanked him and texted Angela — she preferred texts these days — to make sure she was okay. She wouldn't respond for a while. He was sure she had been up late. To his surprise, she responded immediately. 'Pls get me a souvenir! Something classy and cute love you.' He had never before been asked to get a souvenir from a murder scene.

He checked the weather on his phone before stepping out: rain expected. That was annoying. He wasn't sure why. He didn't expect to find any more evidence outside. He didn't like the weather making that decision for him, though. He didn't know if the practice rounds continued in the rain. He thought they would, perhaps unless it got too bad. He stepped outside and the dark air was heavy with the promise of heavy rain, a wet, earthy smell that came down from the sky and up from the ground in a cocktail that only the South could make. Away toward the course, the attendees glanced skyward and carried umbrellas. The weather in Georgia changed just that fast. Soon they would hear the rumble of thunder.

He arrived at the coroner's office and found her in gloves and a smock. Her name was Lauren.

"Come on in," she said and he immediately regretted not doing this by phone. He could smell the formaldehyde and burnt skin and worse.

"Good to see you," she said. "Been a while."

"Yeah," he said, trying to remember his last time down here. He avoided it at all costs.

"You put on weight," she said, looking at him. He sucked his gut instinctively and frowned. "My daughter's trying to fix that."

"Kids are experts at pointing out our flaws," she said, chipper and direct for a woman who dealt with cadavers. Her jokes were often crass, due likely to the fact that there was no one to offend at her work.

She brought him to an ice-cold room with three tables, and on one was Willy Sharpe's body, partially covered by a cloth.

"I owe you for this one," she said. "Most fun I've had in months, maybe years." No apologies for calling it 'fun.'

"Toxicology results were provided at midnight — I had them rush it, any hour I told them. So, he's positive for benzodiazapine. A roofie, Detective Hall. But medical grade, not the stuff you get for prom night. This would knock you right out, and enough of it and you're just dead, but still limber for a while, you get me. So then it's a question of delivery system, right, and so I don't find any in his gut so it's not likely he ingested it. So," She said, pulling a light around toward the man's head. "That's when I saw this, and I'm sorry I didn't before. But see, he has a beard, and sunburn, and his skin is pockmarked from bad acne when he was younger. So maybe you wouldn't notice it right away. But here, just to the back of the jugular line? See it?"

Ryals wasn't sure he did. He cleared his eyes. He had glasses that he never wore and wished he had them now.

"Pinprick, here. Syringe puncture."

"He was injected?"

"You bet," she said. "Acted fast, too — probably was out in a few seconds. Like this, probably," she moved behind him, put an arm around his neck like in a chokehold, and feigned jabbing a needle into his neck.

"Okay," he said, escaping her grip. "So," he tried to clear his head. "How hard is it to get this stuff?"

"The compound isn't impossible to get. A few things you mix together. I can get you a list and where you might find it all.

"Please, and thank you."

Two hours later Jonni was in his prep room in the clubhouse. His dad was there, beaming with pride and twitching with excitement. Dad hadn't known much about golf when Jonni first showed interest. After his mom died, Martin tried to find things for the two of them to do together. They went fishing, they hiked. They tried a local golf tournament together — a friendly game in the community, with a big braai with a variety of game meat on a fire, amateurs and novices and never-played-befores welcome. That was them.

After that Jonni asked to play golf again. Soon his interest in the game went further than his dad's had ever gone. He loved the concentration and how the world disappeared when his head was down and he looked at the fairway or green ahead of him and the path to the hole. He loved the satisfaction of a good swing. Soon he found out he was better than most. He didn't realize that he was good, not at first, but people told him so and then more people came to watch him and he tried his first local tournament as a real competitor. He came in third but the age gap was about twenty five years between him and the next guy.

Dad didn't play with him anymore but he supported it in every way he could. Working as a local banker, his father took on extra shifts to afford quality clubs and trips out of town to other tournaments.

Jonni flourished and soon the bullying at school and rejection from friends — you're just weird, Jonni, why do you stare and why don't you talk to people?— didn't mean as much. He knew he wasn't weird. There was just always a lot of weight on his head, pushing him down, keeping his mouth closed.

When he swung a club it was like that weight was thrown off and he was suddenly light and free. He didn't exactly explain this to his dad but through the teenage years his father didn't know what to say most of the time anyway. It was enough for Jonni that he drove and didn't ask questions and was excited when Jonni did well.

Soon life became about golf. They made money sometimes. Gifts and press. Even when they had to pay their way, it was the most important thing they had going on. Dad got a promotion because his boss was a golf fan and saw Jonni "going places." He ate free at local restaurants. The celebrity part of it was nice because of the way it made his dad proud but Jonni didn't like attention. Especially now.

He was about to confront lots of attention outside. That's what his dad was saying, and what Frank, his new personal security guard, was discussing. "I'm not worried about firearms here," he said in a voice that always seemed to be fighting its way out of a whisper. His eyes were crystal blue and his hair was neat and short. He wore a sport coat over a light blue polo shirt and he wore pants that were light beige. His chest and arms bulged. He was ready to walk the course outside in the heat. Sunglasses hung from his pocket. Jonni didn't like him or dislike him. He hated that someone thought he needed security. He hated that he might need security.

Outside, the security person in charge was talking with Dad. Jonni understood they didn't particularly like someone else coming in. They didn't know this new guy Frank officially. Frank was secured by the

National through a third party security contractor. When he found out Jonni was indeed going to play he called his dad — Martin explained that this morning — and insisted. "Besides," his dad said, "If we could trust the security here, Willy would be with us still." His father seemed bitter and overwhelmed. Martin tried his best of course to manage everything but Jonni's success outpaced his understanding. Martin was a small-town banker who grew up farming goats. Jonni knew he worked hard.

Anyway, now Lawrence, the head of security, was talking to Frank, and Frank seemed to put him at ease. They both spoke about being in the military. Frank wasn't South African but he did some work there. Jonni wasn't sure where he was from.

Buster was in the room now, and he was talking to Jonni about the conditions.

"After the rain it's a soft course. Probably softer than you've played in a while. Which means it's forgiving but you have to bully the ball a bit more. I might go up an iron on the fairway as a general rule." Jonni nodded. He realized his leg was shaking. He needed to pee. He left and came back. His dad smiled at him.

"Ready to practice?"

Ryals walked back to the station running it over in his mind. Willy is somehow snatched and injected, then tied up, but he still pulled on his restraints — so maybe he woke up briefly? Then he's hung. Or he's tied up first, then injected? Or both. Maybe it takes a moment for the stuff to work. Either way he was snatched, somewhere, and by a professional. It happened fairly fast. He thought of one more question and called the coroner back.

"How long between the injection and time of death?" he asked.

He could hear her chewing gum. "Hm. Hard to say. There's traces of it most everywhere in his system, so his heart circulated it at least a few minutes, but probably not longer than twenty. He had food in his stomach that didn't digest, and smoke in his lungs from a cigarette. That stuff might have been cleared out with a little more time. Let's say one hour max, but probably less."

"And he was hung immediately, or before he was dead?"

"Yes, it was fast."

He hung up and thought. That meant, probably, that the injection happened on the course.

Ryals knew something this morning that he didn't last night and that was a good start to the day.

Jonni walked out of the clubhouse to the incessant flash of cameras and a crowd of reporters. But the reporters and the fans didn't shout, they didn't push in, and their faces reflected sympathetic support. Jonni found he could look some of them in the eye and manage a faint smile. Frank walked ahead of him, coolly, watching the crowd and gently keeping people at a safe distance, expertly maintaining an invisible buffer around Jonni. Subtly there came gentle applause. Then more applause. No raucous cheer but encouragement grew as people nearby joined the crowd.

"You got this Jonni!"

"We're with you!"

"All right Jonni!"

He felt a pat on his back, then another, then his dad's hand on his shoulder. Buster emerged dressed in the white caddie's coveralls, topped with his green Masters hat bearing the yellow and red Masters logo. His back read LOMBARD and Jonni's number was on his back and breast. Buster carried his clubs ahead of Jonni. They went out to the first tee directly and soon Jonni stood in front of it and everything was a bit of a blur to him. He was the story — his dad said that — and so he had the biggest crowd. Would have. Until he did poorly. Then they would leave. He felt pressure despite polite and encouraging crowd.

He looked up finally at Buster. He was paired today with Spaniard and former champion Jon Rahm, a tall, bearded man with intense brown eyes. He wore light blue. He smiled at Jonni but as was the custom he kept a respectful distance and didn't talk to Jonni anymore than Jonni wanted to talk to him. Jonni was never much of a talker on the course anyway. Especially a habit since he was often the youngest in any pair or foursome. Most golfers didn't resent him or look down on him but there just wasn't as much to say to a kid.

Buster handed Jonni his driver. The game was now in Jonni's hands. Jonni looked down the first hole; it started high and sloped down and there were pine trees at the end and the sun was breaking over it all out of low morning clouds and people lined both sides and it all slowed down in his mind. He found the flag and he let everything else fade away. That yellow flag, that hole at its base, was all that mattered.

Holes One and Two he worked through at par. Jonni then walked to the Third Hole - Flowering Peach, a 350-yard, par 4 challenge that sloped uphill gently. It was an impossible hole to Eagle, and most players didn't try to drive the full distance. In fact, Rahm teed off with an iron.

The green, in full sunlight up top, was only partly visible from the tee; the flag just barely from where Jonni stood.

He glanced at the rope where the crowd was gathered and saw his father and beside him Frank, the only one with eyes not fixated on Jonni.

Buster continued to speak to Jonni and Jonni finally paid attention to the course. He could smell the trees and the earth as the sun baked the ground and the rainwater evaporated and the ground smelled rich and strong like coffee.

Rahm was not a scientific player. Like Jonni, he played on instinct and feeling. Jonni had heard that before, watching the PGA tour, and had watched many replays of Rahm's play leading up to his 2023 Green Jacket win. Jonni had played in one tournament with him but as an invited amateur and they hadn't spoken. Though his wasn't a technical approach, Rahm spoke with his caddie about whether to use a 9 iron or a wedge on his second shot, calculating yard split and discussing angles by numbers and degrees. Jonni could hardly keep up with the conversation. He listened to Buster's advice, but knew the driver and wedge he was comfortable with and knew about how hard to swing them and then he would just follow the ball. If he tried to think about numbers and meters and ounces he would lose his confidence. Buster pushed him with statistics and Jonni did his best to tune him out so he wouldn't be overwhelmed. Willy had known how Jonni liked to play. Willy gave Jonni tips here and there and encouraged him but he knew when to let Jonni just swing away. Even if it was a bad swing, even if Jonni shanked it, Willy offered little advice beyond "you're trying to push it up there Jonni, try to lift it up and drop it in." Jonni played by feeling, and Willy knew how to tell him what to feel.

Jonni noticed that Rahm watched the growing crowd around them. He imagined Rahm was annoyed by the crowd and scandal Jonni drew. He didn't speak to Jonni except when necessary. He wrote in a notebook,

checked his clubs. His bag held the best of the best in latest carbon fiber
and aluminum technology. Rahm had every endorsement he could ask
for; Jonni's bag held good clubs, to be sure—Titleist--but he was not
sponsored by Titleist; rather, he won them in an Australian tournament.
It was the first bag since the first ones his dad had purchased for him,
on a trip to Johannesburg, at a secondhand shop; even now, sometimes
Jonni wished he played with the scuff-polished, worn-handled set. They
were easier to feel. He knew the names of his clubs now, but his Fairway wood, a Titleist 915F, angled at 15 degrees, with an AD graphite
shaft, was just his Fairway Wood. If he had to think of it as anything
beyond that he got confused quickly. He only knew the name because
Willy had made him learn it. "Learn them all, learn what each one does
and where it came from and why it's like it is. Then forget it and just
swing." So that's what Jonni did. Each innovation in his set was like an
evolutionary design; Titleist did what they did for a reason.

They walked now up the fairway and Jonni knew that he needed
the Vokey Raw Wedge next — He was way off with his drive, outside
the ropes and in the straw; it was a bad shot, but he knew there would
be bad shots. Buster he was sure would tell him to get the ball back in
play with a wedge, but if he had a shot to the green from the rough, he
would put an iron in his hands.

"Don't worry about where his ball is," Buster said, perhaps reading
Jonni's eyes. "Just keep picking your targets. Each one is the only one
that matters." Jonni nodded. That sounded like something Willy would
say. He kept his back to the crowd as he neared the ball.

As he walked, Frank followed with his father along the rope and
they were all cast into the shadow of a heavy cloud as if under the disappointment of the crowd — for what, he didn't know yet, but it seemed

a premonition. He knew his dad would be disappointed. Surely the world would be. The world that was crowded in a half circle around his ball beside the towering pines. More clouds formed now. Several people had told Jonni that tournament weather had been volatile in recent years. Rain was coming.

Lawrence said to come to the security offices. Ryals pulled again into the course, but this time he was turned away at the Magnolia entrance and directed to the next gate down, a maintenance gate. When he checked, he had missed a message from Allison requesting he do so. They wanted to minimize his profile, probably.

He parked after being admitted and he was given a tag for his car to allow easier access. He imagined he could sell it for enough to pay off his car.

It was still early, attendees were still gathering outside on the road and street corners, but it was cloudy now and rain was beginning to drop in light, small drops. He supposed he should have worn sneakers today, or something better for the mud. Instead he wore brown comfortable dress shoes. He made a note to grab sneakers when he returned.

Whenever that was. Even one day on the course felt like protracted time in another world, one in which time passed at its own rate.

He found Lawrence in front of the security office, talking on his radio sternly. Ryals waited nearby. Lawrence let go the radio and walked over.

"Management let someone go this morning and he didn't want to go. I thought I would have to intervene. Come with me. I have something to show you."

They walked back to the video room. At the far end one controller explored video files on four screens. Lawrence offered the detective a chair, but Ryals remained standing.

"Pull it up," Lawrence told the controller. The controller nodded, found a saved file and pulled it up. "This is about midnight on Saturday," Lawrence explained. "Eleven thirty three."

"After lights out?"

"Yes."

The video fast forwarded and then slowed and the timestamp ticked the seconds forward. On the screen, standing in the shadows of trees, near bushes—lighting, then smoking a cigarette. He pauses and doesn't move for a moment. He seems to be watching something.

"What is he looking at?" Ryals asked.

"The course," Lawrence said. Willy stood there, just staring, smoking slowly. Appreciating the view. "But here, watch." Willy exhales, turns to the bushes, and steps that way. It seems he's going to take a leak. "Rewind it," Lawrence said. The controller did. Ryals looked more closely.

"Looks like he's going to piss, right? But look — he says something." Indeed, his mouth moved once. Then he stepped to the bushes.

"And he doesn't come back out?"

"No," Lawrence says. "Easy to miss, though that is no excuse. We're not particularly concerned with a caddie walking around at night. And no one would be focused on him so that they'd not see him walk back. Any camera operator would assume he did his business and then walked away from the camera."

"But he spoke to someone. We can't see who?"

"No."

"He doesn't hesitate," Ryals observed.

"You suspect he knows this person?" Lawrence asked, peering at the screen.

"Possibly. He doesn't show surprise. I suppose someone may have asked, 'hey buddy, give me a hand?'—but how would that not be strange, after the lights are off?"

"It would be strange. But there is activity on the course at that hour."

"He disappears into the woods, and next time we see him, he's — where is this in relation to where he was pulled off the cart?"

"Look here," Lawrence said. He directed the controller to pull up another video. Ryals saw the same truck-bed club car, laden with pine straw bales, parked in the shadows. "Hard to tell, but the same man —presumably — climbs aboard here after loading a bag onto the back. This is about two hundred meters up from where we just saw Willy."

"So he calls Willy in, surprises him, assaults him, bags him, loads him on the car, drives two hundred meters then walks him all the way down to the 12th hole. Then returns. Seems unnecessary. Why the bag? Why not drive all the way down?"

"He's careful with the cameras," Lawrence offered.

"Which means he had to know the cameras."

"Yes," Lawrence said, more carefully. "It seems he does."

Ryals studied the video again. "I'll need copies of all of these, and that bit of video from yesterday," he said. Lawrence directed the controller to do so. Ryals had more faith in Lawrence's team to evaluate the footage than anyone in the department, but he still needed the evidence.

Ryals left the room and walked outside and watched a crowd down the hill clapping as a golfer in white and blue arrived at the course. The rain was beginning to fall now and the golfer held the brim of his cap and looked skyward. Umbrellas were appearing.

Jonni made it through the 11th, White Dogwood, a long downhill par four. Leave trembled with a strong and cool breeze and gently pushed his shot left to right. He rolled his putt in on a fifth shot, and he was lucky, he thought. He wasn't two over.

Jonni now stood facing the Twelfth Hole. He looked down the grade at the bunkers and the flag; all was now in dusk-like light from the heavy clouds. And rain was falling indeed: Jonny felt the big drops hitting him one by one. Rain warm like blood.

He felt sick, and regretted his swing as soon as he hit the ball; it was lazy, dropped fast, short of anything close to a good shot. The crack of that swing, however, brought the rain down heavier, and while Rahm kept walking, Jonni just stood. He trudged, like a man to the gallows, awaiting the call. Surely, they would be rained out.

The call came before he reached his ball. It was nothing but relief to him. A thundering answer to a soft prayer.

FOURTEEN

Jonni sat in the clubhouse reception room, in the corner beside Frank, who texted on his phone, and his father, who was busy socializing in his strongest Afrikaans accent with the other golfers, or, when they ignored him, their managers or caddies. The room was crowded and everyone smelled of grass, rain and pollen. Jonni studied their shoes. All, it seemed, nicer than his; already stained yellow and green with flecks of grass. The deep gray-blue carpet in here was covered with the scuffs from their cleats but somehow, as if by magic, it would be perfectly clean moments after the gathering departed.

All were in good spirits, laughing, using their hands to describe shots on various courses and compare notes. Some held beer. Jonni felt their occasional furtive dagger stares, though. Cutting glances at him, maybe even disliking him. He was glad Frank was near. The game, the crowd, the security people here all surely looked at Jonni as an unfortunate distraction. Someone who brought a murder to this consecrated place. Jonni had played poorly up until the rain shut him out. He was grateful, actually. He could hear it against the windows. Jonni looked at Frank. He was dressed for the rain, or for a hike or anything. He was certainly capable. He made Jonni feel safe, but then again Jonni hadn't really felt in danger. Frank said little but he smiled at Jonni politely as Jonni studied him and then he went back to his phone.

From the crowd, in blue pants and a gray shirt with a white PING hat, Bubba Watson broke free and walked over, shrugging his shoulders as he gestured to Jonni's dad's seat. Asking if he could join him. Jonni nodded. Bubba sat and for a moment he didn't say anything. Finally Jonni looked at him and it seemed Bubba, who was taller than he looked on TV, wasn't sure what to say.

"You know why they call it Amen Corner?" Bubba asked him.

"I've heard the story," Jonni said. "But I don't remember."

"In 1958 Arnold Palmer played through 11, 12 and 13. They say his play was like a miracle. There was a rule, and he had to drop a ball and he went over. Double-bogey five. They say he prayed, argued and they ruled his first ball could play. He won the tournament that year. His entire fate changed right there and then in the middle of wind and rain. Some writer in Sports Illustrated then called it the "Amen Corner." You know, the place Arnold Palmer changed his fate in the trickiest turn on a course any of us have ever come across." Bubba looked over at Jonni, who wasn't sure how to respond. "Funny thing is, I didn't do well in history class," he joked. Then finally asked, "How you doing, Jonni?"

Bubba. nodded as he talked. The way he moved reminded Jonni of a buoy bouncing on waves.

"I'm okay," Jonni said, clearing his throat as he did.

"Tough, the rain, you know." Bubba said. "Guess that's how it's so green down here. I mean, we get it, where I'm from. Florida isn't far. Rains like hell down there. Cats and dogs — do you use that expression?"

"I know it," Jonni said, managing even a slight smile. After all, he was talking with one of his heroes.

"Yeah, I mean half of my state is a swamp."

"You have crocodiles down there, I heard. Alligators, I mean," Jonni said, remembering this from school.

"Sure but not like yours. I did a turn in South Africa, went on a safari. You've got those crocodiles that can take down a zebra, big massive things." Jonni nodded. He knew stories of people killed by crocs. A close friend Jean Rousseau, manager at the famous Skukuza Golf Club in Kruger Park, lost his best friend to a one in the water right at the bridge between the 9th and 1st holes there, one tragic night during a party. Jean was a seasoned club manager, and Jonni had the privilege of playing with him more than once. There on the course, in every way distinct from Augusta; not fenced, populated at night by impala and hungry lions. Distinct except for the game that Jonni could play on both. Distinct except that death hung on both. Jonni wasn't sure why it came to mind at this moment. It was another place that he loved. He wished he could show it to Bubba.

Jonni wasn't sure what to say. He had admired and watched Watson for years. He had never taken a golf lesson and yet he was a world champion. The commenters often joked about Bubba's stance since he didn't play like anyone else. Jonni liked the way Bubba played. Liked that he made the game his own. And Bubba had a Green Jacket. He won the Masters — twice. Jonni tried to figure out how to bring this up. Bubba kept talking. "Kind of a rough time for you."

They both looked around at the crowd. Some looked over. Most were talking amongst themselves. "How are the crowds treating you?" Bubba asked.

"The crowds?"

"Yeah, man. On the best of days they get to me. Don't get me wrong, the crowds in Augusta are the best. In Florida, on PGA events even, they may get drunk, they shout. Here they're decent and polite but I still have a hard time with them. Crowds make me nervous. All those eyes staring at me, man. I don't handle it well."

"It's just a lot of pressure," Jonni said.

"Tim keeps me sane," Bubba said, referring to his caddie. "A good caddie keeps you focused and tells you not to worry about anyone or anything. I've been called rude; really, I'm nervous. I don't think I could play without Tim." Bubba looked up at the crowd but Jonni didn't see his caddie in the room. Jonni wasn't sure what to say to this. He nodded and played with his lace and wished he had more to say to this legend, this idol who was picking grass bits from his pant leg as he sat beside Jonni in a room of legends. Bubba put his hand in a fist and bumped it against Jonni's shoulder. "I'm sure that's exactly how Willy was. I know — we all know this mess is a hard time and I don't know what it's all about. I sure hope they catch the bastard. Just know that we're all rooting for you, and I've got your back if you need anything at all. Cool?"

Jonni nodded, even fighting a smile. Bubba stood up with another knock of his knuckles and walked back into the group. No one else looked Jonni's way, not right now. He knew many of them were talking about him. He could tell when their voices lowered. He sat on the outside of this elite crowd. He looked over and saw Frank looking at him, vigilant as ever. His dad walked back over, a glow on his face from the thrill of talking to these golf celebrities.

Jonni appreciated what Bubba said. He hoped he could remember that moment forever. He still felt alone, though, not one of the crowd, but a distraction to the game, a mar on the tournament like a divot in the grass. That's how they all saw him. He brought this mess here.

And Willy was still gone.

Jonni stood, and told his dad he wanted to get back to the hotel.

Ryals was almost certain that the killer, whoever he was, was long gone out of Augusta. That didn't mean they wouldn't be able to identify him, though, and then pursue him somewhere else. It was hard to hide. Ryals had many files that ended in convictions where the crime was local but the arrest was out of state. It was common for the criminal to flee, to think that the further they were geographically from a crime, the safer they were. Sometimes that was true, but nine times out of ten, evidence caught up with them whether by credit card, ID or cell phone bill. The fugitive was most often found.

Ryals wondered, though, if this one was out of country. A mysterious shroud seemed to cover his identity. He knew nothing, really, and it was an alien and unsettling feeling. The killer was beginning to haunt him.

Ryals thought he should talk to Jonni again. This was indeed a message meant for someone, and Jonni was the most likely person. Ryals sometimes had a gut feeling when someone was lying. He thought the kid wasn't telling all — and perhaps for understandable reasons. Maybe letting it sit for a day would have scared him straight. He checked in with Allison. She told Ryals Jonni had left for his hotel.

Perhaps the hotel was better. There would be less pressure in a place away from the murder location. Ryals was surprised that an actual Masters golfer wasn't staying in the Ritz, but, then again, there wasn't a Ritz in Augusta. The Sheraton downtown, he thought, was probably the nicest. The Partridge Inn, a local hotel with a hilltop view in the old money part of town was perhaps favored. He knew that some golfers rented houses, especially those with families. Lots of homes in Augusta emptied out and rented for the week. Locals with prime real estate could make thousands and take a vacation when traffic was at its worst. A few years back a tech company reportedly rented an entire neighborhood near Savannah Rapids Pavillion. But Jonni was at the

Hampton. Hell, Ryals thought. I haven't stayed in a hotel nicer than that in a long time. But I'm not competing in the Masters.

"I'm proud of you for pushing through. For competing. But you don't have to. It took real talent—and character--to get here. You can do it again," his father said as they drove back. Jonni's clothes were cold and wet. He wanted to be in his bed. His bed back home, not his hotel bed. Maybe, he thought, golf wasn't his future. He listened to the rain on the roof of the car as they drove. That's all he wanted to listen to.

But he did know what it had taken to get here. He didn't want to back down.

In fact it was one shot that got him here; an ace on the 9th in Abu Dhabi. The desert beyond, the wind carrying the aroma of the sea. He took the shot and it felt good and he could feel it pulled by the gravity of the hole but he couldn't see it.

Good shots could be measured by the reaction of spectators. Vigorous applause and congratulatory shouts indicated a birdie; riotous uproar, an unexpected eagle or ace. That day he hit a par four 290-yard shot and knew the ball sank by the crowd's reaction. And he managed a smile before he pulled his hat low again to hide his face as he walked. Willy's hand patting his back, a spring in the caddie's step. "You just made it to Augusta, bud!" he said excitedly. Jonni didn't think much about what that meant at the moment. It took a few weeks for it to sink it. At that moment he just felt the triumph of the shot.

Of course, it wasn't just one shot; it was several wins, lots of practice and hard work, but if all of that had brought him to the door, the ace on the 9th was the key that opened the door.

Augusta was six months from that shot. Jonni had never been here. Some pros and amateurs who made the cut would visit the Augusta National six, maybe ten times to play the course, try out the grass, get a feel for it before the Masters. Jonni couldn't afford that. To travel for tournaments, he often had to raise money — friends, neighbors, local businesses, and once Charl Schwartzl, helped him with the funds to make the trip to Abu Dhabi. After qualifying for the Masters, sponsors finally came to him in a generous way and offered to cover costs

He remembered, two weeks later, Willy looking at him over a fire and saying "Damn it, Jonni, we're going to Augusta!" That was the moment it sank in.

They held a celebratory braai—a South African traditional community barbecue — and raised the money for the ticket to Atlanta. The National took care of everything on the ground, but he still had to get here. The phone began to ring. Interview requests, sponsorship offers from lesser brands — they settled on Oakley and Adidas, but Jonni wasn't in a position to command much in the way of the sponsorships. If he performed well, that would be different.

Willy told him that everything was different now. Augusta would be a whole new level of competition. Willy even said he wasn't up to the task of getting Jonni ready, but Jonni insisted he needed Willy.

He worked out — swimming, running, weights and a stationary bike. Lots and lots of golf. Every spot they could play, every different kind of grass and weather. Every trick Willy could think of to improve Jonni's game. Jonni had never worked harder.

"But kid just do what you been doing. That's all you can do. If it's not fun it's not worth it," he said.

Jonni took that to heart. The sunglasses, the new shoes, the caps either too tight or too loose, the new golf bag, none of it was important.

What was important was just finding the gravity of each hole, the bottom of that flag, into the wind, with the wind, over hills and around bunkers. Jonni's job was simple: get the ball into the hole.

Today it was far from simple. It was press and investigations and cameras and the embellished stories about him and his dead caddie— that's what his dad called it—just "stories"— and it was the pain and loss and Willy was gone. Just gone.

Soon they were back to the hotel and he and his father went to their separate rooms silently.

The phone rang in the next room — his dad's mobile phone — and his dad took the call. He seemed surprised. Jonni could hear the muffled conversation. He realized he was cold; shivering. Jonni turned the shower on so he couldn't hear it and climbed soon into the hot water. He didn't want to think about business, any business at all.

The rain was coming down harder when Ryals drove to the hotel. This time he didn't use his lights, and he turned on the radio to find a station talking golf. He didn't care to keep up except to find out the schedule with the rain — and he wondered if he might learn something that would give him a workable theory. He just could not figure how a murder fell into this world of khakis and floral dresses and smiles and cigars and pimento cheese.

Ryals hadn't announced he was coming to the hotel, and he had Jonni called from the lobby. He waited, fixing himself a coffee from a stand by the bar. He picked a comfortable chair. Every TV was of course on the Golf Channel, though there was no direct coverage of the tournament yet.

As if by some cue, an email appeared in his phone from Ingot. Titled: "Masters Crimes" it contained several links. Ryals clicked through them, squinting at the small screen.

One link: a 27-year-old California man was arrested after sneaking onto the course in 2009.

In 1997, Allen Caldwell III of Martinez, Georgia, committed suicide after his small brokerage failed to deliver 100 promised Masters badges. Ryals remembered hearing about that one.

There was the incident with President Reagan.

A woman, guest of a patron in 2016 lost the badges for herself and the patrons after she drunkenly ran out onto a fairway after a golfer.

In 1977, Augusta National Chairman Clifford Roberts, whom the article described as a racist and traditionalist to a fault, walked onto the Par 3 course and shot himself. His health was in decline — likely cancer.

In 2012, a patron snuck onto the fairway to steal a cup of sand. He wasn't just kicked out, he was arrested.

All that was interesting but not relevant. At the bottom of the email was a note: "Pretty good record over 100 years."

Ryals had to agree. He didn't think a single football stadium or other kind of arena could boast a similar safety record. Perhaps the drunk woman's penalty explained it. Losing the hardest ticket in sports was overwhelming punishment.

Jonni approached and Ryals put his phone away. He didn't stand; he gestured for Jonni to sit opposite him.

"Hell of a lot you're facing," Ryals said. Jonni was pleasant, but his eyes were red and tired, and his arms hung beside the chair like they were loosely attached. He wore Adidas workout pants and a long sleeve shirt. He had very little style of his own and Ryals got the sense that the kid didn't care for that sort of thing.

Ryals wanted to get to know the Jonni a bit. "What is it like where you're from? Different from here?"

Jonni didn't pay attention to a group walking into the lobby, all in golf clothes, and sopping wet. Ryals guessed the course was shut down due to rain right now. They didn't notice them either, perhaps because the bar was still closed at this early hour.

"I guess it's different. More dry, gets real hot."

"It can blaze here, don't doubt it," Ryals said. "What gets me is the humidity, you know, at night it doesn't cool down. Sometimes just stays hot all the way through. Occasionally so thick it's hard to breathe. But this time of year, it's nice," he added. Jonni just nodded.

"You have animals where you're from? Big ones, I mean, elephants and such? I think I read that."

"Yeah, mostly in reserves. Parks, the Kruger. Sometimes they get out."

"What animals?" Ryals asked, genuinely interested. He'd never traveled to Africa, though Angela was determined to go and work with a charity there.

"Oh, giraffe, impala, hippo, elephant, some rhino are left, lions and things. Lots of antelope."

"That's incredible," Ryals said, genuinely. "I would love to see that. My daughter too. She wants to go over to South Africa, since she was a kid. A smaller kid, I mean."

Jonni almost said something but he sat back deflated. Ryals felt sorry for him. Following what had to be the greatest high of his life came immediately one of the worst tragedies.

"I guess you lucked out today — looks like the rain is shutting things down out there." Jonni glanced toward the doors, then shrugged.

"They say it will clear up this afternoon," he said.

"So, I'm trying to sort things out, you know, with all of this.

Doing everything we can. Seems Willy was a really decent guy, and I'm sure a good friend to your family."

Jonni nodded.

"I wonder if you can help me a bit with this."

"How?" Jonni asked, his attitude not surly, not defiant; he just seemed small, is how Ryals had it in his mind. He just didn't know.

"Well, I wonder if anyone has ever approached you. Here, or anywhere. And asked, you know, for you to lose a game, or I don't know, do anything for them. I'm wondering why someone might do something like this. Maybe now something stands out to you that didn't before?"

Jonni seemed to really think for a long moment, as if this idea hadn't occurred to him before. He sat up a bit, his brow furrowed. He looked at Ryals.

"No, nothing like that," he said.

Ryals nodded. He didn't expect much.

Ryals pointed to the kid's wrist, on which he wore several string bracelets with beads on them.

"Those from home?" Jonni nodded. He touched them and moved them around his arm. "Made by hand?"

"Yeah, this spot, near my home. Some girls make them to raise a few rands."

"Do they make it harder to swing?" Ryals feigned holding a club, then gave up when he realized he hardly knew how.

"I'm used to them by now."

"Will they be watching?" Ryals asked. "The people from home. I've heard what they say about you on TV. You're a prodigy."

Jonni nodded. "Yeah, many will." He seemed to straighten up at that thought. He turned to the TV. Ryals stood.

"Well, not much to see today, I guess, as long as this rain keeps up. I better be moving. You have my card still?"

"Yeah."

"Great. If anything occurs to you, just ring me — do it from here if it's expensive on the mobile. Or tell Ms. Roy, she'll get me. I'm sorry again, Mr. Lombard."

"Do you know where he — is? His body I mean, what's happening with it."

"It's evidence right now so they'll hang on to it in case there's something more they need to look at. Then they will release the body to his family. I don't know how that works to return him overseas."

"Okay," Jonni said, seeming to regret the question. He looked sick.

Ryals left him there, walking through the lobby as more people filtered in from the course. Despite the rain, most were smiling. Beside the door was a stack of The Augusta Chronicle newspapers. Ryals read it often but he didn't read golf. Of course the front pages this week were all "The Masters Wrap". He grabbed one, dug down, and found one from yesterday.

As he climbed back into his car he decided that he wanted to know what people were talking about before the murder. What had the buzz been? Ingot and Allison would have good information for him.

His phone buzzed — a voicemail. The team was finished with the personnel files. He called the investigator in the room.

"Finished, yes, but we won't have a report with background checks from the socials we submitted to the FBI until tomorrow morning. What we have now is a reference chart, race, height, gender to exclude some, about thirty percent. But it's tricky because the video doesn't give us a very clear picture. We also have a cross reference of anyone working that area, given a key to a golf cart, some things like that."

Ryals drove through the rain and up the hill into the congestion that grew as he neared the Augusta National parking lot and entrances.

"So how many does that leave us?" He asked.

"About one hundred thirty, in the first category. About thirty working in that area at that time."

"Okay, let's start calling those thirty. See what we come up with."

"We're on it."

The killer wasn't necessarily one of the grounds crew. It was a place to start, a net to cast.

The background checks might give them additional data.

There wasn't much more to do today. Ryals called the Sheriff and gave an update and sounded positive — he said they were "moving in the right direction" which was a political thing for him to say and, he hoped, even somewhat accurate.

There was a natural ebb and flow to investigations. You pushed, then you let off and things worked themselves out then you pushed again. Sleeping on a case often solved it. Constant pressure rarely yielded anything, except in the case of a runaway fugitive or kidnapping.

That was how investigators worked high caseloads. You rotated through. You charged who you could, when you could. You sent deputies to serve warrants. Suspects who laid low reappeared. Lost items became found.

Right now Ryals didn't have anything to do.

He decided to go home for a while. He called Angela, asked if he could pick up dinner.

"Dad," she said, "No deep fried Chinese food."

"Okay," he said. "what would you like?"

She thought. "Wraps from Panera."

"I'm not anywhere close to there," he said.

"Fine. Let's compromise. We can do Thai. I'll call in an order so you don't mess it up and send you the address. And Dad. Did you get me something?"

"What do you mean?"

"From the course. Something? Any stuff." First it was a thing, now it was stuff.

He thought about letting Allison and Lawrence know that he would be unreachable that evening, but then he remembered he didn't work for them.

The last two days had been high paced, and he needed a break, not just physically but to let his mind sort out all he knew. He expected that after a beer, some TV, and rest he would have some better ideas.

He looked at his passenger seat, saw the newspapers. He might read up on golf too.

The rain continued to pour outside and dusk came prematurely behind the clouds. The tournament was postponed at 3 and never resumed. A heaviness held over the National, over Augusta. Ryals was getting nowhere; another dozen groundskeepers had returned calls, but there were no red flags. They still had some, but Ryals felt that he had an instinct about these things and he didn't sense anything would come of these enquiries. If this was a random murder, he might feel about where he usually felt in these cases; put it on the shelf for a bit, run the details to ground, let it wait. The ex-lover was likely to show up drunk at a bar and get into a fight; the suspect would get picked up on a DUI, or someone would come forward and rat out the perp. Things often worked themselves out even in murder; it was usually driven by passion, not planned and executed in sloppy fashion. It made people angry and that threw emotions flying in every direction and it was like particles colliding in one of those laboratories. Eventually a molecule would emerge.

This was totally different. It was planned, sophisticated and careful. Ryals felt that the bad guys were getting away with it, and maybe well away. The usual rules of investigation didn't apply.

As he pulled into the Indian Queen, a favorite, dimly lit bar at the edge of the "Hill," part of town, he thought he should turn it over to the GBI. Or the FBI, if they had reason to take it. Ryals really had no idea.

The bar was crowded, the music low, the chairs were big and comfortable and the air was thick with the smell of rainwater as the crowd around the bar shed water from their raincoats. The bartender had bright red cheeks from running around and the drinks moved fast.

Ryals waited a while at the corner of the bar and took in the scene. He was familiar with this place, and he hadn't felt familiar with anything for a few days now. Leaving the National and coming here was like waking up from a dream. He had to admit it was something of a letdown. There was an energy and something surreal about the course just a few miles up the road. As he listened to the conversations at the bar, he thought he really was onto something with this case, something for the history books. At least three people within earshot discussed the murder. It was the talk of the town. There was endless speculation. His beer arrived. Only a few people here knew him; it wasn't his usual spot but he wasn't usually on this side of town at the end of the day. There were more than a few golf patrons in the bar; it was mostly populated by the rich kids of the Hill, the old Augusta money; some of their parents might be club members themselves. The Masters logo was on a dozen hats and shirts. If they weren't attending, they were fans celebrating. The two TVs in the bar were on replay from the practice rounds.

This was a golf town, it was a Masters town, and the murder was like something that happened in the family. Ryals remembered his barber once saying, "in the South, we don't keep our skeletons in the closet, we take them out and put them on the porch for all to see." 'All,' of course, meant all our friends and neighbors. The southern family. This murder wasn't like that. It was a skeleton people were only whispering about. Like a family secret being exposed. He tried to read their faces. There was no apparent anxiety — he wondered if that would continue to be the case. If they would be afraid for their Sacred Cow, the Greatest Golf Tournament in the World, being marred forever by this crime. Whatever the revelation, if there was one. He didn't see that, though — maybe there was simply too much hype in the air with the tournament on TV and the crowds in town. Christmas and Easter all at once. Holy Week for Golf Fans and the city of Augusta. Sometimes actually fell on the real Holy Week, competing with church activities and forcing some people into a religious crisis.

No, this crowd didn't see it that way, not from what he observed now. Maybe that was the true nature of the South, he thought, feeling oddly philosophical about the whole experience. A part of the country with a broken past, Southerners learned to live with trade-offs, to accept the bad with the good, especially if it meant not shaking their world apart. They were people of tradition who resisted change and if that meant accepting a few flaws and having to live with the sin carried forward from their past, so be it. That was the Southern way.

So maybe a murder on the golf course would be easy to overlook. They could accept it, so long as they could love their game.

Or not. Whatever. Maybe screw it and maybe some rich kids' opinions didn't matter. He finished his beer and realized he didn't want to be stuck in a crowded bar. It was getting hot. He left cash, smiled at the bartender and walked back out to his car. He caught someone watching him as he left; bright blue eyes from a dim corner of the bar. Ryals suspected he would gain notoriety for handling the case. He would be on the news at some point if he wasn't already. He would draw stares.

In nightvision the stars were extraordinary, green but they could be counted by the thousands upon thousands. Bats were illuminated, too, otherwise invisible. This was cheap equipment, with shaky mounts, and instead of a helmet it was held over her forehead and across her hair with elastic straps, but it made a difference. Particularly if she wanted to spot a poacher in the dark African bush.

Kate Chase was just thirty-one, but she had an impressive resume and had managed lots of trips to Africa in the past few years, many helping this group of poaching-fighting rangers via a nonprofit. Of course, she hadn't exactly told her real job what she was up to on these trips, but she was certain they felt fine with a "don't ask, don't tell" policy about the more ambitious activities away from her desk.

Her jet black hair was pulled tight with a bandanna to hide the sheen. She wore a vest and had a camera but no weapon; she chewed gum that had long ago lost its flavor. She did it constantly; in the bush or at a desk. Her high boots were laced tight, made for jungle combat. She was still, but full of energy.

In front of her were three Ugandan Rangers with their team leader a few meters ahead. They looked north across the Kidepo Valley National Park boundary toward the South Sudan border. They were bivouacked, waiting all night, expecting poachers to approach from the east, where they believed there was a fence incursion. The poachers were after rhino horn, which was currently, ounce for ounce, one of the most valuable materials on the planet. More than heroin or gold. Rhino were recently reintroduced to this area from the Ziwa Sanctuary — and new rhino meant trouble. Syndicate-backed militia would cut an endangered animal's face in half to get it, and they would shoot a ranger to keep it.

Kate was tolerated at first, mocked plenty, but she worked hard and didn't slow them down, asking questions only when necessary. She'd been rushed by elephants and stalked by lions with them.

This was a good time of year here; not too hot and the animals were active. Good time, that was, for tourists, though not many of those came here yet. This area was wild. It wasn't protected by tourism nor buffered by hunting concessions. Nighttime was a dangerous time to be crouched in the bush, in grass that hid lions, cape buffalo, porcupines, and deadly snakes. Grass tall enough to hide dangerous militia.

The lead ranger signaled them and she looked forward. With their infrared flashlights, visible only in nightvision, they swept the low area just ahead. For a moment nothing. She thought she heard something, and wondered if it was an animal. It was low enough buffalo might be moving through. Or a lone bull, which was extremely dangerous. She felt her knees burning as she rose up a bit to see.

For several long minutes, nothing. The rangers of course didn't speak; they hardly breathed. They looked through their goggles, which she had provided along with more tech goodies in the bags of equipment she brought.

Then she saw them. Two men, dressed in old and torn camouflaged jackets carrying AK47s with panga blades on their backs. They crossed her field of view in low grass slowly, pausing every few meters. They didn't speak either. Their eyes glowed when they looked toward her, reflecting the infrared light but unaware. The lead ranger signaled. She dropped to the ground, as she was supposed to do.

The rangers moved out quickly into an L shape and they turned on their gun lights, suddenly bathing the poachers in a fiery blaze of white light that blinded them. The lead ranger yelled for the poachers to drop their weapons and to put their hands up.

The poachers obeyed.

The rangers gave the all clear and Kate rose and was allowed three minutes with the poachers to ask questions. She approached with her flashlight, and the two captured men looked up at this strange white woman in field clothes in the middle of the African bush.

FIFTEEN

Wednesday

Ryals felt refreshed today.

Angela was awake before he was and made him toast with egg whites. She had questions about the case; most he wouldn't answer. She asked him about the Masters.

"Today will be another long one," he told her.

"Dad," she said as he added tabasco to his eggs. "I'm fine."

"I'll watch TV, maybe I'll see you," she said. He thought of the man staring at him in the bar. The last thing he wanted was to become a local celebrity.

She was watching it on TV. He kissed his daughter on the forehead and left and took the southside highway to downtown to the station, avoiding the Hill and the area near the National. For now.

There were fewer press vehicles parked out front now — just a van and one reporter — but they would swarm again if there was news. No one inside reacted to him, but the department secretary handed him a stack of opened letters.

"I took the liberty. Loonies, most of them. Nothing I'd give any time to but see for yourself. A couple of people offering to help. One from a journalist asking to tag along." She handed him some messages.

"Anything important we called you about. Other case stuff I passed along.   A couple of restaurants, offering you a free meal."

"Really?"

"Yeah, hun. Including La Maison."

"Didn't they close down?"

"New owner."

"Huh." He'd received thank you gifts before.

"I'd better catch this guy before they turn on me," he quipped.

"A woman certain her ex is the killer, because he hated golf and she hates him, uh— a call from South Africa, not a lot of information, I didn't get the name but there's a call back number."

Ryals took that one.

"And Sheriff wants to see you."

"When did he get in?" Ryals asked.

"He's been in." Ryals looked down the hall to the Sheriff's office. The Sheriff was on his email and gestured for Ryals to sit.

"Hall, what's new this morning?"

"Nothing yet. Getting into it. Background checks should be in soon. GBI forensic report on the room. Final coroner's report. We'll see what we've got, and what comes from dragging the water on the grounds staff."

"Mhm," the Sheriff said, making his own notes. Then he looked at Ryals.

"Hall. Did you go to the press?"

"I'm sorry?"

"At the golf course. Did you go talk to the press?"

Ryals almost said no, of course not, but caught himself. "I did speak to a member of the press, yes. Off the record. Writer, for, uh — a golf magazine."

"What about?" The Sheriff asked, looking over his glasses and angling his gray and silver crew cut at Ryals.

"General background. Gambling in golf."

"You think this is about a bet?"

"I think it's possible," Ryals said.

Sheriff nodded. "Could be, could be," he said. He seemed happy to have something to go on. Despite the trouble, his eyes sparkled. Ryals knew this could define the Sheriff's entire tenure—he likely wouldn't seek reelection but he could talk about this at the golf club for twenty years. (The Sheriff did enjoy golfing, though others said he was pretty bad at it. Ryals had seen him come to work more than once in golf apparel.) "Look," The Sheriff said, "someone there knows you spoke to the press. Whatever the reason, watch our backside on this because the National has been very reasonable but they are looking out for themselves. If they say they want someone else working up there or if they decide they've had enough of us walking around their trees looking for clues, it's going to be a tough argument to win."

Ryals wasn't immune, nor was he insensitive to politics. It was just part of it. It was money politics, racial politics, city council politics, something every time. Ryals thought of politics in investigative work like an infection on the operating table. Best to get in, do the work, and get out and sew the body back up before it happened.

"Oh, Ryals," the Sheriff said. "Don't carry your gun on the course. Specific request from the Chairman. Liability, you know."

"I see," Ryals said. Indeed, all of the rules were different and his jurisdiction was limited.

The Sheriff dismissed Ryals and he went back to his desk and started to go over his daily reports to be sure they were all filed with t's crossed and i's dotted. He remembered the South Africa call and looked at the note and dialed the number. His desk phone couldn't make an international call so he hung up, used his cell phone and tried again.

The phone rang, an unfamiliar tone instead of a ring, but then it simply clicked off. Who knows, he thought. If it's important they'll call back.

Within an hour he had everything wrapped up at his desk and he called the investigator leading the personnel files and — they weren't in yet, on their way — and left a message about the background checks and follow-ups. The investigator called back immediately from the road.

"So we had about a seventy-five percent pickup rate on those calls. Left messages, have some returns this morning. Of note just — hold on — trying to look at the paper here — eh, driving. Anyway. There are a few we couldn't get ahold of. I'll get those names over to you. About sixty from our list are still in the park working the grounds daily."

"Any that would have been working the area near the abduction or murder? Over by the fence?"

"I'll check this morning and get right back to you."

"Send me a list."

Ryals would interview any who were working today. The tournament began tomorrow. Tomorrow, all eyes would be on Augusta, and he was certain the investigation would get more difficult. If only because of traffic.

Ryals looked carefully at each of the three dozen or so files in front of him, spartan as they were. The third investigator, an assistant, was on her laptop looking at social media profiles, anything they could dig up online. Some people left a much more obvious digital trail than they realized. Ryals doubted their criminal was anywhere close to that dumb.

He remembered the toxin. He checked for an email from the coroner.

He found one he hadn't seen. Full toxicology report, and a list of places where the syringe cocktail was available. The list wasn't long.

Hospitals, medical schools, clinical psychiatric facilities, Class 3 pharmacies — "in some of these places you'd have to mix these together on site. See you soon Sherlock."

He jotted down notes.

"Okay," he told the team. "New variables to add into the mix. Anyone here with access to, uh, medical labs, pharmacies, that sort of thing. Spouses, girlfriends."

"So a pharmacist moonlighting as a gardener?"

"I don't think so," Ryals said, leaning back. "I think it's possible that someone falsified a resume as a gardener. Either way, there's easier ways to kill someone." He felt something; like a shadow hanging beneath the trees, deeper than the rest. This was a pre-meditated, dark and intelligent crime.

Ryals needed the FBI or someone else with sophistication to match. He was way out of his league. Ryals didn't back down from a fight, but this wasn't his area of expertise. Augusta was the second largest city in Georgia, but it was a small town, and he was a small town cop.

"Table that," Ryals said finally. "Let's call each and verify backgrounds. Every person here applied and was invited, let's make sure the National did their due diligence and didn't miss something." He had no idea what it took to pretend to be a groundskeeper — as they explained, no one here was without a notable resume in maintaining a golf course somewhere, and he imagined a lot of golf course may be legitimate and even prestigious. So how to fake that?

The truth always came out in details and diligence — the devil, as they said, was in the details.

There was a devil here. Ryals could feel it.

Ryals noticed only after a while that the light outside was dim through the window, as if a premature evening had set in. It matched how he felt. Clouds moved like distant and slow-moving predators; more rain imminent and a threatening storm. His head was down, focused on the calls one after another, and he only noticed when he finished the last one on his list. Half had gone to voicemail.

He only needed someone to verify each resume. One person at the most recent place of employment. He had only to briefly state who he was and where he was calling from and he got compliance. To a person, they all knew what was happening in Augusta. He asked them to verify the name. When they did, he thanked them and moved on.

Unlike on TV, most people wanted to help when the police asked questions. Most were too eager. This was a crowd that loved the course, too, and the game and wanted to preserve it. Their answers were genuine and their respect for the investigation was real. The last man, Course Supervisor from a Pennsylvania Golf Club, had returned to the National for the past twelve years and always worked around the same holes. "I look forward to it every year more than Christmas or my birthday." Ryals thanked him, and ended the call. This would be a long day.

The team made a list of non-answers and they would run through that again this evening.

Real detective work was tedious. Ryals was good at this part of it. He decided a long time ago he didn't care about climbing ladders, accolades, and he didn't carry his cases home. He just did the job.

Rosa Alvarez pushed the cart as she moved down the hallway of the Holiday Inn Express off of Broad Street. It was the very end of her shift, the last late checkout rooms cleaned between herself and Yolanda who now was hopefully finishing the room beneath, or Rosa would have to go down and pick up the slack. She wore headphones as she walked and worked. Music made the day go by faster. She passed the cart as a pair of golf fans walked by carrying an umbrella. This was the busiest time of the year for the hotel; it was a decent crowd but sometimes the rooms were covered in beer cans and torn apart by late night partying. There were spills to soak up and stains to scrub. Occasionally there was a broken chair or table from what she imagined were late night dance sessions.

She went into the last room at the end of the hall and turned the bed over, scrubbed the bathroom, wiped the windows and vacuumed the floors. She emptied the trash cans and replaced the bags and noted it on her chart. Room was cleared and would be occupied again in the morning.

She adjusted the shower curtain, replaced the soaps and shampoo. She left a signed card with her name on the desk, then pulled the door closed behind her while nodding her head to the music. She was nearly done.

She pushed the cart down the hallway which was now completely empty. An awful smell carried through it, coming from one of the rooms.

She walked slowly and the smell grew worse. It hadn't been bad on the way down the hall, but then it had rained and the air had come on and maybe it had drawn the smell out of a room.

She neared the source, leaving her cart behind and sniffing at doors. She found the one; the smell was at its worst there. A "Privacy, Please" sign hung on the doorknob. She hesitated. Her shift was over. She didn't have to deal with this.

She removed her headphones and listened to the door. Hearing nothing, she looked around and knocked. It wasn't exactly procedure but she felt it was her duty.

No one answered. She knocked again and announced herself. She used her master keycard to open the door. The smell was immediately worse, and she took a rag that smelled of window cleaner and held it against her mouth to block the smell.

Inside, the room was neat and she saw a suitcase on the folding stand. She inched forward until she could see the bed and it was unmade with a bottle of water and book on the table beside it.

She took a step back and looked into the bathroom. The smell was strongest there. It was dark, she couldn't see anything. She flicked the light on and screamed when she saw it. A body, in the tub, wrapped in the shower curtain, an empty bottle of bleach beside it; she could smell the bleach but the smell of death overpowered it. Rosa stood frozen for a moment and then she backed out.

SIXTEEN

Through the light in the curtains Jonni could see the steam rise from the parking lot, golden in the morning sunlight, wet from the rain the day before, with green leaves in the road and yellow pollen drying from small rivers in the gutters. Today would be hot and humid.

"I'm sorry," Jonni said. Frank and his father were outside. He spoke through the door. He sat on the bed. He wasn't going.

Jonni turned the TV on but the volume was low. He wanted to turn it up to drown out his father but his father had finally stopped pleading with him. The Golf Channel, available in all rooms. He flipped between channels, including general news. On the Golf channel there was, in the Masters coverage, a policeman and a forensic crime scene woman speaking about Willy. He listened to their speculation. They didn't know him, not at all. They said Willy liked to drink.

That was true. He liked to drink in crap bars, sometimes dangerous ones. He didn't like nice places; to Willy they weren't welcoming, weren't cozy. He didn't fit in. When tournaments included banquets Willy either skipped them or left early, already several rum and cokes down. He could be found at the bar. Willy came from no money and he never had much family to teach him social skills.

Willy also never tried to pretend that he was something or someone that he wasn't.

Jonni didn't know what had happened. Willy sometimes got on the wrong side of someone at a bar. Jonni believed sometimes Willy owed people money. Twice he had asked to borrow cash from Martin, who loaned it to him without asking questions and he paid it back in time.

Jonni didn't know where Willy went or who he crossed, but he must have gone out to some bar, said something dumb, and then one thing led to another. Jonni couldn't imagine anything more complicated than that. In South Africa murder was common. Dad once said golf is how Jonni would escape South Africa. But Jonni didn't want to leave. "A chance I never had, not for a moment. And the country is changing, Jonni," his father had said. Jonni loved his home, though. Nowhere else in the world had what South Africa had. Jonni was proud to represent it when he traveled out of the country.

Of course, now it would be known as the home of golfers involved with murders. South Africans would be known as troubled people, ruining the game of golf and the prestige of courses everywhere.

He saw it last night in the way the golfers looked at his father who tried to socialize with his big-toothed smile. In the way they cast glances at Frank. Even Bubba Watson saw it. He knew the crowd was against Jonni.

The sun was high and bright outside, vapor rose from grass and pavement and the traffic moved on the highway. He knew his Dad was frustrated. Jonni should have been there thirty minutes ago, walking onto the course. He couldn't do it.

All he wanted to do was play. He asked for nothing else from life. He held his putter and flung it across the room and it bounced off the wall and hit another wall. He flung himself down onto the bed and wished he could throw the TV out the window.

Yesterday was a mistake. He could see himself on the TV.

Every mention of him, every shot of him taking terrible stroke after terrible stroke until the rain, thank God, shut it all down.

He rose and closed the curtain.

The Sheriff called a meeting that morning for an update. He was dressed with his tie painfully cinched up to this neck. Ryals couldn't remember seeing him wear a tie before outside of a funeral.

"We're nowhere," he said, his friendly, I'm-your-neighbor demeanor gone. He had been a quality deputy and was a decent man. Now he was a politician. Ryals noticed the bottle of blood pressure medicine on the Sheriff's desk yesterday.

"We don't know that we're nowhere," Ryals answered. "Doing it by the book."

"The suspect could be long gone soon," the Sheriff said.

"He might be halfway around the world already," Ryals answered.

The Sheriff sat back and folded his arms.

"We've got to be ready for the cameras," the Sheriff said. "We'll be in the spotlight soon."

Ryals tried to remember the last time he went to the department gym, or any gym, and wished his paunch was contained. Perhaps, he thought, he was the wrong person for this case.

"What can we do today," the Sheriff said, "what new angle can we hit? I want ideas."

"We're going to continue to work through personnel. The security at the National is tight, someone saw something. There is a detail there, somewhere, we just haven't yet figured out what to look for."

"What about Jonni Lombard?"

"I'll speak to him and his father again. They have personal security now."

"Do you believe they're in danger?" Sheriff asked.

"No. The National gave them security."

Even if the murderer was still around, Ryals didn't think the kid was in danger. This was a one and done crime. The truth, whatever it was, would be a disappointment for the media.

Yet, the killer didn't use a gun, nor a blunt object; but poison. That wasn't mundane.

Ryals could read the sheriff. He feared they were out of their depth.

There was a knock at the door behind them. Another station deputy poked her head in. Sheriff looked up. If she was interrupting, they all knew it was important.

"Sheriff," she said. "We have a body."

He nodded but shrugged. "Okay," he said. Waiting for more. She looked at a notepad. Normally they didn't warrant interruptions.

"Holiday Inn Express, Broad Street. Body found last night, time of death unknown,"

"Drugs?"

"Not sure, Sheriff."

"Why are you bringing this to me?"

"Because according to the hotel manager, the deceased worked at the Augusta National."

It was bright and hot and Ryals shirt stuck to his back even with the air conditioning when he arrived at the hotel at eleven in the morning.

He waited for the Crime Scene team and the coroner to arrive.

The staff kept the hallway clear, and in the lobby were annoyed and angry guests. Word would get out, and the cameras would be here. Every room in town was booked, many with double occupancy.

They didn't yet know anything more than the man's name — Phil Gordon — and the the manager said he was in town as a contractor. The Manager of the hotel had gone to the room, he knew that the guest was booked for the Masters and that he was "working over at it." Ryals didn't take this for granted yet, though. The team went to the room and he went to the front desk to get the man's details from the clerk up front. Ryals showed his badge and soon had the man's details and immediately he texted them to one of the other investigators to check against personnel files. He would also need to speak to Allison Roy.

He went to the room where the crime scene team was already taking pictures and dusting for prints with blue gloves on. The hall outside and the room were crowded. One of the cleaning staff leaned against a wall with red eyes and a pale face. Ryals spoke to her. She found the body. She told him the room was clean already, that there was a 'Privacy' sign on the door, maybe for days. That she smelled the man. She never saw anyone else there nor heard anything. Ryals made a note to talk to the guests on either side of the room.

Ryals went inside.

The stench of bleach and decomposition assaulted him. The smell made his eyes water. Inside he saw the body in the bathtub. Bleach had been poured over the corpse, the forensics investigator explained to the detective. The body was wrapped in the shower curtain afterward, maybe to suppress the smell. Through it he could see the bruises around the dead man's neck.

Ryals wouldn't study the body, not yet. He looked through his belongings, finding clothes, a book with notes about grass and plants and water; sunblock and toiletries and a book. Nothing stood out as unusual.

He took pictures of the man's ID from his wallet laying on the bedside table.

The first question was entry. There was no sign of a broken lock or bolt. The window was intact. The man's room key was in his wallet. Another was on the bedside table in the small paper envelope given at check-in. The crime scene team dusted this for fingerprints.

Had the man let someone into the room? Did he know him or expect him? Or had he simply opened the door when someone knocked? It didn't take much of a ruse to get someone to open a hotel door. Especially if you weren't on the lookout for a killer.

The body was hidden for much of the week. Bleach was used to eliminate material evidence. The killing, though, looked thoughtful and careful and intelligent.

Ryals wasn't certain, but he guessed that in a moment he would find out that the deceased, Gordon, was one of the out of town groundskeepers they had been unable to reach by phone.

He left the room and paced the hallway before he called the Sheriff. Allison Roy responded to his text, confirming that the man inside was a contracted groundskeeper at the National. Contracted for three weeks.

"This just took on a whole new dimension," the Sheriff said gruff and breathy into the phone

"I think," he said. "I think we need the GBI in on this. Full scale."

Ryals did not argue. The GBI already assisted the case through their laboratory. Ryals welcomed the help.

"I agree," Ryals said. He did not believe anymore that this was a local crime.

SEVENTEEN

The crime scene team was done by one p.m. — they took their time, carefully and methodically, almost insulted at the Sheriff's repeated pleading that they "make sure, make completely sure." Lauren, the coroner, took the body away about the same time. Ryals hadn't spoken to her. That was her way. Laser focused. In Ryals experience, her only small talk was during an autopsy.

Perhaps the coroner would turn something up but Ryals was still at the hotel. He had gone over video and they had something — not much — but something. A shape, a man entering the hotel lobby, dressed with a hood and hat and headphones dangling from his ears as if he'd been out running. Clever, Ryals thought. No one would ask someone coming in from a run, and he had an excuse not to reply. His face was down and he seemed to know where the cameras were. His was a vague shape, phantom-like. His clothes were black or dark and just loose enough to give nothing away. Ryals couldn't be sure, but he believed it was the same suspect captured on the National's security footage.

Ryals couldn't be sure it was the same person, but he thought it was likely. The suspect was tall; Ryals could estimate his height against the door frame. Taller than Ryals, by an inch or two.

One camera was aimed into the parking lot. It showed only that the suspect walked across from the alley between the properties.

He entered through the lobby. Then he exited out the side, visible only for a short moment before retreating to the shadows and the darkness behind the hotels.

Ryals had perused countless hours of security video recordings from liquor stores, convenience stores, apartment complexes and traffic cameras. Suspects always believed they were smart, and their luck really depending on the resolution of the video, but no one was smart like this. Even the most clever thugs made a mistake and turned to look out the window or at the camera. Or drove two blocks in front of a street cam or doorbell camera and gave it all up that way. This guy made no mistakes and knew exactly where to look and where not to look. He moved with a purpose. He didn't look like much, but that was the point. He had no features, nothing to identify him. Likely everything he wore was bought that day and burned somewhere after.

Who were these people? The shadow, the devil. The mystery, the prowess.

This wasn't like most cases. The cases where he caught stupid people doing stupid things. This was something he couldn't even define right now.

Jonni slipped out of his room; he didn't see Frank. He made for the stairwell and went for a jog.

The humidity made it like running through soup and he was sweating in minutes but that felt good. Like a purge. He ran along the road that went by shops and connected soon to the busy road out front. Everything was so big, wide and moved so smoothly here. He ran across the highway ramp and up a long hill. Traffic was heavy, much of it headed to the golf course.

No one recognized him, which was also a relief. Not that he expected anyone to. But there in the street were golf fans, a lot. Unlike on the course, they just drove past, heading somewhere else. They didn't gawk, they didn't stare, and they didn't snap photos. They didn't recognize him. They weren't wondering what was wrong with him or what he was thinking or how was he involved; they weren't whispering or casting looks at him like he was a stain, a blemish on the game.

He ran up a long hill, feeling dehydrated but ignoring it. Feeling the sun on his back and the freedom from the confined room and his father's disappointment next door and the reporters in the lobby. There were more this morning, and he hadn't known why. Probably because the tournament started tomorrow.

Jonni ran faster and farther.

Coroner Lauren Josey had already been instructed to make the Holiday Inn body priority "numero uno" and she was nearly done when Ryals dropped by. Based on medical records that were sent from his GP including X-rays of his spinal surgery four years ago, she was able to positively identify Philip J. Gordon.

As she walked around the body she tapped the bright overhead light with two fingers like she conducted a silent orchestra. She used a paint marker to circle bruises and scratches on the man's body, primarily around his neck and collar.

"Clavicle on right side is bruised, guessing an x-ray will show me a hairline crack there. I have finger and palm imprints around the neck and throat — I can smell latex, so presume latex gloves were worn. I also see remnants of black fabric." Ryals recalled the killer — supposed killer — wore black gloves in the video. Maybe he wore latex gloves under something else? That would be dramatic if so. "New theory. On this side of the neck I have line burns from a wire or thin rope. That could explain the fabric remnants. Other superficial items: bruised ribs, left side. Just guessing. Strong corruption by bleach on entire surface of the body. Estimate he's been dead five days."

"That's consistent with video evidence," Ryals said.

"Okay then. I'll perform a tox screen, let you know what I find, but early examination I'm saying he died from strangulation, by a strong individual, no skin under his nails, very little to indicate a struggle."

Ryals looked at the body pale green body, bloated under the lights of the stainless steel room.

"Well," he said. "let me know if there are any surprises."

"The surprise is that he's dead," said the coroner, still moving around the body. Ryals shrugged. He wasn't so sure he couldn't have seen it coming.

Next to the Augusta National. It was mid-afternoon now. The week was moving fast — too fast to solve a crime. Ryals flashed his badge at the guard gate and waited while the guard cleared him to enter. Then Ryals pulled forward and found parking far off beneath pine trees away from the clubhouse. It was a humid day but there was wind and tomorrow was predicted to bring perfect tournament weather now that the rain had passed.

The scope of the investigation was now wider. He was glad now that Jonni and Martin were provided with security. Ryals had to wonder what darkness Willy had gotten himself into, and whether he had brought it to the Lombard's doorstep. Before he didn't think, but it was possible they were in danger.

There was more activity at the clubhouse now and he had to ask two people moving through the operations center before he found Allison again. She was busy, talking into a radio and texting on a phone and for a moment hardly noticed him. Even then he wasn't as important to her, clearly, as he had been a couple of days before.

"I understand the GBI are joining this investigation," she said, and Ryals wondered how she knew that.

"They're coming in to help," Ryals answered. He looked around for anywhere private but there were interns, assistants, people in polo shirts in pastel colors everywhere moving and talking. It was an excited and happy energy.

"Come on to my office." They took stairs and he found himself looking over her desk at the first green.

"What's the latest?" She asked, standing in front of her desk.

"We have added the second victim to the scope of the investigation," he answered.

"Phil Gordon."

"Yes."

"I've pulled everything I have on Phil Gordon here," she said, handing over a folder. She checked her phone. "Lawrence will be here to meet you in a moment."

He read over the file. "South Carolina, highly regarded supervisor of two golf courses, moved last year to Pennsylvania to a ski lodge," she said, "but called in November to say he would still be coming down. The Grounds Supervisor noted it in his file — we keep good records on every employee and contractor, and all are vetted." She was distracted. Kept looking away and outside. He competed for her attention. Things were heating up outside, with more fans, more feverish excitement. He looked again at the file. It offered him nothing he didn't already know. He looked up.

"There was no inquiry when he didn't show up? No one noticed? He's been dead five days."

"I've asked Grounds Director and Personnel. I don't know how that's possible. We're very strict on the gate."

"Strict on who's supposed to come in," Ryals asked, "but maybe not who doesn't?"

"I find it hard to believe someone wasn't at work who was supposed to be. I know it's a big place but we know exactly how many people are here at any time. It's part of our system." Ryals believed it. He looked out the window and leaned to see a small crowd gathering and several caddies in white chatting and Pinkerton guards moving ropes.

"What's happening there?" He asked.

"It's Wednesday, so it's the Par 3 Contest," she explained. "Friendly pre-tournament competition since 1960. Family members join as caddies and the best score after 9 holes wins. Kids walk with the competitors. Some golfers play just for fun and don't post a score. It's all up here on the northeast corner of the course."

"I see," he said. He watched kids running with their fathers as they walked out. The crowd applauded and smiled.

"Lawrence is here." She gestured to her door. "I'm not trying to be too brief, but I'm needed in three places at once. Unless there's something more you need from me?"

"No, not at the moment."

"Good."

She paused and looked at him sideways. "Do you think Jonni will play tomorrow?"

"Isn't he today?" Ryals asked.

"No. He didn't show up." He hadn't heard that. He hadn't turned on the news, though. "He didn't arrive this morning and when we sent someone over he was being treated for dehydration. I thought you had maybe talked to him today. He's all anyone's talking about, though."

"No I hadn't heard that." Ryals almost said he would check in on the kid but that wasn't his job. He looked outside as he walked out. "Dehydration?"

"Apparently he ran too far in the heat."

"I hadn't heard," Then Ryals added, "It's good for ratings and PR if he plays, I assume."

"It's great. Nightmare if he doesn't. But, detective, The National doesn't really care about ratings. We don't turn the cameras on until halfway through the day. Ratings are important, don't get me wrong. But the National is different." she explained as they walked back down, "Tiger was good for ratings. Huge. But this year, everyone, I mean every channel is talking about Jonni Lombard. And he's good. Seriously good. A prodigy. But the murder has made him into a reluctant celebrity. My concern isn't the ratings, detective. If he doesn't play, it's something else I have to deal with."

"How does the director or the board feel about that?"

"It is what it is. Marching orders are business as usual. I do hope you solve this case, though, for all of our sake."

Ryals almost said "Me too," but caught himself. He wondered what the consequences would be here.

Lawrence told him he already tasked his team to pore through footage to figure out anything that could connect Gordon to the murderer. "Trouble is," he explained as they crossed to the security building, "hard to tell who is who, it will take some time to identify

Mr. Gordon and figure out his last hours here. And then I don't know what I'm looking for."

Ryals had been thinking about that.

"The groundskeepers wear those uniforms from the National, right? Like on the video?"

"That's right."

"Are they kept here or do they take them home?"

"They dress here. We do the laundry nightly. Even those uniforms are coveted."

Ryals thought about that. "If I was to try to impersonate one of the groundskeepers and get in here, what would I need to do?"

Lawrence paused and thought long and hard. They stood in sunlight; Lawrence wore his sunglasses, Ryals had left his in the car. "We check IDs and grounds crew have passes that are marked for the specific days they are invited to work." It was remarkable that anywhere else one wouldn't say 'invited to work'. It especially rang true after calling all the golf club supervisors who gushed at length about the beauty of the course. "We have run red team procedures against our own security. KRDL in fact. Spared no expense."

"They don't all necessarily know one another, though."

"You're asking how hard would it be for someone to blend in?"

"Yes."

Lawrence cocked his head to one side then the other. "I couldn't say. But I can ask. I want to say no one can get by that easily, but leading up to the Masters there's extra staff, and we grow every year. I suppose it's possible."

It was a theory; it spoke to opportunity and method. It implied a great deal.

Someone identified the groundskeeper.

Killed the groundskeeper.

Impersonated the groundskeeper.

Snuck on to the course.

Met Willy - who knew this person.

Killed Willy.

Escaped.

This seemed less like a criminal act, and more like something out of a spy book.

He walked back to the car. He felt the weight of not only the investigation but also the politics, the tradition and history of the National. Ryals wanted to hold the door open for the FBI and let them walk in and fix everything. Then he could call it a day, go home and put his feet up. The shadows around the case grew darker. He did not think he was adequate to the task.

He paused beside his car and looked around at the trees and listened to the thrashers and robins and the occasional murmur of the crowd from beyond the buildings. From here the crowds sounded like waves gently breaking and it was peaceful to hear. One found it hard to believe Washington Road, with its traffic, shopping centers, and strip malls was on the other side of the fences and trees.

Within blocks of the course he had often worked cases with the worst Augusta had to offer. Twenty years as a cop gave Ryals a fairly jaded if not truly sour view of the world. Augusta's core had its share of rot. Daily Ryals encountered the disease of criminal humanity and it was hard to see through it. At the moment, he stood in a sanctuary from all of that.

The sunlight was shattered into silver shards through the canopies of the massive Magnolias. White blooms appeared among their boughs like bright dabs of thick paint; with their pink and yellow centers the blossoms were like eyes. Their shell-like structure trapped deep shadows and dense cool air that danced with insects and was a refuge for birds. Cicadas whined from within them like the drone of small invisible machines. He squinted and took in the smell, rich, earthy and something like citrus. Everything seemed to be rich here, like this place was untouched by the world and undiminished. Unblemished. That wasn't exactly true, though. Nor could it be. Nothing could be as pure as the scene seemed to be. The patches of sunlight were scattered over the lane that ran between the rows of trees. They trees were like sentries. Massive and ancient and they seemed to say to Ryals that they belonged here, and he was just a guest.

EIGHTEEN

The Par 3 contest was replayed on the Golf Channel between news reports around the discovery of Phil Gordon's body. The media had all the main facts: Phil Gordon of South Carolina, groundskeeper, murdered at the Holiday Inn. The reports ran under the banner "Murder at the Masters," though one tried "Blood on the Azaleas," (though there was no blood at either scene).

Jonni sat beside his packed bag. He was fully recovered from the run. He didn't know how many miles he had gone, he just went until he was as far away as possible and with each step everything had felt so much more unfamiliar to him. He realized before he collapsed that he didn't like being this far from home. It always made him uneasy and homesick but he could pour himself into the love of the game and let that be his focus and then there was no difference between the groomed grass at home and that of Latin America or Florida.

He didn't have heat stroke. Just exhaustion. He had slept little the past days. Last night he slept.

In just a couple of days though he felt that the love of the game had left him completely. It was a passing fancy. A hobby; and now he was done with it. He could play again on his own away from cameras and everything else. Just for fun. He'd never have to face the scrutiny of a crowd again, nor the inevitable accusations about the black cloud he brought into the game. He would never have to relive questions about what happened to Willy and would he still be alive if Jonni hadn't made it into the tournament.

It was so much easier to walk away.

Dad was upset. Of course he didn't want Jonni to quit. Martin just seemed sad now. He didn't argue anymore. They hadn't spoken in hours, not since Jonni said they could catch the next flight out. Dad merely patted his son's shoulder and said "Okay, Jonni."

The sun set outside. The day ended hazy and orange. Jonni wanted to sleep but he couldn't. He clicked on the TV and kept the volume low and shut the curtains. The Golf Channel was still on; he stared at it as though he was an outsider to the game. He was an amateur who didn't belong in a major tournament, let alone the Masters. He wasn't ready.

Ryals returned to the station at the end of the day and spoke with the Sheriff. In the morning the GBI would take over. There was no mention of federal authorities. The victim was foreign, but the crime was local. That was their view. The Sheriff was clearly frustrated. Ryals said he wanted a backseat. The Sheriff didn't know if that was better or worse for him. Ryals figured the Sheriff didn't want to be the one to say one way or the other who should be in charge.

Of course, they were getting nowhere.

Phil Gordon's toxicology report was on Ryals' desk. He flipped through it. A beer's worth of alcohol. Nothing else surprising. No unusual drug cocktail.

Ryals put it into a folder that he had compiled for the incoming investigative teams. It was all piled on his desk, and in the morning he would come in early, hand it over and offer his full support. That at least was his plan. Now, he tapped it with his finger. He had a strong suspicion that some powers-that-be wanted him to be the one that failed.

There was a message from Mr. Gordon's family asking for details. Those could not be released while the investigation was open. More bad tips and prank calls flooded in. The Deputy running reception marked the ones he had screened as being worth Ryals looking at — they could be counted on one hand. There was another memo from the deputy; three calls from someone called "Kate," which were not marked as 'Urgent' but had the note "says she's federal, arrives tonight, wishes to speak." With a question mark. That was not the deputy's vocabulary; it was written as a quote. Ryals hesitated. It didn't make sense. Why would a federal investigator call him, and not come in and speak first with the Sheriff?

Still he tried the number, which went straight to voicemail. He left the note on his desk. Clicked the light off. Regardless of how he picked it up in the morning, the day was over.

He looked at the newspaper on his desk. Front page above the fold: 'Murder at the Masters.' He wondered what would win out tomorrow — the new body with a headline along the lines of 'The Plot Thickens,' or a full headline of the Masters tournament start, per tradition. He could guess. He bet it would be the first time in fifty years the main story on the first tournament day was about something other than the start of the tournament and the arrival of the crowds.

He wished he had picked up something from the shop while he was there. Something to put on his desk. Regardless how it turned out, he was the first to respond to what would be a case remembered in this town for many, many years.

If and when he went to the course again, he would stop at the shop. Besides, Angela wanted a souvenir.

He drove home past the hospital and stopped to get a burger. He threw away the wrapper so he wouldn't get a lecture from Angela, but noticed the ketchup stain on his shirt beside his tie and realized the lecture would come regardless and he felt bloated and lousy from his first meal of the day.

Maybe he would go on a diet after this. At least he would consider it. Maybe Angela's campaign was winning him over. Or he was more self conscious now about being in the public eye.

He turned onto his South Augusta street as dusk began to fall, his headlights sweeping over the shadows beneath the pecan trees and over the red brick of the former military housing turned forty years ago to neighborhoods. Angela wanted to move across town but he preferred it here, though crime was on the rise.

He didn't want to think about crime right now. He was ready for the day to be over.

NINETEEN

Jonni had fallen asleep with the television on. He had slept for hours. He woke at about midnight. The TV was a blurry yellow light. It was yellow because the TV replayed old warm-toned footage. Slowly Jonni leaned to his side and watched. On screen was The Augusta National forty years ago. Gary Player was there, Jonni of course knew who he was. He was South African as well. He was from Johannesburg. There he was on TV, in 1978, winning the masters in the last nine holes. He birdied seven out of ten final holes. That year was his third win but the most spectacular. He had the lowest score in history that day. The trees and flowers and grass and his green jacket hung on his shoulders were all faded in old footage but were just as fantastic as if it had all happened yesterday.

The Golf Channel continued Masters highlights from the past. Next up was Larry Mize, chipping in the final hole for a Green Jacket win in 1987. It was an incredible chip. Greg Norman appeared to be ready for the win, then Mize walked up to the ball and took a few impatient practice swings, his ball sitting wide of the green. He stepped back, looked up at the green and the yellow flag, then squared up and chipped. The ball bounced and then rolled without hesitation into the hole. In a purple striped shirt he took a run, thanked God above, and went to collect his ball — or to make sure it was there, and he wasn't dreaming it all. Then he calmed himself out of respect for Noman who had not yet holed out.

Then in 2005 there was Tiger Woods extraordinary chip. Winning by three strokes, Tiger slipped into the lead by only one stroke as his confidence dipped. On the 16th in his Nike hat and signature red shirt he stood at the fringe of the green and chipped his ball up the green so that it could take advantage of the lie and find the hole. For a second, it hung over the hole before it dropped as if the ball itself was enjoying the drama.

Tiger shook his fists in the air and high-fived his caddie Steve Williams who just nodded and walked on to the next hole with his champion.

Then the TV played a real throw back. There was no video because it was 1935, but black and white pictures of Gene Sarazan, they called him "The Squire," with his neat black hair and sharp, shaved face and tie under his sweater — it was cold that year — taking one of the "Best Golf Shots of all Time." Using a four-wood from over two hundred and thirty yards away, he made a double eagle on the 15th and climbed three slots to take the lead in the tournament.

Jonni sat all the way up now and watched. He took his water bottle from the table beside the bed and sipped it. He still had a headache, but it was less than before.

More highlights. Jack Nicklaus winning in 1986. He was 46.

1995. "Gentle Ben" Crenshaw crying his eyes out after his win, hugging his wife. His coach had recently died, the TV commentator explained.

2011. Rory McIlroy roaring ahead, sure to win, then losing it all after the 13th hole as his day fell apart.

Greg Norman collapsing in '96; Nick Faldo taking the lead over him. Greg still smiling as he walked off the course. He never won at the Masters — and now was uninvited due to LIV, as Jonni knew. Still, he smiled and waved his putter as he walked from the eighteenth.

Charl Schwartzel in 2011.

Phil in 2010. Vijay in 2000.

Tiger in '97.

And then — Jonni climbed forward and turned the volume up. There was Bubba Watson. Dressed in all white, his hair sticking out of the back of his white Ping visor. He circled the green in a playoff with Louis Oosthuizen. It was a nice and clear day but the sky appeared white in the video. They both made lousy tee shots. Bubba hit his ball right into the trees and pine straw. Watson then recovered with a fabulous shot that stopped only a few feet from the flag. They showed interviews with Bubba, from immediately after the win. His eyes hardly blinking, he looked very much like a kid behind his sun-red cheeks.

"What did you most overcome today?" The interviewer asked Watson.

"Thoughts that weren't on the golf course," he answered. The commentator wrapped up the segment with "History does not forget the men that win the Masters."

Jonni flipped the remote onto the bed and he paced the room. Everything seemed to have left him, instead filled with what played on TV — blurry green, yellow, pink and white, blue skies and gray skies, rain and shine and crowds in styles that changed year to year.

Jonni felt lighter. As if some burden had lifted from his shoulders and some grace had fallen there. He felt energy. He found his putter — he had planned to leave it here, beside the trashcan — and he walked around with it on the carpet in the small room. Then he found a ball under the bed and rolled it out. He tapped it, back and forth. Slowly at first. Then he moved around the room with it. Tapped it this way, then walked to meet it, and tapped it the other way. There was not much space, but he dug the ball out of corners and putted around the legs of the chair and bounced it off of the wall and then set a cup down and rolled it gently into the cup again, and again, and again.

On TV, Bubba was in another interview clip. "If I have a swing, I have a shot," he said. Jonni put his back to the TV and the interview and he kept moving the ball around the room. He tapped the ball to the hotel room door and it stopped there. Walking barefoot in his t-shirt and shorts, Jonni rolled the ball back just enough and opened the door wide and propped it. He grabbed a cup from the bathroom. He putted the ball into the hallway.

Walking several rooms down he placed the cup on the carpet on its side, then returned to the ball and practiced a swing. He tapped it and sent the ball straight and true and just past the cup. He returned to his room for a second cup. He placed them ten meters apart and putted from one down to the other; then he reversed. Someone came into the hallway, talking loudly, maybe a little drunk, but Jonni didn't even look up. He kept tapping the ball one way, then the other. Sometimes catching the cups, sometimes rolling past them. He heard whispers in the hallway and was vaguely aware of several people gathered there at the end near the elevators. Jonni could still hear the TV from his room. He heard the replays and old footage.

When he finally looked up there was a crowd at the end of the hallway; maybe ten people. All had stopped to watch. They beamed at him. They took pictures. He stared blankly back down at them, then he picked up the cups and the ball, smiled slightly, and returned to his room. He didn't know how long he'd been out in the hallway. Judging by the clock it had been an hour.

He felt lighter even than he had before. He heard voices laughing in the hallway now. They passed slowly by his room. He felt something he hadn't felt in days, that seemed so far away it might never be recovered. He felt love for the game.

Soon, he opened his bag and pulled out his shirt and pants for tomorrow. He laid them out, checked for wrinkles. He found his socks. Sunglasses and hat. He laid them all out.

He never put the putter down, never let it out of his hand for a second.

TWENTY

Thursday
First Round of the Tournament

Ryals was up most of the night. He hadn't been able to shake thoughts of the case. The National was in a sense its own jurisdiction, a unique space cut out of the county. The county though was Ryals' territory. He was sworn to protect it. Someone had come into his backyard and had committed two murders.

Angela told him when he came home she was proud of him. She said she'd looked for him on TV.

When he was up and showered Ryals called the Sheriff on his cell phone. He waited as late as 7 a.m. but it was bright out already.

"Sheriff, I want to keep the lead with the GBI."

"I don't want horses pulling in two directions, Hall. You're a bit of a lone dog."

"I get it, Sheriff. I'll coordinate. I've got momentum and I want to keep it going. Just asking you to keep behind me on this."

"Keep me updated," he said finally.

Angela fixed him oatmeal with Craisins, which she patiently explained would go very good on a salad with chicken and pecans as well as on oatmeal.

"So what will happen today?"

He reached over and checked the Craisin bag. "Huh," he said. "It says they don't give you the ability to predict the future."

"Funny dad."

"I don't know, honey. Hopefully we get some clarity."

"I'd think it would be hard to keep a secret on a week like this."

Or easier, he thought. It was possibly the best week of the year to hide a crime. Certainly, if the perp came from outside of town. People came to the tournament from all corners of the world in massive droves. It was easy to hide in that.

"It's like the biggest thing to happen to Augusta ever," Angela said, reaching for his coffee, which he pulled back.

"I don't know about that," he said.

"It's a big deal. Everyone talks about it."

"What do they say?" he asked.

"Well, that it's a conspiracy. Or that they'll shut down the Masters. Or that the Masters is founded by the Mafia and they're going to start killing all the golfers."

"Well, all of that is dumb," Ryals replied.

"That's what I said," Angela spoke with some authority. "But what do I tell them? I mean, you're on the inside."

"I'm on the outside as much as you. All I know are the gruesome, bloody details of the bodies."

"Like what?" She leaned forward, half questioning him and half fascinated.

"Like how they were half eaten, cannibal style. Starting with the fingers and toes."

"Whatever, dad." She cleared the dishes. She was truly a young woman, responsible and mature. He watched her and admired her and was secretly grateful for her mother's genes. At the sink she asked, "So are you going to catch the guy?"

"What makes you think it's a guy?"

"It's an expression, dad."

"I'm trying," he said, rising finally.

"Try harder. I gotta have something to tell my friends."

Sam Ingot sat in the press room and responded to emails from the day before. Sam enjoyed quiet dinners during the tournaments he covered, and for a decade his restaurant of preference was an Austrian-French affair at the far end of downtown. It had been closed three years and he was yet to find a replacement. Last night's attempt was not bad, but was too loud and too crowded to enjoy. He saw several other journalists there, and getting away from this crowd was part of the point. He'd worked too many years traveling from crowd to crowd not to deserve a quiet, fine meal at the end of a day on a beautiful golf course.

So, between emails he searched for new restaurants to try; if he couldn't get a reservation he would remind himself to do so next year. He tried Surrey Center, now he scribbled on a pad two potential options downtown, one old German spot across town, two other options over the river. He was willing to explore.

He then began making notes for the stories today. Of course the events on the course would dictate everything, but Ingot preferred to have a narrative and to stick to it. Most of the men and women in this room would hear the roar of the crowd when someone made a double eagle— on the rare moments that it happened — and their hands would work furiously over their keyboards for forty-eight hours describing the same event over and over.

Ingot didn't jump with the others. His articles went deeper into the lives of players and the journey that brought them to the tournament.

He wrote about their passions on-and-off the course. He liked to pick certain players whose professional arcs moved different than the others that year and follow them closely. He walked outside along his favorite golfers all day long and took notes on their expressions, how much they sweated, if their patience waned and waxed from hole to hole, how often they glanced up at their girlfriend. For two years he wrote almost exclusively about Rory McIlroy, whom he believed — whom he still believed — was one of the greats of all time, but for whom the Masters was a crucible he must endure every year, and surely one day would conquer. Following him in 2015 he walked alongside Rory's girlfriend at the time (famed tennis pro Caroline Wozniaki) who sported pink hair so Rory could pick her out of the crowd. Ingot stayed behind her the whole time, hoping to divine Rory's thoughts when he looked up for her. He rarely looked away from his ball or paid her any notice after the first two holes, and acknowledged no one at all after Amen Corner.

That was part of Rory's journey, inward and outward at once. Sam didn't care at all about gossip, but he cared a great deal about the unity of mind and game. Bobby Jones who designed and founded the Augusta National famously said the game was "played mainly on a five-and-a-half inch course, the space between your ears." Understanding a champion's journey wasn't only about where they hit the ball, where it fell and landed, how many strokes were required. It was about the player's mental state and about his peace of mind.

It was why Tiger Woods could completely redefine golf in a few short years, demolishing competition and records at the Masters, and then fall short, fail miserably in years that followed. It wasn't a physical change, not a limitation. His swing improved, his technology too, he had better coaches and more restful trips to his tournaments with all first-class accommodations. His mental game, though, was compromised.

He could never, it seemed, reclaim that zen in which he played his first tournaments. If he did recover it one day, the story for Sam wasn't that Tiger was "playing just as good" again. It was the journey of his concentration, peace and passion. It would be a story about how he conquered himself.

That was why people were devoted to golf. It was about self-mastery and humility; about submission to the soul.

Ingot looked up. The press room was suddenly alive with energy. He checked his watch. The tournament didn't start for another hour. People were speaking, gossiping.

"What's going on?" he asked. The colleague kept moving as he walked swiftly.

"Jonni Lombard," someone said. The rumor all day yesterday was that he was leaving Augusta; conspiracy theories abounded of course. Lombard hadn't shown that day, and word was passed around that he would withdraw and return home.

"What about him?" Ingot asked another reporter.

"He's here. He's playing."

Ryals arrived early to the station to be ready to meet with the GBI team. They had their own local office, and collaborating with them was not unusual. Ryals poured coffee and sat at his desk.

He found a copy of the Augusta Chronicle and checked his theory about the front page. It read, "Two Bodies in Golden Bell Murder," with a split picture of the 12th hole and the Holiday Inn. There was no evidence yet, other than Gordon's background, that the two murders were connected, but it was a safe bet. Still, Ryals grew twitchy when the media made their own conclusions. Every other article on the front page, save for one, was about the tournament. But the main article was the murder, like he suspected. Down south, Savannah got plenty of tourism for being haunted. Maybe Augusta could try that.

"Going up there today?" One of the other investigators was in early as well. She draped a sweater over her chair and produced her travel coffee mug and placed it on the desk.

"Maybe," Ryals said. "Waiting on GBI."

"It will be one to write home about today. Not often a Masters golfer is a person of interest in a murder case," she said.

"Who, Jonni Lombard? He's not playing."

"Didn't you check the news this morning?" She asked. Ryals glanced at the paper in front of him. Even NPR has it. He's going to play."

Ryals hadn't heard that. He tried to think of what that changed. Not much, except that it would be tougher to interview Lombard again.

Nearly impossible, actually. He tried to remember what time they started playing this morning — teed off, whatever it was. He thought ten. For some reason he was glad Jonni would play.

Also, if Jonni wasn't leaving today, he had some time. He wanted to see what new air the GBI brought into the room.

Ryals checked his watch. He expected the team any minute. He expected the Sheriff before them though. He was late.

"Seen the Sheriff?" Ryals asked the investigator. She titled her head.

"He's in the conference room." The conference room? So Ryals was late. Ryals snagged his jacket and walked over there. He felt territorial. He had aimed to be in first.

But the Sheriff wasn't with the GBI team. The large man sat across from a young woman with dark hair pulled back in a ponytail, no makeup, a khaki jacket over a green shirt and sunglasses that hung out of her pocket. As she stood to greet Ryals he noticed a pocketknife clipped in her front pocket and stringy colored bracelets on her hand. She struck Ryals as a hippy or college protester of some sort who had made a stopover at the Gap. She was fit, tan and freckled.

He took her hand as he glanced at the Sheriff.

"Morning, detective." She smiled, her freckles contrasted against her white teeth reminding him of the summers of his youth somehow. She reached her hand out, her hands were small but her grip was strong. "Kate Chase."

"Kate — can I call you that?" The Sheriff asked, clearly charmed. Ryals sat.

"Sure," Kate said. Ryals studied her. She was an oddity. Somehow too rough around the edges, too tan, her hair too — something. Ryals tried to read her.

The Sheriff handed Ryals a paper. The letterhead read HOME-LAND SECURITY. It announced that Ms. Chase was to be afforded every accommodation in assisting the investigation. It was signed Deputy Director, DHS.

"Mrs. Chase from Homeland Security is here to help us out."

"Homeland Security? Is this suddenly a terrorism investigation?" Ryals asked, looking at Kate again. She wasn't how he imagined a DHS representative would look, not in aprofessional capacity, anyway.

"Not at all," she explained. "My agency has an ongoing interest in any crimes with international connections, or amongst foreign nationals visiting the US."

Ryals furrowed his brow and glanced at the Sheriff. He was careful not to be antagonistic. "Okay," he said. "Are you here with any special resources?"

"Just me," she said, smiling authentically and leaning away just enough not to appear eager, keeping her hands folded in front of her to seem eager to please. Ryals could understand how the Sheriff was charmed. She was both cheery kid and mentor at once. "But I'm happy to help in any way we can."

"Do you know something about this crime that we don't know yet?" Ryals asked.

"We don't, but with next year's Olympics, and other professional sports investigations, we would like to be aware of any kind of crime in professional sports. After all, good, clean sport competition is an international diplomacy of its own." Sounded like a sales pitch to Ryals, and he wasn't sure this girl even watched the Superbowl.

"Okay," Ryals said, but the Sheriff leaned forward and was all smiles.

"We'll be happy to offer you whatever hospitality we can. In the meantime we have — I've explained this to her — GBI on their way in to aid with forensics and other technical aspects of the investigation. Ms. Chase, feel free to shadow Detective Hall and let him know where you can be of help."

Ryals started but caught himself. He was not a chauffeur.

He glanced at the Sheriff to communicate with his jaw and eyes. The Sheriff didn't look back at him.

Kate, surely reading his face, slid her hand a bit over the table and smiled at him. Her smile was piercing and genuine and somehow highlighted her freckles. She reminded Ryals of a Little Rascal.

"Detective, I'm just here to observe and help where I can. So just tell me where to stand as you do what you do."

Ryals wasn't even sure what that was. She would find out soon that he was up against a wall.

He hoped he could push her off on the GBI.

Who had just arrived.

Ryals knew the thin, short, balding man that led the GBI team — his name was Parriot and he had two others in tow. Parriot was an engineer type; thin, balding, slight and bespectacled, he was surprisingly adept in the field, but at his best in a research capacity. Ryals greeted him and they all sat down in the conference room.

"Is this the totality?" Parriot asked, his words metered carefully as the local investigative team brought in their folders of evidence, and laptop with videos. "A footprint, camera captures, secondhand testimony..." He wasn't challenging Ryals; rather Parriot catalogued it all in his head. Through his wire-thin glasses, Parriot was very particular with everything, including each pronounced syllable, and all the way to his ironed polo beneath his jacket. He was thin and fit. The man was a runner, or had one of those metabolisms, and got up early to prepare his clothes. Ryals smoothed his own shirt instinctively as he sat down. Kate took a seat at the far end of the table opposite the Sheriff.

Realizing no one else was going to take charge, Ryals stood. "I know the Sheriff brought you up to speed yesterday," Ryals said to Parriot as he pushed his own folder across.

"Everything you need to know from me is summarized in there. Coroner's reports, interview notes. You know some of the forensics from the first victim."

"Yes," Parriot said, "We'll go over to the second murder site as well today."

"For my part," Ryals said, "I hope something can come out in interviews." Ryals caught Kate glancing at him, almost studying him.

"With the tournament starting, that will be difficult and obtrusive," the Sheriff said.

"I'm speaking with security at the National and we have more personnel, security and groundskeepers that we will interview."

"This one is a pickle on a bun," Parriot said, looking over the folder contents. "I expect we'll get somewhere on forensics and with credit card transactions. You have phone records, as well?"

"Requested, I expect we'll have them from the phone company today."

"We'll start to lay out a grid showing activity of the three persons, Mr. Gordon, Mr. Sharp and Mr. Lombard. My team will design a spreadsheet with all data points. With it we can cross reference and input anything new. Mr. Sharpe's phone, Mr. Lombard's, Mr.—"

"We haven't asked for Mr. Lombard's records," Ryals interrupted. "We don't have cause. He wasn't in the country."

Parriot chewed on this. "Okay. Let's add what we know about his whereabouts to the list. You stick to the human side, Ryals, but I think it wouldn't hurt to request a wider net of alibis, security gate logs, and whatever else we can think of."

Ryals nodded. Unlike with Kate, he didn't want to argue with Parriot. Parriot was like an auditor and he was sharp and unencumbered by his own ego. What Parriot could add would be helpful. Something might shake out as they sifted further through the interviews.

"That works for me," Ryals said.

"As far as we're concerned, this is still a Richmond County Sheriff's Department investigation," Parriot said, looking up through his glasses. "We're here to help." He glanced at Kate. Then extended his hand. "Parriot, and you are—?"

"Kate Chase," She answered and took his hand firmly.

"She'll be helping out as a liaison," The Sheriff said, rising, proud to host these great minds. "But we need the full skills of the GBI on this one," He tightened his tie as he did. He sat, looked everyone over.

"Hall?" Sheriff asked, looking at his investigator. "Anything to add?"

"Let's move."

The Sheriff left the room. Parriot began to collect folders from the table and handed them off to his team outside. He looked at Ryals and Chase. When this tournament wraps up on Sunday night, it's likely that the murderer, if he still is here, will be gone. Along with much of the evidence. Let's keep that in mind."

Ryals hadn't considered that — but up until a day ago, he thought this murder was purely local. Now Homeland Security was here.

Ryals shook hands with Parriot and walked out wondering how he was going to explain bringing Kate along to talk to anyone. He didn't know how to introduce her. Reading his thoughts she offered,

"Call me a liaison, if anyone asks," she said. "No need to tell them the feds are here." That was true. National folks would get ruffled if they heard the words Homeland Security. It could set off a panic.

He sat at his desk to organize a plan for the day. After a moment the girl appeared beside him. The detective at the next desk over checked Kate out from over her glasses. Ryals couldn't imagine what conclusions people would make about her.

"How can I be helpful?" She asked.

Ryals didn't have an answer.

"Lombard will play today. I had hoped to interview him and his father once more. That may not be possible."

"How about we observe him?" She asked.

"Observe him do what?"

"Play. Supposing that this whole thing was a message to him, or someone around him, perhaps we can see who else might be watching him."

"Everyone is going to be watching him," Ryals said, finally looking at her. "Around the world, and more than half that course."

"Of course. I guess I mean, let's step back and get a look at his world as all of this unfolds." Sounded to Ryals like she wanted a free ticket to the Masters.

"I have some other priorities. We can make some time to watch him." He would think of those priorities as they got moving.

The hum outside the clubhouse windows was markedly higher today. Inside was like a beehive.

Jonni's leg bounced nervously but otherwise he was still and quiet. Dad, Frank, two additional Augusta National Pinkerton security — which brought his entourage to five, with Buster standing ready, calm and suppressing a bit of a smile beside him, ready in his all white coveralls and green hat with the yellow logo.

Outside the hallway was clear as other golfers, teeing before him, made their way. The golfers were only allowed in a short time before their tee-off. Jonni was allowed in earlier and saw some pass. Most staff and headset-wearing coordinators did their best to ignore Jonni, but he could feel their looks.

Ahead of him was Sam Bennet. Buster whispered to Jonni,

"Got in here very young, like you. College boy from Texas. He was Low Amateur in 2023. Played through right after his father died.

Shot thirty-two on the front nine. Tied for lowest amateur ever. Then dropped to seventy six. Finished sixteenth and cried as he walked off. No dry eyes around 18th that afternoon I tell you. Great player."

Jonni's tee off came in thirty minutes. He was paired with Justin Rose. They played behind Jaoquin Niemenn and Phil Mickelson — the first time Jonni had ever been on a field with the latter. Mickelson breezed through the clubhouse like he owned the place, a massive smile on his face as he passed. Jonni was not often starstruck but he hoped he wouldn't be close enough to see Phil play, as he would almost certainly be distracted. He felt out of place among these legendary competitors.

Justin Rose was English, about forty years old, and Jonni wondered if they were paired together due to the fact that Justin was actually born in South Africa — Johannesburg, in fact. As if that would bring Jonni some comfort. Justin was across the clubhouse hall. He was friendly. He had come over to greet and encourage Jonni. He had a nice smile and he had won PGA titles and played on the tour frequently. He was tall, too — he stood a good six inches over Jonni; tall and skinny and his nose, cheeks and ears were red from sunburn.

"Players are friendly, but no one minds when you don't go outside yourself," Buster said to him, his voice low, almost in a whisper. "Isn't taken as any kind of offense if you're shut down, keep to yourself. They're all here to focus. This is a head game. Everyone's a pro." Jonni nodded.

Buster smiled. "I once saw the Walrus, Craig Stadler, slap a club member mid swing. Guy threw his club right off the grass and into some bushes. Stadler just walked away. That was him, though. Like a drunk uncle sometimes, but loved every minute of the game." Jonni knew of the Walrus. Big gray mustache, bigger head, with a wicked legendary swing. He was long retired. Jonni had seen videos. He appreciated

Buster's stories. Buster was good at telling them too. Always squinting with his left eye as if to remember each moment clearly. Jonni smiled in cautious appreciation and looked up at Buster. Buster grinned back.

"Want a whiskey before we tee off?" Buster broke a grin. Jonni smirked and shook his head.

A young aide came into the room wearing a headset and yellow polo shirt. She was young, blonde, nervous, excited.

"They're ready for you, Mr. Lombard, if you'd like to begin walking out now."

Jonni rose and drew the deepest breath he had ever drawn.

He stood, ready to walk out and compete in the greatest and most challenging golf tournament in the world. Outside the light was bright. The doors were open to the paradise and the gauntlet.

He nodded to himself, an inward acknowledgement of his skill, a call to self confidence as they walked out. Behind him followed his security entourage, Buster and his father who would watch from the ropes. Dad put a hand on Jonni's shoulder. Jonni could feel it shaking with excitement. Jonni stepped away and between the ropes.

The applause began before he even set a foot on the grass.

TWENTY-ONE

Ryals and Kate could not get through the main gate. They were directed to an off-site parking annex. The lines of traffic were long, the sidewalks crowded with badge-wearing patrons moving earnestly.

"No room in the inn," Kate quipped as they backed away from the gate. She didn't say much else on the drive, but looked outside and was fixated on the view as they neared the course coming up the hill on Washington Road, "This is a rather big deal."

"It is."

It turned out he was indeed her chauffeur, and he didn't even know how to explain her presence in interviews and meetings. "Say I'm on loan from the federal government to help with the investigation," she said, chipper and confident. As if rules were meaningless, he thought. Parriot he knew, and wished he had joined them. Instead Parriot was focused on digital forensics from the office.

They took a shuttle and were dropped off a moment later, not at the clubhouse but at a parking lot not far away. They were escorted to a separate gate where they waited until a security guard emerged and presented them with two VIP badges. They waited a while after that as no one was sure who should escort them nor to where. Security smiled as patrons flooded in and down the long paved walkway past the Par 3 course and through the white gates and metal detectors. Ryals hoped Lawrence had at least pulled some video moments of interest, or had more details to help with the timeline.

He knew he was now in competition for Lawrence and Allison's attention. He wished he'd had more traction before the start of the tournament. There had simply been no time. They now had to compete with a swarm of people coming and going, including the beehive that was the new press building — north of the lot where they arrived and not far from security — with reporters, photographers, assistants, interns and the other Chosen People with the unique privilege to take and share pictures.

"So how many people run around with cameras and equipment here?" Kate asked.

"I don't know. What you see I guess. It's less than somewhere else." Video, though, he found himself explaining "comes only from fixed camera options. The feeds are part of a CBS licensing deal." Ryals was surprised to hear himself say this; he had learned it only a few days before. He cut himself off. He really didn't want to end up playing tour guide here.

Despite the crowd they could still hear the birds. They could feel the gentle and cool morning air. They could see the entrance to the course ahead of them; it was crowded with a kaleidoscope of bright colors as people arrived with barely supressed excitement.

Why not, Ryals thought. It was a perfect day in Augusta, Georgia.

"The weather is great," Kate said, perhaps doing her best to be friendly, perhaps just in awe — she looked around with wide eyes and stared at the greenery. "I expected more humidity."

"It was yesterday," Ryals said as they neared the building. "Haven't spent much time in the South, I guess?"

"No. Virginia is the closest. I'm from Iowa. Dry, cold; nothing like this. This is just lush."

An escort came out and directed them toward the headquarters building. Ryals didn't know why he'd had to wait. His irritation grew. They came to the building and were led to a door, but it wasn't opened.

Ryals buzzed the bell and waited. Was Homeland Security in Virginia? He didn't know. He figured they had offices everywhere. He wasn't even sure he knew what all they did. Plenty at airports, anyway.

Someone opened the door, Ryals didn't recognize him; but he understood immediately and walked Ryals through the lower building to the front bullpen area, where Lawrence was coordinating while watching camera feeds and working in a bullpen that Ryals had only passed by before.

Inside was a zoo of activity. Lawrence's team ran a tight ship; even they were in high spirits. It was as if no murder had happened. How many more staff did Lawrence have this week that were hired exclusively for this week? How did he vet them? He made a mental note to ask.

Lawrence shook Ryals hand. Ryals introduced his new sidekick. "Kate—"

"Chase," she said.

"Welcome," Lawrence said, turning to give them full attention, his eyes studying Kate especially. He shot a glance at Ryals.

"She's here to assist," he said. "a liaison—"

"On loan from the federal government to give any assistance I can," she said quickly. Lawrence nodded but gestured them out of earshot toward the back corner of the room. They certainly drew a few glances. Ryals figured his face was known by now. Kate looked out of place but didn't seem to care.

"Thank you for your discretion. I don't want to distract my team." He looked at Ryals. "What can I do for you?"

"Anything more on tapes?"

"Very little. But one thing. Come on." He led them back to the darkened video room where he saw the same technician from earlier plus three others.

"Pull up what we were looking at," Lawrence directed. The tech scrambled through some files and pulled up another feed from the night of. "It's not much. Just another angle as the suspect leaves. See here."

He pointed and directed the tech to play a video in the top left. Same as Ryals had seen before and had in his file. The killer leaving the shadowy foliage where he had entered, returning to his cart and disappearing from frame.

"That's it?"

"No. Now play the new one," Lawrence directed. A video played on the next screen enlarged. The image was still for a moment, showing an illuminated storage garage, with several club cars visible and bales of hay and fertilizer. "Grounds shed two," he explained. As they watched, another cart pulled in. The same man — head still turned and concealed from the camera beneath his hat — walked from the bay, and out of frame.

"Before you ask, no, there are no other angles here. That's all we got. I'll send you a link to the file. We've been looking all over. The suspect moves like a ghost."

"A ninja," the technician added, shaking his head.

"Can you play it again?" Kate asked. Ryals stiffened. The technician complied. Kate leaned in to watch closely. Ryals watched her more than the video. Typical bureaucracy, he thought. Hire some college kids with the right degree and no sense. Meddle with everything and serve no purpose —

"He texted someone," she said, pointing. Ryals furrowed his brow.

"When?" He caught himself saying, regretting it immediately. Lawrence leaned down.

"Play it again, slow," she said. "If you would."

It played back. She pointed as the man on the screen put his hand into his jacket pocket, and for a split second, glanced down.

"Sent, and I believe received."

"'Job is done'?" Lawrence thought aloud.

"Maybe," she said, watching closely. She believed herself sharper than anyone else, Ryals could tell. She didn't act as if she owed anyone an explanation.

"And?" Ryals said, challenging her. "Not much good it does us."

Kate rose, thinking to herself. She produced a small black notebook with a worn cover. She jotted something down. Ryals watched. He saw that she wrote the time and date from the video timestamp.

"Can you," she said, looking around, "Take me to that spot? Where he sent this text message?"

"Why?" Ryals asked, but everyone seemed to ignore him.

"I can," Lawrence said. "It's not far. But I'll have to be back up here quickly."

"That's fine, just want to see where it was," she said. Ryals wanted to reel her in but he didn't want to confront her in front of the Augusta National Head of Security.

Ryals played along for now but had a few words to say to Kate after this.

They walked to the shed from the video and Ryals looked up to find the camera. Kate didn't.

She stood in place, about where the killer had been on the camera, and played with her watch, which he noticed for the first time was one of those expedition style military watches. Plain looking but full of features.

"Got it," she said as her watch beeped. Ryals had no idea what was happening.

"I'd prefer not to leave you here without an escort," Lawrence said, speaking into his radio and listening to his earpiece. "I can have one come over—"

"No, that was all I needed," Kate said. "Thank you so much. We can go back."

They walked back toward the clubhouse. Kate removed her jacket and Ryals wanted to give her a disapproving look but she never met his eyes. They could see the crowds on the hillsides at a distance as they exited the shade of the trees and walked in the sun. Kate looked overhead, over the hills, everywhere. She was like a kid, fascinated.

Back at the security building, Lawrence turned to face them. "What else can I do for you today?"

Before Ryals could speak, Kate answered. "I know it may be trouble, but I'd like to speak to anyone working security that evening. Not all of them. But a few folks. It doesn't matter who."

"I'll have to get you a list. The night crew hasn't arrived. You can speak to them this evening when they arrive for shift. Starting about six p.m., most of them."

"That's easiest," Ryals asserted. He didn't know why but he felt increasingly deferential. Less and less like this was his jurisdiction as Deputy of the County Sheriff, and more like he was on foreign soil, inclined to ask and hope for permission for every small favor. He didn't want to offend or to lose his welcome.

Well, he thought, it's just good politics. It wasn't like the bureaucracy of City Hall. There was real power here.

Lawrence paused by the security office. "So where are we? Is having a government agency here a good thing for this investigation?" His affect was flat, unreadable, but always edging on cheery.

"We've got GBI on it as well. We're working lots of angles," Ryals said. "We're open to any support."

The security director studied them both for a moment. "What else can I do for you?" Lawrence asked, listening to something in his earpiece.

"Where is Mr. Lombard now?" Kate asked. Ryals turned to her, his neck getting hot under the collar of his jacket. He would have a word with her about interjecting her priorities.

Lawrence asked into his radio and then nodded and thanked whoever responded. "He's just teed off." He paused, looking at Kate. "I would much prefer you didn't try to speak to him until after the tournament. It's not me, it's..."

"Of course, I get it," she said. "I'd like to observe his play," she said. This time Ryals couldn't help but instinctively look at Lawrence as if for an ally. Lawrence himself seemed to calculate the risk of letting them loose on the course. This was, Ryals could read in his face, uncharted territory.

Lawrence shrugged. "Please don't make your official presence known," he said. He glanced at their VIP badges. "In fact, wait a moment." He went into the office and soon returned with two Thursday day badges, the regular sort with holographic foil and a picture of the course worn by all attendees. "Might draw fewer eyes," he explained. They swapped out their VIP plastic. He handed them a paper map as well, and pointed out the first and second holes where they would likely find Jonni.

"Keep the others in case you need to come back and speak to me."

"Pretty," Kate noted, checking the badge out.

Lawrence checked them over, and had a look like he was leaving his child with a babysitter for the first time. "We'll be quick," Ryals said.

"I'll be here if you need anything," Lawrence said, marching back into his compound.

Ryals and Kate were left looking down the sloping hill toward where both the 3rd and 7th tees came together.

He turned to her. "Listen. This place, this organization, has an incredible amount of power in Augusta. I'm working hard to keep everyone happy in the middle of a murder investigation, that includes my boss, my boss's boss, his boss, and probably somewhere down the line your boss. Don't underestimate it and please tread carefully."

"Me? I think you've underestimated it, Mr. Hall."

"Explain that," he said. Thinking, what?

"The gift shop. You know they do one million dollars an hour in business?"

"No, I didn't. An hour?"

"The membership of this club represents a higher concentration of power and wealth than you can find at the top of most countries. Influence not just in the world of professional sports but in global capitalism cannot be underestimated. They say business is done on the golf course? The business done here has global effect. You're cautious about Lawrence's boss. I think there are eyes on us from levels higher than we even know exist."

"When did you become an expert?"

"I read on planes," she said.

"Miss Chase, I don't know what you think your role is here, but it isn't to be an investigator. You said so yourself. So wanting a free badge to go wandering around the golf tournament isn't exactly the low profile I'm trying to keep. It also seems pointless. What are we looking for, exactly?"

She nodded, leaning in, listening intently. Affable and agreeable. He wanted to say more but found himself unable to go on. As if something in her expression disarmed him. It felt like a trick.

"I'm sorry if I stepped over the line a bit in your view, I didn't mean to," she said tactfully. "I'm a few steps behind on this and didn't want to waste time. We don't have to walk down there, but for me it's a bit abstract still, and I'd like to see the kid, see his father, who I believe is there as well. Just to get a sense of them and the atmosphere. I really mean to support you in this investigation and I want to be as caught up as I can so that I can do so."

He looked up at the patches of sunlight coming through the dogwood and pine trees, the animated birds passing through, the blooming flowers. He found himself unable to argue his objections for now. It was this place. It was hard to stay angry here.

"Fine," he said. "We'll walk down there. But anything else — anyone else — I take the lead. I've got a system here, I've been building rapport, and I don't want you coming in and ruining all of that." Even as he said it he wasn't sure how true any of that was. Still, though.

So with Kate again chipper — she had never not been — they walked with the map past the third hole to the top of the fourth, where, once they got around the massive pack of spectators they could see Jonni and another golfer, with two caddies in white jumpsuits, just as the other golfer took a swing with a crack as the club connected with the ball and it shot through the air, its path followed by hundreds if not thousands of eyes, some with hands shielding them from the sun. It landed and the crowd returned polite applause. Ryals and Kate worked their way to the edge of the rope where they could look back and see better. Ryals realized he might ruin Jonni's day if the young golfer spotted him. Ryals saw his father and their security guard. Jonni never looked anywhere, though, beyond the long hill of the second hole, the green grass, and his ball. He kept his head slightly dipped the whole time; his shyness apparently carried to the golf course.

The first golfer nodded to the crowd and stepped back into the shade and after looking for a moment at the tee, Jonni stepped up and there was a palpable hush and buzz of excitement that settled over the crowd. Beside Ryals, Kate watched intently as if studying a map. Ryals found himself unable to take his eyes off Jonni as he stepped up, set his ball on the tee, and then studied the path between the pine trees.

"This is called Flowering Crab Apple," Kate whispered. "Par Three." Ryals looked beyond her. It was a shorter hole. The tee was on an elevated platform, and it descended and ran down to two sand traps on the near face of a slight rise. The yellow flag waved behind the left trap. Rails had interviewed the golfer, heard about his talent, but had never actually seen him in action. Jonni leaned, held his club, inched his feet into the right place; he breathed and his eyes followed the imagined course of the ball and then returned to it. He practiced a swing. Ryals felt a spark of excitement just before the kid pulled back, his left arm straight and his right bending, his elbow rising, his eyes never moving from the ball, and then with a rapid and graceful swoosh of his own he connected with the ball and it shot out. The crowd watched it, and though Ryals lost the ball in the air he heard the murmur of disappointment that turned to polite applause as the ball landed outside the ropes on the left, halfway down.

Kate watched and Ryals looked at Jonni again and saw his dissatis-faction, or maybe it was resignation, as he handed his club back to his caddie. Jonni walked with the other golfer and two caddies toward their balls. Most of the crowd moved with them.

"Okay," she said, stepping away. "I'm ready if you are." Ryals found himself awakened from a trance. He looked at her.

"That's all?"

"That's all I wanted," she said, turning away even as Jonni walked past them. She put on sunglasses for the first time and lowered her face as she moved through the crowd. Instinctively Ryals did the same.

Who was Kate? He wondered. He felt more out of his league than ever. Or maybe she was just pretending to know what the hell she was doing.

"I'll return to interview staff this evening," Ryals said. He meant to emphasize that he would be alone. They left by the entrance and took a shuttle to the annex lot.

"So what now?" she asked.

"Now, we let the GBI do what it is they do."

"Okay, you can take me back to the station then?" Suddenly she was ready to check out. Was she really just here to report on him?

He studied her. "Why did you write down the time of the text message?" He asked.

"If there was a message sent from that spot at that time, maybe I can get the cell tower records — I know you've already requested them — and look for a text sent, or, more likely if he's using a secure messaging app of some kind, a data burst. It's a long shot, but hey, data points, right?"

"What good would that be?" Ryals asked, hesitating before he started the car, despite the heat from the sun shining through the glass. "Plenty of people were probably texting on that tour the same night."

"Yes, but suppose he had a brand new burner phone, or a South African sim card. Either would have a unique signature, and could be traceable. Like I said — a long shot."

Ryals thought it sounded like more than a long shot. He had seen plenty of cell phone records after delivery upon subpoenas. He never saw anything like that on them. A list of numbers and times and texts. That was all he had ever seen.

Perhaps Homeland Security had different options. Patriot Act and all that. He decided not to ask. But he was beginning to get used to being in over his head, and in the dark on his own investigation, and that troubled him.

"So there is one more thing," Kate said as they pulled out. "Whoever you can speak to — I'm not sure if Lawrence is the right guy — Jonni played Tuesday as well, right? Well, it's too soon just yet I'd think but any footage they can give of him from those CBS cameras you told me about, not the TV footage that just cuts away, but the raw stuff of him playing? From today and Tuesday. And maybe plan for tomorrow as well. Could you request that?"

Ryals wasn't sure. "I can ask," he said, not sure he wanted to. He would ask Allison. He doubted he needed to go to a judge for that. Hopefully she would simply hand it over, and hopefully Ryals would figure out why the hell anyone wanted it.

"Chase," he said. "That's a lot of resources for a drunk caddie and a gambling debt."

"Is that what you think this is?" She asked him, incredulous.

"Just because it happened here doesn't meant there's more to it than that."

"It doesn't mean there isn't. I think it's much more than that."

"Oh really."

"Really."

"Based on what?"

"I'm working on that. Detective Hall, I'm not sure you're seeing this the way I am."

"I'm sure I'm not."

"You have politics to deal with. Look past them. Willy wasn't a drunk, he didn't lose a bet to the most clever and murderous bookie that Georgia has to offer. Willy got involved with something much darker, and much more dangerous. That's what I think. And whoever they are, I don't think they're done."

"Meaning what?"

"Meaning I think Jonni and Martin Lombard are in danger, and the killer has shown us that even the course isn't safe."

Ryals continued to ponder. He wasn't a conspiracy theorist. He went on evidence. Of that, there was little.

The GBI team was dutifully at work; they had a small data factory set up on the conference table. Ryals checked in but otherwise didn't bother them. Despite whatever new madness Kate was trying to throw into the investigation, he was nearly certain it would be solved by the GBI team looking for needles in the haystack.

Parriot lacked only a pocket protector; he and his pair of nerd associates would nerd their way through the hay.

In the meantime, there was more on Ryals' mind. Something Kate said — correct that, something he had said to her — he hadn't considered yet. Despite wanting to disregard her wild theories, he was compelled to think further than he had been.

He pulled up his computer and put his reading glasses on. He found the Masters website. He looked for a list of golfers — competitors. He went down one by one, with a pencil taking names:

Branden Grace
Louis Oosthuizen
Charl Schwartzel
Ernie Els
Trevor Immelman
Jonni Lombard

The competitors this year from South Africa. Impressive list, he thought. He had never thought about golf being popular there, because he had never really thought much about golf or South Africa at all. Golf he associated with — where? Scotland? And Augusta, of course.

He wondered if it was possible that the message — if indeed it was a message — of Willy Sharpe's death was meant for another golfer. It could make sense; more sense the more he thought about it. Take a caddie from a junior golfer, make a point to someone else. See what we can do to them, we'll do worse to you. Maybe that was it. He hadn't looked in that direction at all. If so, a South African made the most sense to him.

He googled them one after another. Bios, tournament wins, charitable foundations, families, endorsement deals. How much was an endorsement deal for a golfer, he wondered? He searched. Numbers were hard to come by, though he saw that one of the top paid golfers only made a few million from tournament winnings last year — "only," as Ryals was comparing them in his mind to football and basketball salaries. Certainly, top golfers didn't seem to make anywhere close to those sorts of numbers.

Tiger Woods was — at least for a time — by far the highest paid. Between Nike and championships and commercials and more and more — he made a killing. Not as much now, but for a time he had. He was an anomaly, which Ryals knew because he knew about Tiger like everyone else did. The golfer who became a celebrity outside of his sport. It happened in other sports, but not often in golf.

Ryals googled for twenty minutes and found little. There were few scandals in this sport. He found nothing about DUIs, drugs or sex scandals. No gambling debts or assault charges. John Daly had a checkered past. He was noted for his drinking and arrested at twenty-six for domestic abuse. He was also, apparently, the reason The Augusta National moved its driving range. He hit so far the old driving range couldn't contain him.

Surely there were more scandals than those, but it didn't change the fact that golf was unique — a sport for gentlemen, and increasingly, for ladies.

He leaned back and thought about it. Ingot said it was a mental game. Tiger's fall from the top was a great example of the cost, then, of a distracted mind. Basketball players often performed on the court with ongoing criminal investigations into their misconduct. Many had been charged with crimes. Ryals ventured that wouldn't work with a golf.

Something wicked had found its way into the game, here in its most hallowed corner.

Ryals went back to his list. Supposing there was a connection, how would he figure it out? Indeed Jonni might have no idea at whom the message was aimed. Jonni might be collateral damage.

Short of interviewing each, or pulling financials for all, for which a warrant would be very difficult, he didn't know how else to test this theory.

Ryals guessed he'd need more to go on to get approved to interview more famous golfers during Masters week. Perhaps he could try Kate's tactic. Follow them, see which one looked nervous. Maybe she had tools, ways to get around the limited resources available to Ryals and his department.

Jonni sweated more from nerves than the heat as he walked across the 11th hole "White Dogwood," a par four, to find his ball near the green just short of the pond. It was a long hole, but graduated downhill so the walk was easy. He felt a burden weighing down over him again. He was three over par right now and that number would climb.

"Where your mind goes, you will too," Buster said earlier. It was true, but that wouldn't help him escape today's downhill performance.

Buster talked as they walked. "You know why they call this Amen Corner?" he asked. Jonni shook his head. He had heard the name but he didn't know the story. "It was named by Herbert Warren, a sportswriter. But that's not how it got its name." Buster turned to take in the view and summon to mind the history. "I heard it from one of the older caddies, worked here way back then — 50s. He's retired now, might have passed, I don't know. So, Arnold Palmer was playing in 1958 and he was leading, I don't recall by how much. Then come down to 11th here he was back over, about to lose the lead. It was nice and muddy, due to a storm. He made par here on 11. Then on 12 he chipped over the bank and the ball got stuck in the mud. Just thunk and there it was, not moving."

Buster seemed never to need to catch his breath as they walked. Jonni glanced up, his head otherwise dipped low, and saw the lines of people on the ropes — fewer than the beginning of the day — breaking, walking, or hanging and watching him.

"So he played it but it didn't go well, double bogey, but then the Rules Committee says he can have another dropped ball. He chipped that one up right by the hole, they say he was focused then like a hawk on a fieldmouse. Just put the ball right there," Buster gestured with his hand, sliding it toward an imaginary hole. They were halfway down the hill now. "So that one gets him back on track, but he doesn't know if it counts. So he's walking now with a bit of a cloud hanging over him, goes to 13. Now on 13, despite still having that double bogey, he throws doubt to the wind and goes for it. Eagle, puts that drive right up close and then finishes it up with a putt, 18 feet, right in. He knows then, just knows he's back in the game, throws his hat straight into the air and the crowd is cheering. Everyone loved Arnold, anyway. So then, later on, they tell him: the drop counted. So, "Amen," he says. Or they say he says. Amen because that was it, he had his win. Answer to a prayer. He knew it that moment, everyone did. This corner, your luck changes. Like the wind."

Jonni knew what Buster was doing as he went quiet and they neared his ball. Jonni was afraid of going near the 12th. He played it on the practice round with his eyes closed. Of course he never saw the body there, but he knew. Buster hoped Jonni would buck up, change his own luck coming around Amen Corner.

But the weight of his round felt heavier with each step, and each hole. He tried to make it all fade away, to hear the course only, forget the people, find the hole and bring the ball to it — but he couldn't. All he could do was just swing. He trudged up to the next corner as if to the gallows.

Two bodies, six days, no suspects. That's where Ryals found himself. Kate's theory made him anxious. He didn't need that.

He had no motive — just vague theories. He had no murder weapon. He had no meaningful physical evidence of any kind. The Holiday Inn cameras were dysfunctional. He had no witnesses, no informants, no real leads. Just a few days walking around a golf course.

And an ever-expanding team turning up nothing, and more nothing.

His lies to the Sheriff about "making progress" — the Sheriff of course knew they were lies, and repeated them with a flourish to his superiors — wouldn't hold out much longer.

Then there was this idea of a ticking clock, which wasn't present either until Kate said it.

"In a few days, they all clear out. Anyone you could even think to interview might be gone."

Other than the pressure of "the murderer has skipped town, might be caught up in Nashville or down in Tampa," where he could just put a crime on the shelf and let it work itself out, this one might disappear much farther outside his jurisdiction.

It was late in the day, Parriot was hard at work with no updates of his own and Ryals figured he would get a bite before he went to meet some of the security staff and interview them. He imagined sunset on the course was quite nice.

Kate caught him just as he was leaving the door to the station.

"Food?" she asked. "Beer, maybe?"

He could certainly use a beer. On duty, he wouldn't. He also wore no uniform. He paused but couldn't think of a good enough reason to keep her from joining him. He wasn't going far. There was fast food at the corner.

"I hear the downtown here is nice, any recommendations?" she said as she climbed in the car.

So he found himself sitting at a table at The Bees Knees bistro, a spot he had never tried before but she picked after requesting a tour down Broad Street. He found something on the menu and set it down and she ordered a beer. She was already talking, but it seemed mostly to herself. A musician played; Bo Baskoro, in for Masters week. A world-famous singer, here in a downtown cafe. The Masters was an extraordinary thing. Kate's voice was low.

"Either A, the murderer immediately left town, his deed done, his message conveyed, or B, the murderer remains, the crime being part of some sort of leverage or pressure. In either case, though, someone here knows something. It would be pointless to go through all of that trouble if the message wasn't meant for somebody here."

"It's broadcast worldwide on TV. Maybe the pressure is against the course itself. A threat to advertisers or to the club members?"

"I've considered that," she said. "And it can't be discounted. What better way to tell the money behind a major sporting event 'we can ruin this for you.' "

"Except ratings have only increased," Ryals said. "I assume."

"They definitely have," she said, sipping her dark beer. A bit of froth stuck to her nose. She didn't notice and he didn't say anything. "And that's why that line of reasoning doesn't make sense to me. Besides, these athletes must be insured. Why threaten someone when they could only benefit from it. It seems messy, and the crime itself is anything but messy."

"Mhm," was all Ryals replied. He had considered all of this. There was more though. Despite himself, he was talking, as if to himself:

"Still it's possible the murder has nothing at all to do with Jonni Lombard. He's just unlucky, caught in the crosshairs. It may be personal. Could be this is all about the National, or some board member or investor. Or anyone."

"Could be, could be," she said, and he had the odd feeling that she was validating his theories, and not the other way around. There was something about her — what was the word? Tenacity. That irked him. He tried to think of what it was, tried to look at her and imagine it without being obvious. Something in her manner.

There it was — she reminded him of his daughter. She annoyed him in much the same way Angela did. He wasn't sure exactly how yet, but there it was.

"We cannot forget, though, that Willy seemed to know the suspect. On the video. He was lured out there. Somehow, he was involved. He wasn't a random target."

"What exactly is your job?" Ryals asked her.

"I'm a targeter."

"Which means what?"

"I look for people who don't want to be found. That's my job. Usually by computer. I find my way into the tall grass."

"So can I join you this evening for the interviews?" She asked. Just like his daughter. She knew that if she asked he wouldn't say no. Maybe he was transparent.

Her phone rang. She looked at him, at her phone, and then excused herself, answering and telling the caller "give me five seconds," and there was something in how she did it that was odd.

She didn't move to be polite—she walked out for privacy. Probably nothing, but there was something in her change of demeanor that felt peculiar. He looked at his watch — it was time to go. Kate's beer was empty. He downed his and laid money on the table.

The light was golden and behind the pine trees illuminating pollen like fairy dust.

Jonni walked back to the clubhouse after finishing five over par for the day. Jonni didn't speak. Buster's stories helped get Jonni through the day, but the caddie was quiet now as they walked to the polite applause of a crowd far smaller than he had started with. Still, he had played a tournament day at the Masters. It counted for something.

Twice today, Jonni had looked up to see what Willy thought of his swing only to find that Willy wasn't standing beside him.

Jonni felt bad for Buster. He was nice enough, but Jonni did not want to talk to him. There was nothing he could say that would help Jonni play better. No comfort or support or joke.

Justin Rose was cheery but focused and quiet all day. He gave Jonni space and kept to himself. He played well. He finished at three under. Rose walked with a relaxed saunter as he approached each hole, but clearly his mind was never off the grass. In one of their few conversations, Rose told Jonni that he learned his calm from a coach called McCabe. He said the coach had helped a number of other golfers through anxiety and distraction. "Changed my game completely," he said. He offered to Jonni to make an introduction. Jonni didn't even know how to thank him for an offer to help. But he didn't want to talk to anybody.

From the Thirteenth Hole onward the day was like a dream passing. When they came to the Fifteenth, Jonni was really sliding. He shanked his first shot.

"Kid, good news. No matter how bad you do on this one, you won't beat Sergio Garcia's downright funny meltdown here. You ever watch that?"

Jonni couldn't think of it. Buster continued, "He made a 13 by rolling ball after ball into the water and was in danger of running out of golf balls, which would have added catastrophe to catastrophe. One of the commentators said, I'm not trying to be funny, but the golfers only carry so many balls with them. If he had run out of balls, of course, he couldn't finish the round. Kid you'd have to work hard to have a day like he did that day. Year after he won, too." Jonni managed a smile, if only briefly.

Rose slapped a hand on Jonni's back at the end of the day as they crested the hill on the 18th and saw the Clubhouse emerge in front of them, white and shimmering in the afternoon sun.

"Boet," Rose said in South African. "Sometimes this course beats you for a round. It doesn't own you. Get some rest, I'll see you tomorrow."

Tomorrow Jonni would be paired with someone else. If he made the cut for Saturday, his pairing then and Sunday would be based on his score. The better his score, the later his tee time.

Part of him hoped, desperately hoped, that he wouldn't make the cut for Saturday.

"First day competing in the Masters," his dad said. "Hell of a day," he said. "Five over is more than ninety-nine ought nine percent of golfers in the world, my boy. Be proud."

Jonni walked ahead of his dad, his security guard and his caddie into the clubhouse to wait for his ride back to the hotel. He was sure he would fall asleep in the car.

At the same moment Ryals returned to the staff gate. Contrary to his plan, Kate was in stride.

They found Lawrence as the last golfers walked off the course. Patrons exited on the long pathway in a slow and steady stream, tired, sunburned and ecstatic.

"I have seven people for you; security and grounds staff, folks who were working Saturday evening, stopping by my office as they get in. Take it and do any interviews up there, if that suits you."

Soon in the office Ryals told Kate to just sit in the corner behind him in a chair they took from nearby. Ryals moved the desk chair around to the front of the desk and met with three security and five grounds staff over the course of the next hour and a half, until darkness fell. The conversations were mundane. No one had anything of note to offer. Ryals gave them all a card.

Kate remained quiet and took a few notes. Ryals was friendly, put the men at ease, and they were as helpful as they could be. They knew nothing that could help.

The final interview was the gate security officer for the night. A former police officer from Columbia, South Carolina, he was adamant that he had checked every badge that came in.

Ryals didn't need to ask if it was possible that someone could have stolen a badge to sneak in. Someone had. The officer knew it and was afraid for his job. His leg shook as he recounted the evening. He made excuses.

Ryals cut him off. "I'm just wondering if there's anything else you saw, might have noticed, realized later was off or odd."

"I can't say. I really can't think of anything."

Kate spoke up for the first time: "Grounds crew are allowed cell phones on the course?"

"No. Just radios."

"How do they check for cell phones? Do the grounds crew go through the same metal detectors as the patrons?"

"No, it's just policy." The man twitched. Then he grew still as he talked them through. "I looked at the videos, from the gate and the ones from the grounds, with Mr. Lawrence. I know most of the faces that come in. I believe I would have noticed someone I didn't recognize."

Kate glanced at Ryals. "The groundskeepers looked at these videos as well?"

"He has us all looking, to see if there was anything that maybe stood out to us. Anyone we didn't recognize."

Ryals nodded. Lawrence had already told him this.

"I'm sorry. I wish I could point him out, I just can't. No faces stood out to me."

She closed her notebook, nodded, and Ryals had nothing else.

"I've never seen this," Ryals had to admit as they walked back to get the car. "Killers here are sloppy. Criminals in general are stupid. This guy came in like a ghost. Into an area full of surveillance."

"Back at the station I watched the video of Willy Sharpe smoking. You say you think he knew the killer?"

"Seemed that way. He just walked off."

"Hm."

"You don't?"

"I agree. Though he could have used a ruse. The important point being, Willy didn't react. He wasn't surprised, he didn't run or call for help or call out an alarm. And besides that — what was Willy doing there? At that moment? Just good luck for the killer? No. I think they arranged to meet there, or he gave Willy some notice. My bigger point though is that this killer knew exactly where the cameras were, and weren't. To a few feet."

"Which means what? He was here before."

"He was here before, but he didn't appear on cameras then, either."

"We don't know what he looked like," Ryals said.

"No, but let's assume he doesn't want his face on the cameras at all. It's different during the tournament when anyone can hide in the crowd. Before that he has to assume that at some point, we'd check all the faces, and someone would know who wasn't supposed to be there. What if that happened quickly? Before he was able to get away?

"Lawrence and his guys looked and looked, but saw no one unfamiliar. So let's say, he used a disguise. Shaved. Dyed his hair. Maybe a facial prosthetic."

"Seriously?"

"They went through plenty of trouble. He had an ID. I don't know what he did, but I don't think basic disguises you can get off Amazon are a completely insane idea. Won't help us on the videos, because at that resolution, assuming he never looks directly at a camera, we might not even pick up Mr. Gordon. But regardless. He knew the cameras, which means — if you're asking me—"

Ryals wasn't, but he found himself listening closely.

"—he knows the types of cameras, the field of view, and knew that the irises on these cameras couldn't be simply killed with an IR laser. He had to avoid them."

Ryals was lost. "So what?"

"I don't know. This is just an observation. I think he knew what sort of cameras they had before he even got here. If it was me, I would know."

"How would you know?"

"Not sure. But I'm also not a murderer. Necessity, you know. All that."

"What, you think their computers were hacked?"

"I don't know," she said, shrugging. "Just observing." She checked her watch. "So I got the info on the text he sent."

Ryals blinked and looked at her. "You what? What does that mean?"

"Appears the phone was a burner, purchased here, not long ago. Sim card went active just two days before the murder."

Ryals was perplexed. Federal Agencies operated in an entirely different arena than he had experienced. "So," he found himself asking, "what do we do with that? Can we track him?"

"Well, first, no, it's a burner phone. I can only find out what phones are pinging a tower from this area at a certain time. Too many, of course. I just wanted to filter those for any phone numbers used by burner phones and subsequently deactivated."

"So we can't track his location."

"That's a thing that only happens in the movies, Detective. Well, we can get updates. The phone sends an update to the tower. The tower to a collector. Collector to an analyst. Sometimes it's by the minute, sometimes by the day. No such thing as a real-time tracking."

"Okay," Ryals said.

"We might get more from that line of thinking, though. Let's be patient.

The conversation was absurd. This young lady was schooling him.

Ryals wasn't sure what she meant but he realized that in one day she had gone from "I'm just here to watch" to "I'll tell you when I'm ready." It just made him tired. He wanted to have a beer alone.

Fortunately, it was late enough he was sure Parriot and the others were gone by now. He didn't know where they stayed, or if they commuted back to Atlanta; there would be no hotel rooms available anywhere close. Maybe they decided to sleep at the office. So they had to leave in time to make the 3 hour drive, and make it back in the morning.

Ryals was too exhausted to figure out what Kate was talking about, and too annoyed to figure out her riddles.

"My hotel is on your side of town," she said. "If you're not going back to the station, could you drop me there?"

He turned the wheel dutifully to do so.

"How did you even find a room?" He asked. Not sure that he cared, more sure that he wanted to point out she was foolish to have tried. Even though, apparently, she wasn't.

"There's always a cancellation," she said. No, he thought. There isn't. Not during Masters week.

He found Angela eating in front of the TV, watching replays from the day. "I'm trying to catch a glimpse of you," she said.

"Not likely," he said. "We were only on the course for five minutes. I'm not there to, you know, watch the golf, kiddo." She shrugged.

"Your suspect didn't do too great."

"He's not a suspect," he said, sitting in the room with her in his recliner to watch. She muted the TV.

"Well, you know. The kid. He's cute by the way. Are you going to be able to get me an autograph?"

"I don't get autographs when I'm in the middle of an investigation," he said. "And I don't ask golfers for autographs."

"You're not asking. Your daughter is asking," she said, matter of factly.

"It won't be the first time she didn't get what she wanted."

"Oh, I remember Christmas," she said.

Ryals smiled. He wished he was back in the car with Kate.

TWENTY-TWO

Friday
Round 2

The birds outside were loud and had started at about five in the morning. That was early, and Ryals couldn't sleep through it.

Not as early as Kate, however. Ryals woke to several texts from her, starting at four.

Looking for any similar M.O.'s, international.

Coming up empty.

No dice.

Will think of another angle.

He wasn't just several steps behind the killer; he was apparently several steps behind his new partner.

Before he could pick her up, however, he had a late-night text that he had forgotten about until he woke up. Thankfully the text was from Sam Ingot, the journalist, asking for breakfast. I'm an early riser, let me know where.

Sam took an Uber and they met at a coffee shop with unsatisfying breakfast sandwiches. It was convenient.

Ingot wore a light zip-up wind jacket and a polo shirt. He looked like he might play golf on occasion. His circle glasses with the clear thick rims made his eyes appear perpetually wide, as if he were always surprised, but his demeanor was so relaxed he seemed to exist at one tone, one note and one level of energy. He drank his coffee black and Ryals assumed in the evening he drank gin. He had that gin look about him.

"I was thinking About the Calcuttas. About your case. You probably think I'm an armchair gumshoe. The Calcuttas, the betting, you're talking old, old money. Lots of money. Which is — what I'm wondering is..." He took a sip of water and smiled warmly.

Already Ryals was tired. Between the long humid days and this much education about golf, he was taxed. Ingot produced a notepad with pages covered in scribble. He held it up as if preparing to give a speech. "Let me start again," he said. "Do you know anything about Jones & Roberts?"

"Who?"

"Robert Tyre Jones, Jr and Cliff Roberts. The Founders of the Augusta National and the Masters."

Ryals shrugged, sipping his coffee, thinking of ordering a second cup to have on deck. "Bobby Jones, we have a freeway named after him. Legendary golfer."

"Sure," Ingot said. He had gone from armchair gumshoe to lecturing professor. "The founding of the institution, however, might warrant some consideration as context for your investigation. I began to consider this after we last spoke. If you'll suffer me a moment," he said, flipping over the page on the pad then dropping it onto the table lightly. "I'll educate you on a few of the salient details about the history of the Augusta National.

"Cliff and Jones started this course in the middle of the depression, an extraordinary fundraising feat by any accounts. You'd consider how high the fences had to be just to keep hungry people from seeing where money was being spent. Jones of course was a celebrity, the best golfer in the world, young prodigy, gentleman's gentleman; educated at Georgia Tech and then Harvard. He came from money, but earned his own; he was sensational even as a young golfer. He was the Michael Jordan of his time. This was a time when sports writers were celebrities themselves," Ingot added with a wink. "All of sports, particularly golf was venerated."

"While Jones was the gentleman, Roberts was the asshole. Fundraiser extraordinaire, friends with Dwight Eisenhower, racist. He ruled the place with an iron fist. Cut the pockets out of the concessions staffs' pants so they wouldn't steal. Just a Grade A Bastard, but I think, lonely and kind of aware that he was a bastard. Killed himself after all, on his course, next to the fishing pond he made just to keep his friend Ike visiting him. Died right by the Par 3 course.

"They built it in Augusta . I know you're a local so you know, it was the wealthy elite that lived here, here in the area we call Summerville. It was built mostly for New Yorkers and other out of towners who wanted to winter in the exotic South. It was actually a member of the National who financed Gone with the Wind and Amos 'n Andy, which were fascinating to northerners. There was an allure to the South.

"Eisenhower wasn't the only G-man invited to the club. Dulles, CIA head. You had Taft and Reagan. Quayle. Not Nixon though — because he threw in for Pepsi, and the club was tied closely in with Coca-Cola, whose world headquarters are in Atlanta. The founders were investors, in fact," Ingot said with a bit of a smile.

"The Masters was something different altogether. It could never have happened but for these two men. Bobby's celebrity, Cliff's shrewd business acumen. Elite of the elite, there was probably no greater punishment to a member of the High Golf Society than being disinvited from the club. And of course, just being invited was a gift from Heaven; it was like Salvation: there was no way to earn it. Money wasn't the issue at all. They could charge anything for membership. It was the invitation, the access, the club. Money was behind it, money swung the clubs. Money, and gentlemen. Fall out of line, and lose your invitation. Some would probably prefer death to that.

"There were plenty other bastards in the ranks, plenty of racists — not a surprise in the South in those days, more representative of the population I suppose — but to the course's credit when it came time to get with the times and open the doors to diversity, the National got in line. Jones lived out his final years in a wheelchair, all twisted up with a spine condition, pitiful. The times changed, the founders died, the club became less elitist in some sense, but it will always be the club that Jones and Roberts built. It is about, above all, tradition. And it's "A Tradition Unlike Any Other," — that's the slogan. And it's true. Eisenhower wasn't just a friend of Roberts — he only ran for president because Roberts and his friends encouraged him. Arguably they won him the nomination. The day after he was elected, he came down to the National, celebrated here. Some say The National succeeded despite itself. And there are those that believe that its character died with Bobby Jones, and can never be recaptured."

Ryals had to admit he was more fascinated by the history lesson than he would have been just two weeks ago, but he found himself asking, "What does this have to do with my investigation?" He had, after all, rushed out and botched his face shaving too quickly for a long lecture.

"Just bear with me. The club still does things like its founders. It's beautiful, green, honorable, all that but like any institution it has blemishes, shadows, and perhaps darker shadows than you would expect. As you know, even tickets are an extraordinary business. Do you remember a few years back when those CVS executives were caught with dead men's badges?"

"No," Ryals admitted.

"Yeah, '96? I'd have to check. Corporations have been shut out for fraud. It's Shangri La. Some people think they can buy their way into it. They can't. The point I'm making is, the tradition of exclusivity leads to some extreme measures among very serious entities. There are presidents who are — and who want to be— members. Condoleezza Rice is a member. Top executives of the world's largest corporations. Grudges are part of the tradition here. I know I'm spending a lot of time in the past, but Roberts — more than Jones, but Jones played along — had pro golfers shut out just because they went on dates with local girls that members had their eye on. The power of the membership is near absolute. There's evidence that Cliff Roberts embezzled money for members needs and for his own. No one talked about it then, and no one gets a look at the books today. Not without a federal subpoena, I'm guessing — and good luck with that while senators and White House officials past and present are invited members. Judges, too. Like a lot of other entities, especially back in the day, the National was begun tainted by corruption. Perhaps it's part and parcel of this sort of thing, but there you go. And while much of that is left in the past, not all of it is. Is there gambling amongst these executives, who spend fifty or one hundred grand — as a corporate expense — when they fly down here to do a year's worth of drinking in a week? Are there consequences? Yes, and yes. I don't know where your investigation is, Detective Hall, but I would consider looking into this. In my view there is still an element of darkness here. No ancient satanic order practicing in the shadows, but if a company lost its badges, or if someone was kicked out of the club — and the National is of course very tight-lipped about that sort of thing — that's the sort of offense that, to these men of great means — could provoke a nasty response.

"My point is, people have killed over much less. Imagine a grudge between two members. One could give your killer access."

"Surely there are better places to work out a grudge," Ryals thought out loud.

Sam answered, "There is money here. You may have learned, the shop does one million in revenue an hour during the tournament. And that's not the real money. The membership, that's concentrated wealth like you can't believe."

He looked again at his notes and wrinkled his nose to keep his glasses against his face. Ryals was looked at Ingot, then at his own notes and then up at the cafe beyond, which had grown quiet. Finally, he processed what the reporter was telling him.

"Thank you for this," he said, meaning it. "I don't know where to start with it, exactly, but to be honest we're not very far with the investigation. So any fresh insight helps. If it's two members — which two?"

"Oh, I'm not a detective. I can give you context and a good story."

"Okay."

Ingot shrugged. "Look," he said, "I'm of the camp that doesn't care about the scandal, the history, the rumors; I care about the players and the game. Stats are drama to me. But if I wrote about the Chicago Bulls in '92, I would have written The Jordan Rules. I'm no cynic but context is everything. I hope," he said, reclaiming his notes from the table, "this is some context that helps. Of course, there's plenty of people that hate the Masters, too. Most of them outside of the world of golf, but there are some detractors on the inside. And then there's LIV. That has certainly brought a great deal of ill will into the world of golf. There's tension between professional players and their sponsors. I've heard of lifetime friends on the course, champion level, who are no longer on speaking terms because of LIV." Ryals could see in his face: Ingot cared about this game.

"You know a lot about this," Ryals said.

"I love the game and to love it is to know it. Golf's greatest expression, its most beautiful form, is right here. So the more of it, good and bad that I discover, the more I can love it."

Ryals didn't love it in that way, but it was part of his local heritage. He felt a strange compulsion of ownership talking with Ingot. Ingot loved it so much, but it belonged to Augusta. Didn't it? Ryals wanted it right. He wanted it clear of this blood stain.

Ryals wanted to finish the case.

His coffee was cold. He held the mug on the table. Gripping it as if it might slide away at any moment.

"Hey," Ryals asked, looking at Ingot again. "Was the National built on an Indian Burial Ground?"

Ingot nodded, smiled a bit. "Yeah, I've heard that one. True, apparently. Augusta is a town because it was a trading crossroads by the Savannah River. When they dug the ground for the course, they found bones from several Indian tribes, as the story goes. Didn't know what to do with them."

"Where did they find them?" Ryals asked.

"Under the 12th green," Ingot answered.

TWENTY-THREE

Ryals left the breakfast meeting with his head in a fog. Somehow everything seemed darker. Ticket scalping was one thing, and everyone knew the National brought in plenty of money, but to think that powerful forces and old money and big money lurked in the shadows of the Golden Bell and that Willy was an unfortunate pawn in a chess game between sinister forces was like a dark fantasy.

Then again, the South was haunted. Everyone knew. There was pain in the roots of the Magnolia trees here, tragedy behind the street names and Antebellum homes on The Hill.

He picked Kate up. In her lap was a Fedex package. She removed a small black zippered case.

"What's that?" He asked.

"Gift from a friend," she answered. She put it away into the backpack she wore over her shoulder. "Might help us if we get close enough to these folks."

"You think the killer is still anywhere close, do you? These guys are pros, they wouldn't hang around here," he said, reiterating the conversation he'd had with the Sheriff.

"Actually," she said, "I do think he — or they — are still around. Maybe sticking very close."

"What makes you say that?"

"Just a hunch," she said. She went on looking out the window, as if appreciating a foreign country. Cheery again. Just as irritating as before. Never giving a full answer. She acted as if everyone should already know what she meant and was thinking. He twisted the steering wheel. She was well under his skin at this point, and he wasn't about to walk around the private golf course with her while she waved her magic cell phone wand about and got them both in trouble.

It took him half of the drive to realize the other thing that was gnawing at him. He was afraid he had completely misread this crime — what if the killer was indeed hanging around? Ryals had assumed the killer was long gone from Augusta. Maybe there were more layers to this, and something was just beneath his nose.

He glanced at Kate, her freckles, bright eyes and the way her knees came together in the car, much like a child. No, he thought. He had years of experience investigating murderers.

Jonni was paired today with Sergio Garcia from Spain. Sergio wore Adidas in navy blue, his whole outfit sponsored.

They walked to the first tee slightly apart. Jonni felt conspicuous with a bodyguard following him around. The only confidence he had walking on to the first green was that the worse he was likely to play, the smaller the crowd would be around him and the less he would appear on TV. Likely he would be cut after today, and not playing the final two rounds.

The sun rose quickly here; at home the weather was about the same, though the nights cooled more at home.

Just before they got to the ropes, Dad gave him a hug around the shoulders and told him, "Do your best out there, Son. The world is cheering you on." Jonni smiled and nodded, saying nothing. The excitement he felt, watching those replays on TV, those magical moments in history, was slipping away.

"Today," Buster said beside him, talking low as they walked through the ropes held open by the Pinkerton guards who smiled at the golfers, "Don't think about your score. Don't think about the cut. Just think about the course, the grounds, the ball. Enjoy it. Just take a stroll. All this," he said, glancing at the people along the rope line at the top of the hole, "doesn't matter."

Jonni stopped as Sergio adjusted his belt and swayed back and forth, moving from one foot to the other. They both looked down the fairway as runners ready for a marathon. He listened to Sergio breathe in the air deeply and exhale. Jonni did well, holding it in with the smell of flowers and foliage and evaporating dew. It didn't smell so different from the warthog-trimmed grass of his home course. From the summer mornings in Bela-Bela.

Buster was right. Jonni had to ignore the people on the sides with their hats from tournaments past, the ladies with the wide white brims shielding the sun from their faces, holding maps up to protect their eyes, men with cigars and the young men joining them, sweet blue smoke twisting slowly into the heavy air like milk mixed into tea, others already drinking beer from clear and green cups, as if any rules of society didn't apply here, as if the course was where a clock existed only to separate tee times; their necks leaning over the yellow rope and wide eyes as they looked at him like curious antelope, unblinking, ready to follow the ball after the snap of the driver; none of it mattered. It wasn't why he was here. Jonni closed his eyes and breathed again, just like Sergio.

For a moment, and just a moment, the sound disappeared and he could only hear his breathing, and he was anywhere, on any course, and not just here.

Then he opened his eyes and it returned and Buster was talking to him. His was the first swing. He didn't look as Buster handed him the driver and a ball and smooth wooden tee and he knew instinctively as he stepped up, feeling his father's gaze, then all the other eyes reaching out to him like soft small probing fingers, that he would miss the shot, that it would be far left, wide, maybe over the rope between the rough and the footpath. He sighed, this time full of anxiety, and his feet grew heavy as he stepped into position.

Kate asked to be let off at the course when Ryals said he needed to go to the station. "There's nothing I need to do at the station. You can just update me. Drop me wherever."

Ryals wanted to argue. He wanted badly to reign Kate in, keep her on a leash. She didn't work for him, though. He had no authority over her at all, but he wasn't about to let her stomp all over his crime scene, even if ten thousand other people were.

He took her in and introduced her to Allison, and Kate politely asked to spend part of the day following Jonni and "keeping a low profile, no invasion or investigation." Ryals noticed she didn't mention the device in the satchel around her shoulder; it looked like a small purse.

"Of course," Allison said, "and I'm here should you need anything. All smooth so far today. Everything is on autopilot," she said it as if a rehearsed script, her eyes and mind elsewhere. Ryals took his leave, and hoped Kate wouldn't ruffle feathers.

At the station he went in to see the Sheriff before he met with Parriot, who was already at work with his team in the room set up for them. Ryals explained everything he could about Kate. When the local and state politics came raining down, it was best to have some shelter. The Sheriff listened and nodded, his face serious, but unsure of himself.

"Hm. Call her office and request some official documentation," The Sheriff said. He pulled out the letter she'd provided. "It certainly looks legit."

"It may be, but it's on us if she's cutting any corners." He and Ryals were clearly on the same page, but per usual, it was more work for Ryals. "Don't throw any mud on it. Have the department federal liaison request a clearance order, or whatever they may send."

Ryals sent an email before he sat down with Parriot, who was at work between papers, statements, a map on the wall and a laptop.

"Morning," he said, full of energy. He was drinking tea, not coffee. He needed to detox from caffeine.

"Where are the others?" Ryals asked. Parriot was alone in the room.

"They'll be down shortly," Parriot said. "It's a one man job until later." He directed Ryals to the map on the wall. "Question for you," he said. "Working through Mr. Sharpe's travel card usage on Saturday."

"Something there?"

"Maybe," Parriot said, sticking a pin into the map. "Here he has coffee, on his way to the course, presumably, geographically it's obvious.

Right here, Starbucks, not far from his hotel. Apparently he preferred it to his hotel coffee, or just wanted a stroll. He buys the coffee at 0732."

"Okay," Ryals said.

"His pickup time to go walk the course was 0800. We have no reason to think he wasn't there or that he was late." Using a pencil, Parriot drew arrows between pins on the map, with times beside them.

"Okay."

"Then we presume — I don't know how much you have verified this by video, but we presume he's at the course until he checks out at 1600. Now," Parriot said, glancing at some papers. "The car service, or shuttle, supposedly returned him to his hotel."

"That's what I've been told," Ryals said.

"But here's the odd thing, and I need your local insight on this." He moved to another pin, on the other side of downtown. "His next card swipe was here, at a smoke shop just east of the downtown area. Now, I did a google maps look, and there's nothing there. It's not a pleasant place, and it's not on a main thoroughfare. So, first question: is this a place someone would chance by if they were out exploring the town in the evening?"

"No, it isn't," Ryals said. "Someone might go down and walk Broad Street, maybe even Telfair here. On a Saturday night, sure. The River-walk, along the Savannah river here, is popular, but..."

"This is several blocks off the beaten path, so to speak," Parriot offered.

"It is."

"So why is he there? There's a spot a block this way, a bar, the Fox Hole? A dive?"

"Fox's Lair."

"You've been?" Parriot asked him.

"Years ago," Ryals said. "I'm aware of it. It was a dive, but under new ownership it's turned around, or so I've heard. It's still not in the best corner of downtown, and its off the beaten path

"Would Mr. Sharpe have been aware of it?"

"I don't know. It's a long way to go for a beer. I wouldn't have recommended it to anyone."

"Okay," Parriot said, making a note on a small pad. "So then there's a second question," he picked up a credit card statement. "He used his card at the small shop, but not for a taxi, and not for anything else in the area. Perhaps he used cash. Though that's inconsistent with how he paid at the convenience store."

"Yes," Ryals said, thinking through it. "Perhaps a per diem? He could use it for food, travel, but not for cigarettes?"

"Possible," Parriot said, making another note. "You would need to ask Mr. Lombard about that." Parriot studied the map.

"Or someone else paid."

"Indeed," he said.

"I'll get on the ground and figure it out," Ryals said. "But most of that stuff isn't open until this afternoon."

Parriot shrugged. "We'll keep working. It's all we've found so far."

Ryals had several hours to do paperwork but he was far more inclined to join Kate on the course. Being there was a vacation in and of itself and today the weather was perfect. On the other hand, he didn't want to deal with Kate. He checked his watch. He started to call his daughter, then remembered when she told him "Dad, no one calls anymore. Everyone texts. And don't text too much. Just a few words is all you're supposed to do."

So he texted Angela: lunch?

He picked her up and brought her to the Village Deli, a favorite of hers, closer to the Hill and across from the municipal small craft airport. She had a salad, he had a sandwich with fries. He ignored her judgmental look when he scanned the menu and did just what he wanted. He was enjoying today. He enjoyed seeing Angela on workdays and he was enjoying the weather and he was going to enjoy some french fries.

Fortunately she was smiling at him when he handed his menu over and when the food came.

"So," he said. "How is your day going?"

"Reading a lot. I jogged."

"Which way?"

"Up the hill, past the convent like you said."

"Good," though of course he would prefer if she ran into a convent.

"How's the case?" she asked, sipping her unsweet tea. (It was important to specify if you wanted your tea unsweet in Georgia, and Ryals rarely did).

"It's going," he said.

"It's going to be big, I know it. I mean, it already is. And it's yours."

"It's the department's," he said, defensively. "It's yours" felt like more a curse than a blessing.

"Sure, but they'll interview you, won't they? When you solve it. The Murder at the Masters. I bet they'll call it that."

Ryals shrugged. "Who knows. We have other people helping now. It's not just mine,"

"Like who?"

"GBI, DHS even," he said, raising his eyebrows. He wasn't sure who he was trying to convince. Certainly not her.

"Wow," she said, but she couldn't hide some disappointment. She wanted her dad to get the credit for this. To be the hero. That's not how it works, he wanted to tell her.

"Tonight," he said, lowering his voice. In fact, he could have been followed by the press. He glanced around, suddenly aware of that idea. "Tonight I have to figure out where the victim went the night before the murder. And today I'm working with this woman from Homeland Security."

"That's so cool."

Their food came and she didn't eat immediately. "And," she said, "you got to go all over the Masters. I've been watching it all week. Jonni Lombard is awesome. And he's cute."

"Cute?"

"Yeah, of course. And his accent. I heard an interview." Ryals winced. "It would be so cool to meet him and get an autograph."

"I don't think that's possible," he said.

"I know, I know," she said.

"Maybe I can ask for an autograph, though," he said, winking at her.

"What happens if you haven't solved it when the Masters is done?" she asked between bites of lettuce.

"That depends. He's not a suspect so he can go home," Ryals said, knowing of course how ice cold the case would become after Sunday. He felt suddenly guilty for being here with his daughter. If there was press outside, the picture of him leaving a restaurant midday would play well when they didn't solve the case.

They finished, paid and walked to the parking lot. He put his sunglasses on and climbed into his Dodge Charger, a fairly conspicuous police vehicle with the government tag and grill strobes. Angela loved to ride in it — at least he believed she still did.

As he turned the car over he noticed it — in the rear view mirror — a car parked a line behind him, a new model with tinted windows and inside a man who did not move.

"Dad?" Angela asked, looking up from her phone.

"Sorry," he said, and backed out of the spot and out of the parking lot. As he passed the car he tried to get a look; if it was paparazzi, Ryals would like to have a heads up if someone planned to publish or post pictures of him and his daughter. Surely he was imagining things. No one wanted pictures of him.

When he passed the guy, the guy wore a hat, and dipped his head — was he wearing a hat before?

He pulled into traffic and drove away while Angela connected her phone to bluetooth.

Kate knew very little about golf but she was learning fast. She stood near some men smoking cigars, listened to them talk and asked them a few questions as they followed Jonni Lombard along from the par four Seventh to the par five Eighth. Ryals was right, it was hard to spot anyone. They spectators lined up along the rope lines and crowded near the flags. The crowds were devoted to this game with a passion and respect that surprised her. It was hard not to get lost in it.

"Remember Tiger's shot here in 2015? We were here, right on it. Al were you here?" One of the guys asked the others. They were what Kate thought you would call "Good Ol' Boys."

"Al wasn't. Didn't make it that year."

"That's what you get for moving out of the South," the other said.

"You guys are local?" Kate asked as they walked, following the golfers.

"Born and raised," one said, puffing a cigar. Another said,

"Evans," he said. "Greater Augusta area."

"So you come every year?"

One touched his badge. "Lifetime badges," he said. "Came from my dad."

"How's that work?" she asked.

"Doesn't anymore," he said, looking at the others. "National changed the rules. Used to be about local legacy. This was ours, here in Augusta. You got badges, they stayed with the family. Not anymore," he said, bitterly. "I'll probably lose mine after this year."

"Why don't they want to keep that going?"

"Commercializing. Slowly, but surely. You give away one custom at a time. Soon it's all owned by Wal Mart."

"Food is still cheap, though," she said. She'd read about that. "They still offer the same pimento cheese and egg salad sandwiches for a buck fifty, beer for four bucks. The same cracker jack snacks."

"Mark my words, one day that will change, too."

They walked on past her, breaking off to find beer at one of the concessions houses. She kept with the crowd that followed Jonni Lombard, his head hanging, hands in his pockets. She had spotted his dad behind the rope a few times, trying to keep a brave face, but full of doubt. Kate understood from the Good Ol' Boys that if Jonni did poorly today, he wouldn't make the cut to play tomorrow. There was a lot riding on him. He was three over right now, and he walked like he was going to a sentencing.

She wondered who wanted him that way. Or was it indeed just collateral — this kid's confidence and livelihood, just caught in someone's crossfire.

She felt for him. She reached into her satchel. Meeting Allison first was a way to get through without going through the metal detectors. She had brought a tool sent to her from a friend working with a small tech company that contracted for the government. It was the same tool she used in the bush when looking for poachers. She wanted to test it. This was one thing this course and the wilds of Africa had in common. She hoped it would give her the advantage in the wilds of Augusta, just like it did there.

She needed to do some things on her own. Ryals seemed to be a good cop but Kate had her own agenda and didn't want a chaperone — she just needed him to do his job so that she could do hers.

Ryals drove downtown after lunch. He exited Riverwatch Parkway and continued down Telfair to the far east side of downtown. He first visited the small convenience store where Willy bought his cigarettes.

He parked across and down the street and sat for a moment and watched. Sitting outside was the usual riff raff. A bum sat on the corner, a thin man smoking. They stood in a shadow. The door opened, a pair of school-aged teenagers emerged with bags of forty ounce beers. Ryals had worked this street before as one of his first beats. It wasn't pretty. Downtown dissolved into a slum, parallel to the Savannah River, past the train tracks and under the highway overpass. There was no reason for a professional golfer's caddie to come here for cigarettes.

Ryals exited the car and walked to the shop. A young Middle Eastern man stood at the register behind plexiglass. He didn't react when Ryals showed his badge. Ryals asked if they had cameras. The man pointed; there was one behind him pointed at Ryals.

"How far back does the footage go?"

The young man shrugged. "Gotta ask the owner," he said. He wrote down the number for Ryals who took it and walked out. All that he wanted to see was confirmation that Willy had been here. He would go in and ask about security camera footage but first he drove around the block, first north, then south.

Four blocks one way were two strip clubs, and then began Broad Street's worse end. A block the other way was the Fox's Lair which to his surprise, looked fairly decent. A gem at the edge of the slums?

It was closed now but a sedan was parked outside. He went down and knocked. A woman past her prime in jeans and a large black t-shirt answered. Ryals showed her his badge. He asked if anyone was there who might have worked a week ago.

"I wasn't. Stevie was. He's in the back now," said the older woman, looking sideways at his badge. She was pleasant, her gray and russet hair was pinned behind her head.

Ryals stepped in and found the place looked and smelled far nicer than he remembered. Apparently upstairs was a Bed and Breakfast now. Or had it always been? Certainly, it had improved since his last visit.

"Do you have cameras here?"

"At the entrance," she said, pointing. The camera looked from the entrance toward the bar.

"Do you have footage from last Saturday?"

"We should. What do you need it for?" she asked, somewhat suspicious.

"Trying to piece together a timeline, is all. We don't believe any crime was committed here, but we're looking for someone who may have come here in the evening that day."

"Video goes to the office upstairs. If you'd like to check that first?"

He would, he said. He followed her into the back, dungeon-like office area, past a kitchen that smelled of grease and bleach.

In the office she retrieved video footage on a laptop.

"Disappears after today," she said. "So good thing you came in."

He chose the correct hour and watched as the video loaded. He let it play, directed her to fast forward ever few seconds. Eventually she let him control the keyboard.

Late in the evening, according to the footage, he spotted Willy Sharpe. The caddie walked in and sat at a bar, his head low. He ordered a drink.

Soon another man entered. He waited a while across the room, watching Willy from afar. He wore a hat. He approached Willy and sat beside him at the bar, his face always away from the camera.

The newcomer ordered only water. Willy hardly looked at him, but they appeared to speak. A bartender passed back and forth. Willy didn't seem friendly, and finally the man turned and left, leaving cash on the bar. He continued to look down, away from the camera, as if he knew where it was.

"Can I have a copy of this?" Ryals asked.

She gestured. "Help yourself." He figured out how to save it and send it to himself.

He didn't know what he had learned, but he had confirmed that Willy came here, and met with a man — was it the suspect captured on the cameras at the National? Ryals wasn't sure. The man in this video appeared thinner to Ryals. That could have just been due to his wardrobe.

Ryals took a picture of the video with his phone as well as the copy he emailed himself. He asked to speak to Steve, the bar back.

When he showed Stevie the picture on his phone, the kid squinted at it. "Eh, maybe. I sort of remember them. Yeah, I do."

"Do you remember anything about them, or their conversation?" Ryals asked. "Did you overhear anything?"

"Naw, too much noise in here, ya know. You know what I do remember, that guy there, the one that was left, I thought he was going to cry. Full grown man, looked like someone killed his dog or something."

"He did cry?"

"Naw, just looked like it. You get that look you know. Then he just left and didn't drink. I guess normally customers only cry after they drink all night," Stevie said, cracking a smile. Ryals just nodded. He took out his notebook and wrote those details down. He had more information, but he didn't really know anything new.

Outside clouds had moved in quickly, and rain was starting to fall. In the summer, you could almost set your watch by the regular thunderstorms that came through, rolling like a scheduled freight train and often as frightening. Thunder cracked and heavy, warm drops slapped down and then it was gone by evening as the humidity spiked all night.

Ryals drove away in the rain, up Broad Street and headed toward the station. Then he read a text message from Kate: ready for pickup. As if he was her chauffeur. He fumed for a moment, but could hear the lecture coming if he told her to catch a cab—which would take her a full hour, at least, in the end-of-tournament-day-madness.

He took the ramp up John C. Calhoun expressway toward Washington Road, knowing the traffic he would face.

He turned the radio on, found the sports station, and listed to the end-of-day Master's coverage. He wanted to know how Jonni was

doing, or how he had done. The rain was coming down harder now.
The station discussed other golfers. Ryals was surprised he recognized
more than a few of the names now. He was picking things up.

His phone rang. He answered. "It's Debbie," said the department secretary.

"What's up?"

"I called DHS like you asked." she said. His wipers were pumping,
it was hard to hear her. He put the phone to his ear. "They don't have
a Kate Chase, nor Katherine Chase working for us in a liaison capacity.
They said you must have the name wrong."

"What?"

"I called the Atlanta Office, who staff the Bush Field office here, I
guess." That was the Augusta Regional Airport. "They don't know her.
They called Washington, D.C., who told them the same thing."

Ryals was confused. He was trying to think of a response when
through the rear windshield he spotted it; no headlights, moving fast
at an odd angle, he had just a glimpse before he felt the impact and the
immediate lurch of the car and the wheel was yanked from his hands.
He felt the G force as the car spun out across lanes; he heard a screech
and saw the guard rail come up fast and then he slammed to a stop and
he saw mud and grass cover the windshield before he blacked out.

TWENTY-FOUR

Ryals woke up just seconds later, his neck and head aching and he tasted bile. He looked up and saw rain on the windshield, and through the orange flashing hazards of a parked vehicle, someone emerging and shouting at him. Asking if he was okay. He looked for his phone but he couldn't find it.

He felt around the seat and released his belt. He could see the front of his Charger was destroyed, likely totaled, but he was right side up. He landed in mud on the embankment. Hydroplaned out, spun a few times. Steam hissed from the radiator. Rain drummed on the roof. The airbag was deployed, and his face ached and burned from hitting it.

After a moment he released his belt, breathed, and emerged from the car. He was okay. Bruised, maybe. He didn't feel like anything was broken.

The woman who stopped stood at his window. She said she had dialed 911. Ryals opened the door.

"He just, just hit you and kept driving," she said, and he processed this a moment before realizing he needed his phone. "Don't worry," she said. "I called an ambulance, they'll be here in just a moment." There was little traffic headed north, but cars were slowing to see the accident.

"No," he said, slowly, still catching his breath. He could taste bitter adrenaline in the back of his throat. "I don't need that," and he went back to his car and found his phone. He wasn't sure who to call.

He called Angela. Told her he had been in an accident, but he was okay. She started to cry but he talked her down.

Then he called the station and reported the accident to the charge deputy. The deputy said he would have a unit by to pick him up "right away."

Ryals stood against the car in the rain. He had a rear camera but the car — as best he could remember — hit him in the rear quarter panel. He checked it, saw the dent, dark gray paint left behind. Was it an accident? That was just how highway patrol was trained to stop a car in a pursuit.

Ryals dipped his head and spit blood.

"We're on the lookout for a gray sedan with a dented panel — calling it a hit-and-run," The Sheriff said, Ryals drinking water across from him in his office. "So, was it?"

"I don't know," Ryals admitted. "Might have been," but he was thinking about the guy in the parking lot at lunch. The car could have been the same one. Had someone tried to intimidate him?

Or he was just paranoid and it was raining on the highway and people were morons.

Ryals was about to say something else to the Sheriff when Kate walked in. She'd been told. Ryals studied her. Her hair was wet, she still had her satchel, wrapped in a plastic bag.

"How are you?"

"I'm okay," he said. My radiator, not so much."

"Wasn't yours to begin with," Sheriff said with a weak smile. Parriot walked up behind, a bag over his shoulder, ready to leave. Ryals looked at him, then excused himself to talk with Parriot. "Car accidents aside, we're making progress."

As he left he looked at Kate. "How did your little project go?" he asked.

"No dice," she said, studying him. "You didn't get a good look?"

"Not really. Too busy hydroplaning."

"Cameras?"

"We checked. Can't see much. Water, angle. By the time he's ahead of the car I'm spinning so no plate."

He needed to talk with Parriot. Then he needed to speak to someone at DHS.

Kate sat in and listened as Ryals told Parriot what he'd found at the Fox's Lair, and opened the download link for the video.

"He was emotional?" Parriot asked.

"Said he looked that way," Ryals said, rubbing his neck. He had a headache like shrill ringing.

"We have at least one, perhaps two unknown agents at work; we know they planned and executed a multi-stage crime over several days. Which required significant advance intel work — knowing where Mr. Gordon was staying, et cetera," Kate said, not looking at either of them, her gaze distant as if thinking about something else entirely.

"Willy meeting an individual at the Fox Hole—"

"Fox's Lair," Ryals corrected.

"—right, tells us one very important thing."

"Which is?" Ryals head was still cloudy. He was having some trouble keeping up.

"Willy Sharpe wasn't a random target; whatever this crime, we can presume now that he or the Lombards are connected to it."

"That he was emotional — though it's only the impression of someone in a crowded space — could be significant. Perhaps there was pressure on Mr. Sharpe," Parriot mused, looking at his paperwork.

"Or he knew he was going to die," Kate offered. Ryals wasn't sure why she would say that.

"So then did he recognize the same individual at the course that night?"

"We can take measurements to compare height. Go to the Fox's Lair, then to the course. Measure head location on the camera."

Ryals was familiar with the technique, and it was tedious. She could do it. He just wanted a shot of whiskey and a powerful painkiller.

"Excellent," Parriot said. He jotted a note. "One of my team can do that tomorrow. We'll need to call ahead." Thank God, Ryals thought.

"Can we speak with Jonni tonight?" Kate asked.

"Why do you want to?" Ryals asked her.

"I think in light of what we know of Mr. Sharpe's whereabouts the night before, and possible emotional state, it's worth asking him. I know it's the night before the third round, but he may still be up for a while," she said.

"Will he play tomorrow" Ryals asked Kate.

"He made the cut," Kate answered, "Finished three over, and they confirmed it a few minutes ago." There was a spark of a smile behind her words — he wasn't sure if it was because she was happy for him, or happy that the Lombards weren't leaving the country tomorrow.

Ryals didn't want to, but she was right. Parriot grabbed his bag. "I'm crashing here tonight, thanks to the Chief's cramped guest room futon. So I'll be nearby. I may go check out the Fox's Lair this evening. If that's acceptable," he asked Ryals.

"Go for it," Ryals said. "I'll rally and speak with the Lombards."

Parriot departed and Ryals and Kate were left to study the room. He realized both looked and smelled like rain, he the worse. He kept a jacket here, comb, all that he needed to sharpen up. He was reluctant to go to the hotel, but the alternative would mean waiting twenty-four hours.

"Let's go," he said. "But you'll have to drive."

As she drove he was quiet, letting his double-dose of Tylenol slowly ease the throbbing in his temple. His neck was tight now as well as his lower back. Angela called twice, he texted her he was fine and that he'd be home after work.

Kate drove with both hands on the wheel. Her posture was perfect, and she was alert. She continued to irritate him. He confronted her with the call regarding DHS. It was fuzzy.

"I can forward the email from my office," she said. "I provided it to the chief."

"You may need to send it again," he said, reading her expression, which was inscrutable. She was a young woman with an agenda. He didn't know what to think about her, really, and wasn't sure he wanted to dig into it.

They arrived at the hotel. True to the southern rhythm, the storm had passed and the air smelled of ozone and wet pine.

In the hotel he rang Jonni's room from the front desk. His father answered. Ryals could hear his disappointment — no, aggravation — when he announced himself, all the more so when he requested they come to the lobby.

Martin asked instead for them to come upstairs.

Soon the four of them sat in Jonni's room. Martin was in excellent spirits, talking animatedly about his son's playing, and how much better he would do the next two days, now that he knew the course, and had momentum, and had the crowd behind him. It was hard not to share his enthusiasm. Even through his thick accent they could hear how proud he was of his son.

"You're playing against odds, Jonni," he said.

Jonni greeted them with a half-smile, which for Jonni was animated.

"I know it must be important to focus right now. We want to check in. Ask a few questions."

"Of course," Martin Lombard said, sitting opposite them on the suite sofa as Ryals took a chair and Kate sat on the windowsill. Martin eyed her, trying to figure out why she was there and who she was. Jonni met their gaze, and did not seem disheartened by the visit. Ryals thought his father's enthusiasm lifted Jonni's spirits.

"It may seem like nothing new to you, but we're tracking a few things. We know Mr. Sharpe met with someone, and that perhaps he was disturbed by that meeting. I can't say much more, but it was here in town the night before the crime occurred. Has anything come to mind since we last talked?"

Martin shook his head. "No. We said what we know. Willy drank, sure. He gambled? Sure. He was an Afrikaans farm boy. He wasn't a criminal."

"Do you know anyone he may have planned to meet in Augusta?"

"I just can't think of anyone. Of course, the caddie circles, the same comings-and-goings at golf tourneys all over the world, you see some of the same people. Surely he knew some people who would be here. I don't know why he would plan to meet them, not before Jonni played. He would be devoted to the upcoming tournament."

"You live in Hoedspruit, right?" Kate asked.

"That's correct."

"Get down to Joburg much?" She asked.

"Just occasionally. Use the airport plenty."

"You stay over at the City Lodge there?" She asked. Ryals just looked at her.

"I have before maybe once or twice, early flight but usually we drive right in. Only do it if someone's covering the bill."

Kate studied him, but her look was kind. "You always travel together?"

"Usually. Jon's done one, maybe two tourneys alone with Willy."

"Pops usually travels," Jonni said. "He doesn't let me go around the world alone."

"Of course," Kate said. "Augusta is a long way from Hoedspruit. But I guess Mr. Sharpe did it alone." Jonni nodded somberly.

Kate straightened up, took out a notepad. "Anyone ever approach you, Mr. Lombard, in South Africa or somewhere else to discuss smuggling of goods out of the country?"

He straightened up and looked at her. As did Ryals, who decided that her gumption had finally gone a bit too far—the line that she had crossed was a half mile behind her. He gave her a sharp look. She nodded, tucked away her pencil and notepad, and leaned back, done with her questioning.

"We're still exploring many angles," Ryals said.

Jonni was troubled, his brow twisted, and Ryals saw that Kate continued to study the player. Ryals felt his headache growing worse. He could feel his neck and spine tightening with every moment he sat leaning forward in this chair, and he wanted today to be over. To him this had been a wasted visit.

"We're here to help, but Jonni needs to rest," Martin said. Ryals rose, shook their hands, and stressed,

"Forgive the intrusion, we want to figure this out."

"Absolutely," Martin said.

Ryals waited until they were in the car and away from the crowded lobby before he said anything.

"Listen," he growled, ready to unload on her, but before he could say anything, she calmly put her hands on her knees and looked at him.

Always cheery. One of those kinds of people who couldn't be deterred and never got moody.

"Mr. Hall, can I buy you a beer?"

He blinked. "What?" He asked. "No — I want you to explain to me why you're asking questions about Jo—jo—"

"Joburg. Johannesburg. Yes, I'll explain. I think it should be over a beer. You've had a hell of a day. Besides I'm famished."

Soon they at a local Mexican restaurant called Veracruz a mile away. It was noisy tonight with the Masters traffic. They found two spots at the bar on the end, and everyone was talking loudly or watched the replays on TV. Everyone was drinking. Kate ordered two tall beers. They came fast and cold. She downed the chips. He had no idea where the calories went. She was like a hummingbird, he decided. Active lifestyle, active metabolism.

Kate nearly downed hers as Ryals looked at his beer. He felt himself growing impatient, though, as she perused the menu. He regretted coming here. He should have kicked her to the Sheriff. He had beer at home, and a recliner.

"Today wasn't a hit and run," she said.

"You care to explain?" He asked her. She set her glass down and laid her hands flat on the bar.

"I spend much of my down time, you could call it, in southern Africa. My employer knows about it, but isn't really interested in what I'm trying to do. See, up north, in say, Kenya, the State Department has a significant interest in elephant ivory, in poaching. You may have read, five years back, that a GPS transmitter hidden in a tusk was tracked over the border to a Boko Haram militia hideout, and ultimately to Kony himself."

Of course Ryals had not.

"Now, what do you know about rhino horn?" She asked, munching her chips loudly with her hand cupped to collect the dripping salsa. It was loud in here but her voice was perfectly calibrated, somehow, to cut right through the noise and yet still isolate their conversation.

"Nothing," Ryals said, eagerly drinking his beer and feeling suddenly very tired. He thought this young woman might be crazy. What was he doing waltzing her around his investigation?

Who was she?

"Gram for gram it's the most valuable material on the planet," she continued. "More than heroin, cocaine, gold even. For no good reason, of course, but that's beside the point. In South Africa, rhino poaching is rampant. Southeast Asian syndicates are behind much of the hunting and trafficking, hidden by many degrees of separation. There is of course enormous money in the horn trade. But the State Department isn't interested in South Africa, neither is my employer. They claim there is no evidence of connections to terrorism, but obviously that's wrong. For one thing, there are terror cells all over the country, and they never engage in terrorist acts in areas that can provide horn. Rhino horn is plentiful — or was — and so it's a local cash crop. I spend plenty of time off working with counter poaching groups and nonprofits, interviewing poachers and looking for evidence of what I know is really going on: terrorists are making money from poaching rhinos. No question. It's just a matter of exposing it."

Ryals looked at his beer and tried to understand what was happening here. The bartender checked in on them and Kate ordered another round. Someone came out of the bathroom near them and Kate hid her face subtly for a moment and said nothing. She glanced around the room. She had said 'employer,' which sounded strange for some reason.

"I don't follow," he finally said. "Rhino horn? What does Homeland Security have to do with South Africa? With animal parts?" He really felt tired now.

"I never said I worked for DHS," she said. "The Sheriff said that."

"What about the letter?" He asked.

"What about it?"

"Is it real?"

"It's really a letter. It's really from DHS. My people can get their people to write a letter."

She had a confident smile, and watched the TV before looking at Ryals. In this light her eyes were bright and she looked suddenly older and more mature than before. Still just a kid, but he saw in her something competent. He also noticed for the first time a significant scar against the side of her neck.

"Who do you work for?" Ryals asked. "DHS says that they don't know you. I'd be justified to report you. I'm considering it."

"I'm an interested party, and I work for a government agency. I have permission to pursue this investigation," she added, then paused as the new beers arrived, "but this isn't strictly an official trip."

"CIA?"

"Something like that," she answered.

"So you're a spook."

"I don't think I come across as spooky," she answered dryly.

"I need more than that."

"In Southern Africa I operate under U.S. Fish and Wildlife. Who, by the way, do phenomenal work. In fact, DHS has recently opened an office to support the same wildlife protection and counter-trafficking mandate. I work out of various consulates and move between these agencies. So, for all intents and purposes, I can claim DHS."

"But you're not with them."

"No, not technically. But I am here to help, Detective."

Ryals watched the restaurant and looked for some of his coworkers and tried to remember if he had picked this place or if she had. He felt like he was being pranked by the boys at work. He expected to see them raising a glass from a table across the room. They didn't. He didn't know anyone here.

He looked at Kate again. He shook his head.

"Listen," he said. "Just because you don't get the information you want doesn't mean that someone is lying. No one has to be lying for someone to be uncomfortable with your questions. Investigations require patience and take time. There's not a bogeyman behind every corner. This guy drank and gambled. It's between the lines of everything they say. That's what they're hiding. They don't want to speak ill of the dead. And Martin doesn't want his son filled with doubt while he's out there competing. I don't know who you are, or what you're doing here, but you're not a detective and you're affecting this investigation."

"While this case may be of national agency interest, I'm personally invested."

"You're some kind of cowgirl," he said. "Running around the world."

"Actually my job is pretty boring. My desk, as if I actually had one, covers Southern Africa. I love animals. I would have been a vet if I hadn't studied political science. Absolutely. Probably be working in the field right now helping injured impala. I'm an admitted crusader. I prefer to be in the field."

Ryals tried to study her. He held his wallet. He just needed the bartender. He didn't intend to finish the second drink, which he hadn't even ordered.

"What does any of this have to do with my case?" He asked.

"Trafficking is trafficking," she said. "It may be rhino horn today, but once there's a smuggling pipeline opened up, everything flows through it. Children, drugs, weapons. These are well financed enterprises and backed by international syndicates who are in it for business. They are a business and they are constantly looking for new ways to make a profit. It's very, very hard on the ground to get a glimpse into their organizations at a high level. I can interview a poacher but he doesn't know anything. He was recruited by a friend, who was recruited by a friend and on and on. You hope to get lucky — sometimes you are when they're carrying a rocket launcher you can trace."

Good lord, Ryals thought, finally catching the eye of the bartender. This girl talked a lot. His vision grew blurry.

"Over the past year I've heard stories about some of these syndicates going higher up the food chain. They bribe government officials, and they corrupt legitimate businesses. Not just in South Africa, of course. But I met the cousin — stay with me here — of a professional rugby player. World Cup champion. Who said his cousin was in trouble, got involved with the wrong people. Said his cousin confided in him that he had been approached, and offered a substantial sum of money to use his access in and out of the country as an athlete — they're never searched or stopped— to smuggle stolen microchips out of Taiwan. That may seem innocuous, until we explored further — and found two charter jet companies out of Europe that made back door deals with athletic clubs to put extra bags into hidden compartments. Add to that corrupt low-level airport employees, we discovered two major trafficking operations. We discovered two — we don't know how many we hadn't discovered."

"Athletes would risk their career for this?" Ryals said, finding himself interested. He held back his money and put his hands on the table, seeing as how he had a little beer left anyway.

"One horn could fit into a gym bag, and that could be worth a million. These aren't the Michael Jordans of the world. These athletes aren't all sponsored. Money talks. But it's not always athletes. Sometimes it's part of their team. A coach, an assistant."

"A caddie."

"Precisely, maybe."

"So that's what you think happened here?"

"I have no clue. I heard about your case; everyone over there is talking about it. Virtuoso kid in the USA playing golf and his caddie gets murdered. So I'm thinking, maybe. And if so, if so," she sipped her water. "I might have a chance, on US soil, to get a glimpse into one of these organizations and maybe even offer asylum in exchange for information. Or something. But I don't want to get ahead of myself," she said.

"So why do you think they're still here?"

"Willy Sharpe isn't the only piece to the puzzle. This was a public slaying. It was meant to send a message. To who, is the question. Someone across the world watching? Maybe. Or, someone here, right now. Someone has something that the bad guys want, and they mean to get it before the tournament is over."

Ryals still felt sleepy, and dizzy, but what she said kind of made sense. At least in as much as she didn't sound crazy by the end of it — except how fast she talked — and this very well could be a theory that explained what had happened.

Of course, if she was right, she didn't seem to have anything that would help his case other than a good story.

He chewed on his cheek and thought that he was way out of his depth.

"Where did you get the scar?" He asked, referring to her neck.

She removed her jacket and pulled her collar down, revealing her shoulder and clavicle and several scars there. "Adolescent lion; the mother was poached, had her paws hacked off. Little guy was upset — little I mean, weighed almost as much as me and didn't like me trying to help him." She put her jacket back on. He had to admit he didn't know many people with lion scars. It was maybe the first thing about her he was able to verify.

"If this is true," he said, "What do you recommend? I don't see how it helps me catch the killer. In fact, if what you're saying is true, this is some international organization and the killer is far away."

"Maybe," she said. "But two things. One, I think Jonni Lombard knows more than he's telling you. He and Willy were confidants,"

"And two?"

"Two, maybe they're gone, maybe not. You were hit today. I don't think it was an accident. Do you? I think you were targeted. Were they trying to kill you, was it a warning? I don't know. We have no idea how many people were involved besides."

"I don't know."

"Neither do I. Maybe Jonni isn't into it, maybe he's young, and if he was approached by a criminal organization, he might be scared and, if we play it just right, willing to talk. The way he's acting, though, I think there is still pressure on him, and I think it's up close, somewhere."

"And in two days everyone leaves," Ryals said.

Kate nodded. "And the killers likely will too. Doesn't seem — again based on his demeanor, the fact that Sharpe wasn't happy — that the bad guys are getting what they want. If they were, they'd be quiet, invisible and you would be at a movie with your daughter."

"I'm here to help. Help me keep a low profile, and I'll do all I can."

"I see," he said, trying to think if he really did or didn't. He needed a walk. No, a long night's sleep.

"So what's next?" he asked her, realizing he was nearly through his second beer and he was feeling much more relaxed now. He might even order food.

"Next," She said, opening her menu, "we keep digging, and if we feel desperate, I think we try to force the bad guys out into the open, like park rangers do with poachers."

"How does that work?" He asked.

"I have an idea," she answered.

Kate dropped off Ryals at home. He needed Tylenol and lots of sleep. Angela waited for him; she wrapped her arms around him and had hot tea ready for him and an ice pack. He didn't need any of it but he accepted it and after assuring her he was fine and taking a long, hot shower he laid down and hoped that most of today had just been a dream.

TWENTY-FIVE

Saturday
Round 3

Jonni was up well before dawn. He twitched with nerves as if ants crawled up and down his skin. He held his putter between his knees. Buster told him yesterday that when he was back in his room he should close his eyes and imagine each hole, glide his way through it, going over every detail so that when he got there it felt more familiar to him and less daunting. He did that now, but he didn't close his eyes. He had the TV on, no volume, and there were more famous replays, but he didn't need to watch them now. He needed quiet.

He didn't expect to make it to today. He had done so by one stroke, which wasn't much. Something happened, though, on the 17th and 18th holes yesterday. For a moment, for half of an hour, perhaps, the world had faded away, he'd felt the gravity pull of those holes, and he played golf like he loved it.

He could play like that again. He had to. It was the only thing he wanted to be good at, and he didn't want it taken away from him.

He was dressed and ready and soon his father would knock on his door, and security would be waiting for them downstairs, and they would go meet Buster. He was cold in the room; his leg bounced in part to warm him up. Soon he'd be in the sun and feel the humidity and heat, and he couldn't wait.

He was paired today with Brooks Koepka, the American player from Florida. He was PGA Tour Player of the Year in 2018. The year before that he'd won the U.S. Open. He was just a couple of years older than Jonni.

For the first time this week, he was excited.

Kate was waiting outside when Ryals, feeling extremely hungover from the accident, medication and beer; feeling sore and a little bit cranky, walked out of his house to the car. The air was cool, the dew was heavy on the grass. The weather today would be perfect. He was instructed not to drive, but told the Sheriff he wanted a vehicle ready for him. He'd need it, and he would be fine behind the wheel. Climbing into her rental sedan now, he wasn't so sure.

He hadn't yet processed anything she'd told him the night before. Was she telling the truth? Was she crazy? He wasn't sure. Yet here she was at his house, picking him up as if she was his partner. He didn't ever work with a partner. He preferred to work alone. Besides, the Richmond County budget wouldn't accommodate one.

He wanted his pain, totaled car and stress-filled week to be worth something. Before they drove out, Angela came running with a small bag for him. She hugged him.

"You should eat something," was all she said. He checked — she'd made him an egg sandwich.

"Here's what I'm thinking," Kate said. "The fact that Jonni is playing, and that the whole world is watching, is something we can use to our advantage. Either the killers or their representatives are on the course or they are watching."

"So," Ryals said, digging in to the sandwich, and finding himself hungry.

"So, if they think Jonni's made a deal with us, or that he's talking to us, they'll get angry. Presumably."

"And do what?"

"Hard to say, but it might force them into the open," she said, her short nails tapping the steering wheel.

"If they think Jonni's betrayed them, they might try to kill him," Ryals said. "They've done it twice."

"They might, yes. Which is why he has security."

"So you want to use him as bait?"

"We have a short window to draw the bad guys out. We have to be proactive."

"What do we do? To make it look like we've made a deal."

"I'm not sure. It may be enough that we walk with Martin Lombard for a while. I presume you can't let him off the course to spend a couple of hours in the station."

"No, not a chance."

"We'll have to devise a plan. Assuming they are watching."

Listening to her, Ryals now felt no longer inadequate, no longer in the dark, but for a moment inspired.

Her idea was foolish, though. He would be reamed out if the Sheriff saw him on TV walking around the course during the tournament.

"No," he said. "Walking with him is not an option."

"Something more subtle?" She said. "We must assume they're watching closely. What if we simply accept something from Mr. Lombard. Tell him to give us something. A phone number. Take it from him on TV. They would see that. It might be enough that they would at least approach him." Jonni had been reluctant to talk to him. The killers had made a public show, and responding to them in a public way could call their bluff.

"I don't like it," Ryals said. Then admitted, "but time is against us."

"And," Kate said, her tongue in her cheek as she turned down the highway, forcing the gold morning sunlight bright in their eyes, "the cameras aren't always on him. We'd have to make sure that they are. How do we do that?"

"We hope he starts doing well," Ryals said. "Then the world will be watching."

There was a hush over the station when Ryals and Kate arrived. He learned quickly it was due to a visit from the Mayor, who was in the Sheriff's office with the door closed.

"Is that bad?" Kate asked.

"I'm sure it's not to congratulate us on our quick work," Ryals said, watching from his desk before Parriot waved him over.

Parriot had progress to report. He'd brought two boxes of Krispy Kreme donuts to the station. Ryals took one self-consciously, glancing at Kate, and sat back holding it while Parriot briefed them.

Parriot pulled out a few pages of scribbled notes on a yellow-legal pad. He paced. Ryals yawned and felt his neck contract in pain like a tight rubber band threatening to snap. He should probably be in a neck brace. "I don't have much. No calls to Sharpe's room phone. I'm sure Investigator Hall, you knew that much. We've tried several cab companies to see if one picked up Mr. Sharpe the night after he met at the Fox's Lair. One — City Cab — has a record of a pickup a block from there, with a return to Mr. Sharpe's hotel. Which confirms the timeline, and lets us know whoever he met didn't offer him a ride.

"Based on the location, we assume this was not a chance encounter. We do not know that for sure. Possibly Sharpe wanted a drink and didn't want to be seen having one. In that case, someone would have followed him to the bar." He pulled out two photographs with notes on them. "I went last night and measured the height against the wall to have some metrics on the unknown individual."

"Did you do the same at the National?" Ryals asked.

"Didn't need to. I had a frame of reference on the footage based on a parked Club Car. From the wheel height, according to the online specs I was able to measure the height of suspect on the National security videos. Considering also the other physical attributes — basic build, skin color, drab dark clothes — I can say with confidence we are looking at the same individual in both locations. Both measure five foot ten," he held up a picture of the security camera footage from the Fox's Lair, a picture of himself on the cameras in the same position beside it. He had some math and the height scribbled on it.

Ryals studied the first. The man in the hat. Stocky. Wide shoulders, thick neck. He remembered the man in the car yesterday. Thinner, dark green hat. He didn't think it was the same person.

If the hit wasn't an accident, he was being followed — he wondered for how long.

Which meant — what? They were waiting for the right moment to hit him? It could have just been an accident.

It wasn't what he expected from a hit and run. Ryals was certain he'd been targeted.

Ryals heard a peal of thunder far off. He remembered Allison mentioning the rooms were reserved for Club Members. He doubted that inquiry would be well received. Especially after what Ryals learned from Ingot. Ryals didn't speak up, though or argue with Kate. He just reminded himself to step out of the way in the event of political fallout. "At one time," Parriot said, "Only ten percent of the club was allowed to be from Augusta, according to the internet. Is this still the case?" he asked, to no one, apparently.

"There's is something I'd like to suggest we consider in regards to how the suspect breached security and accessed the course. There are two bungalows and ninety-four rooms at the National. They are reserved for club members. I am certain it is a very tricky proposition to find out who was staying there the night of the murder."

"That's an understatement," Ryals said.

"If we learn anything more about the perpetrator or perpetrators, we can go to a judge to support a request of flight and rental car records, but to be honest, if the suspect or suspects came from Atlanta, there's no point in even looking unless we have a suspect identified. That said, we have asked for a list of any males renting cars out of Augusta the day Willy Sharpe arrived; he arrived via Augusta Regional himself. Assuming he was followed in, we can see who else came in that day and rented a vehicle. The rental offices provided us with twenty-eight names and numbers to look into."

"They just gave that information to you?" Kate asked.

"They did."

"Twenty-eight is worth investigating," Ryals said.

"Indeed. Starting in ten minutes, before people shut off their cell phones for the day, we're going to begin calling the provided numbers, and we may be doing some hotel visits. Time is ticking."

Ryals offered his investigative team. "They're standing by to help."

"Good. We'll start with calls, then we'll be knocking on doors."

"I'll do my share," he said. "I just need to find what vehicle they've made available for me."

Ryals was impressed. Parriot might actually be getting somewhere with his data. It seemed a much surer shot than Kate's imaginative intrigue.

The meeting broke as the Mayor, a tall, black man with a signature look in a dark suit and a blue tie, walked through the bullpen of cubicles and detective's desks and lieutenant's offices and out the front door. The Sheriff came out and nodded to Ryals who went into his office.

"Shut the door," The Sheriff said. Ryals did.

"You won't believe what I just heard," The Sheriff said, more smiling than irritated, though he was shaking his head. "He thinks it would be better if we never solved this case."

"What?"

"Said it would add to the mystique of the National, books would be written, people will talk about it, it would invite more tourism, haunted tours — he had a list. If we solve it, he claimed, people will just forget it and it will be a stain on our heritage. If it's unsolved, it's a mystery, and 'that's a good thing.'"

"You're kidding. He can't advise us not to pursue this investigation."

"Oh, he was careful not to advise anything. He said he was just musing, you and me, he said."

"Is pressure coming from the National?"

"Directly or indirectly, I'm certain," The Sheriff said, tapping a carved and painted wood duck that ornamented his desk.

"He came in person," Ryals observed.

"Yes he did," The Sheriff agreed.

"He might have been advising us for our own sake," the Sheriff said. "It's something to consider."

"Are you giving me advice, now?"

"No. I am not. I'm only informing you."

I'm down the rabbit hole, Ryals thought.

Jonni felt claustrophobic. He sat in the waiting room with Buster, his tee time today at 10:15 a.m. Twenty minutes out. After ten minutes of sitting he took a walk out the back and into the shade of the magnolia trees. A few minutes after Buster emerged after him and placed a stick of gum in his mouth. He offered a piece to Jonni, who declined.

"I don't chew on TV of course," he said. "Used to dip. Did it for fifteen years before doc told me I was headed for gum cancer so I quit." It was the smallest of small talk but Jonni found that Buster was a calming presence. He liked the guy. He began to feel he might miss Buster after the weekend.

"You're gonna make your mark today, kid. I can see it."

"Yeah," Jonni said, entirely unconvinced.

"Do you realize what you did yesterday? Up to this moment?" Buster said, standing alongside Jonni and looking up to the treetops. "Be proud, and build on your success. You know once when I was just a kid it was my dream to play pro. I took lessons. I tried. I love playing. One day I realized, I just wasn't good enough. It wasn't meant to be. You, though.

You made it to the third round of the toughest golf competition in the world. One percent of one percent of everyone that picks up a club doesn't even come close. You've already made it to heaven, kid. Now you just gotta dance with the angels."

Jonni watched the sunlight through the magnolias. Beetles of some kind jumped from leaf to leaf. He could smell the flowers. Jonni breathed in smells that were foreign but that somehow also smelled of home. Gold mist swirled in a prelapsarian mist.

Jonni was meant to play the Masters — not just play. He was meant to compete. That's what Willy told him, one week ago before he left for the airport to come to Augusta.

Jonni smiled at Buster, the biggest he could manage. "Yeah," was all he could really say, but he nodded. Buster slapped him on the back.

"Let's go show Arnold Palmer who's boss," Buster said. They walked inside together.

TWENTY-SIX

Ryals dropped Kate off on his way to the first hotel on the list. He was given six, starting out in Evans, a forty minute drive from the course. It was likely pointless, as anyone who had flown in for the tournament would be at the tournament, but he had no choice but to try while the patrons remained in town. Ryals had a list of addresses and names and started at the top.

Today the sky was clear blue with porcelain clouds edged with silver moving past like herds of floating cattle. Ryals remembered a morning, some summers back when Angela was in elementary school and they went to the park and did that thing where you look for shapes in the clouds. She saw everything, imagined everything. She was far more creative than he had ever been. He saw turtles.

Perhaps Kate was that way too. Seeing more than he could. Maybe he was meant to be little more than a beat cop. Knocking on doors.

He found no one at the first three hotels he visited. Those visits brought him to lunchtime. He left messages with the desk for each guest to call him when they returned.

He went — as if on autopilot — to a drive through window at a fast food joint, but found he wasn't hungry. He drove right through.

The next address on his list wasn't a hotel but a residence in a Northwest subdivision. Ryals knocked and found two men there, one Australian, one Chinese. Ryals stepped in and spoke with them. They were both attorneys, they were the odd men out in a group of six that rotated to the tournament on four badges.

Ryals realized quickly how out of his depth he was. He didn't know how to ask them at all about international smuggling or figure out if they were part of a Southeast Asian crime syndicate.

Focus, he reminded himself. The crime was local. He pressed them for timelines, alibis, listened for motive.

He walked through the steps, jotted his notes.

There was nothing here. The men had alibis, and whether it was the table of liquor, the guy in his pajamas or the empty pizza boxes, these guys didn't strike him as master criminals. They were also lawyers, which they had authenticated with business cards and websites. When they discovered why Ryals was there, they were more than happy to help.

It's a local crime, he reminded himself as he walked back to his car. A murder is a murder is a murder. Motive, opportunity, and all basic principles of an investigation still applied no matter how complex or grand the scope of the criminal activity.

He plugged the next address into his phone and drove to it, his mind anywhere but on the road. Which was how he didn't realize the next address was Jonni Lombard's hotel until he pulled into the parking lot.

He paused there a moment and looked at it from the same space he'd parked in yesterday with Kate, right up front.

What were the chances? He wondered. Fairly good, he thought. This was a decent sized hotel in close proximity to the course.

Inside he phoned the guest on Parriot's list. There was no answer. He asked for the room number; the manager offered to take him up but Ryals said no. He only wanted to knock on the door and be sure.

He climbed up the stairs, his knees stiff. He needed an SUV or a truck to drive. Twenty-eight years in squad cars, issued cars, driving constantly, climbing in and out, sitting at his desk that was too low for his knees in an uncomfortable chair was catching up to him. A long career that began as a Sheriff's Deputy hadn't turned him into a seasoned gunslinger; instead he was a tired, underpaid paper-pusher and door-knocker with knees that were getting bad and whose gun saw less use than his white-out.

He checked the printed list again and knocked at the guests's door. He saw someone down the hall return to another room in gym clothes. Ryals knocked again, and hearing nothing turned to leave. Then he paused. From within the room — maybe — there was a slight sound. A shift of weight, or slight scoot on a bed, a foot on the carpet, something indistinct. Just air turning on?

He moved to the door, slowly, and listened. He looked at the peephole, saw only light. He was nearly against the door and completely still. He listened to the air on one side, feeling fatigue.

Then he felt something, for the first time, something as if it had been here the whole time, perhaps behind the drifting clouds, or their shape he hadn't been able to see. He felt, or he imagined evil on the other side of the door. He could fathom a dark presence, something awful that had descended to Augusta in the form of a quality of criminal; a presence like a wolf on the prowl in a neighborhood, a rabid coyote in his backyard. This entire crime, this enterprise behind it was sinister. Ryals felt the malice and darkness behind heinous criminal acts before. What he sensed now he had never experienced before.

He listened. Was there indeed a presence in the room, or was it just fatigue and his body aching and his imagination?

The feeling dissipated. Ryals looked up at the door, saw no change in the light in the peephole and heard nothing inside. He had waited at least five minutes in the silence of the hallway.

He returned to the elevators, feeling a strong sense that the other side of a door was as close as he would ever come to the criminals who murdered a caddie at the Augusta National. He wasn't sure why. They were smarter then he was; they had a plot and were several steps ahead of him. They could see everything while he was in the dark.

Back at his car, he felt humid wind coming from the river, and it was comforting. He climbed into his cruiser and began to back out of his space when he saw a small folded paper under the wiper on his windshield. He put the vehicle in park and stepped out to fetch it. He looked around the lot, found no one lurking in a car. He read it in the driver's seat:

> *$50,000, paid over time - untraceable - to drop case. Leave note on car anytime if interested.*

This was new. Ryals read it over and over again, then he looked around the parking lot once more, but nothing stood out as suspicious. Maybe, he thought, Sam Ingot was right. He heard something like echoes down the great dark halls of the old institutions, the shadows hung beneath the magnolias, their waxy, heavy leaves now joined overhead on the long drive to the clubhouse that Roberts and Jones built. The whisper of the founders, the titanic forces at work, pushing and pulling.

Ryals knew he wouldn't spot them but he turned in all directions again. They were watching him. Some they. Anywhere he went, whatever he did. Leave it on the car, anytime. They would see it, anytime.

The specter and the darkness.

Then there was Jonni. Ryals couldn't find a way to reconcile these two ideas. Ingot's story was compelling. One wanted to believe it was true, wanted to see the bones in the foundation. How was the kid a pawn in that, though, when the evidence showed Willy meeting someone else?

Was it possible, Ryals wondered, feeling the air conditioner blow cold and his skin tighten, that the National was fixing the entire game? That there was a game behind the game?

He looked around again, hoping to find someone watching him, perhaps the man from lunch, hunched down in his car, his hat low. Or perhaps it was better that he saw no one.

He would bring the note to the station. He handled it carefully, finding a notepad to slide it into to preserve any evidence. He doubted he would find anything.

As he pulled out, checking every car in the lot in the fierce, bright midday sun, he wondered less about who had written it, and more about what would happen when they knew he hadn't accepted the offer.

Allison alternated between mineral water, Vitamin Water and Tums. If she ate she knew she would slow down.

She retreated to the clubhouse and her office and watched the tournament continue to unfold from the operations center, checking the screen with an electronic readout of the course leaderboard, watching the ticking numbers indicate steady progress, and another set of numbers that counted how many patrons were on the course or in the shop and which competitors had departed or were arriving.

For a while it had felt to her as if there lay a pallor over the tournament, like a morning fog that did not dissipate. Indeed Amen Corner, the lower south side of the course, had once been a swamp, and on spring mornings often hung silky mist in the hours before sunlight, a reminder of its pre-history.

The Director had met several times with the board members, and had entertained visits from several high-ranking club members. She sat in on a few of those meetings. Most were encouragement, questions, offers of support. The murder seemed to be less important to supporters, patrons and members since the tournament was underway without further incident, with even the press starting to lose interest in it. Still, a couple of them just wanted assurance, as one member put it, "that there ain't some other badger in that hole about to bite our goddamn hand."

She agreed. What was at first an apparent suicide now perpetuated into something more complicated, but so far the investigation hadn't yielded anything that she had been made aware of. Allison liked control, and she didn't like surprises. She suspected there was something else down that hole, and she didn't want to find out the wrong way.

It could be disastrous PR. She had spoken to the National's head publicist and marketing department. She shared with the director her fear that the investigation could drag on for months or even years. They might continue to face scrutiny. There was no hoping the crime would fade into obscurity; while no one had leaked a picture of the caddie's body hanging over Amen Corner, she was sure it was inevitable. That image would forever be tied to the tournament and the club. Nothing else on the course was made public, no gate was open, no interview given or picture allowed between the end of one tournament and the beginning of the next. The Masters press must — and always did — carry water for three-hundred and fifty-nine days.

Between tournaments the National members expected privacy, anonymity and elite exclusivity. A great weight was over her shoulders to ensure the Club did not fail to meet those expectations.

A few years back, before Allison's time, protestors took to parking lots nearby to decry the men-only membership policy. The club changed that policy (because it should, not because protestors said so), but the membership did not appreciate the attention. They were content for the Augusta National not to appear in the press at all between tournaments.

Allison's earpiece buzzed. "Mr. Lawrence," her assistant announced. "He's down here."

"Send him up, " Allison said. She checked her watch. She had twenty minutes before she was due to meet with the director again. She watched a pair tee-off from her window. From her window she thought it was Vijay Singh and Patrick Reed paired. She hoped Vijay had not complained about his pairing. If he had, she hadn't heard it. Lawrence arrived at her door.

"How's it so far today?" She asked, carefully placing an empty bottle into a small recycling bin beside her desk. Lawrence wasn't always clean shaven — in the winter months he sported a neatly trimmed beard — but today he was. He looked as if he was in the military again.

"Two thrown out. One daytime badge, drunk. One was on a lifetime patron's badge. Friend from out of town."

Allison shook her head. It was tragic to lose a lifetime badge, if it came to that. It would fall to her to deliver news to the badge holders. When she had to do it, she felt it was like telling someone they had inoperable cancer.

"You have the details," he said.

"Lombard security?"

"No complaints. They're blending in. They've noticed nothing out of the ordinary."

Occasionally they offered extra security to a golfer — depending on his hot streak — and they sometimes provided it for dignitaries attending. Of course Tiger Woods had to have a security detail, especially on his return to the game following the hiatus. The Pinkertons were glorified ushers now, not the investigative, presidential-level detail they had once been. That was how the National preferred it. Wrongdoers, like the drunk and disorderly, were simply escorted politely out. The National needed no more security than that and certainly didn't want to give the impression that it was necessary. As a former director had put it, "everything facilitates the experience between the patron and the player. The only thing that should get between them is a yellow rope."

"How is he?" She asked.

"What do you mean?"

"Jonni Lombard. How is he?"

"I haven't checked in on him, just his security detail. I believe he's played through Two now." This murder had happened on her watch, and she felt responsible for Jonni Lombard. She had barely spoken to him yet, but a great deal of her mental energy was devoted to his well-being as their guest.

"Anything from Richmond County?" she asked.

"Nothing today. His federal liaison, the young woman, is here again walking the course. My guys say she's keeping a low profile. I've continued to cooperate but I don't believe they know much more yet."

Allison nodded and looked just outside the clubhouse in the shadows of the live oak and great magnolia, where families of club members stood or sat in chairs, isolated from the crowds.

"I hope to God they solve this thing," she said. "After the tournament is over…" she trailed off.

"The killer will be long gone," he said.

"Yes. That too." She was thinking of the news cycle.

"You think the Chairman really wants it solved?" Lawrence asked, his tell-tale — or diplomatic — wry smile appearing.

"Why do you ask that?"

Lawrence didn't respond.

She truly didn't know. The Chairman was a kind man. He was thoughtful and honest. But he was a shark when he needed to be. She couldn't imagine there was a consensus amongst the board members or club members of anything except a desire for the killer to be caught and prosecuted.

Conspiracy theorists would claim that the men and women at that level knew all of the answers already. Allison didn't think so.

She turned again and looked out past the first tee at the rest of the course, a vivid green with patches of pink and white, and alive with pastel people moving along the rope lines.

Kate stood against the rope watching Jonni Lombard. She was learning plenty of the nuances of play, both from observation and listening to nearby conversations and asking questions of other nearby patrons, as she had yesterday. All were eager to talk about the mechanics of the game or the stats of each player. Patrons watched with excitement and etiquette.

Of course some whispered about the murder. She listened closely to those. No one knew anything and wild theories were shared.

Though she had never wanted to attend a golf tournament she did enjoy sports, and it was hard not to wait with bated breath to see the drop of the ball. When Jonni prepared to swing she was afraid to blink. This was not like basketball, where players could take shot after shot, trying over and over for points; here each swing was victory or death. Nor was it like football or rugby, which by comparison were brutish games. There was one chance for a total of three or four points, at most, the difference between a bogey and birdie was celebration or demise.

She would have enjoyed observing many of the players, but was mostly interested in Jonni. She studied his expression. His pace. She wanted to see who he talked to, though it seemed to be only his caddie, and they didn't speak often. Still, Kate believed people revealed a great deal if you watched them long enough. She watched wildlife for hours, learning what she could of the behavior of wild dogs, for example. No book could tell her what observation could. As he walked from the third to the Par 3 fourth hole, his caddie whispered a few words in Jonni's ear, almost like a jockey encouraging a thoroughbred. A security detail walked with Jonni along the ropes, Kate could identify two of them. Pinkerton guards held ropes open as the players and the caddies passed between them. Martin stayed near one of the bodyguards as well, his eyes never leaving Jonni. For the most part - Kate caught him occasionally glancing at the security, as if for comfort, to know that they were safe.

The security guards were easy to spot in part because they were the only ones not watching Jonni—for the most part. The guard beside Martin did look back and forth over the crowds, especially those nearest Jonni, but he also intensely watched Jonni play. She looked carefully at him. He wore a shirt with a tree on it, a logo of some kind with the letters "BRG." She didn't know who had chosen that security contractor, but she found him to be a bit obvious and too often distracted by the gameplay. She had seen many security companies pass through Africa, protecting diplomats or high net worth individuals. Some were professional, maintaining a low-profile and always in control of logistics. Others were loud, distracted, essentially off-duty cops (the worst she ever experienced were the DPS officers assigned to Texas officials). She was not impressed by this bodyguard. Then again, what threat could really manifest during the tournament and on the course? Even she couldn't ignore Jonni's game play. She couldn't blame him for watching Jonni too.

Kate was hungry. Today she had only the peanuts offered at concessions. She didn't want to leave Jonni. If she had grown good at one thing on stakeouts, waylays, sitting in an office at work, it was patience of mind, gut and bladder. Ryals didn't think she had much to offer. She knew what he thought of her. She learned long ago, as almost always the youngest in the room, to never argue her case; only to prove herself.

The young South African prodigy would, too. One way or the other.

Jonni walked up to the fourth tee — which Buster had explained yesterday was called Flowering Crabapple, pointing out the low-branched, pink blossomed trees behind them. "As a kid," Buster said yesterday, "we'd chuck the fruit at one another, hard as we could. I'd have welts like tomatoes." Buster was effective at keeping Jonni focused on the best parts of the competition.

He could feel his play teetering on the edge of collapse, after a terrible putt with a disappointing bogey.

Buster told him that ANGC favors those who cut the ball smaller than a slice. The National favors those who can control their fade, "but," he said, "you are losing them into destructive slices. If you can limit the slice, you can compete here. Keep your grip and focus past the ball."

Jonni focused. He knew a slice was caused when the club met the ball off-center, creating a spin that drove it astray to the right. Buster had added, "But the other thing about this course is you can come back from a slice." His encouragement and advice were getting through, but Jonni wasn't finding his footing, or his spirit in this tournament. He'd resigned himself to play again next year — he wouldn't give up. He may fail badly this year. Who could blame him? Maybe he'd get it together, if he were invited back.

His partner watched and the patrons hushed as he stepped up to the tee and looked two hundred and forty yards straight down one hill and then up the next toward the small yellow flag waving to the right with a gentle breeze. Two bunkers were on either side of the hole, like guard dogs before a tomb, Jonni thought.

"Don't think about the bunkers," Buster said as Jonni stepped back and watched. "They're not even there. Just find the hole and guide it in. The sand is only there to distract you." And it did. Bright white, growing bigger in his eyes, he felt there was no way he could escape. He stepped back to the tee and drew his breath and focused on the ball. He could hear the whispers of some in the crowd, the crack of a ball at a nearby hole, echoing off the trees; the sound of the breeze and the blue jays. The crowd again, breathing, whispering, shifting; all around him, crowding in. He closed his eyes a moment, shut it all out, and swung.

He'd overcorrected. It wasn't a slice, it was a hook. Far to the left, it landed near the bleachers, past all the watching fans.

TWENTY-SEVEN

The Sheriff read the note from Ryals' car, now in a plastic evidence sheath.

"Enough to retire on," the Sheriff observed.

"Almost. I thought I'd negotiate," Ryals quipped. The note was in a plastic evidence bag. The Sheriff set it down on the desk. Parriot stood behind Ryals, deep in thought.

Parriot said what Ryals had already considered: "If the point is to avoid embarrassment, I think the National has the most to fear."

"It could have come from a member. Not directly." Ryals said.

"If that's true, we're dead in the water," The Sheriff said. "Let's not even consider that."

"How did they find your car?" Parriot wondered.

"Followed me all day, if I had to guess. I've moved around. Surely they had to."

"Can we see it on the dash cam?"

"Wasn't on."

"Should we make the National aware of this?" The Sheriff wondered, perhaps asking them, musing out loud. No one answered him. Finally the Sheriff declared. "This is our investigation, not theirs."

"We hold it as evidence," Ryals said.

"Maybe we can run a sting," Parriot asked.

"Either this isn't a real offer," Ryals said, "or it is, and it didn't come from the bad guys. If it's real, it came from a member. Or maybe someone who doesn't want the National smeared. I don't think a sting is going to catch the killers. This isn't their m.o., not from what we've seen."

"It's still criminal," the Sheriff said. "No matter who wrote it."

"I'm not against the idea," Parriot said, "But I agree with Ryals, it's not worth committing resources to it right now."

"Where's Chase?" The Sheriff asked.

"On the course. Doing her thing," Ryals said. "Whatever that is."

"Perhaps we can loop her in on this," Sheriff said again.

"Sure."

Now Ryals had to find Kate on the course. He parked a half mile from the staff entrance, walked the distance to the staff lot, and took the shuttle in from there. He used the VIP badge, and informed Lawrence he was on the property. Ryals looked at the clubhouse; he could see one of the bungalows Parriot had described in the trees to the east. He noticed more details each time he came here, particularly seeing things in new light since his conversation with Ingot. Not darker or more sinister, but if a painting it was as if it had more definition, depth, character. There was more than met the eye at every corner here. Here men who changed the world stayed, relaxed, socialized, and undoubtedly made deals. Others changed history on the manicured, surreal grass. Here patrons harbored grudges and forged friendships and dined and smoked cigars.

A true plantation, it echoed with southern history. Augusta, Ryals knew, lost much of its workforce in the 1950s when industry attracted substantial numbers of the black population to the north, as industrial factories were willing to pay significantly better than did agriculture across the south. Then there was a period of "white flight" from the city to the suburbs in which much of the wealth of Augusta disappeared and the city decayed. It was decades before it began to assimilate into a healthy economic state again, thanks in large part to Fort Eisenhower and the Savannah River Site, where nuclear materials were refined. The National survived the economic downturn; it had survived periods of racial injustice and political upheaval.

Ryals looked the clubhouse over now, studying its facade as if a faced lined with history. Ryals tried to imagine — he was sure there were pictures somewhere — what it looked like in its first years. He pictured when Magnolia Lane was lined with young saplings. When the clubhouse was newly built. When Bobby Jones and Cliff Roberts stood together and breathed in the air of the first spring over their newly christened course. Ryals wondered if they had any sense of what the future would hold for their project, of how it would command the world's attention.

Surely they did, since they built a suite and office specifically for a U.S. president to use while staying over. Bobby Jones was already by then world famous. They had to know his home course would be, too.

Ryals made his way onto the course, past the large leaderboard, the same style it had been for nearly a century. The names of competitors and their scores were advertised by large placards and rotated by hand. Ryals didn't know where Kate was. She would be a needle in the haystack, or at least in whatever throng surrounded Jonni Lombard. The leaderboard listed Jonni's progress as 'Thru 5.' He could find Jonni on the 6th, then.

Ryals didn't check in with Allison — he would only do that when he had something significant to report or ask — and so he went past the clubhouse and through the yellow rope, the eyes of several Securitas staff — they watched the administrative buildings, while the Pinkertons maintained order on the course — following him as they spoke into their radios. The ghost of Clifford Roberts was in the administration; the ghost of Bobby Jones was on the course. This quality of security on a golf course made sense when he kept in mind that at any given time a billionaire or a head of state might be in the clubhouse.

Or that a nearly-invisible killer had infiltrated the grounds, and his whereabouts were completely unknown.

He found a small white wooden stand in the shape of the clubhouse that provided tee times as well as a course map. Jonni's pair started ninety minutes ago; Ryals wasn't sure what that meant but he couldn't be far. Using the map he walked the course for the first time following the holes. Tea Olive, Pink Dogwood, Flowering Peach, Flowering Crab Apple. Along the way he asked who was playing each; Vijay Singh, Martin Kaymer, Si-Woo Kim, Doug Ghim, Ryan Moore... some names he recognized. Ryals walked down the hill, keeping along the north edge of the course as one green led to another tee. He came finally to the sixth, a Par 3 called Juniper. It hosted another white leaderboard against the trees down by the far end, and a row of brilliant pink azaleas ran along the fairway.

Ryals finally saw Jonni. The player leaned on his club waiting for the other player he was paired with to hit. Together they watched the ball whistle through the air; Ryals couldn't see where it had gone.

Applause followed, and the trance was broken and Ryals searched the crowd for Kate. When he finally laid eyes on her, she was waving at him and smiling.

They walked together with the crowds, following Jonni to the seventh. Before any mention of the investigation Ryals found himself asking in earnest "How's he doing?"

"Not great," Kate said. "Sitting at six over, will probably get worse." Her tone was upbeat as always. She spoke matter-of-fact. "He'll rally." Her hope was genuine.

"What's up?" She asked. He looked at her small satchel; she held one hand over it.

"I got a note." He said. He showed it to her on his phone, keeping it close to him so as not to draw scrutiny from patrons.

"Hm," she said, as if she wasn't really listening. Then after a moment she asked, "Does your department provide any SDR training?"

"Any what?"

"Surveillance Detection and Reconnaissance. Methods to spot a tail. Highway lane changes, pulling into and out of parking lots, stuff like that."

"I just watch out," he said. Then, feeling challenged, added, "I know the streets. I would have spotted someone."

"They have some way of keeping an eye on you, if they want you to leave a response. Interesting."

"Yeah," he answered, feeling more spooked now talking to her.

"It might mean you're getting close to something. Not sure what."

"Maybe not. Could just be a member of the club who wants to put the matter under the rug."

"True. But does that sound like the sort of behavior becoming of a member of the business elite?"

"How would I know?"

They arrived at the 6th hole near the tee, and they kept back and out of the players' view. Jonni patiently evaluated the hole, a 180-yard par 3 that fell down the hill and rose up to the green and the flag. Ryals felt a wind pass over them from the far end of the fairway. It felt good; he was sweating after his hike to find Kate. Everyone else here, including her, seemed far more comfortably dressed than he was.

"What's your next move?" She asked, then held up a finger to quiet Ryals before he could respond, as the kid stepped up between the cleanly sawed pine branch sections laid on either side of the tee box. He shrugged his shoulders to loosen them, then squared his feet and readied his swing. They waited while he went through the prologue to his shot. Ryals spotted his father Martin watching eagerly from the rope beyond them. He hadn't spotted Ryals; he was laser-focused on his son. He wouldn't notice Kate or anyone else in the crowds. Then came the deep breath, the swing, the crack and the whoosh of the ball. Applause soon followed as the ball landed near the rope but a good distance from the green. He heard a few disappointed mutters. It was a polite crowd and they wanted Jonni to succeed. Kate clapped.

"So," she asked, stepping back with him. "What now?" She watched Ryals as the second player prepared to tee off.

"Still working on everything else. Was hoping you had some suggestion."

"There are fewer and fewer options as time goes by," she said. We just need a little luck," she said.

"We're not lucky. We're not anywhere," Ryals snapped, frustration mounting. He wasn't sure why he had hiked all the way down here to find her. She wasn't helping.

The crowd went silent, and so did the two of them. The other player swung, fairing better than Jonni had. Ryals felt for Jonni. He also briefly relaxed as he focused on the game.

"My advice?" She said. "Keep hitting those hotel rooms, look for anything odd. Follow the kid like a hawk when he leaves here."

"Like you're doing."

"I will stay on him. If they're watching you, they're watching him."

The detective hiked back up the hill — sweat slick down his back, his shirt stuck to his skin, his jacket on his shoulder now. He felt he stood out. He stopped at the fairway crossing over the sixth hole as the gallery guards held people back while a pair of golfers passed. Ryals saw a man in a wheelchair beside him, pushed by a younger man, presumably his son. The elder wore a hat — 101st airborne, World War II. Korea. The younger of the two gestured to his father. "All he ever wanted was to come to the Masters." His son was both proud and, somehow, relaxed and elated. As if years of effort had finally paid off.

He fought through two wars to get here, Ryals thought. People had a lot riding on this tournament.

Ryals returned to the parking lot by way of the shuttle and he stood in the shade of a tree and watched the parked cars. The lot was patrolled; one security guard sat in a car, another walked the lot. No one else came with Ryals on the shuttle. Across the street there was nothing; a wooded wall with a Richmond County deputy parked watching traffic; down a bit, a shop that once sold camping gear and now antiques. Outside of the Masters lot there was nowhere for someone to be parked, to watch him or wait for him. He scanned the cars in the lot, shielding his eyes from the glare of windshields. He looked for the silhouette of someone watching him from a vehicle, but there was no one.

Whoever they were, they remained a ghost.

Ryals continued to his car, turned the air on and cracked the window but the hot leather seared through his damp shirt.

He'd seen far worse crimes than this one — domestic assaults, murder-suicides. Of course most of his day job was hit-and-runs, bartenders stealing credit cards, more low-level offenses. On more than one case he'd been threatened. Rarely credibly. Learning how to spot a tail, and how to evade one — those were new ideas to him. They were not new to Kate, apparently. He had an uncomfortable sense that she was actually leading the investigation. Based on the last conversation, that might be true.

TWENTY-EIGHT

The sun was well above the Ninth fairway. Pine shadows dropped beneath the boughs. The grass glowed as if supernaturally endowed. As if this place were something out of fantasy, built by enchantment. Jonni squinted. He couldn't recall ever having to shield his eyes against the glow of grass before.

"Put it behind you. Here we are," Buster said, knowing that Jonni's mind was on the previous green, where he'd missed a twenty foot putt, sliding the ball a full two meters above the hole, and much too fast; a putt that should have been easy, but that Jonni botched. The 8th, "Yellow Jasmine" was a par 4 straight shot with short, gentle undulations like ripples in a mountain stream. But there was nothing gentle about Jonni's performance right now.

Buster was right. He was on the 9th, though he was eight over par now, a number he knew only by looking at the leaderboard as they passed.

The Par 4 9th, "Carolina Cherry" was a long climb up between rows of towering sentinel-like pines. It rose toward the clubhouse again. He could feel the watchful eyes of the clubhouse on the top of the hill, exerting a god-like presence. It was not just the people, the club, the members or the Chairman. It was the Legacy, which was sacred and he feared he would ultimately tarnish it.

He took his next drive too fast to control his body. He got too far in front, finding the bottom of the swing arc inches behind the ball.

His nerves crushed him, resulting in a humiliating shot that flailed under a tree just off the tee box.

It lay out of the sunlight and in the shadow. Then the sun over the fairway was dimmed by clouds overhead.

Ryals went first to the station and sat across from Parriot beneath the air conditioning and stared at the spread of papers on the table.

"Getting anywhere?" He asked.

"Nothing compared to your exemplary field work, Detective, but in my experience cases are often solved at the desk." His desk — makeshift desk— was covered in lists and mini-dossiers of Augusta National members.

It felt to Ryals like radioactive debris, like something from inside one of those nuclear labs at the Savannah River Site — down the road, where Parriot's father had worked.

"Of course it's not recent, nor a complete list," Parriot said, following the same gaze. "It's based on a leaked partial membership list in 2002, along with a few names added from interviews or admissions found around the web. I've crossed off the names of those who have died, and a few others that seem irrelevant. What remains — even of the impartial list — is a who's who of who's who's."

"Like?" Ryals, like all Augustans, knew rumors, a few facts perhaps.

"Former Secretary of Defense, ambassadors, Hollywood notables, local physicians, a few sports chiefs. CEOs and other officers of Exxon Mobile, Coors, Continental, General Electric, Coca-Cola, Texaco, IBM, AT&T, and a host of smaller companies: J.R. Butler, Moses Contracting, Allied Operations Group, even a few non-profits. There are Georgians, but longer lists from most other states; some local Augustans. It's impressive by any measure." Parriot stared at it a moment. "And," he said, "a list that could get anyone —including me — fired. One way or another."

"There might be something here but I have no data to cross reference it with, except South Africa. At least half of the list has business all over the continent, including South Africa. That was partially based on surface-level connections, but it's likely more." So the data was not very helpful, even if they knew what they were looking for.

"This case lacks context," Parriot said. "I'm whistling in the dark." Ryals agreed.

Context. The course murder, the motel murder, the meeting, the note, car accident. A chain of events. One act leading to another. Like a series of golf swings moving the ball down the fairway.

"Where did it all begin?" Ryals asked in a sigh.

Parriot shrugged. "Before Willy Sharpe got on a plane. We may have to be prepared not to have that information."

"Then maybe the murderer isn't here anymore."

"Someone is here. The murderer? I don't know."

"Right," Ryals said, suddenly ready for tomorrow to pass, and the Mayor to have his wish; for this to become another twist in the winding vine that is the history of the Augusta National.

Ryals' phone buzzed. Angela. He would call her back in a moment. He returned it to his pocket.

"What is Ms. Chase doing?" Parriot asked.

"Attending the Masters."

Ryals was about to mention her theory on the killer. His phone rang again. Angela. He answered.

"Hey, Ange," he said.

"Dad," she said, matter-of-fact but he could hear strain in her voice.

She spoke at a high pitch, reporting news she knew he didn't want to hear. "There's a man in a car in front of the house. He's been here for a while; he's just sitting, and watching the house. It's really creepy, dad."

Ryals' heart skipped.

"Lock the doors, stay near the window," Ryals was off the chair in a heartbeat, Parriot suddenly alert. "I'll call you right back. I'm on my way."

"Dad," she said. "Dad, he's out of the car, and he has a gun."

Ryals knocked his chair over moving toward the door.

"Lock yourself in the closet. I'm coming," He hung up and dialed 911.

"What is it?" Parriot.

"Someone's at my house with a gun," Ryals said. "My kid is there alone."

"I'll drive," Parriot said. His sedan had police flashers, Ryals temporary vehicle did not. Ryals shouted at dispatch to get a car to the house, nearest available patrol.

"It would be ideal if they can hang back until we get there. We may be able to learn more."

"It's my daughter," Ryals replied severely, his square jaw set.

They pulled into the neighborhood, rounded corners fast enough their tires squealed. They came to Ryals home and saw just a black and white unit out front — the first responder.

Ryals bounded out of the car and across the yard not even stopping to ascertain any threat. He got to the door where a uniformed deputy stood with Angela.

"He just left," She said, her voice a bit shaky. She hugged her dad.

"I didn't see anyone," the deputy told Ryals.

"What happened?" He asked Angela.

"I noticed him out front. He was in the car and he wasn't moving for a long time. Then I called you, and I saw him walk up. He had a gun in his hand. He didn't ring the doorbell. He just..."

"He left this," the deputy said. Holding it with gloves, she lifted a black plastic pistol with an orange tip. A toy, an Airsoft gun.

"He wanted to frighten you," Parriot said.

Instead he frightened Angela. He pulled his phone and checked the doorbell camera, hoping it had recorded. It didn't always work.

He found the video. A man with a mask over his mouth and nose. A hat. Walked to the door and stood in front of it, the gun invisible out of frame. He didn't move, he only stood there. They could see his eyes; piercing crystal blue. Blonde hair beneath. He finally crouched then walked away, no longer holding the gun.

"Why a plastic gun?"

"It's all he needed to intimidate," Ryals answered Parriot. They stood in the station now. Angela at a chair, still frightened but listening to their debate.

"Also doesn't have to pass a background check."

"Which, if he isn't a citizen, he can't."

The gun was on the desk, ready to go to forensics. But in the video the guy wore gloves.

They played it again but now on the laptop, hoping to get a glimpse of the license tag. As the vehicle pulled away, they got it. Parriot jotted it down and immediately put it into the system.

"Hell," Ryals said. He pointed.

"What?"

"The front end. Smashed headlight and quarter. That's the guy that hit me."

"I hope he got the liability policy," Parriot said. "That is a rental. We can work with that."

Ryals may be in way over his head, but this ex-high school football star, college wrestler, twice deputy of the year and father of a tough daughter was not easily intimidated.

They scared his daughter.

He would solve this case.

TWENTY-NINE

The putting stroke was smooth and rhythmic, propelling the ball along the perfect grass, down the most famous slopes in golf, until the ball lost momentum just on the lip of the hole. As the ball briefly rested there, the sunlight gleaned on the dimples until one brilliant ray pushed the ball another quarter inch, falling into the cup, followed by a legendary roar of The National.

Jonni watched as his partner picked up his ball and waved it briefly in the air as he walked away, smiling at the birdie. Jonni's embarrassing display a moment before was, hopefully, forgotten by the enthusiastic crowd. Neither of them was going to win, but there was a toughness in the imbalance of their play, which drove a distance between them as well — one would not be dragged down by the other.

Perhaps one could be encouraged, but in every drawn breath, every whisper of wind and sip of beer and puff of cigar and "ooh" and "aah" Jonni felt his energy drain; drained in front of the world he wished would shrink until it was just Jonni and Buster alone on a patch of grass. Or Jonni could be standing in the sun at home and far away.

And of course, his every swing, every putt and every step was an insult to Willy. That Jonni continued to play took away from Willy's legacy and whatever love he was owed in death. That Jonni even played without him felt like some kind of betrayal of his mentor and friend.

He thought about Willy. About chowing down on a burger at the golf club restaurant, the vervet monkeys climbing down to steal the sugar packets from the coffee trays; or even better, the schnitzel, Jonni's favorite, a beer, like his first with Willy, laughing about girls and the time Jonni farted when he swung and then the many times thereafter when Willy imitated the noise just as Jonni was about to take a swing until Jonni would break into a laugh and couldn't swing. He practiced too at the Skukuza golf course, run by Jean Rousseau (who then went on to manage Phaloborwa's Hans Merensky destination golf resort) and learned how tricky and unique grass could be.

The chorus of voices — the many locals, supportive, the older gentlemen offering tips until Jonni's handicap dropped and then watched and admired and bought him a Dry Lemon and Tea when he walked back to the shade of the restaurant and club. He and Willy.

He'd never had many friends, but he enjoyed friendship with Willy.

As he walked through the ropes, held by the men who guided the patrons, Jonni trembled; he felt tears welling and he forgot where he was for a moment and lowered his head and he, for the first time, took the sunglasses from his pocket and pushed them on, so hard they scratched his face, and Buster knew that he was upset and didn't put a hand on his shoulder but just walked along beside him.

Allison sensed a migraine coming from the stress and the adrenaline of sustained anticipation. She wasn't drinking enough water. She was cool under pressure. She had to remind herself of that. She drew breath and calmed her nerves. She continued to the clubhouse.

Her radio crackled and she heard one of her coordinators speaking; the transmission was faint and broken. She paused outside her office and asked the coordinator to repeat herself.

"Say that again?"

"I said the Chairman," the girl said, "he's on his way down."

"On his way down where?"

"To the — I don't know. Bottom of the course. He's in a cart."

"What?"

"And he asked for them to stop play on the 12th."

Allison didn't know why he would be out of the clubhouse right now. She didn't bother making a call to figure out what was going on. She left the clubhouse through the rear door. There were no golf carts parked outside the entrance to take. She decided to walk it.

Jonni looked up from the grass at his feet. He didn't know where he stood; he couldn't be sure what hole he played now. He was in a daze. He looked across the patches of sun on the fairway; that look like a splattered watercolor, duckling yellow and jacket green. He could hear the birds but he couldn't see them. A soft breeze swayed the boughs and sunlight sparkled gold on pollen-heavy needles and leaves. Banks of pink and white azaleas like frosting on the foliage ran around the green in hanging shadow. He could hear the murmur of the crowd, and saw the rows seated up in the stands that overlooked Amen Corner. He was drawn to retreat into the nature and beauty opposite them, and ignore the pressure the spectators represented. Of course now he knew where he stood. He was at the curved corner that he had faced twice this week before in torment: the 12th hole that stretched down and across Rae's Creek and ended in bright sunlight. To Jonni this turn of the course still looked as if it descended not to the famous creek lined with perfect grass and crossed by a stone bridge, but a dim dark entry to doubt, a water not crystalline but rather opaque and foreboding. His energy and momentum were sucked from him. Twice he had braved it, but now, he felt it all coming apart before he had teed off. He wished nothing more than to turn and leave. He thought he could master the game. Instead he felt the opposite was happening.

He hadn't seen Willy's body, but he could imagine it now, hanging from the TV stand, grinning at him, a last joke, untold, in Willy's throat held by the rope. Jonni's breath came in sharp gasps. He could hear nothing from the crowd, from Buster, nor from anyone. It was as if time had frozen for a moment and he was held in a dreadful limbo.

Jonni looked up after a moment, though, and found that, indeed, everything had stopped. It wasn't just his imagination. The crowd murmured, but in a different way now, and they all looked not at Jonni but toward a place between the stands and concessions lines. Many were asking questions in whispers. Even Buster and, everyone else looked away, back to the rope, at something that was happening there. Jonni looked up, curiosity overcoming his crisis of doubt. Koepka and his caddie also stood and looked toward whatever had caused the stir.

A golf cart had parked and a tall older man wearing a green jacket ducked beneath the rope and was walking right toward Jonni. Jonni caught a glimpse of his father, mouth hanging as the man passed him. The older man had silver hair and sunglasses which he removed to reveal piercing gray eyes and a wide tan face and a brief ivory-white smile. He walked toward Jonni as if meaning business. Jonni recognized him but the weird improbability of what was happening made him slow to remember the face. He heard Buster say quietly, "Well you have a fan."

It was the Chairman. Jonni had met him at the dinner, and now recognized him. He was head of the Masters and the Augusta National and now he interrupted the play and walked toward Jonni.

He extended his hand, not to shake Jonni's, but gesturing that the kid take a step — maybe a walk — with him. Jonni looked at Buster, then found his father, then looked again at the Chairman. He found himself walking away with his club in his hand. For a moment they strode the fairway in full view of everyone and the chairman said nothing. He just looked, breathed it in as if he wanted to take a moment to appreciate where they were.

"You know, Jonni," the Chairman began in his soft Georgia accent. "Bobby Jones didn't care for caddies except to carry his sticks. He said once that if he needed a caddie to tell him which iron to use he might as well have the caddie swing it. Of course, his was a genius that we've never again seen the likes of." The Chairman took a breath and looked off at the trees and the nothing beyond, because when here, on the course, nothing existed beyond its borders; it was the entire world.

"Of course, most golfers, even our best, aren't that way. Our patron saint left and won't be incarnate again. We like to think of golf as a sport played, as Bobby said, on a five inch course here," the Chairman tapped two fingers against his temple. "And it's true, for the game you play on the course. But the world outside affects what's up here."

He now offered a wide grin, then after a moment he grew more serious. "I believe no course in the world requires more of you, more focus, more faith. Faith in God, in yourself, in your swing. No other course than this one. It's alive, probing you, and it seems like it wants to take you down and ruin your game. It matters who you have on your side. It matters that your family is behind you. It all matters. You can't pretend it doesn't."

Now they stopped and looked down to the bottom of the hole, to the edge of the course itself hidden behind a picture-perfect Georgia forest. Everything was still as if it were a painting.

"Mr. Lombard, you're a fine golfer, more than fine. Spectacular skill. What's happened this week is nothing short of tragic and that it happened on my course, the course where I am currently the chief guarantor of our legacy. That is not something lost on me. It may seem that this course is out to get you. The National isn't meant to defeat you; that's not its purpose. It's meant to bring the best out of each competitor. Those that fail to rise to its challenge fail only themselves. And they may return the next year. It doesn't want failure, however. It wants your best. Son, I don't want anything from you but your best."

Now the Chairman looked at Jonni directly. Jonni raised his head and looked the man in the eyes.

"I can't imagine what's going on between your ears. We owe you a deep apology for inviting you into our home and allowing this tragedy to happen. I want you to know that I know you're a fine, fine golfer, and for the hours you're swinging a club, that's all you should be. If you pack it up here and go home, you go with all of our respect. But here you are. Don't worry about the leaderboard, about the score, about anything. Find the flag, find the hole, and swing."

Jonni didn't speak. He didn't have any reply. The Chairman turned to face the rising hill and the entirety of the National up to the clubhouse and Magnolia Lane.

"Bobby once said 'golf is the closest game there is to life. You get your bad breaks from good shots, good breaks from bad shots. You have to play the ball where it lies.' I've had that on my desk for many years."

The Chairman put his hand on Jonni's shoulder then departed. The old man walked past Buster, past Koekpa, both to whom he gave a slight nod. He climbed again under the rope and walked to the waiting golf cart. The crowd murmured in wonder. He knew that the entire world of sports was watching this hole right now. Jonni breathed in the grass and felt that breathing was somehow easier. For a moment he stood frozen, not sure what to do or say until Buster walked over to him and, also not sure what to say, cleared his throat and simply asked, "You ready to swing?"

Jonni watched the golf cart turn back up the hill as he went to the tee and turned and felt the cool shaft of the contoured driver in his hand and the light pitted ball and tee in the other. He looked down the long slope of gentle green from the tee to the blue-black of Raes Creek, the grass-topped stone bridge; the sun-paled splashes of pink, rose and white azaleas behind it; the yellow blaze of the Golden Bell plant; the white sand bunkers scooped out of the grass revealing that it was all just a tableau made of marble, the whole course cut from stone; and beyond that the wall of pine and dogwood trees and deep jade shadow as the sun passed behind. The flag fluttered, just up and to the left.

Jonni carefully placed the ball onto the tee and forgot that Buster was standing beside him and that yesterday this was a painful wound that wouldn't heal. All faded away. He rose and squared himself in front of the ball and looked at it, then he didn't look at it, he just looked at where he wanted it to go and after a practice swing he maintained a steady breath as he imagined the ball take off over the 12th fairway and past the pines. This was the only shot he had to take today, this was the only hole had to face. Finally he inched forward and he swung and felt the solid connection that sent the ball in a high arc that crossed the wall of pines in a small white flash.

Kate didn't completely understand this tournament but she knew something significant had happened. Everyone around her was talking about it.

"That was remarkable," she heard a woman say.

While following the Chairman's interruption the patrons had all been abuzz with speculative chatter, they now gasped and broke into loud and fervent applause as Jonni's shot — she could see it now sailing impressively close to the green — dropped, bounced, and rolled toward the flag and the hole in what Kate knew, even without knowing golf, was a remarkable shot. The ball came to rest just feet from the hole, and she couldn't help herself but join the applause and look at Jonni's face as he, for the first time since she started watching him cracked a very faint smile.

"Well look at that," said a man beside her who removed a cigar from his mouth.

The energy over the course had changed, and already Allison could see streams of people migrating toward Jonni, necks craned to watch, feet shuffling quickly. News spread between patrons quickly. Now no one wanted to miss Jonni Lombard, who had just had a private audience with Allison's boss, the pope of the Augusta National.

Investigating the rental car seen on Ryals' doorbell camera led only to a dead end. The car was rented under the name of a dead child in Ohio who had never been to Georgia.

"Put out the APB," Ryals said. "Maybe he gets pulled over and we get lucky."

Parriot agreed and shrugged. "So they want us to know they're watching you. Which means they want you to think that worse things may come."

"No one intimidates my deputies in my town," The Sheriff said, pulling up his belt against his paunch. He at least pretended now to be leading the investigation.

"They haven't," Ryals said firmly.

"Here's the thing," Parriot said. "They began to put pressure on us. On you. Which means you were getting somewhere. So what changed? Why now?"

"Nothing. We have no breaks."

"That we know of. Maybe we know something and don't know it."

Ryals thought a while. All of them did. "Or they want me distracted because I'm about to find something."

It was true. They'd kept him occupied. If he hadn't been hit, what would he have done yesterday? What was he about to stumble on?

Parriot shook his head. "There must be something. They were in the shadows, now they've twice risked exposing themselves."

There was only one new thing. One thing he had not gotten to. "The video," Ryals said. "There's something in the video from the Fox's Lair that we didn't catch."

They crowded around Parriot's laptop, Angela in the back craning to see, but everyone so focused they paid her no mind. The Sheriff buried his chin in his fingers. They pulled up the same grainy image they had watched before. Parriot fast forwarded to when Willy walked into the bar. Met with the man. Became agitated. Left.

Parriot played it again.

"I don't see anything new," Ryals said, memorizing every pixel of the grainy scene.

"They come, they meet, they leave... maybe it's not about the video," Parriot observed.

Ryals felt it had to be. There was no resistance, intimidation, anything until now. There was, before that, the man in the lot at lunch (Ryals looked back at Angela thinking about it), but he didn't think the man meant to be seen then. At that point they were surveilling. After going to the Fox's Lair, they had changed tactics.

So there had to be something to the Fox's Lair meeting, something worth them getting excited about.

They had to have made a mistake. But what?

"Play it one more time," Ryals said.

"'Play it again, Sam,'" Parriot quipped, rewinding the footage. Ryals leaned closer. Watching the other patrons in the bar. Were any watching Willy? Was there someone else who didn't wish to be identified?

They observed only casual drinkers, a pair of men in suits, rednecks and old timers. Nothing was out of place.

"I don't see anything," Ryals had to admit. Parriot shook his head. "Maybe there's another angle we didn't get. Maybe they got it first."

"If they did, why worry about me?"

"Ryals stared at the frozen image. The empty barstools. Willy came all this way to meet at this spot. The man knew exactly which one was Willy, exactly where to go...

"Press play," Ryals said. Parriot looked at him, then hit the spacebar. One thing they hadn't done yet, was watch further than the meeting.

The video went on for another couple of hours, and they had watched just far enough to confirm the meeting. Maybe...

"Fast forward," Ryals said. The video sped forward. A pair of girls came up to the bar, ordered, left. Someone occupied a stool and talked to the side.

A man, dark hair, Asian, came and sat, ordered a drink.

"Wait. Back up. Let it play," Ryals said. That sixth sense that got him in an investigator's chair, that study of old fashioned human normalcy and deviancy, was activated.

"What do you see?" Parriot asked.

"That guy. He ordered a water. See," Ryals pointed. They backed it up. The man ordered, the bartender poured—no booze.

The Sheriff grunted. "Designated Driver?"

"Driving for who?" Ryals asked.

On the screen the man got up and left, with cash on the bar — a twenty.

"Big tip for a soda," Parriot said.

"Go back," Ryals said. Parriot wound it back. Ryals looked closely, perusing each grainy pixel like satellite pictures in a spy movie.

"There," Ryals said. Parriot froze it. "Slow," Ryals said. They watched. On screen, the Asian man set his drink down, and his hand disappeared under the bar for a moment, and came back holding something. He'd pulled it from beneath the table right by Willy's seat. Then the man put his hand in his pocket, produced a twenty, and left.

"Blink and you miss it," Parriot marveled.

"What is it?" The Sheriff asked.

"They recorded him," Ryals said. "They recorded the meeting."

"Who? And why?" Sheriff asked.

"I don't know," Ryals said. "But they didn't want to be seen. They realize we have them on video now.

"We have a glimpse of men behind the curtain," Parriot said.

Ryals stared at the man in the video. Short blonde hair under a hat. Neatly dressed in a dark shirt hanging over a dark t-shirt. Dark pants. The more he looked at it, the more the individual stood out.

Kate's theory was suddenly more relevant.

Somewhere there was a recording of the meeting.

"Let's get the video to GBI. Maybe FBI," Parriot said. Ryals had other ideas. He wanted to see what Kate could do with it.

He emailed himself a copy.

The Sheriff answered his mobile, and after a moment put a hand up, indicating everyone standby. He hung up.

"Cleaning staff reported suspicious characters at Martin and Jonni Lombard's hotel floor. One wore a mask."

"On our way," Ryals said. He told Angela to stay where he was.

Characters. There was more than one.

THIRTY

The 13th Hole, Azalea, was a Par 5 that ran five hundred and ten yards from tee to green around a knee-bend with thick trees walling both sides and flashes of white dogwoods over the pink sprinkle namesake flowers behind the green, which the players couldn't see from the tee.

The 13th was a recent a dramatic example of how the National evolved to remain unpredictable. "They changed it last year. They moved the tee box here thirty-five yards back. It was the easiest par five on the course. Now, it's the toughest of them, in my opinion," Buster explained.

Jonni remembered what Willy told him about the 13th: "It used to be you went for broke here. Now it's a hole you lay up. The hole ran five hundred and forty-five yards.

Jonni stood between flowers, leaning trees and a rock wall. All for a moment was still. He thought about what Willy told him, and Buster's advice now. He looked around the bend, imagining what lay at the far end around the green.

Jonni aligned his toes. He gripped his driver. He went for broke.

The crowd's response began with applause, then to a crescendo. Jonni didn't stare in disbelief, he didn't marvel at himself or pump his fist, though he could see Buster smiling.

But he felt, for the first time this week, like he belonged at the Masters.

Running at the National was a certain way to get kicked out of the tournament.

Still, he moved fast downhill, and Sam Ingot was glad to find he wasn't the only one moving. Many patrons migrated to Amen Corner like rainwater flowing downhill.

Sam was going to write about this Masters, about its history; and what was happening now — from afar he heard a chorus of awe. Crowd reactions at the Masters could be measured specifically according to Par, Birdie, Eagle, if one knew what to listen to.

This is why he wrote about golf. Sometimes, lightning struck.

He passed the concessions and elevated bleachers. Ingot, red faced, stood beside the grandstands just above the reserved space for members' folded chairs and he looked between patrons at the green. The players were still at the far end of the rough and approaching the flag.

Koepka and Jonni neared the green now following their second strokes. Jonni strode up to the ball, some sixty yards or further ahead of his partner, and from where it sat on the edge of the fairway he could see the yellow flag a bit uphill, as if it were waving at him, inviting him to the hole.

Jonni didn't delay. He looked with confidence toward the flag.

He swung. The ball began its journey effortlessly from the head of Jonni's hybrid club, and it didn't just drop suddenly but seemed to float down, like a landing biplane; it didn't bounce so much as skip deftly onto the green, where it kept its pace as if on an errand it meant to finish; and finish it did. It rolled knowingly to the hole and disappeared.

The spectators roared.

They spoke first to the manager, and emphasized the need for discretion; they couldn't let this get out. The Lombards did not yet know.

They spoke to the cleaning woman. She told them someone emerged from a room in the hallway and shoved her aside. She couldn't give a description other than that they wore masks, and she feared they might hurt her. She identified the room as one of the Lombards, but she didn't stick around. She rushed downstairs.

The detectives got into the elevator and went up.

Ryals put on gloves, so did Parriot.

They walked into Jonni's room first. They inspected the lock, Parriot using a pen flashlight. The lock had been drilled; a tiny hole passed through the chassis. The door pushed open with a slight turn of the handle.

Inside nothing seemed amiss at first glance. Stepping in slowly Ryals took in every detail. The closet door was open slightly. He pushed it. Inside was the safe, and it was open. He crouched.

The safe was also drilled with precision, and it was empty.

"I'll check Martin's room," Parriot said, and went out to the next door over. Ryals scanned the room, but nothing was obviously amiss. The drawers were closed, suitcases neatly arranged.

"Same deal over here," he called back. "Safe is cracked, empty."

"Yeah," Ryals said, barely speaking to Parriot. He felt he was in the presence of a ghost. A shadow, a specter.

"Uh, Ryals. Ryals!" Parriot shouted.

Ryals instinctively reached for his gun. He ran out into the hallway and to the next room. Parriot bumped into him as the agent backed quickly out of the room.

"I didn't see it at first," he said.

"See what?"

Parriot pointed. Ryals looked past him. He also saw nothing at first. He moved into the room slowly, gun low but ready.

"Not seeing anything," Ryals said.

"In the corner. Under the curtain," Parriot said.

Ryals saw it. A silver-black snake. Curled and watching them. Uncurled it was probably more than a meter long.

"Poisonous?" Ryals asked.

"Venomous. And I'd assume so."

"Let's get animal control," he said.

They waited for them in the lobby.

"You think it just found its way in there?"

"Absolutely not," Ryals said, but he couldn't be sure. Animal control arrived quickly; their office was not far. They went up to the room, and came back down within twenty minutes with a closed plastic crate. One carried it out to their vehicle. The other stopped to speak to them.

"That was a first," she said.

"Snake in a hotel room?"

She shook her head slowly and looked away from the room. "I had to look it up to be sure. That's a Black Mamba."

"A what?"

"Very, very dangerous African species. Unlike anything we have here."

"So it didn't just crawl through the window."

"I can't answer that," she said.   "But if it did, it's a long, long way from home. We don't even have a protocol for this thing. I wouldn't have attempted to get it if I knew."

Parriot and Ryals climbed into the car after putting uniformed units in the hotel to watch and wait. The Lombards wouldn't be staying here tonight.

"I'd call that attempted murder," Parriot said.

"Breaking and entering,"

"What was in the safes, do you think?"

"At least their passports, I'd wager."

"So they want to kill the Lombards, too. Or intimidate them. I cannot divine what it is these people want."

"They may think that Willy gave something to the Lombards. They're looking for something. They think the Lombards were meant to have it, or can get it."

"Why kill them, then?"

"Why kill one of them, you mean. There was only one snake. To put pressure on the other."

"You think Jonni really knows something?"

"No, I don't, but that clearly doesn't mean his life is not in danger."

Jonni played Fourteen for par, but on Fifteen, Ingot watched as lightning struck twice. The par 5, at 530 yards, Jonni completed in just three strokes, leading to a crowd explosion uncharacteristic even for Masters patrons. Dozens more had now amassed around the pair. The curiosity of the week was becoming a phenomenon.

Moments like this were more rare than lightning, which in the South in the summer was frequent. Ingot wrote that line into his small notebook for today's article.

The interesting thing about golfers who got on a tear at the Masters, Ingot knew, is that they rarely did it halfway through. When lightning struck, wildfire started. Players suffered extraordinary meltdowns when they did badly, and they rarely corrected themselves from the slippery slope. On the other end, though, a rising star could take off in a blaze of cosmic glory.

Competitors lost their fortunes midway through this course, not the other way around. Many had lost it at Amen Corner. Few had gained it there.

Jonni Lombard was just three holes into his trajectory but he was already blazing hot. Ingot took notes on a small notepad. He noted the view, the shadows on the grass and the feel of the air. Any journalist could describe the facts of the day and the play. But to be there was an inimitable experience that couldn't be faked for all the poetic vocabulary in the world.

Sam watched Jonni walk the pathway from the 15th, his head high now, a modest smile on his face. Koepka was playing exceptionally well, but he was not the spectator focus at the moment.

Number 15 was "Fire Thorn," and Sixteen named "Red Bud." A a dark water pond lay between the tee and the green on the 16th. Many players took a safe route around the pond. Ingot could already tell

Jonni wouldn't do that. He would hit the ball high and let the hole invite it back down.

The crowd pressed in against him but Sam was not irritated. A gentleman's tournament, it was still, and always would be a sport. The thrill was real, it was tangible and it was impossible not to share in the exhilaration. The thrill of a hot streak was in the air like electricity.

Kate felt the excitement. She had never played team sports. She was a cross-country runner. Still she was enthusiastic at university games. Later during grad school her interest in professional sports grew. Now she enjoyed rugby when abroad, and had little time for anything when she was back in the States.

After two days she was invested in this young South African prodigy. These were not the raucous crowds she encountered in other sporting events. Even so, the crowd around Jonni had begun to grow in fervor. The group that followed Jonni paraded to the 17th, pushing ahead to gain the best vantage point to watch what the kid would do next. There was an eagerness.

She found herself, of course, not watching the people around Jonni — as she had been, but rather watching him. He was a changed player. Whereas before he walked as if dragging invisible chains, so heavy they cut through the grass behind him, now he glided, eager to challenge the next hole. It was a remarkable sight, and where she had cringed before when his shots crash landed in pine straw now they landed just where they were meant.

She stopped in the shade of oak trees — the sun was lower now, but the intense afternoon light remained strong — beside a group of young women in sun hats and summer dresses. Kate couldn't see Jonni as he squared up at the ball, but every face was turned toward him like sunflowers to the sun. Using her binoculars, she scanned the front row, where the VIP chairs were arranged. She found Martin standing at the edge. Beside him was Jonni's security guard. She couldn't pick out the other guard from his detail.

Thwack. Jonni took his shot. Kate did not follow the ball with her eyes. She watched the stout, square man; the security guard. He didn't watch the ball. He watched Jonni. He watched the crowd as if looking for a threat.

She studied him. His hairline was wide; his shoulders sloped down from his neck. When he turned toward her his bulging eyes were focused like a hawk. She made a mental note to pull background checks on anyone in his detail.

It was time to leave; she had seen enough here and had a plan.

She had learned something important here. It was time to put a plan together.

THIRTY-ONE

Jonni finished the day eight strokes lower than his noon score, which was a dramatic turn of fortune and skill.

The National discouraged press and downright forbade certain activities during the tournament such as autographs and shouting, but that didn't stop a swarm from rushing up as Jonni walked off the 18th hole and through the line to the clubhouse. Every face that greeted him beamed encouragement. His father kept a hand on his son's shoulder the whole time and more than once pulled him close into an embrace. Buster for his part repeated the same catchphrases for the past hour:

"Well I'll be," punctuated occasionally by "Historic." He concluded, "I'm watching history in the making. Be proud."

Jonni allowed himself — slowly, inch by grassy inch — to feel good. To feel like it wasn't a betrayal of Willy's memory to compete. He was encouraged; he felt he had permission to play The Masters.

Jonni breathed in deeply and shuddered slightly with emotion. He felt overwhelmed and he didn't know what to do with his positive emotions any more than the negative ones.

He would have the chance soon. His father knew his son and insisted. "We have to get back," he said. "Get you rested so you can do this again tomorrow, my boy. You gave them a taste today. Tomorrow you're going to serve them up the whole damned meal!" Dad was sunburnt but beaming with pride.

They walked through the clubhouse, passing aides who smiled at him and Club members in green jackets who greeted them.

Jonni didn't see the Chairman but knew he watched Jonni's every move. Jonni asked for the car right away, and it was ready when they emerged through the front. Jonni hugged Buster inside the rear of the clubhouse. Then he made his way through the hallways to the front. He felt exhausted. He would sleep well; and he had to. Tomorrow he had to be rested.

When Jonni came to the lobby, he saw Detective Hall waiting for him.

Ryals offered a black and white unit, and two deputies to escort Martin to collect his things from the hotel. Ryals presumed it was an upgrade to stay at the Augusta National Clubhouse. Whom they had displaced for Jonni he couldn't imagine. The president of France maybe.

He stepped outside to find Kate waiting for him. How she knew where to find him, he had no clue.

"Come on," he said. "We'll talk in the car."

After the long walk from the entrance they climbed into Ryals' sedan.

"Want to grab your kid?"

"Please."

"Then a bite?"

"Sure. Anything new today?" he asked.

"Very interesting day," she said, but didn't elaborate.

"I have something for you," he said. He handed her his phone. She opened the screenshot in his email. "Look familiar?"

"Should he?"

"Yes." She looked closely. Peering at the screenshot as if expecting him to do something.

"Care to elaborate?"

"He's the reason I'm here. Pull over somewhere."

"I just told Angela I'd take her out to eat."

"We'll pre-game a beer then we can get her."

He diverted down a side road and parked by Sheehan's Irish Pub. She left her phone in the car, he noticed. She pushed it under her seat. She told him to do the same.

They took a high-top table in the front corner. She ordered a stout, a water and a basket of fries. Ryals was glad Angela wasn't here.

"The man in the photo is Xian. He has a number of aliases. He's a bottom feeder trafficker, frequently connecting bad people one to another. He exploits people and is often found where things are dirty and sticky. People lose money around him. He's ruined more than a few lives and there's more than a few truckloads of pangolin scales, lion paws and rhino horn among other illicit materials that he's either stuffed behind bags of rice or found a way to profit share. I've suspected for some time that he's wanted to break into bigger business. Punch above his weight class, so to speak."

"So you knew he'd be here?"

"No, I didn't, but he's among the usual suspects. I recognize him."

"Why is he here in person?"

"There could be only one reason. He stands to make money."

"Or lose it."

"That, too." She sipped her beer. She was no dainty gal, Ryals thought. She also didn't stand on any ceremony and her eyes moved constantly. He noticed only now they were bright green, but contrasted nicely with her Irish freckles.

"He's got friends in a number of governments. Gets things smuggled. U.S. Fish and Wildlife have gone after him before. So has Homeland Security. He's a slippery eel."

"How does this help us?"

"If we find him we can have him detained. On U.S. soil he's not likely to have many friends in high places. We might get him talking. I think you're right, though."

"About?"

"He's here because he stands to lose money. Otherwise he wouldn't have risked it. If we can get him we have a shot at doing more than solving the murder."

"Okay," he said. "Well, I have more to tell. That's not the strangest thing that happened today."

"A mamba," she said. "Jesus. You should have led with that."

"Is that meaningful to you?"

"It's meaningful to them. It's notable in Africa. It sends a statement. My guess? It's Xian. Sounds like his brand of b.s."

"What's the statement?"

"I don't know. We're after you. Maybe, 'you can't escape'. Or 'we're lethal.'"

"Is that something you've seen before?" He asked, and he realized he'd begun to lean on her experience.

"Not exactly. It fits with Southeast Asian syndicate tactics," she said. "Intimidation, strange signals. Xian isn't known as the shrewdest operator, but he's learning. The entire trafficking of wildlife parts is based on folkloric medicine. They exploit traditional beliefs and superstitions. They like spooky."

"This would fit."

She looked Ryals in the eye. "You almost certainly saved Martin Lombard's life."

"Been an eventful day," he said. She nodded. For once she wasn't smiling and laughing.

"So you're watching Jonni?"

"I have been, yes."

"They're coming after the kid."

"They are. Honestly, Hall. Here's what it looks like to me. Willy got into debt with the wrong people. They want their pound of flesh. They'll kill to get it."

"We need to know what Willy owed."

"Owes. They're still here."

They left together to get Angela. Ryals had introduced Kate to Angela, but felt he needed to again with all he was discovering about Kate. Angela, however only asked Kate questions about Jonni. Angela had a crush.

"Where to?" Kate asked, interrupting Angela's barrage of questions.

Ryals directed her to a greasy spoon joint but Kate had her own suggestion— Arsenal Taproom — and so they drove up Walton Way.

"Wanted to try this place," she said. "Someone mentioned the name Arsenal was part of Augusta history," she said.

Ryals nodded. "They made confederate weapons here. There was a factory at the edge of downtown. Vitally important in the Civil War." He didn't know much, but he beamed with that fact. Finally, something he knew, and she didn't. She was unusually chipper considering they were in the twilight of an investigation they were about to lose. Ryals ran through it. The bad guys had every advantage. They would at least protect Jonni and Martin. They could at least do that. Maybe that was all a local Detective could do in a case like this. Ryals was determined to do more.

Kate commented on landmarks and streets. She turned down Monte Sano Avenue, passing Jake Ellis Lane.

"Would make a cool character name," she observed.

"He was a Masters golfer, way back when," Ryals said, trying to recall where he'd heard that. Angela began to offer her own tour commentary. Ryals wondered what Angela would think if she knew more about Kate's background. He wondered what else Kate would tell her. Clearly she already liked Kate. Ryals didn't mind. Angela needed good women role models.

They pulled up at the Taproom, which Ryals had never been to before. They were back on the hill. The Indian Queen was about his speed; but this place bordered too much on the fancy part of the Augusta world — and he wanted to stay clear of Masters traffic. Pulling up they found the Taproom was swarmed with patrons.

Somehow the trio found a bar table; it was crowded and he was glad to see Angela wasn't the only kid. Ryals was sensitive to raising his daughter too fast. She acted like a young woman, but she was still a kid.

Ryals found he was famished. Kate ordered another basket of fries to start. Angela didn't make a comment about counting carbs.

After the day he'd had — two days — he felt claustrophobic in the bar. He also still stewed with anger after Angela's call.

Kate and Angela ate the fries. Ryals wondered how Kate stayed fit. He gave Angela a look. She swatted his hand when he reached for one.

"I ran Willy's cell number," She said. Ryals didn't know how she'd gotten it.

"And?"

"Nothing interesting," she said.

Food arrived in stages. They didn't talk about work. Kate described Jonni's gameplay today. Angela absorbed it. Then Kate talked about Africa and Angela announced to her dad that she wanted to go on Safari.

Ryals realized he hadn't had lunch today; he inhaled his burger as Angela looked at him disapprovingly, then at Kate.

"My dad is racing toward a heart attack," Angela explained, matter-of-factly. "He doesn't realize there's no prize for coming in first."

Kate smirked. Ryals ignored this jab and shrugged and stole one of Angela's fries in retaliation.

The bar was packed and getting more so. At a corner near to them the bar counter was two patient patrons deep, waiting for the sweating bartender to bring beers. Ryals studied them. It was all a sea of white and green ball caps, some dated from tournaments past; polo shirts and t-shirts, all according to the Summerville uniform, some, who had been at the tournament, wearing sunglasses on neck straps or on their necks backward, faces and necks sunburnt. There were the regulars as well, local diners who hadn't been on the course. This wasn't a redneck bar, though in Augusta there was no fence between rednecks and any other sort of local. Among the patrons were at least a half-dozen nation-alities; an Asian group and two Indian families dined near the bar. The bar represented at once the old and the new, but also the neighborhood regionality of the old Arsenal town.

Near Ryals was a man not enjoying the day as much, dressed more darkly and standing drunk and sullen against the bar. He spoke to no one. He was the only one Ryals couldn't label in the crowd. Kate rambled on about something or another with Angela. Ryals tuned out the day for a moment in casual observation of the bar life.

The man at the bar glanced at him, then looked past, perhaps waiting on someone. His eyes, though, weren't red, glazed with drunken stupor like Ryals expected them to be. When the man at the bar looked around, his gaze was sharp, piercing and observant. Was he waiting for a date? A friend? He was well built, dressed in dark jeans or some kind of work pants, wearing dark boots, which also were distinct from the white and colored sneakers worn by the rest of the crowd.

The man held a clear drink with a lime. Ryals thought at first it was a gin or vodka. He saw the way the bartender poured drinks, though — this man had a plastic cup. He was drinking water. Ryals set his beer down on his table and thought about the video from the Fox's Lair. Like the figure in the video, this man wore a ball cap low over his brow. Ryals couldn't see the man's eyes now as the stranger kept his head down. Ryals began to ask himself questions. Was the man here when they arrived? Ryals looked past him at the TV so as not to be caught staring; he kept the figure in his periphery. Ryals couldn't remember if the man was already there, or had walked in. He hadn't noticed.

Ryals looked the stranger over once more. Then he noticed his boots. Salomon, they said, black on black. And the logo was a small "S," and it was familiar but for a moment he couldn't figure out why. Where had he seen that before?

The man turned, and his eyes caught light and for an instant flashed over Ryals' face. They were crystal blue, and suddenly he recognized the man.

"Kate," Ryals said, his voice low. He looked at Angela.

"Yep," she answered, a step ahead of him, or at least keeping pace. The bar was noisy and the man was far enough away that Ryals could speak without being obvious.

"Your five o'clock?" Ryals said, low, lifting fries to his mouth, trying to appear casual.

"Spotted him a moment ago."

Angela stopped eating and Ryals tapped his daughter's hand so she wouldn't stare.

"He came in a moment after us," Kate said, getting a look as she turned to check the TV. "He's watched us since he walked in."

Ryals didn't know if the stranger knew they had noticed him. His gaze, when Ryals caught it while acting casually, was both unfocused and yet still somehow probing.

"Let's pay," she said. "And call for backup."

They wrapped their meal, and Ryals could tell Angela was on edge. He went to the restroom, dialed 911 and had Kate take Angela to the car, intending to pull the stranger away from the girls. He waited a moment in the restroom by the sink, watching the door, but the man never came in. When the door did open and a pair of loud beer buddies pushed their way in Ryals left. In the bar the man was now nowhere to be seen and Ryals suddenly panicked that maybe the man had followed his daughter, and his attempt to separate them was a bad mistake. He went fast out the front door, right toward the car in the dark parking lot, and saw Kate and Angela safe in the vehicle. Kate shook her head. She hadn't seen the man emerge.

The attack came from the left, from the shadow in the eave of the building. Ryals had a sudden impression of blur and menace, and instinctively he went for his gun. Before he could use it he felt the blow of a fist into his ribs and he was spun around and hit the ground and faintly heard Angela screaming behind the glare of the headlights, muffled by the sealed car. He rose and tried to get a look at the man but felt another blow to the gut and he doubled back. He was dizzy, he couldn't seem to get his hand to his gun.

He could hear Angela scream. His pistol bounced in his palm. His grip was uncertain. A flash of metal flickered as a knife appeared. It came at Ryals and he felt searing pain across his chest and ribs. He saw the set jaw, the narrow nose and the blue eyes bright like daylight. He was thin but moved fast, nearly too fast for Ryals to block the second stab. Ryals grabbed the man's arm, lifted his leg and kicked as hard as he could. The attacker went tumbling back, but did not fall over and rebounded and hissed like a vicious cat. The man was on his feet dashing again at Ryals. Ryals turned so that he faced only the empty parking lot and farther drawing the attacker away from Angela. A vehicle turned at the intersection behind and headlights swept over them. Ryals aimed and fired and the sound was explosive. It clapped back into his ears from the pub wall. The attacker bounded back. For a moment they all froze. Ryals felt the sear of pain from the cut and he felt hot sticky blood under his shirt dripping down his side. The blue-eyed man didn't drop. He was ready for another attack.

Suddenly Kate appeared behind him, she lifted a small device and shoved it into the man's throat and there was a popping sound as she tased him and then he dropped.

THIRTY-TWO

The stitching in the trauma center went quickly. The crime scene was handled by the Sheriff directly. The mustached emergency room doctor explained the knife hit Ryals' fourth rib, and if it hadn't, he wouldn't be leaving tonight.

"No jumping jacks," the doctor advised. He wasn't sure he could reach his arm out in front of him, let alone do calisthenics.

Angela hugged him when he emerged and he howled.

"Sorry, dad, I forgot," she exclaimed. "Sorry!" Kate had left with the suspect back to the station. Parriot had called. When they got to the car, now nearing nine p.m., Ryals called him back. A deputy waited with a car outside to take Ryals home.

"Guess they took it up a notch from intimidation," Parriot said.

"Yeah," Ryals said, surprised to find that his voice shook. "What's the story there?"

"I'm downtown," Parriot said. "Ready to interview your new friend. He's not saying much. I thought we should wait on you. Kate looks ready to pounce, though"

"I definitely have some questions," Ryals said, and directed the deputy to the station.

The Sheriff told Ryals to go home.

"Sheriff, we have a day to wrap this up. Or it's both our jobs. I'll heal when the tournament is over." The Sheriff acquiesced, but he wanted a doctor's note. Ryals promised one. He'd get it in a few days. By then he'd also have to go through paperwork for discharging his weapon. The investigation delayed protocol for now.

A black and white gave him and Angela a ride. Inside the station she plopped down at his desk and turned on the computer. Another detective got her a soda and a snack.

Ryals met Kate and Parriot.

"I'm not much of a shot," Ryals said.

"You scared him. And only hit dirt. We have a suspect in custody. I'd say that's a positive."

"Thanks to Kate," Ryals said.

"Purely a good citizen. But I did figure that the safest place was right behind him," she winked at Ryals.

"Where is he?" Ryals asked now with an edge.

"Room two," Parriot said. "No ID, just a phone. Hasn't given a name, hasn't given anything. Running him through a facial recognition database. No hits yet."

"Let's see what he knows."

The three stood and faced the suspect. He had short, choppy blonde hair. He had a tattoo over his neck, hidden just beneath his collar. It was in a language Ryals couldn't read. His eyes were an unsettling blue and his nose was narrow, almost to a point.

Kate studied him as if reading his body language. She said nothing. Parriot and Ryals sat across from him.

Ryals began. "What do we call you?"

The man was silent.

"Where are you from?"

Still nothing. His only movement was when he licked his tongue over his teeth. It was almost a menacing gesture.

"You threatened my daughter," Ryals said. "And you tried to kill me. You're toast. There's a sliver of light, just a sliver. You give us everything you've got."

"Lawyer," the man said with a thick accent. "International lawyer." Ryals looked back at Kate. It hurt to turn. He wondered if she picked up the man's accent.

"I cannot help you there. Some public defender will show up, at some point. Bureaucracy can be slow. May be a few days."

Parriot tapped the table with a pen. In front of him was a folder. "We have camera from the bar. From his house," he said, gesturing at Ryals. "We have enough to charge you with all we need right now. I can count at least six charges. Given the preponderance of evidence and eyewitness testimonies. I'm not sure how much room an attorney has to wiggle here. I'm guessing a public defender is simply going to tell you your best case is a reduced sentence. Oh, and we have federal investigators involved, so hopefully you'll have the resources to navigate a federal charge."

The suspect looked away from them toward the wall, toward the door, and he shrugged. Ryals thought he should feel angry. He didn't. He didn't feel frustrated. He wasn't sure why.

"Do you know Willy Sharpe?" Ryals asked him. He said nothing.

"How about this man?" Parriot said, and pushed the image from the video of the Chinese man in the bar. The suspect glanced at it, but didn't react.

Ryals and Parriot looked at one another. Ryals glanced again at Kate. Her faced revealed nothing. He thought he picked up something in her expression. Focused anger, maybe, as if she were carrying a grudge. Ryals thought it was a little puzzling, but he didn't stare. She gave no indication she had any questions for the suspect. Finally, she looked at Ryals and gestured for them to leave. They rose and left the room.

Outside Sheriff Vinson waited for them.

"What do we have?"

"Not much."

"What do you make of his accent? South African?" Parriot asked.

"No, not South African," Kate said. "I'm not sure. Australian, maybe."

"So we have a murder suspect from nowhere," Ryals said. "Though, he may not be our murder suspect."

"He's not," Kate said.

"She's right," Parriot answered.

"Why not?"

Parriot turned his laptop around. He opened the footage from the National the night before Willy was found. Kate simply pointed at it.

"What am I supposed to see here?"

"His height," Parriot said. "Our perp is taller than this man. By a few inches."

"And the shoes size doesn't match," Ryals sighed, looking over the intake form.

"There's that, too," Kate said.

"Then who did we catch?" The Sheriff asked.

"I'm certain we'll learn more from his phone," Parriot said.

"We hope," Ryals said.

Outside she spoke. "You can keep working on him. I'll try another avenue. Parriot, you can rip data from his phone?"

Parriot nodded. "I brought my Cellebrite machine."

"That will help," Kate said.

"Help what?"

"Help us find the others involved."

They tried to question the suspect once more and got nothing. They left him in the interview room. Kate then said she was leaving. Ryals realized he had no idea where she was staying; staying; she claimed to have found a room last minute, but where was just another of her mysteries. Angela slept on a sofa in the deputy lounge. He roused her. He was grateful that he'd only been injured and that Angela was safe, and for a brief moment he felt confident that, if he could indeed rest, they might solve the case. But they would get nowhere with the suspect in the interrogation room. He took Angela home for the night. The morning would come quickly enough.

He turned on the TV in his bedroom briefly. He checked the local news. The last thing he remembered was seeing the Sheriff in a late night press conference, announcing the arrest of a person of interest in the murder at the Masters.

THIRTY-THREE

Jonni laid back on his bed, already showered and dressed and he stared at the ceiling as the first pale aquamarine light came in through the crack in the curtains. It was a blend of the vibrant green trees behind the hotel and the velvet blue dawn sky. There was a peace this morning unlike any he could remember. It wasn't just that he no longer heard the busy road outside as he had in the hotel; it was something deeper. There was no sound at all in the rooms. On the wall was art; drawings of the National. They were original, signed by the artists. The bed was large, the curtains soft and rest on it was heavenly. Coffee was delivered to the antechamber, and he hadn't even noticed, though he was awake for some time before it was even light out. He rose finally and poured coffee; the mug was cream-colored with a gold print of the clubhouse.

For the first time this week, Jonni was hopeful. He was ready to compete.

As the dew-laden grass warmed with the first flickers of Sunday sun, the aroma of spring rose from the flora; they sailed on a placid morning breeze that ascended from Rae's Creek where honeybees danced over the flower. Allison breathed in the calm before the storm — and glancing skyward, she could see those high, silver-sheen stratus clouds that foretold weather. With obsessive frequency she checked the weather app on her phone, and — weather patterns in the South this time of year being so volatile — the radar and wind maps. Fifty-fifty there would be storms today. A storm delay could be accommodated. The Masters had extended to Monday in the past five times. Everyone made significant profits when that happened, though logistics became a challenge. It was a possibility she had to consider. They would not allow gameplay after dark.

At this hour, however, the day was pleasant and perfect. There was energy in the air, but it wasn't from a coming storm, rather the final round of the tournament.

She met with her staff and department heads, spoke briefly with the Chairman. Staff migrated to their stations to prepare grounds, concessions, gift shop, bathrooms, gates, parking and media. The well-oiled machine sprang into action on the final day of the eventful tournament.

The investigation was a distant concern to this morning. They had provided to the police all that they could. Last night Richmond County made an arrest. The Chairman was confident that would begin to put it all to rest. The Chairman had assured her the investigation would not interfere with the final day of the tournament.

Then as she walked out to the grass for the first time her phone rang. It was Hall.

"Detective," she answered. "What can I do for you?" she said, masking anxiety and irritation with cheer.

"We've had some progress. I need something from you."

"It's a busy day, Detective. What can I offer?"

He explained his request.

As she listened, Allison looked at the sky and checked her weather app again. Still a 50% chance of precipitation.

Ryals returned the call from home after the message from Kate that waited for him when he awoke. He couldn't imagine when she slept.

Dressing for the day was a difficult. He nearly had Angela put his shirt on for him. He did it with one arm while his body protested every move. He put on a light polo shirt and jacket and gray slacks. Easter was a week away. Today was Palm Sunday, and in Augusta the crowd would migrate from church to golf course, or the living room where they could watch it on television.

Angela would go to a friend's house for the day. Ryals drove to the station using one arm. He walked in to find the Sheriff and Parriot, but not Kate. Someone delivered trays of muffins. He reached for one, then hesitated. Angela wasn't here to scold him, but still he skipped the muffin and went to the cabinet and made oatmeal.

Kate arrived. She carried a backpack and set it down.

Ryals greeted her. "I spoke to the Operations Director. You'll have anything you need today."

"Great," she said. She was in high spirits. She handed Parriot a small thumb drive. "Phone records from the suspects phone, from the past six months."

He blinked at her. "That's more than I got through my extraction."

"I figured. Maybe it helps," she said.

"We should interview him again," Ryals said. They agreed. They went downstairs for a second round. Ryals had a renewed vigor for the interrogation. He seethed.

The suspect sat opposite them again, disheveled, greasier, but he wore the same scowl.

"How did you sleep?" Ryals asked. He shrugged. "We're here to give you another chance to cooperate," Ryals said. "The window for that is very narrow." Ryals noticed Kate shifted, as if she had something to say.

"Now," he said. "Anything you'd like to share with us?"

"Lawyer," the man said. His voice was gravelly. He had slept poorly.

"I'm sure someone is working on that," Ryals said. "Help us in the meantime."

"Lawyer," he said. He closed his eyes as if to take a nap. Kate tapped her foot. Ryals was irritated by it now. He looked at her. She tilted her head, saying 'let's go outside.'

After a few more minutes of no responses, they walked out.

"What is it?" He asked her.

"You're getting nowhere."

"We'll wear him down."

"No, we won't. He answers to someone else, someone with lots of money whom he believes has his back. "But after last night, we have information that can and will help us." She said. "If you'll allow me, I have an idea. There's just no time today to sit around and hope that he comes to his senses. And anything he might give us we would have to verify. He could easily send us chasing our tails."

She led them upstairs. Ryals glanced at Parriot. Both seemed to wait for the other to decide when it was time to rein her in.

"What do you need for your plan to work?" Ryals asked suppressing mild irritation.

"It's what you need. And this," she handed him over a small gray device.

"And this is?"

"You'll use it on the course. I won't be there."

"Where will you be?"

"See this?" She pointed to an LED light on the side and a LCD readout with signal strength indicators. It was the size of a handheld radio. A small boxy thing with a flat plastic antenna.

"This does what, exactly?"

"This will tell you if a cell phone is active nearby. It will show you what tower it uses, and how close it is."

"What will this do?"

"It will show you who's using a phone at a place where no one is supposed to have a phone."

"So you want me to use this? What will you do?"

"I'll be on the course with you. The problem is..."

"His phone isn't very helpful," Parriot admitted.

"Yes," she said. "He scrubbed his calls, or had multiple burners. That doesn't give us much to go on. There's another option, but you aren't going to like it," she said, looking at Ryals.

"Why not?" He asked, and looked toward the interview and holding areas where the uncooperative attacker still waited. Kate gave Ryals a knowing look.

"Absolutely not," the Sheriff said. "You're not taking a suspect and letting him go."

"Mr..." Kate began. "Sheriff." She didn't know his name, Ryals realized. Nor did it seem to be relevant to her. "It's the only way to make something work on our timeline. Any other effort simply doesn't give us enough time."

The Sheriff looked at Ryals, who stood at the door. "I don't like it either," Ryals said. "Hell, I'm the one he stabbed. But I think it's our best bet. Going on the assumption that anyone else we need is going to slip out of town within twelve to twenty-four hours, we have to get creative. We're still several steps back."

"No harm? He attacked one of my detectives. He may be responsible for murder."

"He's not," Ryals said.

"Not that one, anyway," Kate added.

"What?" The Sheriff asked.

"We have multiple incidents and multiple perpetrators," Ryals said. "Eyewitnesses and cameras telling us of at least three distinct individuals in four different locations. We're out of time and she has a plan. We were willing to accept her help, this is the way to do that." She gave him a look of gratitude. He didn't return it. He knew her ambitions were her own. He was okay with that only so long as their interests converged.

"Look," the Sheriff said, a single thick finger on his desk to anchor his point. "Ryals, you're compromised. You shouldn't be out there anyway. And yet you're responsible. For this multi-agency effort," he said. "You are responsible for what happens to that suspect from the minute he leaves the room. I just held a press conference, for God's sake."

"I know, sir. We'll keep an eye on him."

"GBI is okay with this?" The Sheriff asked Parriot, for safety.

"I can make the case of uncertainty in the ongoing investigation," he said.

"We expect him to do what? Take us right to the killer?"

"No, sir," Kate said. "Hopefully, when he's released he'll make a call, and we can identify who he calls."

"A phone call to who?"

"To whoever is involved in the plot," Ryals answered.

The Sheriff shook his head. "I look forward to your positive results," he said diplomatically.

THIRTY-FOUR

Sunday

Jonni's final drive down Magnolia Lane for this tournament was quiet. To avoid having to hide his thoughts from his father, he told Dad that he wanted to go in early, and alone, to prepare for his final day. He knew his dad was earnest and well meaning, but he put pressure on Jonni. Jonni could barely work under the pressure of the millions whom he didn't know. His dad was the one person left he didn't want to disappoint. But he needed to breathe.

Jonni knew, as he stepped out of the SUV in front of the clubhouse in the shadow of the early-morning sun, that if he were to play well today, if he were to compete at all, he had to sequester his thoughts.

As he went inside the pro room and lockers where his clubs would be waiting with Buster, walking the long green carpet and eggshell-white walls with perfectly posed pictures of the institution's history, he knew that if he were going to compete today, to find the green, let alone regain yesterday's momentum, he had to do it alone. Alone in his thoughts and alone on the course. Buster would be his companion, but he had to shut everything and everyone else out.

Frank waited just outside the pro shop. Jonni didn't make eye contact. It was best to ignores security and the implication that danger stalked Jonni. He no longer believed that it did. Buster sat by Jonni's bag reading a small prayer book which he folded and put into his pocket.

"It's gonna be a good day, a real good day," Buster announced, smiling with a squeaky-clean shaved face and neat hair ready for his green caddie's ball cap which rested on his knee. Other caddies were in but Jonni was the first golfer; he was given entrance earlier with special permission. He didn't like that he was constantly a special case, but he was here, and it was time to compete.

"Coffee? Water? Anything?" Buster asked. Jonni shook his head. No, he didn't need anything. He had grown to appreciate Buster. Buster demanded nothing from him, and was quiet when Jonni needed him to be.

A good caddie, some old man at a clubhouse once told Jonni, was a telescope. He helped his golfer ignore all that was irrelevant and focus only on the goal.

"Nothing, thank you" Jonni said, as he drew a deep breath then sat beside Buster.

He was surprised to find that he meant it. He felt relaxed now. He breathed deep. He could do this with Buster at his side. He could tune out the rest. Look through the telescope and find his way on each hole.

"Back home," Jonni said, "We have these braais. You know, cookout in backyard, everyone gets together. I never know what to say or who to talk to. I usually go off to the side and take a putter or wedge and hit a ball around. Always keep them with me, dirt, grass, pavement. Willy was the only one who would walk up and say anything to me. Everyone else knew to leave me alone." More words out loud than Jonni believed he'd spoken all week. Buster nodded, tapping his fingers on his knees.

"Sounds like me at family reunions," Buster said. "Go watch the game or play with the dog. Rather talk to one than twenty. Why I like being a caddie, you know. Focus on one person, not ever have to live in a crowd. I like being ignored when the game is done." he said. Then he looked at Jonni a moment before reaching out to adjust the way the clubs sat in the bag, one by one. "No one is gonna replace Mr. Sharpe for you, not ever, Jonni boy. I suspect, though, he was a good enough caddie to you that he's always with you. Still in your head, all he taught you. This is, after all, a game of legacies. He left one. You will too."

Jonni smiled. Jonni agreed, and without other pressures he could believe it, every bit of it. Frank outside was a ghost, he didn't matter, didn't exist. Whatever happened on the course today happened there and existed there and everything else was a different reality. Jonni stood and listened as the door opened down the hall and more golfers arrived, competitors, a fraternity into which he was invited, and would compete, and would excel.

His tee off came at midday. He was partnered today with Larry Mize, who, in his sixties, was significantly more seasoned than Jonni, and who wore today a pale blue polo and who, nearing the end of his competition days, had a real legacy of his own here to preserve and defend. Larry announced his retirement in 2023, but had returned for one more tournament. Larry played better in this tournament than any he'd played in the past decade, and Jonni knew the real story of this year's Masters, if it wasn't for Willy's murder, was Larry's performance. He'd shot a seventy-one and sixty-seven the past two rounds. Larry greeted him with a bright smile, and seemed to take no offense at all to the way Jonni was sure to detract from Larry's last round at the Masters.

"He's from right here in this town," Buster said with a hint of pride, giving Jonni a background on Mize, "Went to Georgia Tech then started playing golf as a pro. Won the Masters in '87 after a three-way play off. He tapped this dream of a chip from a disadvantaged spot outside the green for an impossible birdie, beat Greg Norman. As a young guy, then, too," Buster said, now whispering as they drew near. Jonni remembered that shot; he'd seen it on more than one highlight reel, including in his room the other night. He greeted Mize, who smiled with easy-going eyes and he looked like he might preach at a country church on Sundays. His eyes moved constantly under his Srixon hat and beneath his white hair. He hadn't an ounce of fat on him at six feet and Jonni could still see in his smile and step and blue eyes that matched his shirt the same youth and energy and focus that won him the green jacket years ago that he saw in the grainy video when his hair was black.

"Good to see you," Mize told him, his Southern accent heavy but his step light. "Pretty day for golf." That was it for now; he strode over the grass to talk with his caddie and surveyed the greens and Jonni agreed it was a good day, though the air felt full, and he thought he could smell rain. He didn't mention his return to the tournament, his imminent retirement. He was here to play and he was cheerful about it.

Jonni turned and caught a glimpse of his Dad on the rope line, smiling at him confidently. Frank stood beside him, and the second ANGC security man was nearby as well. Jonni wasn't sure his name. Jonni smiled at his dad — Martin had never missed one of Jonni's tournament games.

Jonni looked past his father, at the leaderboard that stood just down the lane from the gift shop, still blank and ready to broadcast today's competition. Jonni saw the names of those going before him, and then his name and Mize's now, appearing beside the words "THRU 1." The blank spaces on the board would soon populate with numbers trending red or green depending on each player's fortune.

Mize had the first shot, and Jonni saw for a moment as the veteran player was about to take his first drive, the crowd already gathering for the pair, and he knew of course that Mize deserved it more than he did. He was a son of Augusta, and this was supposedly his last tournament. Still Jonni sensed many watched him with dark curiosity.

Ryals and Kate drove to the National, sipping coffee in travel mugs.

It was left to Parriot and another detective to release the suspect when given instruction. They would tell the suspect that they did not have enough to hold him and would give him his phone.

"How do we know someone will call?"

"Call, or text. More likely text. Whatever our knife-wielding attacker is going to do next, his job isn't done. If they mean to come after Jonni Lombard, they will do it today. We know someone has threatened him, and is watching him. They will be on the course."

"And we'll find them with this?"

"With a little luck," Kate said.

"Luck," Ryals thought. They just released the man who attempted to kill him, hoping for a little luck. Ryals tried to remember the last time he solved a case with luck.

"What if someone else has a phone? An employee? Staff?"

"I don't think they will. No one is allowed one. I read that ANGC performed a security audit of staff, not during the tournament but some other time in the year. They found one employee hid a phone in his lunch between two slices of bread. He was fired. No one gets away with it."

They arrived to find the parking lots densely packed. They parked and walked more than a mile to the entrance. Once again, they found badges waiting for them — this time, they avoided the metal detectors and followed a security escort in. They both had phones, they had the device, and Ryals had his duty Glock 17 on his hip. His sport coat today would just conceal it; he did not want to draw attention, but he couldn't risk being without it.

Jonni stayed at par until the 4th hole, "Flowering Crabapple." There, the haze overhead turned to steely white cloud cover and the sunlight disappeared. Jonni's first stroke with a long iron landed just shy of the twin bunkers that defended it, positioned at either side of the green. The crowd, already feeling the energy of the day, cheered his first shot louder than was customary at the Masters. To Jonni, as he got into the zone, the crowd, even Buster's congratulations, were increasingly just white noise. Though the wind was moderate but gusty, it was as if he cut through it. Mize's tee shot was deftly hit as well; he read the wind and dropped his ball ten yards north of Jonni's.

After the long walk downhill he chipped the final ball in gently for a birdie, not even hesitating, believing simply that the gravity around the hole would pull his ball in, that he had only to offer it up and it would sink where it was meant to.

On the 5th hole, "Magnolia," he swung uphill with his driver sending the ball past the intimidating fairway bunkers. He heard gasps as the shot sailed slightly over three hundred yards. The ball had flown into the white void overhead and then came coasting down gently in the center of the fairway, well clear and farther beyond the trees where his ball had fallen yesterday. He was within reasonable striking distance of the green.

Even Mize whistled at his shot as they walked. Jonni lifted his chin and marched up the hill. Buster handed him an iron.

Kate used binoculars and kept her small satchel with the device around her shoulder. Ryals watched the way her eyes swept the crowd, and looking toward Frank and Martin Lombard but never directly. Always past them to see who might be looking on. Ryals did the same, and found he quickly removed his jacket to let his polo breathe and so as not to stand out among the spectators — or patrons, rather. He wished he had a place to store the jacket. He worried his cut would start to bleed. He wore a dark shirt today for that reason, a sport blend that wicked moisture. He still wasn't comfortable.

It was hard as well not to get excited along with the crowd. He applauded as others did. He struggled not to be lost in the moment. Comments were passed around with praise for the kid's performance:

"About the best five-iron shot I've ever seen."

"Against all odds."

"Born to play this course."

The crowd shuffled and grew ever larger from the Fifth to the Sixth then to the Seventh hole, which was where Ryals felt the first heavy raindrop slap his folded forearm. He looked up, saw clouds growing thicker and darker like the lowering of a shade. The rain fell now just in occasional drops; over-eager before the appointed time this afternoon. That time, though, seemed more near and inevitable with each passing moment. Umbrellas were held at the ready, rain ponchos opened, ready to to get drenched.

Kate checked her device.

"It picks up our phones," she said. "We'll have to turn them off."

"Now?" He asked.

"Not yet," she said.

A crowd followed the young South African from hole to hole, hurrying to keep up, not wanting to miss a moment of Jonni's performance. Sam Ingot was in the crowd again; he carried a pen that he kept clipped to his lanyard and kept his small notebook clutched in his hand.

He joined in the applause — he was fair-minded, as a good journalist should be, but he was first and foremost a fan of the game. Jonni's performance was fine and his attitude laudable. Similarly, Larry continued to surprise and cut his score down with a competent and smooth performance played with the ease of someone who had victories already behind him, with nothing to prove, taking bold chances, the kind, Ingot thought, one would take when he had nothing to lose.

Jonni's play didn't slow even when the fast greens were wet and heavy as the first sheets of rain passed over them ahead of a storm that threatened them from the south. Jonni played an energetic and confident game.

Sam had written about similar streaks, some historic, some he had been present for: Bobby Jones' Grand Slam, Tiger Woods' 6-year climb at Pumpkin Ridge; Kevin Streelman at the 2014 Travelers' Championship, Byron Nelson in '45, 17-year-old Lydia Ko at the ANA invitational — plenty of moments came to mind, exciting and inspirational, rare solar flares in the golf solar system.

Jonni nearly undershot his drive to the 12th, swinging hard and clearing the creek, but he walked up with confidence and used a pitching wedge to chip his ball to the flag, the crowd erupting in applause when they could see the line was true and perfectly paced. Mize patted the kid on the shoulder and Jonni handed his wedge back to his caddie as they walked out of the furthest corner of the course, rain now coming down steady but gentle.

Jonni had gone from four over to six under and his name card and Mize's flipped up toward the top of the leaderboard.

Sam took his notebook out and described the flashes of sunlight that appeared through clouds. He described the details of the experience, including the dense pine needles underfoot, the spark of raindrops on the leaves like tinsel as the players passed beneath them. He described Jonni's mud covered sneakers.

The rain had not truly begun to fall yet, but it would. Jonni smiled as he left Amen Corner.

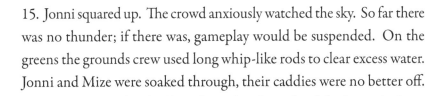

15. Jonni squared up. The crowd anxiously watched the sky. So far there was no thunder; if there was, gameplay would be suspended. On the greens the grounds crew used long whip-like rods to clear excess water. Jonni and Mize were soaked through, their caddies were no better off. Buster used a small umbrella and towels to keep the clubs dry in the bags.

"They're gonna get sloppy now," Kate heard several of the patrons observe, but Jonni's shots cut silver streaks through the rain.

Mize sliced the last hole, sending a water-slinging ball off to the side where it bounced off a tree and skidded in the wet grass, but it landed advantageously. He was able to putt it in for a surprising birdie.

Kate watched Jonni, and Frank, and Martin on the sideline. Frank watched Martin more than he watched Jonni, and kept one hand in his pocket. No one else, save for Ryals, seemed to notice. He was perhaps concerned that Martin was exposed to the crowd. Jonni was protected by ropes and gallery guards and the watchful eyes of hundreds of patrons; someone could easily get to Martin in the dense throngs.

Ryals looked at Kate, who was soaked through like him, but her clothes were made for it. Her sneakers were all-weather, and her socks were low and wool. She did not seem to mind the weather. His cotton jacket was heavy and his socks squeaked in his shoes. His ribs and his back and his knee hurt, and he regularly took Tylenol. Standing was a chore; he wished he could sit.

"If there's thunder, they'll stop play. Maybe for the whole day."

"Would that good or bad for us?" He wondered out loud.

"I don't know," she said.

She didn't know whether to hope for a rain delay or for the sky to clear up. Jonni didn't smile anymore; his last shot was wide and landed in the trees. The rain was making play tough.

"What's that?" Ryals asked, turning to her. She listened to the sky for thunder. It was faint, distant.

"Thunder?" she said, hearing it. "It's faint. May be an airplane."

"No," he said. "That," and he lifted her arm to hear it better — the tone from her device.

"Turn your phone off," she said. They both did.

The machine was quiet then emitted a tone.

"Someone has a phone," she said. "It may not mean anything."

They scanned the ground. The device was quiet again. They saw no one; but the crowd was dense. The rain and dark clouds reduced visibility as well. The players walked up the fairway. The crowd moved with them. Kate and Ryals followed.

Jonni's ball sat about three yards outside the green on Fifteen, beyond the bridge and past the pond where rain seemed to dance on the surface. Kate watched as Jonni walked up to the ball and Buster handed him a wedge. Jonni waited for Mize to take his position and then Jonni lined up for the shot. Kate watched Jonni's shoulders relax. He eyed the green, practiced his swing then squared up against the ball. But then his shoulders seemed to tighten. She could see something in his body language. A hesitation in his arms. He looked at the ball and seemed to glance toward the crowd. Or maybe he just meant to shake water on his hat. She knew something had changed though. He hesitated. He was uncertain.

He swung and caught grass. The ball spun up and twisted in the rain. It missed the hole, moving too high, too fast. It landed over the hill. He'd duffed it.

The crowd was suddenly uneasy. Kate looked around at the discomfort, the shifting of weight and scratching of noses. Jonni, irritated, returned his club. Then he pulled it back out. He knew he'd need it again; the ball had rolled too far beyond the flag. He waited for his partner. Mize took a long time before making a perfect shot; he beat Jonni to the hole.

Then Jonni walked to his ball to shoot again. And Kate could feel a change in air pressure. The rain had paused but the clouds were heavy. Jonni swung too fast, too impatiently, and the ball went wide again. Toward the water.

Into the water. The plop sent ripples that rolled outward in concentric circles. Jonni stared. She could feel the energy change in the crowd. Jonni stormed toward the water.

"Oh, no," Kate said under her breath.

But Ryals touched her shoulder. The device. She looked at it. Studied the crowd again. Someone was sending messages.

"How close is the phone?"

"Within fifty yards," she said.

"Can we adjust it? Make it so we know if it's closer?"

"Yes," she said. She changed a setting on it.

Ryals said, "Let's walk and see what comes up."

They moved through the crowd, step by step. She watched her device. Ryals wanted to see who moved with the crowd, who didn't. Who watched the ball, who watched Jonni.

Kate looked up just long enough to see Jonni take another swing. And his ball went astray again.

"He's melting down," she heard someone say, their voice trembling. She could feel it.

THIRTY-FIVE

Each step up the hill was more brutal than the last; the pain in Ryal's side was excruciating and he looked at the water rolling down his side expecting to see it running pink with blood. They kept fifty feet or so behind the crowd. The device was quiet.

"You think they're gone?" Ryals asked, suppressing a grimace from the pain in his ribs.

"No," Kate said, her eyes wide and straight ahead like a cat stalking prey, "I think someone is here. They're communicating with their man on the outside."

Ryals wanted to turn his phone on and ask Parriot where the suspect was. If he'd run and they'd lost him. Kate said no phones.

Ryals lost his balance as one foot slipped on wet pine straw and he slipped and fell on the slope. Kate tried to catch him, then helped him stand. "Ow," he said. His injuries were getting the best of him.

"Gotchu," she said. By the time he was up and checking himself over the device pinged again. They were close to Jonni. They stopped at the rope line. The fairway was ten yards across here; the phone could easily be among the spectators on the far side. There they saw Martin and the bodyguard. The bodyguard glanced into his pocket, then at Martin, then at Jonni again.

"Did you see that?" She asked.

"Yes. The bodyguard has a phone."

"I don't believe he's been given special permission to keep his."

"Certainly not," Ryals answered.

Then they saw something they hadn't noticed or hadn't seen before. Jonni hit his last putt of the hole and walked off with Mize. Everyone else broke up to move — but not Martin, and not Frank.

"Watch them," Kate said. Ryals looked closely. The bodyguard gripped Martin's upper arm and whispered something. His words were clearly menacing. It all happened quickly. If they weren't looking for the phone, they wouldn't have seen it at all.

"Remind me. Who hired his security?" Kate asked.

"They came recommended by the National. By a member, I think."

"Interesting. He seems a bit familiar and a bit unpleasant."

"I'd say someone has insurance on the Lombards."

"And Martin knows it."

They walked again. Suddenly Martin and the bodyguard were gone.

"Lost them," Kate said.

"Me too," Ryals admitted. Steps were painful, especially against mud slicks.

"There," Ryals pointed, catching the pair further off the rope line. "Look at his shoes," Ryals pointed lower. Frank wore Salomons. His steps were careful and firm.

"Want to make a bet on the size?" Ryals asked.

"No, I don't." Kate said. "I think you may be right."

"That's our murderer," Ryals whispered to himself. Kate didn't contradict him.

Ryals powered through the pain, ignoring the mud slick on his leg. He heard thunder and felt rainwater streaking over every joint.

They paused at a crossing over a fairway and waited for the gallery guards to pull back the ropes and let the crowd cross, some of whom looked to be escaping the weather. Ryals followed Frank, and Kate was directly behind Martin now. Ryals could see that the bodyguard checked his phone as he made his way to the edge of the crowd. Ryals lost sight of Kate. The crowd was compressed on the muddy path under the pines. Everyone was pushed together and they all bumped and occasionally slid. It was a jovial group; his mission among them was not so agreeable. He continued his pursuit; the bodyguard led him up the hill and off the path to the right toward the deep shade of a more dense group of trees. They moved south of the 18th hole. He hadn't spent as much time on the course as Kate, but he had a decent sense of geography.

Rain fell in sheets. Ryals saw white bungalows hidden in the pines further into the wood. He moved along the path like a coyote hunting its prey. Ryals thought to reach out to Lawrence, but he couldn't stop now. He walked as naturally as he could but at a quick pace. He limped along, between his slip in the mud, and the stitches and aches from the car accident, he had trouble. Frank looked left and right but never behind him at Ryals directly. They came close to the tree line, where gallery guards were posted at intervals. They walked along them. It was dim as if it were early evening beneath the foreboding sky dark as lead.

They continued past the restrooms, moving with the stream of patrons, but the bodyguard broke for the trees. Ryals was thirty yards behind; he left the path parallel to his suspect. The bodyguard seemed to be on a mission, but he aimed between the bungalows in an area where there was nothing but trees. Ryals was surprised they hadn't been spotted and stopped by security; but with the crowd and the rainfall everyone was distracted. He didn't want to spook the bodyguard, but they were now the only ones moving through the wood. Somewhere in the back of his mind Ryals knew that something was off. Ryals felt searing pain and believed he'd popped at least one stitch. He kept going.

He passed the same bathroom and came to the line of towering pines
and into the shadowy wood beyond. He heard thunder.

Kate continued past the first green toward the clubhouse where Martin
showed his pass and walked into the Member's Only area and toward
the inside. He had left his son behind.

She removed her pass from her bag and showed it and was allowed
to follow him.

She found him in the locker room, water dripping onto the floor,
other golfers standing around, their day finished.

She waited in the hallway out of sight. She decided not to confront
him. To wait and see what followed. This place was safe and secure;
nothing violent would happen here.

Kate backed into a busy office where radios buzzed and staff ran in
and out and with many discussing the weather; rain and thunder in
hushed tones as they watched screens. She picked up a radio and held it
to blend in; no one paid her any attention. She glanced into the hallway
and Martin emerged. She followed him to the front of the club as he
looked at his phone. As far as she could see he carried nothing—except,
maybe—a small paper in his fingers.

She backed away before he could see her. She waited out of sight.
When she peeked again he was gone. He could only have left the way
he came in, so she again exited the building into the dusk-like shade
beneath the massive oak tree. She caught sight of Martin to the north
as he walked quickly past the clubhouse and pro shop and toward the
course main entrance. Kate pulled her badge out to hang on her chest

as she held the stolen radio to her ear to look as if she were working while she walked.

Martin looked all around, but didn't seem to notice her — plenty of patrons, staff, interns, agents and press moved to and fro, and he was more concerned about something else. Martin and his bodyguard had split up — she wanted to know why.

There was a rain delay and some patrons aimed for the exits. Kate glanced at the leaderboard; many competitors hadn't finished their round. She took note long enough to see that since she had left him, Jonni had added two strokes to his score. Mize continued to do well. Umbrellas and raincoats now were as common as pastel polos and sun dresses had been earlier. Patrons were prepared for rain. Most wouldn't give up a few hours at the tournament just because of rain. Some stood waiting on the storm to clear and play to resume.

Ryals paused by a tree and rested against it; he tried to catch sight of the bodyguard again. The mysterious man had disappeared in the woods. The sky was covered and the sound of the tournament seemed distant. Here in the woods Ryals felt he was a world apart from the competition. He was still on the National's grounds. Surely Lawrence could see him on camera. He hoped he could.

There was no sign of the bodyguard. Somehow he'd disappeared. Ryals leaned against the tree for a moment and caught his breath, and felt the searing hot pain up and down his side. He was sure he'd popped another stitch in the fall but he didn't want to check. He looked at his phone. Parriot was on his way. At least here he was out of the rain.

Ryals stepped forward, glad that he had his gun with him, but at the same time he knew that if he were to use it on the course that would be the end of his career, one way or the other. He should feel safe here, but in fact while he was far away from Amen Corner, he was deep in the same ominous wooded boundary where Willy had been murdered. The pain in Ryals' side was excruciating; each heavy breath threatened to pop more stitches.

He pushed himself away from the tree. He couldn't let his suspect get away. To the left, through the trees he could see the white facades and porch lamps of the bungalows not very far off. There was activity there, but how many people and what they were doing, he couldn't be sure. Had the bodyguard gone into one? The nearest was perhaps forty yards away. Ryals tried to identify footprints. It was as if the bodyguard had simply disappeared.

He started toward the nearest bungalow.

Ahead through the trees, to the west of the bungalow Ryals could clearly see a pond, water dark and alive with the rhythm of rain, and beyond that was manicured green; he believed it was the Par 3 course — it was empty now, perhaps a good place for a meeting, maybe the bodyguard had gone that way—

The attack came from behind him, with horrifying swiftness; he dove senselessly, reacting to the muscular body and menacing pose of his attacker, whose outstretched arm held something metal that glinted even in the dull light; it wasn't a blade, no, but rather something more sinister — his mind processed it — recognized it — he fell into a tree and gasped — slam! He was knocked down — he saw what the man held — it was a syringe — a needle — coming for him.

Jonni watched his chip bounce over the top of the bunker and finally onto the green on the par 3 16th hole, "Redbud." The thunder had ceased and play had resumed. He had to clear the pond that separated the green from the tee box. His first shot was too far north, to the left of the pond on the side of the steep hill. He slipped on the treacherous embankment as he looked for his ball, then finding it he hastily hit the ball toward the green, where Larry had already sunk his ball. Jonni was frazzled.

The crowd that watched him had shared their enthusiastic energy; now he felt they added weight to his game; an unhelpful pressure. He felt he couldn't breathe. He felt the urge to retreat again, to hide from public scrutiny. He looked for his dad among those at the rope line, but he didn't see him. He felt alone.

Think, he told himself. Buster — was it Buster, or was it Willy? — told him it was half math, half art. No, that was Willy. When you couldn't solve it like a math problem, you got creative. You just followed your gut. Jonni tried to ask his gut — but he felt everything pushing into his head now. The crowd, the memories, the thoughts — it was all pushing to get in. He couldn't think. Time was passing.

How much? He looked around. Looked for Buster. Maybe it had been five minutes. Maybe it had been an hour.

The afternoon had grown dim, the rain had ceased for a few minutes but returned now with greater intensity. Buster earlier had gone on about the rules about when they would shut it down. On the 14th they paused play. Now they pushed through the rain.

Jonni now stood at his ball, taking a putter from Buster as Larry watched patiently, standing in the rain. Jonni didn't make eye contact with anyone. His first putt missed and he finally sank the ball on his fifth stroke.

Kate's switched her phone on. She only followed Martin now; she didn't look at the device. She kept her voice low.

"It's Parriot," he said.

"Where are you?"

"Entrance. Where do I go?"

"Gift shop. Get here quick." She was in the gift shop, having followed Martin in. It was a big space, upper level with more expensive gifts, the yellow Master's flag everywhere; it was fairly busy and the merchandise light on stock but still organized. She browsed and even picked out something to buy. A cap. She tried on one after another, looking around the room via the mirrors. She could still see Martin. He was not really looking at anything, just wandering aimlessly. His face was white and his expression distraught. She put several other items in her bag. After a while someone approached him —a man, southeast Asian by the looks of him, wearing a black jacket and dark hat and he simply extended his hand and Martin shakily handed him a small slip of paper. The man stared at Martin a moment, who didn't seem sure what to do next, then he departed quickly.

Kate stayed with the stranger. He seemed to linger, picking out two items seemingly at random which he took to the cashier. Kate did the same, purchasing a cap which she put on to change and conceal her profile as she exited the gift shop. But the stranger stopped at the Check Counter, where customers could have their souvenirs held during the day.

That was the safe place, she realized. That's where it was. This was a handoff. Something had been placed there among patrons' purchased merchandise. The stranger handed the small slip he'd presumably received from Martin. As Kate watched in her periphery the stranger exchanged his ticket for a large clear, green striped bag — its contents impossible to see from where she stood — and immediately departed for the exit.

Kate put it together — the bodyguard was there to make sure Martin went through with the exchange.

She called Parriot, hiding her phone as best as she could.

"Where are you now?"

"Walking up," he answered.

"I'm coming your way. Target is black jacket, black hat, clear bag. Walking fast. I'm on his six. Do we have a vehicle on standby?"

"I'll send one of my guys to it now," he said. "Should I call the police?"

"Not yet."

Within seconds Parriot was in view, standing at the entrance. She looked for the buyer, or the bag man, whatever he was. Martin should soon be back on the line by his son to see the end of his game. She spotted the bag man again. He was through the turnstiles. She pointed; Parriot nodded.

Parriot smartly turned to walk ahead of the man and enough patrons were leaving all at once through the gates ahead that no one person stood out. She counted two additional GBI agents; one woman and one man. She hoped the target hadn't noticed them as well.

Outside the gate they walked the bridge to the parking lot, which was mostly unpaved and now muddy. The man walked past several lines of cars until he spotted one, idling, headlights on.

"There," she said into her phone. "Silver sedan."

"I see it," Parriot said, breaking off. "Cut him off at the entrance?"

"Yes," she said.

"On it," he said, and pointed one of his agents to run to the vehicle.

As Parriot's man went into motion, she realized their error. The bag man had too much of a lead. They wouldn't block him in time. She found a Master's parking attendant and told her that someone had just stolen a bag. She pointed to the silver sedan, into which the bag man had just climbed. The sedan pulled away into the line of exiting traffic. The GBI vehicle was too far behind. The parking lot was too busy.

"Where's your car?" She asked Parriot.

He led her at a jog, aware of the predicament. They ran for the vehicle.

"Put out an APB," she said. "Did you get the license plate?"

"No, it was out of view."

She jumped in and they spun the wheel as they ran out of the lot.

They pulled out onto Washington Road and accelerated. The sedan pulled away. They weren't aware they were being pursued.

"My agents are just behind us," Parriot said.

"Just hang there for now. Let's see what he does."

So they had four against — well, she wasn't sure how many were inside. Parriot carried his pistol.

THIRTY-SIX

Ryals gripped the tree and spun around it like some sort of jungle ape. There were two men in pursuit; where the second had come from, he had no idea. He was barely ahead of them, and only thanks to having knocked the bodyguard with the syringe against a tree. Every step was a stumble and every breath was excruciating. Ryals ran toward the pond and the green grass outside the woods; some voice in his mind telling him that if he could just find the right place to turn and face his opponents he could best them; like the charge of a football offense at the scrimmage line, but another part of his mind knew that it was two against one and there was one needle. His gun had fallen or been snatched. It wasn't in his holster. He had to run. A single prick of that needle and he was done for. Providence alone had protected him a moment ago.

He could hardly run in a straight line; he listed left, toward the pond.

He could feel the attackers behind him. He gripped a thin tree, slick with rainwater and he spun sideways and was flung onto the manicured grass alongside it away from the pines. He clutched at the grass and his nails dug into the mud and he saw the men approach and he had no other choice but to lunge at a pair of legs. It was the thicker man, the bodyguard, who he saw only when the man went down, his head smacking into the earth, but Ryals hadn't incapacitated him.

"Richmond County Sheriff!" Ryals shouted weakly, "you're under arrest!" But the words were pointless and pathetic. He wheezed them out.

He rolled with the bodyguard, delivering a blow to his chin but it seemed to have little effect. He punched again, knowing that his only chance was a desperate determination and not giving this man a second chance but he also knew that he would feel the prick of a needle full of paralyzing, heart stopping death serum any second. The bodyguard managed a sharp punch and Ryals was flung off. Then he saw the second attacker; the blonde man with blue eyes, the more slender, the man from the car, the man — yes — from the station, whom Ryals had arrested, the man who frightened Ryals's daughter and then sat in the station, smug in the face of the Sheriff's authority, so certain that wherever he came from, he existed above this little town, above the Sheriff's department, above Ryals and all of their rules. The fiend wore a Masters badge, and how he had obtained it when so many people fought to have just one struck Ryals as sacriligious, and Ryals felt a volcanic rise of adrenaline and though he saw the needle emerge from the man's jacket he charged, gripping the suspect's arm and throwing a punch as hard as he could at the man's neck, but instead catching his throat: his wet knuckles slid up brutally along his windpipe to his jaw where he cracked the man's head back and seemed to punch through him and then together they went down again.

Ryals turned to the bodyguard as he righted himself in tear-inducing pain. He had snatched the syringe and held it as if he meant business. In the distance he heard shouts.

"Don't move!" Ryals said and he was sure the guard knew he meant business. He held the needle ahead of him like a dagger and the body-guard kept his eye on it. "Onto your knees!" Ryals commanded and he moved around the man as he pulled the cuffs from his belt. They were slick and dirty but they worked.

They went tumbling as he was hit again from the side.

Ryals felt the wind knocked out of him and he heard a ringing in his ears and he realized then he was done. Clearly he knocked the other man out and now they were both on him and in seconds the needle would be in his arm or shoulder and that would be it. He tried to summon the strength but his body said no. He slid in the grass and rolled onto his side.

He could only hear his own labored breathing.

And then, slowly, he realized that nothing happened. For a sickening moment he thought he was already drugged and dying. And he heard something else; other voices, short and curt and loud. He had a hard time turning but he finally did, and rose, and saw men in jackets swarming them. A dozen at least. Ryals rose, he was barely able, and backed away from the two men who now lay on the grass in surrender, and Ryals saw Lawrence standing among the Pinkerton's who surrounded them. Lawrence gestured and one of his guys moved in to help Ryals, clear him away, and then they moved in on the assailants. Ryals set the syringe on the grass.

Jonni felt the uneven give of the wet grass as it bent and slapped back against his putter. He pushed the head forward; it connected with the ball and together they moved as one, like the moon and sun in eclipse, and then gently he stopped the stroke and the ball continued, the exchange of inertia complete as his putter stopped and the ball rolled in a sharp curve just above the hole then driven by gravity and the weight of the collecting water and against the laden grass. But then the ball went too fast and passed the hole. Jonni had made an impatient, frustrated shot. He didn't even hear a gasp. Didn't hear the sigh of the crowd.

They knew. He was losing now. His score ticked up another stroke. He barely felt the sting this time. His feet felt like lead as he walked up to the ball again. Dragging his shoes through the wet grass

He let the putter swing and connect and it was once again too hard and he practically pushed it into the hole after that. Buster didn't even say anything as Jonni walked past him and tried to avoid the gaze of the crowd.

Finally, they stood at the 18th tee, and there was a new kind of tragic hush to the crowd, as if it were the eve of Good Friday, and the rain had finally stopped and a chill set upon the course. The afternoon light was fading. Precipitation fell through the air in intermittent mist like a curtain. The mood was somber for Jonni, but a fervor had grown around Larry Mize, who played what was certain to be the best round of his career. Jonni was glad to no longer be the center of attention. The crowd was dense; they celebrated Mize.

But when he stood at the tee, looking up the long final 465-yard stretch called "Holly," named for the several varieties of American holly bushes along the narrow fairway with its dogleg bend. He could feel the disappointment from the fans. He looked up at them only to identify his father in the crowd for reassurance. He did not stand a chance to win, but he would try his best.

Larry swung. His drive shot through the air with a miraculous lift in the cold, wet air. It whined and climbed the hill and Jonni was sure he had never seen a shot like it. The crowd erupted up above, and that was soon echoed below.

Jonni took his place. It was like walking the plank, but then he thought of Willy. Willy once told him, nothing matters but how you play the game. He didn't say the game mattered. He didn't say that winning mattered. Willy said how Jonni played mattered. Dad reinforced that to mean that Jonni must always play to win; their economic security depended on it. Jonni's career trajectory depended on outperforming everyone else — on outperforming himself. That wasn't what Willy meant at all, though. Jonni realized it now. Willy meant, it matters where you are in your head when you take your swing. It matters that you enjoy it.

He looked over his shoulder; behind him the sky was clearing. It glowed fiery pink and orange in a band beneath the storm clouds that now were passing by to the west. The sunset illuminated water drops on tree leaves like glitter. Jonni thought of the strand of lights yellowed from years of use that hung all year round on the side of Sam's clubhouse restaurant. He longed to be there.

Jonni looked up the hill only once and he nearly closed his eyes. He took a practice swing. His breath was deep and resonated in his ears; he could have been alone in a small room. Everything faded away; he was alone on the course with his club, the ball and the manicured grass over the final hole at the most extraordinary and challenging course in the world. He knew his score. He couldn't win now if he tried. Not even with a hole in one. He could still do his best. He could finish with dignity. He took his shot.

The ball rose high into the Augusta sky and came down far and away above him. The crowd wasn't ecstatic; there was no roar. But there was lively applause.

"That's it, Jonni," someone said, encouraging him.

He extended his club to Buster who took his driver from him. Jonni nodded to Larry and together the quartet of golfers and caddies began the steep climb to claim their final shots.

He found his ball beneath the last hill. He stood by it as Larry prepared to take his own.

Larry did, chipping the ball in a high and graceful arc that landed just above the flag. It wasn't done. The crowd's expectant mumbles turned to gasps and then a true roar as Larry sank his ball. It was an extraordinary feat. Had Mize's lightening struck twice? Jonni knew what it meant, or he was nearly certain. He first had to take his own.

He swung. His shot was wide. There were two hills on Eighteen. The green sat on a tricky slant. From the dip beneath it, and between the two hills a tall man could see the clubhouse. This Buster had pointed out two days ago; it felt like a lifetime hence. From a TV stand high above he could see the cameras watching him and he could hear, beneath it, the snapping of the photographers' long-lensed cameras.

He found the ball barely on the grass with no obvious angle to the hole. For his second shot he used an overly aggressive 8-iron at Buster's suggestion. He took the club from his caddie and swung. He couldn't see the hole. He thought he could feel it, though. The ball landed near. A good shot? He wasn't even sure. The crowd was quiet.

If he wanted to play the last strokes as best he could, he would swing for par. He would pitch the ball up just above the hole, giving it enough force against gravity that the ball would roll back down lazily, and he had only to pitch it a yard to the right for it to fall in the right line toward the flag.

Larry sauntered over to him. Just close enough. They had spoken only a handful of words to Jonni today.

"This is the start of The Masters for you, Jonni. Not the finish."

Jonni stepped up, readied his putt; he breathed, listened to the hush that fell over the course all around him.

He remembered Willy once told him that the best time to sneak up on a lion was when it was about to pounce. It was laser-focused then.

Just the lion and the wildebeest. Nothing in its world exists but that prey. It's whole world is oriented around the wildebeest. Its senses are fully occupied. See your shot, Jonni. See nothing else in the world. Willy hunted lions, or at least had hunted alongside them. Be like the lion, Willy said. Whatever problems there are in your head, sneak around them while they're distracted. Go after it.

Play because you love it, Willy said.

Jonni breathed, he crouched to study the path to the flagstick and the hole.

Jonni looked at the grass beside him, as if to see Willy's thick saliva there as he spat, ignoring whether or not it bothered Jonni.

Jonni shut everything out of his mind, not by force, but by falling backward into the only comfort he knew; the only thing constant and true: The Game.

Like a lion, he thought.

He swung hard and sharp and stopped quick and his ball buzzed into the air and though he couldn't see it he felt it was true and for more than that he looked at the crowd to study their reaction as they waited, craning, straining. They began to clap. It wasn't a remarkable shot, it wasn't a game-changer, but it was good. The ball rode along the glistening grass as if alive, moving at its own pace, with somewhere to go.

It went. It sank.

Jonni felt the weight of the entire day, the week, all of it, he felt all of it sink with the ball. It was done. He turned to face Larry. From the reaction of the crowd he realized what he, in a daze, had only suspected. A cheer went up around the rope. There was excitement for Jonni and what he had done, there was immense support from the crowd.

But Larry had won. He hugged Jonni. They waved. Jonni felt tears in his eyes. He cried. He saw his Dad as the two gallery guards opened the ropes. Jonni walked forward to embrace his Dad. Then he was in the crowd.

There were hands on his shoulders. He heard his name called. He walked off the grass and past the rope.

Everything that followed was a blur. He felt light and elated, that is, until he saw the policemen waiting for him at the entrance to the clubhouse.

THIRTY-SEVEN

They sat in silence until the light knock that sent Martin nearly jumping across the room. Ryals rose to let Parriot in. The Sheriff had called Ryals several times, which he just noticed, but he put his phone away and opened the door. Ryals looked like he'd ridden a hurricane. He requested gauze on his side and a National on-call doctor had patched him up. He was streaked with dried mud and bits of pine needles and grass. Jonni hadn't come in yet. Lawrence aided in the arrest of the bodyguard and secured both of them and helped Ryals back. The deputies now had both suspects in custody. Ryals would get to them later.

He found Martin outside with Lawrence's help. Now they sat in a small conference room. He waited for Martin to speak.

"My son can't know about this," he said. "He doesn't know. He knows something, I mean, maybe. Just not the full deal." He wrung his hands, began to stand and then sat again.

"I can't promise anything," Ryals said.

Martin wiped his face with both hands. Ryals stared through the pain he felt in more places than he wanted to count. "Lots of corruption in South Africa, lots of smuggling out of the country, one way or the other. They wanted us, they approached us. A business deal. I took the deal, I was stupid. So stupid. I took the endorsement from Adidas,

I took the sunglasses and the shoes, all for Jonni. This was just another one, I thought."

"What was the deal?" Ryals asked.

"It was simple things at first. Carry this, carry that. Envelope, box on a private flight. Successful delivery meant a bonus. Take it on a private flight, in places you won't be searched. We have access, you know. Treated differently. Nothing big, not a lot, whatever it was. I said yes. Jonni loves this game, but golf doesn't pay much, at least not at first. It's nearly impossible, and the world is so expensive for a South African. I gave up everything for my son to pursue this dream. Sold what I could. This would help. I want him to win. I want him to be the best. I had to find a way to make that possible. He deserves it."

"Then when Jonni won the Latin American and we were invited to The Masters, they reached out again. They came and met me. This was more serious, I could tell. What could I say at this point?" Martin looked carefully over them all, and then at his son. His lip quivered. "They said a friend would meet me, I would do the trade. They gave me a bag, I never looked at it. I wrote them and told them no. I said I would bring it back. Then..."

"They killed Willy Sharpe," Ryals said. "To put pressure on you?"

"Yes," he said. "It's all my fault." His voice trembled, his hands shook and he looked at them as if something, some physical manifestation of his guilt might suddenly appear in them. "They wanted me to go through with the deal. They said they would ensure that I did."

"They met with Willy first, though," Parriot said.

"I didn't know that either. Not until you told me. They must have asked him to convince me. Maybe they thought he could get to the bag."

"What do you think he said?" Asked Ryals.

"Willy? Willy wouldn't stand for that kind of thing. He would have said no, or shove off. He didn't call me. I don't know who he called. I don't know why he met them."

"So he didn't know about this arrangement?"

"No," Martin answered, his voice lowered, almost a whisper. "Not at all."

"So he doesn't help them, and then they kill him," Ryals said, feeling the pain in his side sharply as he sat up. No position was comfortable. He still felt dizzy. He didn't want to get up, though, even for water.

"They killed him, but first a groundskeeper so they can get to him, killed him in such a way as to make a very clear statement to you. Somehow they lured him out that night." Ryals thought, as a threat also to anyone else with whom they were working, who might get cold feet. In this or other deals. With a glance he knew Parriot was thinking the same thing. "And you didn't go to the authorities?"

"You're the police, here, I mean, in this town, your country. These people, they're all over. Not South African, that's for sure. What can you do when they can follow me over borders anywhere in the world?"

"What did they want you to do with whatever it was they wanted you to carry?" Ryals asked.

"They would call and tell me."

"Did you? Carry something over?" Parriot added.

Martin said nothing. His eyes looked around as if he needed a safe place to rest his gaze. He found none and his eyes just seemed to lose focus in defeat. His personal space was invaded, there was nothing he could do about it.

"Yes," he said. "But."

"But what?" Ryals asked. "Where is it?"

"They can't find it."

"Where is it?"

After a moment, "I put it in checked items. Someone just picked it up."

Ryals phone rang. He answered Kate. She told him what was going on.

"I'm sitting with Martin now," Ryals said. "He's confessed. Is confessing." She told him they'd call him back. They were in pursuit of the bag man.

"Other investigators are looking now for the buyer."

"They'll kill me or Jonni back home, if you interfere."

"We'll do our best to make sure that doesn't happen," Ryals said, not feeling in a particularly good humor.

"How did the seller, this group, how did they first contact you?"

"A man bought me a drink at a tournament. Back home. Dressed nice, began talking to me about business deals. One thing led to another. They're Asian. Chinese, I think."

Ryals looked at Jonni, who was deflated but relaxed. Outside was a flurry of activity, elation and cheer around the tournament coming to a close. In this room the group was somber. Jonni did not look angry. He did not yell at his dad. Ryals did not believe that Jonni knew any of this. Jonni simply looked tired.

Night fell. The clouds cleared slowly from East to West, breaking apart like arctic ice. Kate and Parriot had nearly lost the silver sedan but were on it again as it took the long curve of the wide interstate perimeter designated "Bobby Jones Expressway." Traffic was dense but Kate kept her sharp eyes on the suspect vehicle. Parriot told his agent to let up a bit and let the silver car pull ahead, just enough. He didn't want to give away their position, if it wasn't already. They merged and kept their distance, focused on the taillights of the suspect vehicle.

"What's this way?" Parriot asked. Kate was already looking at her map. "That airport," the agent said. He pointed at a sign as they passed. "That's what I thought," Parriot said. "Okay, never mind. Let's gun it."

In ten minutes they pulled into Bush Field which was flanked by a marshy wood and air thick with rain-released petrichor and smell of the swamps and pine forest.

They parked against the curb and as they emerged, Parriot called the Sheriff to arrange official backup. "They're on their way," he reported when he lowered his phone. "I'll go in first and speak with security."

"You want them held?"

"I want to be sure we see them all. If they're waiting on someone else I don't want to miss them."

They walked in separately. Parriot found a TSA agent, showed his badge and explained the situation. Parriot had to twice tell the young man to keep his voice down as he radioed the supervisor. The airport was relatively small, but busy with the tournament traffic. Parriot could see the tarmac through the windows; it was occupied with several commercial aircraft and a row of private jets.

He watched as the suspect in the jacket passed through security with his driver. They didn't appear to be waiting on anyone.

"I need to get out there now," Parriot told the man. "Ground the planes, no one leaves." The agent stared at Parriot dumbly. "Tell your supervisor. And have him meet us outside." Parriot led him — and Kate and his agent close behind — through the security corridor, guided by the Homeland Security officer mumbling his way past others. They got to the gate area, spotted the pair of men leaving through a private exit.

Parriot could see them through the window walking out to a waiting jet — which was whining as the turbines began to spin up.

"Come on!" Parriot said, and they broke into a run outside.

They were met with the blast of air as they circled the back of the plane, the TSA agent pleading voicelessly in the singing of the jet engines. Parriot had his gun out. Kate her badge. They ran to the front of the plane, just as the door closed and the men climbed in. They clearly meant to begin their taxi out.

Kate stood right in front of the nose of the plane and simply held her badge out. The pilot stared at her curiously, then he sat back. Parriot was alongside her, gun drawn but not aimed, badge high. He shouted; they couldn't hear him, but that was fine. They needed to know he meant business.

The pilot looked back, shook his head and clearly said "Sorry," and then the turbines began to wind down.

THIRTY-EIGHT

This was not where Jonni expected to relax after the last round. He stared at the wall in the Sheriff's conference room, his father beside him with his head lowered. He knew his dad was sorry, sorry for all of it — he'd tried to say something but there was nothing to say. Jonni saw a TV through the glass window and saw himself on replays. It felt like that; like it was all in some other small reality away from this one. His dad wasn't in handcuffs. Jonni wondered when those were coming.

The detective looked as if he'd been hit by a train. Bits of grass were in his hair, and his pants were stained with mud. He wore a large sweatshirt from the Masters; it was green and it read PATRON and he winced as he moved and sat across from them. He was obviously in pain. He explained to Jonni that neither he nor his father had been charged. "I don't believe we have good cause to. We have the killers in custody."

The Sheriff came in and spoke to Ryals. "Parriot has the others in the GBI field office. He'll speak to them but they demand a translator." Jonni wasn't entirely sure what that meant.

Someone else arrived —a tall, handsome man with black hair. He was introduced as the District Attorney

After some silence Ryals finally spoke. "Here's what we know so far," he said. "The men who attacked me are being held and will be indicted on a host of charges, and that's just for attacking an officer of the law," he slid his hand on the table as if laying out an invisible map of what that meant, "Frank is former US Military. Both are mercenaries hired through a security firm here in the U.S. The FBI has apparently had the firm under investigation following suspected illegal activities in Mexico three years ago. Our best bet—they aren't saying much—is that they were hired by whatever group wanted, or wants, to put pressure on you.

"We will expect you to testify," the district attorney said, sitting opposite. "We will work with your state officials on details, and on witness protection for you both if that's what you want. You'll be invited to stay here for the duration if you believe your life is at risk."

Jonni dipped his head. He closed his eyes and thought about his game that day, about the rain skipping off the ball and the glowing line of bent grass as it landed in the rough. "But I see no reason to charge either of you with any crime. You are, at best, accessories who operated under threat, and it is the interest of Richmond County to bring to justice those responsible for the murders of Willy Sharp and Philip Gordon. I believe with your help, we'll be able to do that."

He opened a folder and went through several pages, everyone waiting quietly. "we have some paperwork to get through tonight," he said, "but it will be a while as we interview the suspects and coordinate with the GBI team."

Martin reached out for Jonni's hand and held it. Jonni didn't pull away. "Could we— we've skipped the tournament dinner, you know. Could we—"

"I'd prefer you stay close," the DA said sharply. Ryals the investigator looked up.

"How about if I take them out for food? My supervision. We won't go far."

"That will be fine," the DA answered. He looked at Ryals, then at the Lombards. He seemed about to say something else, but stopped himself. Ryals could read his expression and shared the same sentiment. Everything about the investigation was unexpected and peculiar. No one knew exactly what to say just yet.

Parriot laid out every document he had in front of the four Southeast Asian businessmen, and he knew — as they waited on their attorneys — that he had major players in custody. All four had been on board the jet, which was bound for Hong Kong by way of Hawaii. Parriot's hope was to make something stick to them and keep them from going anywhere. They were the invited guests of an international corporation based in Sydney. There was no indication they were fans of the game.

They refused to speak until their attorneys arrived — Parriot had already received a call from a congressman who wanted to know what the problem was. To Parriot that indicated levels of corruption on U.S. soil even he hadn't imagined. That wouldn't deter him. Kate was in the other room with one of their other suspects and Parriot thought that between them they could make something stick quick enough to keep anyone from traveling. These men were wealthy and did not like to be detained and the State Department, he was told by the congressman, didn't like it either. Parriot responded that he didn't particularly like murder for hire in his state.

Parriot was no expert but in the souvenir bag, hidden in a shoe-box size disguised as a gaming console was what he was nearly certain was a missile guidance system. With it was a small bag of gemstones whose worth he couldn't begin to imagine.

He had placed calls already to Homeland Security — Kate gave him the number — and the FBI. They reported the arrest and the evidence they had to anyone and everyone. They wanted all eyes on this case to alleviate the potential for corrupt influence.

Still, Parriot doubted he alone could keep them here long. He would have to work quickly. He needed a federal charge to really anchor them. He was sure he could identify one.

Kate left Parriot with the jet passengers. She found Ryals as he was leaving with the Lombards and his daughter, Angela.

"Join us," he said, walking like he was an arthritic geriatric. He was covered with bruises. She'd heard the details of his ordeal by phone. She knew he had two men in custody.

"I'm going to sit in on the interrogations," she said. She wanted to speak to Mr. Lombard as well but she didn't think he could help her get anywhere she particularly wanted to get to in her own personal investigation.

In reality she went to the break room and waited for a while. She napped briefly. She didn't want to be in the room with Parriot. He had his business.

She had a little bit of her own.

After a while she rose and found him between interviews. She looked down the row of doors and windows. She knew which man she was looking for. It was the entire reason she'd come here. He was in the last room. Neatly dressed, boyish good looks, unassuming gaze. He sat with hands folded. She waited a long time, and saw no sign that Parriot would return soon. Lawyers had come and they had gone.

She opened the door and slipped inside. She put her satchel onto her lap. She said nothing at first.

"You don't know me, Mr. Zhao. I know you well. I've been looking at your work for years. You were arrested in Nairobi, again in Cape Town, in Singapore too, I believe. Yet somehow you always manage to slither right back out."

She watched him. He looked out at her from under his brow like some predator. Just enough attention to her now that she was a threat.

"I've seen an infant rhino cut out of its mother so that the nascent horn on its small face can be provided to your network, exploited by your wholesalers, sold to those who don't even have the money to afford it but believe it will magically save their life from disease. Or that of their child. I've stood at intersections where vehicles are still smoking from machine gun fire, bodies dead inside. Or destitute Mozambican poachers crossing borders into national parks only to be trampled by elephants. There are young girls who have suffered unspeakable horror all thanks to you and your pipelines. Destruction and suffering follow everywhere you go. We fight these things on the ground, meanwhile you move place to place in a luxury jet. Those other men, they're just along for the ride, I'm guessing. You're the guide here. Top dog."

She took her phone out and a small folding stand for it. She turned the video recorder on and turned it on the table. Then she pulled out her small satchel.

"Do you know what a Naja is? Ever heard of that?"

He shrugged.

"Doesn't surprise me. Why bother yourself with the dangers faced by those you exploit? You just send people. You don't care who you hurt, not on either side.

"But this week your man put a black mamba in someone's room, and I'm guessing you thought that was clever. Because why not play games with people's lives, I suppose. A naja is a Mozambique spitting cobra" she explained. He rolled his eyes.

"See I know you, Mr. Zhao. I know how you exploit local people. It's one thing to be recruited when you're desperate. You, and people like you come in offering to help. A year's pay for a weekend's work? The third world is your playground. Disposable labor.

"Anyway, you liked snakes. You trafficked that mamba, did you? Or just found someone who could?"

He said nothing. "Maybe not. Maybe you'd have to know something about snakes. Me, though, I did smuggle something out of South Africa. I am also a very big fan of snakes. They are fascinating to study. The mamba is dangerous, but it's not what killed my boyfriend when he was on patrol with rangers in Zimbabwe, responding to attacks that you funded."

She pulled out a small tube of toothpaste from her satchel, along with a toothbrush. She unscrewed the cap, producing a hidden eyedropper.

"The naja is a snake found in southern Africa. It's quite common. You might know that if you ever stepped foot out of the airport in Africa. Fortunately for us, you stepped out of the one in Augusta, so allow me to educate you. As the name suggests, the Naja spits at attackers," she said, rising, and holding the dropper carefully. Now the man watched her with sharp eyes that tracked her every movement. His breath quickened and she could hear his heart beating. Suddenly suspicious. Alert. He was cuffed to the chair. He could move but not much. "But I've talked to several people who have been attacked. They spit into your eyes, you see, and everyone describes the pain in the same way. They say it's like having a hot coal taken out of a fire and laid atop your eyeball. If you treat it, flush it out, you might not go blind. If you don't..." She looked at him. "You're going to scream after this so let me tell you what I want — the first of two things. I want to know your network, all the pieces you can give me. You'll write it down, or you'll explain it. I'll take it from there. You don't work alone. You've spent two decades building your empire. Even then, you're still a middle man, aren't you?"

His eyes whipped back and forth and he yanked on his cuffs but in one swift motion she grabbed his hair in her fingers and yanked his head back and held his eye open and released a single drop into his right eye. He did scream.

She walked around and waited a minute for his shrieks to turn to whimpers and she turned on the camera.

"Now, let's have a conversation."

Angela sat across from Jonni and asked him a million questions. He at first just stared with an exhausted look but soon it turned out Angela's unbridled enthusiasm for his celebrity was exactly the tonic he needed. Ryals wanted to hold her back, but hadn't much energy to do so. Soon they were talking, and Ryals was surprised at the questions she asked. Even more so at how much she knew:

"Rory Mcilroy made his comeback, winning three majors in a year. And Jordan Spieth had that crazy game at the British Open a few years back but he took it! Right at the end." Ryals stared at her. He'd never heard her talk golf before, and she sounded like she knew what she was on about. There was a lot about his daughter he didn't know.

Sitting in the corner table of the Waffle House they drew stares, some due to Ryals' appearance — he was still disheveled, bruised, bandaged; but mostly they recognized Jonni.

Jonni didn't want anything to eat. He barely spoke and ordered nothing. Then Angela told him about the chocolate milk. So he got one.

And then his appetite appeared. He looked at the menu. He began to talk to Angela. To answer her questions. She asked golf tips and he answered. She asked about South Africa, and he answered.

Ryals had little to say to Martin, but for all the insanity of the week the men had two kids with a connection for a moment and for their fathers that was enough.

The waitress came and Jonni ordered an All Star Breakfast. Angela interrupted Ryals to order for him, but he talked over her.

"Egg whites," he said. "Wheat toast. Tomatoes. Coffee. Please." He looked at Angela, expecting some praise. She just nodded then returned to deep conversation with Jonni. The two were now like old friends.

He leaned back and let his eyes flutter with the exhaustion of the day. He watched the traffic on Washington Road. Taillights were blurry. His home town felt foreign. Or he felt like he was a foreigner. It was all different after the past week. He closed his eyes and thought he might sleep. He couldn't believe he was at a table with a Masters competitor at the end of a murder investigation. The week had ended very different than it had started. Martin looked out the window, and his face was troubled. Ryals studied him then said quietly,

"You'll have lots of questions to answer, you know." Martin nodded, his expression told Ryals that Martin wasn't sure he'd escape jail. Ryals just nodded at him. "But not tonight."

"Not tonight," Martin said. He turned and put his hand on his son's shoulder. It wasn't rejected, and Ryals could read the relief.

"Seems incredible," Ryals said.

"What?" Martin asked.

"That all of this would happen here. At the Masters. With the eyes of the world on this place."

"What better place?" Asked Martin, almost in exasperation. "There is nowhere like it. In the whole world. We have been all over. It is its own world. Its own rules and laws. Closed off, you drive just down there, and you wouldn't know its on the other side of that bamboo." It was true. On that course things happened that could happen nowhere else. For better or worse, Ryals was now part of that long and complicated tradition. He had never asked to be. He hoped Jonni would return and give them something else to remember. It seemed impossible — that a murder at the world's most famous golf tournament could be forgotten. Then again, the Augusta National controlled its own history in a way that few other institutions could. It was indeed a tradition like no other.

"By the way," Ryals asked, suddenly realizing. "Who won the tournament?"

"Dad!" Angela exclaimed. "Larry Mize! He birdied 18."

"What a way to retire," said Ryals.

"He earned it," Jonni said. Their food came.

Ryals phone buzzed. He checked the text. It came from an unknown number. A video file loaded.

A single message came with it: Pleasure doing business with you. See you maybe never. PS, poor guy has pollen allergies I think.

Ryals frowned. Then played the video, holding it close to his face to hear it over Angela and Jonni's conversation.

On the screen the Chinese suspect, seated across the interview table against the white wall sobbed. His eyes were red and his face was flushed.

"Yes," the man cried. "I paid him. I paid him to kill Willy Sharpe."

EPILOGUE

Perhaps the most spectacular shot in the history of The Masters was Tiger Woods chip on the 16th in 2005. The ball lay at the edge of the rough as if it were just venturing out into a public arena. The greatest golfers can see the rough, fairway and green as one tapestry. They had a relationship with it. The course was alive to them. It was as if a living entity with a relationship to the golfer; a relationship often friendly, more often antagonistic. That relationship was moody and shifting and unpredictable.

There, just beneath the transition between distinct shades of green grass lay the ball and Tiger in his red shirt and black cap walked around the green like a cat stalking its prey. At 13 under Tiger hovered at the top of the leaderboard with confidence. His concentration as patrons smiled on was invincible. Verne Lundquist's voice shook through the CBS broadcast as he softly but hurriedly described what he seemed preternaturally to know was about to happen. The trees reflected against the pond beyond him, deep green over the water dusted with pine pollen. Dogwoods among the shadows bright as if glowing with support. Not a soul on the course did not tremble with expectation. This was the second shot of the Par 3 on a stage set just inside the pine shadows cast beneath golden afternoon light that flared between boughs. The great competitor of that day completed his arc and stood just outside the green. He tilted and practiced his swing. Looking briefly up he watched the still scene as if seeing his forthcoming shot unfold, as if he could divine what was about to come and watched what no one else could see. The curve of the ground was invisible to most, it revealed little to those who could not see what he could see. Tiger looked again at the ground, took a step forward, and chipped the ball with a short swing. It briefly rose as if into some kind of ethereal light, and then dropped and rolled above and seemingly wide of the yellow flagstick. Then gravity kicked in and the Woods' strategy revealed itself as the ball patiently proceeded on a predetermined path to the hole. It came to the lip of the cup and hesitated, like a thing awaiting the permission of its master. That apparently granted, it dropped and the crowd, and the TV commentators, exploded.

Sam Ingot had been there that day. He was a junior staff writer then for a golf magazine. He felt that scene was much like observing something not meant to be seen. TV cameras caught it and preserved its brilliance for posterity. There was nothing like being there, though. In that golden light, on that perfect day, observing the perfect shot. No other place in the world could offer what was there manifested.

The Augusta National humbled veteran players while elevating new-comers. Every player served the course. Ultimately it was the Master of every golfer invited to play there.

The Augusta National, Sam Ingot wrote, took several internal steps to address the series of crimes committed around and related to the

Masters Tournament, and while harsh and thorough, they were completely private.

Sam wrote his column from the airplane. Of course he didn't know at the time how the crime had turned out, but he didn't need to.

He wrote what was important to him, the world of golf and the Masters: the story of a boy who, despite all odds, fought that battle "on the five-inch course between his ears." He fought it, bravely, and ultimately won — not a green jacket, but perhaps himself. Besides, coming in second at the Augusta National is nothing to apologize for. Especially for a Rookie. Jonni Lombard would have many more chances.

It really was something to watch the young South African golfer play, let alone in the throes of the most sensational crime ever committed at any golf course, much less, the National.

When Ingot posted the article he then reached out to Detective Ryals Hall at the Richmond Country Sheriff's Department.

"I'm not digging for dirt. I just want to know — what did the National say to you, after the fact?"

"She — they — thanked me. Profoundly."

"What does profoundly mean?" he asked.

"Well," Ryals said. "They gave us a care package of gifts. And invited my daughter and me to play the course."

"Did you?"

"I told them give me a month. We're going to take some lessons first. I don't want to waste the opportunity."

Sam wouldn't add that part to the article. The Augusta National was a special place, and while he wasn't swept into the magic of the legacy as some were, what it preserved holy in the game of golf he also, as a patron and fan had a duty to preserve.

Six Months Later

The hippos groaned their signature guttural sound from the pond where they relaxed as the sun heated the water. Jonni could smell the schnitzel from Sam's kitchen where lunch was starting to cook in the kitchen. There was a small crowd, some to watch him play. He ignored them, squared up against the ball and tapped a long putt over a dried-out green much slower than the ones a few thousand miles across the ocean where his career was lit, like an open flame in a windy field.

Though here Jonni wasn't even aware of his celebrity, not unless he opened his computer or pored over his phone. He'd rather be out swinging over dry Africa grass. His dad fielded most of his phone calls and emails. The phone rang constantly, interviews were scheduled and conducted; Jonni traveled and played other tournaments and spoke little to his father for the first few months. Dad had begun carrying a gun on his hip, or in his jacket, but nothing had happened, not yet.

Jonni still occasionally grew emotional when he played. The investigation into the parties responsible for everything was ongoing. Willy was still gone.

He finished his game and walked to Sam's and there he saw a woman sitting alone with a small coffee and sunglasses. For some reason she was familiar but he wasn't sure why. Her hair was brown-red. She seemed out of place but still somehow blended in. She waved to him.

He stopped at her table before walking through the dining room.

"Mr. Lombard," she said. "I'm Kate. We met in Augusta."

He just looked at her. He did remember her, but he wasn't sure exactly what her role was there. He didn't know if this was a friendly meeting or an interrogation.

"If you wouldn't mind, I'd like to buy you a coffee. Do you drink coffee?" He hesitated, then sat. She waved a coffee over. "I'm working with the American government, and I'm here to help you. Do you mind if we chat about Augusta a little bit?"

She slid him an envelope. "I've identified them."

"Who?"

"The people behind everything. The crimes in Augusta and abroad. They're still at work. In fact, I've heard they're quite active in the Middle East now. I plan to look into that."

He listened to her but he said nothing. She seemed young for this work. He looked confusedly at the envelope, and then around. No one was looking at him. He heard the hippos again. The soft rhythmic whooping of the hornbills. "What do you want?"

"I want your help," the woman said. "Just let me tag along when you play. On occasion." He looked at her, held the envelope. "What's this?"

"The men we're after. They'll make an appearance sometime soon. For a long time I couldn't do much about it. Thanks to you, my government is interested now. It's a win-win for me and them."

"Win-win?"

"I enjoy watching you play," she said. "It's really something."

Kate and Jonni will return in

THE PRO

About the font:

Garamond is a group of many serif typefaces and embodies the elegance and sophistication of Renaissance typography. Named after its creator, Claude Garamond, this serif font exudes a sense of classical refinement and balance. With its slender, graceful letterforms and subtle contrasts, Garamond is beloved for its readability and versatility across various mediums. From books to advertisements, its enduring appeal lies in its ability to convey tradition and craftsmanship, making it a staple choice for designers seeking a touch of timeless beauty in their compositions.